D0975077

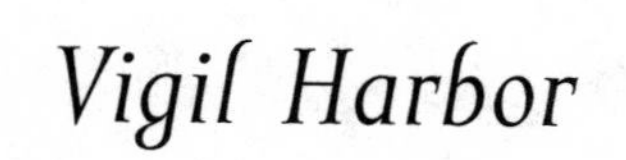
Vigil Harbor

Vigil Harbor

Julia Glass

PANTHEON BOOKS *New York*

This is a work of fiction. Names, characters, places, and incidents either are the product of the author's imagination or are used fictitiously. Any resemblance to actual persons, living or dead, events, or locales is entirely coincidental.

 Published in the United States by Pantheon Books, a division of Penguin Random House LLC, New York, and distributed in Canada by Penguin Random House Canada Limited, Toronto.

Pantheon Books and colophon are registered trademarks of Penguin Random House LLC.

Library of Congress Cataloging-in-Publication Data
Name: Glass, Julia, 1956– author.
Title: Vigil Harbor / Julia Glass.
Description: First edition. | New York : Pantheon Books, [2022]
Identifiers: LCCN 2021033121 (print). LCCN 2021033122 (ebook).
ISBN 9781101870389 (hardcover). ISBN 9781101870396 (ebook).
Classification: LCC PS3607.L37 V54 2022 (print) | LCC PS3607.L37 (ebook) |
DDC 813/.6—dc23
LC record available at https://lccn.loc.gov/2021033121
LC ebook record available at https://lccn.loc.gov/2021033122

www.pantheonbooks.com

Jacket image by Matt Anderson Photography/Moment/Getty Images
Jacket design by Jenny Carrow

Printed in the United States of America
First Edition
2 4 6 8 9 7 5 3 1

For Dennis, Alec, and Oliver:
my family, my harbor,
my home

Any apparent somewhere which you may inhabit is always
at the mercy of a ruthless and omnivorous everywhere.

—E. E. Cummings

Vigil Harbor

Let's say it's true that geography is destiny, place entwined with person. Would living on a peninsula—promontory, headland, bluff—make you peninsular by nature? Not someone who sticks out but someone who likes backing up to a body of water, who finds a cul-de-sac comforting, not cornering? You'd miss out on casual, unpredictable commerce with travelers merely passing through, because your town would be a place of beginnings and endings, of retreat or stasis, and after a while you'd likely notice a sameness to your neighbors. You'd all *be a bunch of proud peninsulites: privileged, but also myopic.*

That's how some outsiders see the people of Vigil Harbor, a town that thrusts itself into the Atlantic Ocean, all but completely enclosed by restless water, deflecting the longshore current like a crooked foot aimed straight toward the rising sun. On a map, the harbor itself resembles a long blue parcel held snug beneath a muscular arm against the Massachusetts coastline. At the big toe, two of the town's oldest roads rise toward a park with a view raised high by granite cliffs. The shoreline here is rugged with rock, nothing like the bygone aprons of silken sand that once turned neighboring towns into summer playgrounds, much of that sand recently eroded by pummeling rains and swallowed by storms that no longer repay the ground they borrow.

That park is where residents gather every year to watch their fireworks on a Fourth of July that lasts for days. In spirit, not much has changed on this day for a couple hundred years—not through depressions, recessions, pandemics, and definitely not during wartime. In wartime, town pride swells like a spinnaker in a sailing race at the yacht club.

It begins at dawn: for two hours, the bells of the three remaining churches ring with abandon. At eight a.m.—shame on those who sleep in—veterans of wars and invasions from Vietnam to Venezuela march the twisting colonial ways or wave from an antique trolley, the high school marching band preceding them with off-key pomp and drumming. The Girl and Boy Scouts follow in turn like a ragtag militia, and a small fleet of jewel-toned vintage automobiles creeps along behind, klaxons blaring, the caboose to this train a 1969 powder-blue Volkswagen convertible owned and driven by the longest-standing elected official, a fourth-generation Harborite named June Smithson.

The parade ends at the Old Burial Ground, where four hundred revolutionary patriots—most of them fishermen who tossed aside their nets to form George Washington's navy—lie beneath slabs half-swallowed by the earth, their epitaphs worn thin as a whisper. June lays a wreath on the grave of a different soldier every year, his name pulled from a big mason jar of names by the town historian.

Local merchants—the chowder café, the ice-cream parlor, the yarn shop, and the nestlike boutiques owned by women wealthy enough to lose their silk shirts on the bottom line—put their wares out on the sidewalk. They offer compostable cups of lemonade, along with the molasses cookies whose recipe dates back to the town's first innkeeper.

The Episcopal church hall displays local artworks and sells them to benefit a vaccination campaign or a refugee camp in some remote, far less fortunate country that few of the artists or donors could place on any map. Roving bands of tankard-wielding reenactors sing sea shanties and use their role-playing as justification to drink too much rum at noon. The blazing sun makes them drunker still.

If the summer's catch is decent, somebody runs the Scholarship Lobster Raffle. Tall-masted sailboats swan around the harbor, backyard grills ignite, and families turn from feuding to playing horseshoes and croquet. As day seeps into the folds of night, streams of sunburnt Harborites converge on foot at Emmons Head; spread their blankets, some seasons hem to hem, others distanced like tiny islands; and open their bottles of wine. Before the fireworks begin, they clamber to their feet, older folks feeling the kinks in their joints, and they sing the town song (first verse only).

Take to your boats; oh, men, take to the sea!
Hoist anchor, loft sail, like your fathers 'fore ye!
Leave behind hearth; oh, leave behind brides;
We are sworn to the ocean, our fate in her tides.
This be our fortune, the bounty down under.
Leave whales to New Bedford; 'tis cod we shall plunder.
Women and babes, let thy vigilance burn
Until to the harbor your mariners return!

People who now make their living from forces unseen—chips and codes, chromosomes and neutrinos—are moved to tears by a cornball song from an era they count their lucky stars never to have lived in. In the picturesque gloaming, they stand and sing and shed all sense of irony, skepticism, threats of despair. It is an intimacy both true and artificial.

As an almost-island, Vigil Harbor has not suffered as badly during waves of contagion as other, landlocked towns. It has so far, you might say willfully, remained aloof from political extremes. Town Meetings remain bipartisan in a cantankerous but ultimately collegial fashion now regarded as arcane in most parts of the country. In the last election, only seventeen residents registered as members of the EndTimer Party, the angry spinoff of the failed campaign to elect Kip Kittredge to the White House.

But unsettling times will unsettle everyone. Struck by a recent rash of divorces, beginning with a pair of well-known yacht club members who swapped their respective marriages for a shared membership in a survivalist commune, Vigil Harbor is a little less secure about its resilience. Because love, as firmly as war, is stitched deep into town lore. Approach by water and, at the mouth of the harbor, you must circumnavigate Ruby Rock, originally Arabella's

Rock, Arabella the widow of Samuel Thesper. They were married hardly a month when Samuel launched his fishing dory and small crew to challenge the entry of a British ship in search of patriot outlaws. He meant to hold them off long enough that a meeting of rebels in a local sail loft might disband and hide. But he was shot through the chest by a hotheaded Regular equally intent on breaching the harbor. Samuel fell overboard, and his body washed ashore on the island, a place used for drying cod on vast wooden racks. Two days after he was buried, Arabella swam to the island and threw herself from a ledge on the far side. Three women who had rowed in pursuit made it there only in time to bring her body back. She was interred next to Samuel, near the peak of the burial ground.

Such stories, though always a little suspect in their fairy-tale pathos, are countless in a town like this one. Towns like this one are, after all, mostly the sum of their stories, or the voices that tell the stories. Add to those stories this one.

Brecht

Like every basic Saturday night, the windows in my room are shaking in their frames. Not an earthquake but my stepfather's music. He stays up way late and plays it so maxed up, basso profundo, that the walls in the living room vibrate clear to the third floor. It pumps through my veins, frazzles my nerves. He gets a river of random heritage tuneshop flowing along, *thumpa thumpa thump*, everything from Nina Simone to Code Dread, and whether there are guests or it's just him and Mom or even just him, he dances. Austin is a dance maniac. He says dance is his number one narcotic. But sometimes he also breaks out that champion leaf he gets from he won't say where. He promises Mom it's throwback, the kind they swear won't pickle your judgment, and it does have a smell more like some weirdass tea, less like skunk. He only smokes if it's just him or he's only with Mom, though I don't think she smokes. Austin would never smoke with clients, and all friends, he claims, plus even strangers you pass on the street, are future if not past or present clients. So the whole basic world is a client.

Sometimes I vext him to turn it down. Maybe he does, by a margin that doesn't matter.

He'll yell up the stairs, "Earplugs, dude!" in that diluvian-but-who-cares tone, and I'm like, what if I slept through something asteroidal? Austin says don't be melodramatic. He says I'm a doomseer, too typical of my generation. He says it lightly, in a faux-jokey voice, but when he doesn't think I'm in earshot, I've heard him refer to Generation F: failure, fuckup, fatalist; take your pick. If you want to get poetic, flotsam. Others call us Generation NL (out loud, *nil*): No Life, as in having no lives worth living, or maybe as in Get a Life, which it's true a lot of us cannot seem to do, or not according to some fossil definition of "grown-up." As in, going out there to Be Something. People who are hard on us like that tell us to look at the kids who came of age in the pandemic years, the ones who survived and even, somehow, figured out how to live lives of their own while ducking in and out of lockdown during the surges.

Austin, who has no kids genetically his own, says our allergy to independence (that's what he calls it) is the fault of our parents, but collectively, not individually—because he wouldn't want to get Mom too far down. I was twelve when she married Austin, so there wasn't much he could do, he says, except root from the sidelines. As if me and Mom are some kind of sporting event.

It's so obviously not her fault that I boomeranged home, that I'm in this state she sees as deep limbo, but she's always felt responsible for who I am. I think she can't help feeling guilty about us losing Dad—which is nuts, but I get it. Maybe it's also middle age and the whole mortality thing, but she's in this fragile place right now.

I guess we are doomseers, me and Noam and the rest of us, but why shouldn't we be? We're not Timers, we're not *that* stooge. No way would we flee to the deep woods just because we're afraid the next bomb will flash-fry our own town square, the next virus turn that town square into an emergency graveyard. Nor are we desperate enough to join the Restitution Corps, forget the army! But we see that the bar's going up on surviving what's to come, some of which is certain, some not. Like the growing list of Hot Spots on the Global Climate Watch. (Picture a map punctured with cigarette burns.) I heard one of Austin's clients saying that his son's college has a major called survival studies.

Me and Noam have a bet going. It's about the next tsunami, the one that some seismologists are sure will be set off soon, maybe even tomorrow, by a slip in plates that meet somewhere off the coast of Spain. The projections show it pointed in our direction. So we've taken positions on exactly what date the big wave will rise, on how much time it will take to cross the ocean, on how long a stretch of coast will take the max hit, on the number of fatalities. We're allowed to change our minds as we please. It's a subject we like what-iffing.

We know that unless there's some futuristic warning system in place, we might not be alive to see who wins. Our town is bull's-eye center of the wave's projected path. (Farewell to Cape Cod, or what's left of it.) Anyone who thinks that our being up on a cliff will protect us, that the wave will just crash politely into the granite ledge and slither back, is *totally* stooge. The wave will roar up and over Emmons Head, then horizontalize its King Kong fury, probably even smash off parts of the ledge. All the fine old antique houses? Four centuries' worth of driftwood in a flash. My stepfather's clients' brand-new houses? Lethal sheets of fractured steel and glass turned into shrapnel.

The Big T, as we call it, would make Cunégonde, that monster storm from three years back, look like a fairy princess. On Back Harbor, Cunégonde ripped every dock off Harrow Point, blew out nearly all the windows, toppled a dozen power poles, sent three roofs flying out to sea, and buckled two new houses cardboard flat (houses not designed by Austin, he'll be quick to tell you). On Ruby Rock, the bunkhouses must've vaporized; not even the kiddie toilets remained. The summer camp was toast and lost its insurance. They put a FOR SALE sign on the island, but the sign's now totally covered in guano. Me and Noam took Austin's tender out there last summer: what a wasteland. I never went to that camp—we moved here when I was too old for stuff like that—but Noam said it was a cool place if you were little and liked running wild: bows and arrows, camping under the stars, bonfires and ghost stories, dissecting dead fish, Huck Finn stuff. Now the island's been conquered by seals, refugees from the Cape, which lost miles and miles of beach, megatons of sand. Some afternoons, they make such a ruckus, barking, squabbling, yodeling, you hear it from all over town. Some people think they're a nuisance, other people say they bring us "closer to nature." But conservation rules give them squatters' rights.

Where there are seals, you're always warned, there will be sharks. Big ones. But Noam says where there are seals, there will be selkies. He says if you hide out and watch super close, and if it's one of the rare days they strip off their silky fur pelts, all you have to do is poach one on the sly and, jackpot!, you've got the naked maiden who owns it. She is yours, so long as you keep hold of her skin and take good care of it. She will do your every basic bidding (though not sure I like the medieval sound of that). And just try to picture the two of us sneaking a pair of feral maidens up to my parents' third floor. We could do it when Austin's stoned, but no way would Mom fail to notice.

I told Noam that story's got to be from a children's book, and he said it is, okay yeah, but the story in the book is based on a million stories from history, nautical *facts* recorded in ship's logs. I asked him when did he ever read a ship's log, and he said he totally did, in fact he read *several,* back when he had to do a research paper in American history class for Ms. McCarthy. He went to the town archives and dug up this crazy stuff. No way, I said, would Ms. McCarthy ever let a paper be about mermaids. First of all, Noam told me, selkies aren't mermaids (*those* are fictional, he says), and second of all, he wrote about ship's logs from cod-fishing voyages back like four hundred years ago. Those guys were at sea for months on end, I told him: all sailing and no sex, never mind sanity! But okay, I conceded, we'll call it history. Besides, what harm is there in looking out for naked girls on Ruby Rock? And if we get lucky, we will pounce. I do like Noam's brand of eccentric.

Noam is a year older than me. We both went to the High, and we lucked out on being young enough that we didn't have to yo-yo on and off screen through those years, but we didn't hang out. Maybe we had a math class together; we can't quite remember. Afternoons, I ran cross-country or track, though I was no star; he played basketball in winter (he *was* a star), took after-school marine tech in spring. He thought he'd go to a maritime college, maybe get to be a naval mechanic, but he had a GPA blowout. I only found this stuff out much later, when we became friends.

I went to college for almost three semesters, but now I honestly wonder, what's the logical point of it, really? It was a college with a major price tag, and Austin joked once too often about "potential ROI." Also? I was in New York and my sophomore year was the year of the Union Square attack. All those innocent people just buying roses and pumpkins and fancy beeswax candles, or playing in the playground with their kids; I heard the explosions from my dorm. When I decided to take a break, go home for a while, Mom didn't argue. She said I could return to school when I felt ready, but it's been a year and a half and I'm pretty sure I lost my place.

What throws us together now, me and Noam, is that Noam wound up back at home, too, but his mother had turned his old room into an office. So Mom offered to put him up here. She doesn't even charge him rent, and it's not hard to guess why. She doesn't like my being alone too much. So now I am practically the opposite of alone, because Noam hardly ever leaves the house. He reads a lot, and he says he's boning up for tests to get him back on track for the maritime college, the Coast Guard, anything that will send him to a job at sea. That's where he's happiest, he says—out on the water—which would help explain why he has fantasies of bagging a selkie.

He would drive me crazy, except that I'm out working most days—since no way was Austin going to let me come home without getting a job, so he made sure that happened. I work for this guy who does landscaping and tree work, a lot of it for Austin's firm. I know my stepfather hopes I'll go berserk with boredom and decide to finish my degree, maybe somewhere close, maybe just the remote-classroom thing, and while the job can be boring, and it doesn't offer what Austin calls *prospects,* there's a basic sense to it, like even a "goodness." We plant and transplant things. We keep living things from dying, fight the blight. (To put it biblically, the blights are legion: beetles, moths, fungal shit, bacteria and microscopic worms carried by alien birds blown astray from their migratory groove.) We organize stones into walls—garden walls, property walls, walls to hold back water. (You sleep like a champ after a day of walls, even through Austin's house-quaking music.) We're "doing no harm," you might say. And there is plenty of harm going on out there. Plenty.

Celestino, as bosses go, is pax. I told Noam one time, "That man has the patience of moss." Noam just about choked on his beer. We were blowing my pay at The Jetty. He asked if maybe I should go back to writing poetry, the way I did at the High, when I had Mrs. Tattersall for creative writing. I said I just might! I still keep my word book, my random thoughts on the nutzoid pretzeling of English. Like take the word *match:* how can it mean, all at once, a sports competition; a way to start a fire; and the perfect partner or twin, like your soul mate? How can *tender*—the word for Austin's little boat—also refer to both softness and money?

But for now I'm an apprentice at something more or less unwordly.

Celestino likes teaching the things he knows to other people, which is not something you can ever assume in a boss. He's maybe more serious than ideal: doesn't joke around or even take much time off. He doesn't seem to put much stock in conversation (no wordplay for him), and it's got nothing to do with his English, which is practically perfect when you listen past his accent. Not that he says a lot. But if he's fitzed about something, he lets you know, even calmly. The air is always clear.

He seems like a great dad, too. Once in a while, if we have a loophole in the day, we stop by his house, where Connie, his wife, runs a home school with a bunch of other families. Celestino's there to sneak a hit of his kid, Raul, who would be in third grade if he went to normal school. The house is pretty small, and even eight or nine kids fill it up fast, like a flock of ducklings. There's this big glassed-in porch set up like a classroom, with an actual olden-days blackboard, baskets of paper books and wooden puzzles; the museumy smell of chalk! But most of the time, no tronics allowed. Which is either genius or totally not.

Celestino's wife calls it "going retro." Mondays and Wednesdays the kids work onscreen, because how else can they grow into this world, into the *connectivity*? But every other day they put their tronics in an old wine crate beside the front door. They read from those pulp-and-glue books, write and draw on paper. They make music with real instruments, not audioware. They build real things in real space.

While Celestino gets in time with Raul, maybe fills his thermos or consults on married stuff that's none of our business, Connie will give me and Finn, who does the gruntwork with me, lemonade or cold tea and some kind of treat she's made for the kids. Even with all that duckling chaos, the house feels like a good house, a happy house. I get a little jealous, but it's just my imagining what it would be like to live with parents who don't wonder why I have no ambition. Never mind parents who are both your original parents. *What is your signature passion?* was a question on a sheet handed out by my freshman writing professor at college. I wanted to write, *I haven't met her yet,* but instead I wrote, *Making things that don't fall apart.* It just came to me then and there, like horseshit that's accidental wisdom. Or maybe I poached it, unconsciously, from Austin. But it felt pretty true.

Here is another thing about Celestino, though nobody would ever say it out loud, or not anymore, not since the visa raids: he's one of the very few not-white people who actually live and work in Vigil Harbor. Which would have to make anyone self-conscious, especially if you saw that fascist shit unfold around you. I'm guessing he was sponsored, like Samson and Ayeh, the couple who run the bowling alley—but even they don't live here. They take a bus from somewhere near Boston: let's be honest, somewhere a whole lot more real than this town.

It's none of my business, but when I see how much he sticks out, I hope he's secure. This town, where you will meet any number of people who claim to be *thirteenth* generation—as if it's a brag to have loitered forever in the place where your diluvian max-greats settled out of total desperation—has an isolated feel, or more like protective halo, even though we're only thirty miles from the city. People who live here tend to never really leave—or they come back, even when they swore they never would. (Connie is one of those people.) My parents are unusual: neither one grew up here. So it's a bit like a Mobius strip, this town.

When you're somewhere out of state and people ask where you're from (like when I was in New York) and you say Vigil Harbor, either it means zero to them or they kind of light up, as if you've said you're from Camelot or Palm Springs or Blue Hill: somewhere once-upon-a-timey, somewhere tricky or impossible to find. Or gone. "We live in Brigadoom," says Mom, whatever that means. Me and Noam joke that, come the tsunami, we just might be the next Atlantis. Vigil Harbor is like a place that's obsolete but nobody knows it yet. I'm fine with obsolete. Not dead, of course, but outmoded. I've never cared about mode. Mode puts you in the crosshairs.

Maybe Noam moving in with us was a bad idea in unexpected

ways. Because we have each other, we become stasis. We are a physics problem from Mr. Clevenson's class: Brecht + Noam X (same politics + shared bathroom) = Inertia. We colonize the third floor of this house, like those seals on Ruby Rock, and even if we dent our heads on the low ceilings and the idiot rafters, we have the best views of the harbor. We even get an eyeful of the VHYC on the opposite shore, its fat-cat porches, its foofy kite-tails of dainty little banners that represent a coded wink-wink system of who's welcome there from other yacht clubs of the world. (*Burgee:* there's a word for you, one meaning only, though not to be confused with *bungee.*) And all summer, on party nights, I get an earful of the worst wedding bands on the planet. (Austin: "And you complain about *my* music?")

We also have a pact, me and Noam: no more gaming. Read, listen to music, debate life, maybe check the news just enough not to be stooge out of touch. I was done with games after that therapist my mother made me see last year prescribed this VR situational thing called Moodroom. I'd stand in the middle of his office and enter this mansion of emotions, one per room, and tell him what images popped into my head as I roamed through the feelings. Horseshit. It reminded me, in fact, of how I feel when Austin's music is turned up too loud.

Noam's company is therapy enough.

All basic things considered, why would I go anywhere else? And did I say that my mother is a very fine cook?

I did say that she's fragile, though, and this is something I can only sense. Fragile as in lonely, even when she's at a party. (I know how to read Mom's eyes, expressions, ways with her hands.) Which stands to reason, a little anyway, with how hard Austin's working these days, meaning Celestino works hard, meaning I work hard, meaning Mom's on her own a lot, since she mostly works from home. Sometimes she leaves meals out for the rest of us before she goes to bed.

I know her better than most people know their moms because we lived together, just the two of us for four years, in a shoebox apartment in the city, before she married Austin and we moved out. For all my complaints about him, she made a good choice. She's smart; she just hasn't always been lucky. My actual dad, who I remember but not well, died in the original corona surge. He was young, but he had asthma. (Mom claims the chaos of the hospital is what killed him. She couldn't get his body back for months.) In photos where he's holding me on his shoulders or pushing my swing at the playground, he's almost scarecrow thin, body like a spear, smile so big and bright in his tall skinny face that his head looks like a lantern. I have his bushy black hair, also his long nose and hands, not so much his height. There I'm pretty average.

Austin's work bonanza happened like this. Last year, suddenly, like so suddenly you could feel the air crackle with it, couples around town fell apart, splitting like trees struck by lightning. Some kind of rise or fall in the atmospheric love pressure, a virus of radical discontent. (You can have an emotional epidemic, I've heard. Or maybe it was dormant stress from home repairs after Cunégonde. Mortality panic syndrome: if the jig's up soon, I am partying NOW.) It started with the Tyrones, who, to spite each other you can be sure, both hired Austin to blueprint their do-over lives or, to be more exact, the places they'd live in to do it all over.

Thaddie Tyrone is easily the richest man in town. He has a papal bank account, so his do-over was your dream house on slam, perched cliffside (prime view of the ocean from which that tsunami will rise!), the kind of work any architect lives for. At the same time, Ex–Mrs. Tyrone (Lucia? Felicia?) asked Austin to perform a luxe gut job on the Federal mansion she held on to in the squalling. A deal with the devil, he admits. He does not like obliterating that kind of history. But some checks, Austin says, you're stupid not to cash. They're more than money. And I think he's salvaging all the details: paneling, floorboards, mantels. He rents an old sail loft by the town landing, just for stockpiling things like that. The woman from the history museum who gives the walking tours claims it's the loft where the rebels were meeting on the day Sam Thesper saved their lives—and lost his—by distracting the British ship sent to root out the treason. Austin says that's apocryphal BS, since he's sure the original part of the building was built after 1800. No harm in coloring a little out of the lines, I told him. Don't be so sure, said Austin. Of course, to an architect, coloring outside the lines is dangerous. The draftsman's lines are what keep the buildings from falling down.

All around, though, principles are shakier these days.

High-profile stuff, those two projects, the stuff of both gossip and news, after which word goes out that Austin Kepner is the architect to hire if suddenly you are facing the domestically uprooting shock, whether rude or welcome, of postmarital solitude, and if your attorneys, accountants, therapists, and mediators leave you with a nickel to your name.

So he's been taking on clients left and right, like the female castoffs of the Vanderhoff-Cho, Rosenberg, and Tattersall splits, also Stanley Guardini (ditched by his younger husband; you could see *that* one coming) and the poor, totally humiliated good guy Mike Iliescu, whose wife, it turns out, was boffing Mr. Tattersall—yeah, my English teacher's husband—and is supposedly running off with him to one of those psycho wilderness camps. The Tattersalls and the Iliescus are members of the yacht club, so the whole thing was max tectonic, socially speaking. The kind of thing where you couldn't not take sides. Or so says Mom. And she is the fairest of the fair.

Right after Tyrone showed Austin the site for his new bachelor château, Celestino took me and Finn up there to see the literal lay of the land. "Up there" is right. It's out near Harrow Point on a spot where a much older house burned down decades ago. The heirs hung on to the land until someone—that would be Tyrone—offered them the right price. So Austin's building him this total testosterone palace. It'll look like a massive ship with its prow aimed straight toward the incoming nor'easters. Austin says he's designed it to cleave a storm like a sailboat's bow divides a wave when you take it straight on. The wind's gotta be champion fierce up there, and right now there's nothing growing but one big-ass oak that Celestino says isn't long for this world. So plantings will be tricky.

Trees, of course, were one of the "sentinel alarms" Senator Kittredge listed in that stooge convention speech. Like what people who are old enough to vote haven't seen the years and years of death-watch headlines eulogizing coral reefs, honeybees, songbirds, frogs, bats, and just about all tropical fruits? "Play Noah's story backward," he said, "and that is where we are, folks. We are unbuilding the ark!" Clever. Talk Bible and you play to both sides of the room. But listen, rich old boy who gets to geyser on about your platinum ideals, talk about doomseers! After hearing your max-dire prophecies, who wouldn't *rather* live in what you call "end-stage denial"? Because what are you supposed to do, adopt a bat? Not like I didn't vote for the guy myself—I still have that PURGE OR PERISH biodegradable badge I got at the rally—and not like I didn't zone on the delusion of him as president, but when you think about it, who sanely thinks some old-money beekeeper-poet, from a part of Maine that's practically Canada, could begin to run a country as deranged and post-traumatic as this one? So I'm over it. I'm here in Brigadoom. As for Kittredge, he's back in Maine, CEO of a geothermal energy conglomerate. So much for *Cooperate Over Corporate.*

The frame on Tyrone's boff palace started going up last week. So I got the idea I could camp out there some nights and who would know? If Mom and Austin go to bed on the early side, I grab my sleep roll, a couple of beers, and hike on up. I go home at sunrise, and if I run into Austin, who's always up way before Mom, he's not going to ask where I've been. Not like I have a curfew. We do the *hey dude* wave and I head straight upstairs.

Clear nights up there, the stars are killer, and even if it's raining, I'm dry. The surprise is that I've got a crow's nest vantage on the night trawlers, or that's what I figure they are. You can't exactly see them—even if you have snipersight, they're just these voids of space—but I have amazing ears, and the first night I was up there, the surf was satin calm and I became aware of a mechanical hum, way out past Ruby Rock. Next time, I borrowed Austin's fancy binoculars, and sure enough, I could make out these ghost-boat shapes up top near the horizon, like paper cutouts on the moon-striped water.

Word is that the Coast Guard's totally overstressed on storm damage and drug traffic, that they've given up on policing black-market seafood; as crimes go, it's trivial. Or they're looking the other way. Austin says palms are being greased. It's not like the fish, or the ones everybody wants to eat, are ever coming back south. The notion of quotas is quaint. You hear about these old-world dories they use, heading out in buddy-system pairs, one the operator, one the decoy to fool the enforcers—if they show up. But if the boats are old-school, the diving gear and track-nets are hypermodern. They're equipped with life-seeking gizmos but undetectable, using some kind of military ghosting technology. Hackers of the sea. So if it's out there, they will catch it. And of course there's shark. They're off-limits, too, even if, thanks to the seals, they're not so scarce.

First night in my lookout, I stayed up way late just watching the dories slip to and fro, beads on a wire. They run parallel to the coast, sliding way up north for days, or that's the rumor, to the underwater banks off Labrador where the last fish hang out. Fun to picture the crews on those boats like old-timey pirates in a picture book I had as a kid: rings in their ears, patches on their eyes, pegs for legs, colorful parrots draped on their shoulders. *Argh, matey!*

The second night, Noam caught me sneaking out. I told him I was meeting a girl, and when I consider that lie, it's not a bad idea: I could hook a girl—my own secret fishing expedition—and take her to that place and she'd be totally, if she was worth it, awed and thankful. When the second level's framed out, I could bring her to the same spot where Tycoon Tyrone plans to plant his king-size bed. My wingmen? The stars above. (Nobody's figured out how to endanger the stars.)

But some things are better off not shared.

So last night I was up there, eyes on the horizon, eating Mom's cheesy turnip pudding (the dill from her garden makes it), sipping an ale from Austin's bougie Bev-rij, and I notice something new. A boat with a light—faint but sure, a tiny beam like a golden pencil. It's headed my way, in toward shore. Its passage is marked by a seam in the sky that means a naked mast: a sailboat under motor. It's dark-hulled, not white, so it's murky. No one on deck that I can see. Then it veers close around the end of the point, out of sight.

Weird. But weird things are the norm. Weird weather, weird politics, weird relationships. Another reason I like my routine, my own not-weird norm, however dull it seems to others. I show gratitude for it when I can. I do stuff I never used to do, voluntarily, like weed Mom's garden or do my own laundry. I heard Mom telling Austin I'm taking steps toward getting back in the world. But, *Mom,* I wanted to yell downstairs, I *am* in the world! This is my world, not some fantasy she might have of my living a "life of the mind" in New York or wherever. I am making *this* world mine, and I like it. I like it fine. If I were a bird, I'd be lining it with dead leaves and dryer lint and random cozy shit. It's a version of safe. Wave or no wave, that's all I basically want, though hell if I'd admit it to anyone. Safe.

I'm hoping work on the palazzo goes slowly. The nights are getting warmer, and maybe I'll loosen up and invite Noam. I can't tell if he resents that I've been keeping it to myself, claimed it like an alpha dog keeps that bone between his paws.

And then there's this: Austin's been a little sidelined by a journalist from some architecture institute who's following him around to write a profile or tribute. She's from Texas, says Austin, and though at first he was skeptical, he doesn't mind her company, and she doesn't get in his way. She sees him as an overlooked genius, which even though I'm not exactly qualified to judge, I basically doubt. That's the way she was talking when I met her in the office yesterday morning.

I was picking up my lunch. Mom does that sometimes, packs me lunch and drops it off at the firm or sends it in with Austin, since Celestino usually picks me up way early. He says early hours are the most productive (and, as summer looms, definitely cooler). He's right, since roads are empty and there's nobody holding you back with random chitchat, but I think it's mainly because he likes getting home early, back to Connie and Raul.

So Mom packs healthy food in these little steel containers she got at some Euro kitchen boutique when we still lived in New York. She's making sure I eat things like seaweed salad and apples and her excellent meatless meatballs, but she puts in cookies or cake, too. Her cardamom blondies if I'm lucky. Last year she bought up all these spices and froze them, right before the new tariffs happened.

So Austin was at the big table in the open area the offices share. He's not the kind of honcho who takes clients to an inner sanctum for private meetings—even though his office is the best one, giant windows from which you could dive directly into the harbor. But he goes in there pretty much only when he wants to do something solo, regeneration and creativity shit. He likes it when everybody at the firm works together in a "flow." He's got this fake-rustic wooden sign by the water machine that says OPEN DOORS, OPEN MINDS. So Filene and Troy, the baby architects, leave their doors open, though I notice that Hap, the guy who does all the digital scutwork, tends to close his. (His work, to me, is the definition of dull. And he's ten years older than me. *There* is somebody with no life.)

Austin was at the table with this woman, and they looked up when I came in. Austin's giant laptop was open, on its screen the plans for the new façade to Ex–Madame Tyrone's Federal mansion. I wondered if he'd take the reporter into the Vroom, this windowless closet-nook with a soft chair where you can put on a headset and tour the house you dream of that hasn't even been built. Fictional furniture and curtains. Sometimes Austin throws in a virtual pet. It's Moodroom minus the cheap psychology.

"My stepson, Brecht," Austin said to the woman when I walked in. "He's on our landscape team. Out in the field today, as you can see. You might enjoy tagging along with them, too."

From the state of my clothes, I looked like a mudslide survivor. Plus I nearly smirked at the notion of being on a "team." Yeah: Celestino, plus me, college dropout, plus Finn, whose brain I am certain was pixelated by weed. Go, *team.*

But she stood right up like I was a VIP, and the first thing I have to say is *fuck* was she ever tall. She's maybe fifty, but sleek fifty. She had on a long coat, made of something light and swishy, the color of fancy-ass cashews, a swoop of a coat that's more about style than warmth. Her hair was the same color as the coat, thick and braided like a helmet around her head. She looked like a warrior goddess, even her white skin bronzed—I guess by time in the Texas sun.

"Happy to meet you, sir," she said in this Technicolor Southern accent, a shock by itself, but "sir"? As if I wasn't half her age.

"Brecht, meet Mrs. Coyle."

"Petra," she said. "Please."

I told her I was happy to meet her, too, and sorry for my grubby appearance.

She clapped her hands together (nails tapered and polished copper) and said, "No sorrys for good hard work, young man! *Il faut mettre la main à la terre,* my Huguenot great-great-papaw liked to say. He had a modest grapefruit plantation, and I suppose he had an entourage of pickers, but he is reputed to have had his own hands in that soil the whole season through."

"Quite the history," said Austin, sparing me the need for comment when I had none. Though I did wonder how picking grapefruits would involve sticking your hands in the dirt. More like standing on ladders. But I excused myself and went to the bathroom to wash up. Celestino had us rebuilding a terrace at a house overlooking Calico Beach; the slate flagstones were jumbled all to hell by the last storm, not even a big one. The client wanted us to replace all his dead rosebushes, too, though not with roses. Roses are a bad bet. February was freakish: subzero for days, then a week of warm winds, then back down into the teens. (Except, says Celestino, you can't really call it freakish anymore.) The rugosas survived, but most hybrids caved, heirlooms frostbitten back to the rootstock. Celestino's shown me the chart he keeps of temps through every winter. It helps him predict which plants will survive in which gardens, which will seem dead for a while when they're not, which ones leaf out fine but fail to bloom. Wisteria, he says, will be flowerless for the third year in a row. Not that the vines don't still spread like armies on a mission, splitting clapboards off houses and strangling drainpipes.

While I was in the bathroom, I listened; hung out at the sink, washed my face, tried to get a comb through my wildman hair. Mom says it's more like a mane, though she doesn't tell me to cut it. I know it makes her think of my dad.

I heard Mrs. Coyle say, "Look at what you've done with these curved dormers. And this clerestory! My oh my. Flattery's not my job here, but who would've dreamed up such graceful lines, marrying the new to the old? Ingenious."

"Not to the purists," said Austin. "I'm afraid what I'm doing is highly inauthentic, but the commission has lost its teeth. The Antiquity Commission."

"Teeth? What teeth?"

"The ability to do more than strongly suggest restrictions on exteriors. The ability to enforce. To tell rich white people what they can and cannot do with their money."

"Progress will have its way," said Mrs. Coyle.

"As will regress, I'm sorry to say. Sometimes they march hand in hand," said Austin. "But if you come back in a couple of weeks, we'll be starting the actual work."

"I have nowhere pressing to go," she said. "I am taking my time on this project because I'm enjoying it. I hope you don't mind."

"How could I mind?" said Austin.

On my way out, I nearly forgot to pick up my lunch, but Austin stopped me. "You're on the Frankenheimers' terrace?"

I nodded.

"Finish today, do you think?"

"Should," I said.

"Splendid." A word he'd never use if it was just us. "Tomorrow I promised Tyrone we'd make a site visit with Celestino. Brainstorm trees." I knew this was his way of getting himself to a place where he could mention the boff palace in front of his visitor. Which, why shouldn't he? I figured this woman would now be along on that visit. But while me and Austin traded a few more logistics, I saw her staring at me, like she was unpeeling me (as opposed to undressing; more a psychic than sexual thing). I was spooked, though Austin would tell me it's just the doomseer in me, on post-traumatic alert. (Can I tell you how tired I am of all this PTS talk?)

Her eyes, unlike the rest of her, are a sharpshooter blue. Blue like the sky before the bomber drove his little death truck into the farmers' market and filled that sky with flash and then smoke. Smoke, but also flying fragments of so many things, things that shouldn't have been, blown to smithereens. That's the most vivid memory I have: the sky filled with every conceivable color of smoke, me standing at a high window that might or might not have been in the room where I lived. I can't really tell you where I was for a lot of that day.

Petra

The Texas ruse was an affectionate wink back at Carly, dear Carly, but what the hell was I thinking? That I could exist round-the-clock inside this saccharine bless-your-heart clown suit for days on end, maybe weeks? You don't do an antebellum accent these days, at least in these parts, without courting ostracism. Though I admit it: I was also feeling nostalgic when I cooked up this new persona, challenging the me of olden days who went from audition to audition, eager to land anything from the sufferer in a laxative commercial to a toga-wearing member of the Greek chorus in Off-Off Euripides. And I did get to play Marguerite Gautier back in my college days.

But that left-field remark about the Huguenot grapefruit-growing grampa with his hands in the dirt? Did I think I was in improv class or what?

"Darlin', you are impulse incarnate," Carly once said to me, and she meant it kindly, since had I not been impulsive, I'd never have marched right up to her in the lobby of the Manhattan Theatre Club and told her (half-whispering) that the extent to which the dress she was wearing showed off her profoundly enticing derrière was downright dangerous. We were each alone, each sipping champagne at intermission while pretending to be engrossed in the headshots of that night's all-queer-female cast, and when she turned and stared at me, widening her clover-green eyes in slow-motion shock, I thought, *Well, at least I'm not going to be slapped.* But then she said, in her plush San Antonio accent (one I could not have rendered for the role of a lifetime), "Let's not discuss what your dress does for your heavenly tits."

Off came those dresses that very night, to lie in a slippery pool at the foot of Carly's king-size bed with its view of Manhattan's closest thing to a forest primeval. (Honest Abe, I had no idea!)

We were together for the next twenty-one years, until five months ago, when Carly had a mushroom cloud of a stroke—at the hospital, of all places, in the middle of Grand Rounds. We had barely unpacked from the trip we took to celebrate her sixtieth birthday at a four-star Mexican hacienda in the lap of a majestic volcano that exhaled subtle sparks by night, ethereal plumes of tulle by day. I thought of that idyllic week as our honeymoon, too, since we'd married, without pomp or circumstance, a few months before. As if she knew what was coming, Carly insisted that she'd begun to lose sleep over the need to ratify my place in her life should she drop dead.

"Your ass is nowhere near dropping dead," said I. "Your amazing ass."

"You don't like to face that I am the older woman," she said, ignoring my bait.

"By six years. Big deal."

"And the rich one."

"I hate it when you bring that up. You know I don't give a fuck."

"Why not? Why on earth, darling," said Carly, "shouldn't you be glad that if you have to mourn me, you can do so in material comfort? I'd definitely give a fuck if I were you. In fact, if you don't give a fuck, then I should be fucking somebody else, somebody who appreciates the trips we take, the restaurants we frequent—"

"Carly, Carly, you know I love, love love *love* all that. You know it. I'm sorry. I just don't need the rock on my finger, my name on your accounts."

Legalities honestly didn't matter to free-spirit me, and I suppose a teeny sprite in some nook of my better self stubbornly wanted Carly to be damn certain I wasn't with her for her money (or her terraced two-bedroom lookout on Central Park West). Because I wasn't. I am quite certain we'd have been together even if we'd occupied a cramped, drafty walk-up on Avenue D (not that such places exist anymore). But not giving in to her pragmatic proposal began to seem ungracious. So we did it no-frills: city hall at ten a.m., no flowers, no rings—though we did have lunch at a favorite French restaurant we fondly called The Overprix (rhymes with *dicks*). That was less than a year ago now. No wedding anniversaries for us. And now I wish we could have had at least one—dozens. Is there a lesson in my adolescent resistance to tradition?

But as hard as it was to lose Carly without a moment's warning, let alone a loving if painfully lingering farewell, that's how easy it was to sell the apartment and transfer the assets. Somehow, against all logic in a place that's proven so vulnerable to catastrophes both random and malicious, a view of that park still sets off a bidding war (even if the view now includes the new flood basins, underscoring just one reason so many people have fled). In the weeks before the closing, I sold off the few valuable objects we had acquired on our travels and called Carly's hospital's thrift shop to pick up the furniture. Clean slate, new life: I didn't know yet that I'd be veering back full circle to settle old scores.

I turned fifty-four three weeks after Carly died. Friends sent cautiously festive messages by all the too-many means of connection we now have; I answered none of them. I started the day in our pink-tiled shower, where it occurred to me that I had now lived one year for every card in a full deck, if you count the jokers—and count them you always should. Looking back, I could actually regard some years as red in feeling, others black. Some years had been as sparse in luck or joy (or, conversely, as chaste or serene) as an ace of clubs on a field of white, while others were byzantined with patterns designed to complement a woman's cunningly jeweled tresses or conceal a knave's fist clutching the hilt of a dagger. Queen of Hearts? The year I met Carly. Jack of Diamonds, the year I got that one decent film role, the one I thought might turn my fortunes around. But oh, if ever there were a joker in the pack, it would have been the year I turned twenty-nine, the year of Issa. Or was that one my Queen of Hearts? Treason to Carly, that I should even waver. Which rates the greater score in love, the queen or the ace? How about hearts versus diamonds? To those who'd misread me as a gold digger, I suppose Carly was my Queen of Diamonds.

After my birthday shower, during which I cried a Venetian canal,

I went out and ate an uncharacteristically enormous breakfast at a place on Columbus that Carly and I had never set foot in, or at least I hadn't. It was a fern-filled bistro renowned as a heterodominant pickup bar in the evenings, a young-mothers rendezvous after another kind of pickup: that of the kiddies from preschool. So it was still mostly empty when I took a booth by the window and found, on the seat, one of those thick shiny architecture rags that have so far survived the encroaching death of print. In a state of pure sloth, I paged through it without much interest while I waited for my Lumberjane Special (pancakes, eggs, yogurt with pinecone granola—more calories than I'd generally consume in an entire day). Just as I was about to toss the magazine aside, I happened on a spread showing a house tucked into a hillside overlooking a meadow confettied with flowers. Desirable as it might have been, it wasn't the house that sent blood rushing to my face; it was the headline, or, really, just the name.

VIEW BECOMES VISION:
ANOTHER AUSTIN KEPNER GEM

I read every word of the article, and at the end, I looked into the face cameo'd against another picture of the house and said, "So there you are." Here he was, a man I had met only once, in passing, decades before, yet for whom I had dreamed nothing but daggers. (Was Kepner my Jack of Spades?)

I consider it no insult to Carly that I am on a mission to avenge if not track down Issa. Sometimes I tell myself that all I want is to know what became of her, not to reclaim her. Twenty-five years ago, after she disappeared (I do not buy the story that she killed herself; I do not believe she would have or even *could* have), I went so far as to hire a detective, though the only one I could afford in my pre-Carly life did little to impress me—he was, after all, another underemployed actor—and when he came up with the lame verdict that she probably did drown after jumping in the river (as the dull-witted cops had concluded), her body swept by the river currents clear out to sea, I thought, Well maybe, but that would not be the end of Issa. At worst, she would have returned to her underwater origins, her true clan. (Call me demented. I've been called worse.)

Having unpacked my bags, I inspect the room at the inn that Austin Kepner recommended after buying my story. Maybe, deep down, I was hoping he wouldn't, but egos are so inflatable, aren't they? So here I am, all at once a freelance writer commissioned to do the groundwork for a possible documentary called *Building by the Sea in a Time of Tempests*. In digging down on all things Austin, I read an interview in which he was asked if he identified as an apocalyptomist. Kepner's answer was that he considers himself "a master at defying disaster," a coy way of saying that he's fluent in the new, more resilient materials used to construct coastal buildings in the post-Cunégonde era.

Not lost on me is the irony that this building, the Twin Chimneys Inn, has surely withstood any number of storms over close to four hundred years—without all the newfangled stress-proof metals or vulcanized synthetic rubbers. It's one of those authentically colonial mansions spilling over with by-the-book organic charm. Thanks to the warping of wood through a long life of seasonal swellings and constrictions, every angle is crooked, the doors hang loose in their frames, and the skewed floorboards creak beneath the rug every time I cross the room. Even the windowpanes distort the outside world—and probably leak cold air in the winter. The glossy doors of the antique wardrobe do not quite click shut, and the mirrors on the outside are stippled and foxed. In the closet masquerading as a bathroom, I have only a shower to wash in and only a skylight for ventilation. And these Shakespearean rafters, for God's sake: I'm going to behead myself when I have to pee in the middle of the night.

But it does open onto a private foyer, from which two steep flights of stairs take me to the ground floor, a warren of small common rooms and a tiny bar outfitted to feel like the cabin of a sailboat. In all likelihood, my room—now called The General's Retreat, according to a silly brass plaque on the door—was once an overcrowded crash pad for servants.

Yet it also reminds me of a hotel room in the Alps that I shared with Carly in the rosy days of our falling in love. Carly was in Switzerland for a conference, and she paid for me to tag along. By day, while she rode a gondola to the top of a mountain to meet in a glass-walled conference center with other physicians bent on thwarting the spread of tropical plagues, I roamed the town—a skiing enclave on summer hiatus—eating sausages and chocolates in a vain effort to quell my hunger for Carly. We would meet for dinner, sometimes in the company of her colleagues (English the common language, though I wouldn't have cared if it were Swahili), and then stay up half the night making a riot of our expensive, monastically pristine bedsheets. Every morning of that week, I awoke in the lint-colored dawn to see Carly, naked except for her reading glasses, poring over sheaves of footnoted tables and graphs spread loosely across the cloudlike duvet.

"Graph me," I'd whisper, removing my lover's Ben Franklin specs.

I loved Carly, and I'll miss her forever, but Carly loved me more. We never said so, but we knew it. Unlike me, she wasn't tugged at by any unresolved historic passions, and she repeatedly declared her gratitude to whatever cosmic forces had schemed our collision. Her devotion anchored me in so many ways. She even paid, without expectations or conditions, for half a dozen years of acting classes and later, when that damn virus extinguished my ambitions once and for all, as cleanly as a cigarette snuffed beneath the heel of a boot, supported me during the embarrassing period I think of as The Breakdown, before I lucked into my consolation vocation as a designated shopper to the filthy rich at one of the city's new membership-only men's stores. How happy I am to leave *that* behind.

I contemplate lying down on the large, inviting bed, but no. I want the rest of my first day here to be entirely constructive. I must study those images I've gathered of Kepner's houses, from sites like Architectonomy and Domiphile. But first, I appraise my views. The inn is in the middle of what my map calls the Village District, my room on a corner. From four crooked windows, I survey a helter-skelter of steeply pitched rooftops, two church steeples, and the absurdly narrow roads twisting hither and yon. The wooden houses are painted in a fauvist range of colors, as if, in defiance of its architectural stodginess, the town has delusions of Bermuda in its glory days.

Directly below the side windows I also see the walled garden abutting the inn, one of those spots where young couples will pay a fortune to stage a fairy-tale wedding. At the moment, a gardener is raking dead leaves out of the flowerbeds. For a moment, I feel as if I'm back at that luxurious hacienda, because he might well be Mexican; maybe he's one of the lucky ones who found a sponsor early on. I'm reminded, painfully, of how we lost Manuela, Carly's longtime housekeeper, despite Carly's best attempts at bribery and string-pulling. Naively—stupidly—we thought we were somehow immune, and by the time we got our paperwork together for Mani, we were told it was too late. The paltry quota of sponsorships for our district of the city had long since been filled. That Carly was on the board of the opera with a district judge (a fellow dyke with whom we sometimes partied at the Fig and Leaf) helped us not one bit. We suppressed our upscale white guilt by sending Manuela money for a few years, but then we no longer heard back. Eventually, we could not tolerate sending money for which we received no acknowledgment. I wonder sometimes where most of that money went: to cartels, to postal clerks, to corrupt policemen on the take? But that is one of my worst faults: fretting over past choices when they have been chiseled into history.

After he finishes raking, the gardener stands back to look at a small tree, then goes to a truck parked on the street, brings back a stepladder and a set of pruning shears. I watch him for several idle minutes. Perhaps in this back corner of the world, you can hide your Latino workers, your island nannies. Perhaps in a place like this, you can pass them from one employer to the next, like clandestine hand-me-downs, no paperwork, no records. I wonder if I've fallen into a closed society; narratives ranging from the Narnia chronicles to *The Stepford Wives* spring to my overactive mind. Were we in New York, someone would have snitched on this fellow a while back.

Why is it that I'm now far more conscious of people's skin tones, and the implications thereof, than I ever was as a suburban adolescent, decades back, in hip-hop-era New Rochelle? How foolishly we talked ourselves into believing we were "enlightened," even equal. Prince and Ice-T *ruled.*

The inn does not have a restaurant, so I'll need to inquire about delivery or take my drawl and my Lois Lane small talk out to some sit-down establishment. (Oh-so-helpful Kepner, that scoundrel, gave me a list.) I do seem to have a small fridge in my room and will have to stock it with whatever I can fit.

I've been ignoring my phone, since no one knows I'm here; theoretically, I'm on a no-fi yoga retreat and then visiting my elderly mother in her Scarsdale condo, where I've also claimed I'll be offline, too busy with Mom's demands and frailties. But I check it anyway, by habit, and see that, speak of the devil, there's a vext from Kepner, sent an hour ago. He wonders if I want to ride along tomorrow for a site visit. And his wife hopes I'll come to dinner one of these nights.

Oh, a wife. A wife. *Why yes indeed, darlin', yes, I'd be tickled magnolia pink to accept her invitation.* And I vext him back to say how much I'd love to do both. *My schedule is yours!*

All right then. Now to put myself out and about, explore the terrain, assess the battlefield! *Oh you drama queer,* I hear Carly tell me, her casual laugh a sign of her approval. *You laugh like cashmere,* I told her in our days of ravishment. And yes, I did tell Carly about Issa, but not the whole story. If I had told her everything, even Carly would have thought I was raving mad. Or perhaps especially Carly: a doctor, a scientist, a disciple of the empirically sound. And if I were ever to tell it out loud, to anyone, probably I would reach the same conclusion. But that final night I spent with Issa—that precious, indelible, brokenhearted night, one of only two—I know I witnessed her other self, her primal self. I suppose I should, rationally, call it her supernatural self, but it felt nothing other than natural, our coming together that way, that final night. Could I have saved her? That's the question I asked myself for months after her disappearance, but how grandiose. Perhaps she saved herself. From dirtbound human stupidity and skepticism. From all things corrupt. From men like Austin Kepner.

I look down at my bare feet. I flex my toes against the worn rug. My toenails need repainting. With a pang, I think of Issa's perfect feet, how I wondered, when I kissed them, if they were counterfeit feet, hallucination feet. Did it matter? Issa was the love of my life.

Austin

I used to think that the apex of any successful architect's career—and I'm not including the Mile High Club: the Gehrys, Venturis, and Wrights—would be the imagining, engineering, and building of his dream house. Mine would have been a far less aggressive version of Tyrone's: on the coast, yes; great expanses of glass, yes; a high perch at the edge of the world . . . but mine would lie close to the earth, a single-story form, sinuous, sprawling, more like a sleeping cat, my bedroom the tip of its tautly curled tail, looking both out across the water and back toward the body of the house, so that when the sun rose (I've never wanted to live on any coast but this one), I'd wake to see both the taut cord of the horizon and, if I turned my head, the fiery illumination of my other rooms, urging me to get up and loop my way through the curving cherry-paneled hallway, past another bedroom, into the belly of the cat—an ovoid living room crisp in the early daylight—and on through a narrower dining room into a south-facing kitchen. A house not vast, not grand; just singular. It would hold me and a woman I had yet to meet, and there we would know how to be both alone and together, we would entertain friends and associates, we would do our work. This was after the catastrophe of my time with Issa, a handful of months that weighed on me, on my willingness to share my life with anyone else, for years. Yet I knew I'd grow out of that cautionary solitude. I knew I'd meet someone: someone sane and stable and settled.

In a way, the dream of the house was both consolation for and distraction from my folly, shame, and unavoidable guilt.

For ten years, I maintained two accounts for my dream house, one in the bank but the other, the important one, in my head: an accrual of details; of angles, surfaces, and dimensions; of materials neither cheap nor flashy. I didn't know where the house would be—in what town or even state—but if a business trip took me somewhere coastal and I saw a piece of land for sale, I'd plant my fantasies there. I was far from affording such land, but I was working my way up at the firm, inching closer.

Superstitiously, I kept my house in the ether of imagining; I opened no files for it on my computer, created no virtual models. When the time was right, the place secured, I would dive in deep.

And then, like everyone else, I watched the world shut down around me: lost jobs, lost dreams, lost lives, lost . . . gravity. By which I mean, all assumed connections to the ground beneath our feet. A house takes its foundation for granted, you might say. A person, too. In the second month of the first surge, both of my parents—who'd been so pleased to find that retirement community not five miles from the house where they'd raised me near the Jersey shore—became infected and died.

Swiftly, one by one, the firm's active projects had stalled. A number of junior architects, those I thought of as just below me on the ladder, were furloughed. I took my Cadillac of a desktop monitor home from the office to my apartment. Within days, I stopped dressing as if I were still entertaining clients. I began to wish I had a dog.

My father called about my mother two weeks into the lockdown. No, there was no point in my renting a car (if I could get one) and driving out from the city. No, I would not be able to see her, not even after she fought it off, as he knew she would. *Strong woman, your mother.* He was strangely calm about it, and I let myself be reassured by that. My parents were always level-tempered, rational people. I spoke every day with my older sister, marooned in her own house arrest, with husband and children, out in Milwaukee. We spoke more in two weeks than we had in two years. We found artificially common ground in our sense of sudden, shocking impotence. There was nothing we could do but wait. Then our father stopped calling, nor did he return our calls. Five days of silence, after which we heard from a woman we'd never met, a stranger telling us that our father was on a ventilator, our mother gone. She was so very sorry; the nurses were overwhelmed, some of *them* now ill; she would help us make arrangements, but no, we could not come; *please don't endanger yourselves and others.* (How I remember that "others.") Would we like to speak, over the phone, with our father? He wouldn't be able to speak to us, but he'd hear us. Yes, one at a time would be best. Could she call us each back?

That day, every bit of it, every twist and turn, I remember, from the breakfast of yogurt and apples I couldn't eat to the dark blue shirt I wore for the Zoom call with two of my associates. We were going over options for structural downsizing and cost-cutting measures in a corporate athletic facility—dwindling budgets were already having a domino effect on buildings still in the planning phase—when the call came through, my chance to speak with my father (in fact only *to* him), maybe for the very last time. But before the sympathetic stranger could set up the call—and how, really, would I know that she was putting the phone to Dad's ear?—I had to sit on hold. I'd taken the phone into the bedroom, and I sat on the edge of my bed, taking in all the flawed details of the walls and windows I would have overhauled if I owned the place, while into my ear flowed a version of "Skylark" as cheaply crafted as the mullions in the nearby window. And then I was being told, ever so gently, that she, the stranger, was going to lay the phone next to my father and put me on speakerphone. On speakerphone, I sobbed my way through the platitudes of a probably-but-please-let-it-not-be last farewell. *You taught me everything worth knowing. You and Mom showed me what love should be. But I will see you soon. You'll make it. You're a warhorse.*

That summer, I drove to New Jersey to retrieve my parents' cremains, arrange for their burial in the plot my old-fashioned father had purchased decades before. Nearly a year later, when I returned to working in the firm's office, I was so shaken that I started spending any free day I could get driving north and west to look at houses on the market in any small town lush with trees. I drove up into the Hudson Valley and out past the Meadowlands, as far as the Delaware Water Gap and even into eastern Pennsylvania. Everywhere, as if to stoke my yearning for escape, I saw the ubiquitous blooming of azure hydrangea and volleys of flame-colored lilies. I was surprised to find that the prices hadn't fallen, not at all; they had ballooned. I was in no shape, financial or mental, to buy any of the houses I looked at, but I had a burning resolve.

After two months of this fool's quest, I became exhausted and surrendered to the revised rhythms of doing business in a world overshadowed by a cat-and-mouse plague. Those few years are, to me now, a claustrophobic blur.

And then I met Miriam. We'd been seeing each other for a few months when we confessed to each other that we were done with the city. I had a classmate with a thriving small-scale firm in Cambridge, and he said he might be able to take me on as a consultant. He lived in a seaside town from which the commute to the office was, he confessed, a living hell, but he could do much of his work from home. He suggested that I book a room at a nearby inn. I hadn't been there more than an hour when I realized I wanted this town more than I wanted the job.

And like an omen, there it was, just a few blocks from the inn. The house was small, old, emphatically vertical, with a long narrow lawn that ended at the property fronting the harbor (a neighbor to take the brunt of swollen tides). Strong trees, handsome antique windows, a sheltered view. Looking through one of those windows, I could see that the owners had already left. Standing on the tiny lane that ran past the front door, I called the agency on the sign and booked an appointment for later that day.

The agent, no fool, saw through my attempt at nonchalance when I spent so long in the medieval crawl space of a cellar. "You oughta know, you're looking at a bidding war," she told me when I emerged. She lowered her voice. "But also, because I have a hunch you'd be a good fit here, at a market where the pressure is to sell inside."

When I asked her what she meant, she told me that old-timers on the town's select board were making it clear, discreetly, that Vigil Harbor was now in danger of becoming a haven for urbanites seeking a new kind of refuge, a place to flee that was close enough to civilization yet, socially speaking, kept to itself—and kept an eye on itself. "We like believing"—she chuckled—"that we're all the progeny of mariners. I mean, go figure."

Would I live in a place with such an insular attitude, all because I wanted to live with this lawn pouring almost directly into the sea?

I called Miriam from the lawn while the agent caught up on her texts in the kitchen. I told her about the risks I was willing to take—and those I wasn't. Ironically, considering that we both wanted out of dense city living, what felt reassuring to me about a house in a true, old-fashioned village was the surroundedness. Suddenly, I knew that I no longer saw my happy future self as the lord of a small private manor on a windswept cliff. If I was ever to face sequestering again (and I was pretty sure we would), I wanted the comfort of being walled off from yet surrounded by others in the same plight. I was humbled not by a sense of community but by a coming to terms with the limits of my own independence. Or, let's face it, with my lack of go-it-alone courage.

At dinner that night, I told my classmate I wanted the job, and I wanted his connections in this town.

We live in that house now, and in it I feel both anonymous and free.

The insularity, however, is haunting at times. It's hard to know if it was always there and that insidious remark by the agent who showed me the house was simply the paranoia of the moment. Some things changed forever, some veered back to how they were, or seemed, before, but I know this: I have very few clients who come from far away. This visitor, the woman writing about me, reminds me of that with her *Streetcar* accent, her sleek self-conscious clothing, her intent ogling of everything and everyone around her. She is, as my mother used to say, "a bit much," but I have my own vanities, so who am I to talk?

But Brecht's return is also a reminder of the town's commitment to a kind of baseline "normality." I know people talk about him. Oh, they pity him. (And they pity us, Miriam and me.) They thank their lucky stars nothing so awful happened to any of their children out in the world (not yet, I could rudely point out), but it's Noam's mother they pity the most. Miriam used to call her now and then, even suggest a walk or a glass of wine, but the truth is, we pity her, too, and she knows it.

I won't deny that a yearning for some mythical normality may be what drove me away from New York, though hadn't I already embraced it simply by falling for a woman like Miriam, who'd sailed through some pretty treacherous waters to emerge without cynicism, neurosis, or unreasonable fear? I told her I wanted to make my own way, apart from the hivelike firms where I'd worked since getting out of school. "All I want is to build houses," I said. This was a little disingenuous, and she knew it, because she said, "But not Monopoly houses."

I wanted to build houses for people who were well-off enough—just enough—and discerning enough (well, more than enough) to want to come home every day to somewhere not quite like anywhere else. My classmate, with his small but selective clientele, gave me a foothold in that world.

But I've never been interested in building modern-day castles, "estates." So I've compromised myself in this project for Thaddie Tyrone, which is, if not a bargain with the devil, a tutorial on the epitome of modern sin: domestic decadence. I caved, I like to tell myself, because to say no to a man like Tyrone would be to sabotage too many meaningful local connections. And now that I'm well rooted here, I like to keep my business local.

The house he wants isn't large by the standards of his income bracket—living space will measure under four thousand square feet—but he wants it to be crafted of the rarest materials, and he doesn't want salvage. No floorboards or window frames or bathtubs once walked upon, gazed through, or languored in by anyone before him. Always be careful, I have learned, when clients tell you to spare no expense. Either they will, in the end, balk at that expense or their standards will become stratospherically impossible to meet.

Miriam told me, at the beginning, I'd live to regret saying yes, but since I did, she hasn't said another word. He visits the office at least once a week, asking her to let him in the Vroom so he can gloat once again about his palace in the sky—and so he can tell me that maybe we should reconsider this or that chamfered edge, this or that depth for the closets; and isn't the stone I've chosen for the terrace too blue? Doesn't it compete too much with the color of the sea? Each time, I nod and pretend to ponder, then placate or reassure him.

I've handed over more of my "lesser" clients—that is, the smaller jobs—to Filene and Troy than I normally do. But it's good for them, and makes them happy, and it streamlines my emotional interactions with the likes of Stanley Guardini and Mike Iliescu, both so rudely and publicly betrayed by their spouses.

I'm no stranger to facing the heartbreak of watching someone you believed was your soul mate suddenly turn childish or brutally mean or even stark raving mad. It takes a long time to recover, because the person you no longer trust is yourself.

Mike

As I stand among my flotilla of boxes, staring out at the meager triangular park by the meetinghouse, its half-dozen maples struggling from salt-poisoned roots, its benches commemorating citizens worthy but long dead, I try to convince myself this wasn't a mistake. Staying in town—not fleeing to some primitive retreat in the windblown middle of nowhere, as chumps like me deserve—is something I've done largely at the urging of sympathetic friends. The collective refrain seems to be, *We refuse to let you out of our sight, so don't think you can run away.* She *is the one who ought to leave town. At least she's doing something right!*

I'm genuinely surprised so many people have stood by me in my mortification, though I imagine it's Margo Tattersall who rallied the troops. "Listen, buster," she said the second time she knocked on my door, "the fuck with this woe-is-me Quonset hut vision—as if a softie like you could even survive in those conditions."

Reluctantly, numbly, I followed her advice and put myself in the hands of a so-called relocation consultant—no mere *real estate agent*—whom I secretly christened Broker Babs. Her jewelry alone told me the price range of the properties she is accustomed to selling, and she clearly thought I was ignorant or stupid when I told her that no, I didn't even want to look at the place with the harbor view. "Don't want it," I said. "Don't want to pay for it, either."

"I want you to know that we are talking *priced to sell,*" she argued. "Three bedrooms, two baths, grandfathered PV hot tub—nobody puts *those* in anymore. Gray-water cycling, outdoor shower on the waterside deck. *Max* closet space. And listen: the view will knock you flat. Plus, as I need not tell *you,* Dr. Iliescu, we are sitting pretty here, well above the floodplain. Are you a morning person? I'm guessing you are. Because the sunrise over the ocean—"

"Anything but the godforsaken ocean," I said, and if I were a believer in any deity, I would have meant that literally. "As I said, two bedrooms, the usual amenities, that's all I need." Twenty or thirty years ago, I might have opted to live on a boat, but nowadays only a fool would choose to live in a floating home. Sometimes I think of my father, standing in the basement of our suburban ranch house after a mighty summer cloudburst, staring at a dark shape on the concrete floor as it spread slowly toward us from the bulkhead door. "Son, remember this," he declared ominously. "Once you become a homeowner, your number one enemy is water." How much more right he's become as time marches on.

Not that living inland, where flash floods and tornadoes and blizzards make their own mayhem, is much less risky, but I'm with those who realize that the romance of living at the water's edge has waned. It's exhausting, like living with a spouse who has a bad, unpredictable temper (come to think of it, what it must have been like for my mother to live with my father). Even the salt marshes I am trying to salvage seem to lie in wait. In ocean-hugging towns like this one, sailing remains glamorous and addictively intrepid; the older yacht clubs still have waiting lists for membership. But sailors with any sense resemble swamis, shrouded in solarproofed fabrics, faces layered in Asian ointments yet to be approved by the FDA.

We were in Broker Babs's car, parked by the building containing the purportedly idyllic apartment, when I told her *no ocean view,* and for a moment she looked at me the way I once saw my wife, so many times over so many years, look at our two teenage children.

Which provoked a wishful twinge: now that I was being forced to give up the house they knew (thanks to the mother they would probably forgive, whom I should probably *want* them to forgive), would they ever come to stay under my roof again, together? I thought of their visits home from college, half a dozen years ago, when their high school friends traipsed oafishly through the house, speaking in post-adolescent, post-millennial vernacular, tracking slush and mud across the carpets, making locust runs on the refrigerator, leaving damp beery patches on the furniture. I still recall, with a perplexing nostalgia, the endless plinging of their various devices (devices whose sleeker, more cunning descendants I now use compulsively myself). How doltishly ungrateful I was for their presence back then. Now Marinda, like some latter-day Persephone, has been sweet-talked away to Cal North; her husband, as he declares so often, could never live anywhere else. (How much was the man drawn to my daughter's accidentally Californian name?) Egon, who seems to shrug off the escalating risks of New York City, is closer to home, but just to maintain his bare-bones existence, he holds down two or three shifting jobs. Forget a casual visit from him.

So here I am, under a new roof, tossing sleeplessly on a new mattress, having put my cyber signature on all the necessary marriage-sundering e-forms, when a mere month ago my life looked like any other lucky suburban stiff's empty-nester humdrum existence, wife sharing bed, mortgage paid off, antibodies good and diverse, blood pressure A-okay.

I turn my attention from the living room window's view to the worn-out miserly kitchen (part of the reason this place was such a "steal"). Once again thanks to Sergeant Major Margo, a very young woman named Filene, an eager-beaver associate from Austin Kepner's firm, has just left the premises after taking countless pics and measurements with her toylike Dij and asking me a series of questions to give her a "design vision" for my "culinary habits," "aesthetic preferences," and "domestic social needs" (a less duplicitous wife, anyone?).

She pointed that tiny device at me to record my answers, and if not for her gamine cheer and pretty smile, I might have lost patience and told her to just do whatever the hell she wants to my kitchen. Spray-paint it gold! Install a fountain! Pave the floor with rusty nails!

Her final question was "How do you feel about red?"

"Well, it hasn't offended me lately," I said. "That I know of."

She laughed more ardently than she should have, but her amusement seemed genuine. "So there's this max-new zero-impact surface we've been using, and it comes in a fabulous shade of carmine. Max durable, too! In a really big room, it might overwhelm, but in this sweet nook of a kitchen—"

"Sounds perfect," I said.

"I'll get you a sample. Others, too, for sure. Think of it like an inspiration kit."

An inspiration kit. All my problems solved!

I'm guessing she's in the latter half of her twenties, and I almost asked if she grew up here, if she knew Egon or Marinda in school. But did I want that conversation? Of course not. I thanked her and saw her out the door, watched her descend the flight of steps to the street level, and waved goodbye.

Just then, on the chipped granite counter soon to be transformed by a "fabulous shade of carmine" (since I do not plan to spend a minute with that inspiration kit), my phone buzzes. Weirdly, I find myself thinking it might be Margo, about to issue another set of orders. I realize that as much as I resent her edicts, I welcome them, too.

At least I can be sure it's not Deeanne. And why would it be? I'm the abandonee. When she has anything to convey, she contacts her lawyer, who contacts mine, who contacts me. In shedding her past, she's even changed her name. Modesta, she signed on the docs severing our union. Christ, does Tom have a new name? I'm thinking Brutello.

"Dad? Where are you? Are you in your new place yet?"

"Marinda. Sweetie." Saying her name gives me such pleasure these days. Hearing her voice even more so. "I'm standing in my new kitchen. Or old ugly kitchen. Which is getting a makeover. The rest of me is mostly in storage."

"So the house . . . ?"

"Everything's out. The agent doesn't want to show it with my scruffy guy belongings. The things your mother left—"

"You dumped them, I hope. Your right, that's for sure."

How quickly she's gone from interrogating me about what I did wrong, nearly accusing me of dynamiting the life I had with her mother, to condemning Deeanne outright. As heartily as I want to agree with her, I say, "You and Egon may want some of her things, down the road."

"Those pretentious tapestries and Louie Whatever armoires and settees? Fat chance, Dad. All they remind me of is how *careful* we had to be when we had friends over. 'No drinks without coasters!' 'Shoes off in the parlor!' *Parlor.* Like we lived in somebody else's house."

Again, I resist the bait. "So it's staged. You wouldn't recognize it. Not exactly cheap, but the sooner it's off my hands, the better."

"Whatever it takes," says Marinda, and I detect in her firmness a repressed energy of some kind.

"How are you, sweetie?" I ask. "How's Harkney?"

I can actually hear her draw a deep, shimmering breath.

"We are good, Dad. We are very good. We have news."

She's pregnant. I know it before the words are out. Yet her rapture is subdued, even tenuous, as if I might mind that she's happy, as if I might wish that everyone else were mired in self-pity.

"Oh my girl. My grown-up girl." The first sob erupts as I speak, like a stone rising from my chest, freeing space in my heart.

"Are you ready, Dad? Ready to be"—such joy in her laughter—"a grand-pa?"

"Sweetheart. I am ready as I'll ever be. Why not."

Marinda begins to cry. Before I start in, too—if I let myself go, I won't stop, I just might *bawl*—I say, "Your mother knows?"

"No way would I tell her first." I'm gratified to hear the rasp of anger in her voice. "And it's a girl, Daddy. I can't wait to take her out with you, on the boat. I miss sailing with you." *Daddy.* When did she last call me Daddy?

"You're my best crew. You know it. You've got those mermaid feet." This is a joke dating back to her earliest years. *But, Daddy, mermaids don't have feet!* I picture Marinda's small, plump torso engulfed by one of those old-fashioned puffy orange life vests. Last week, during the move, I came across one, furry with mildew, in the bottom of a trunk at the back of the mudroom. Beneath it lay a tiny pair of boat moccasins, the leather dry as wood. Some creature had made, and long since deserted, a nest in one of the shoes. I wiped away tears as I stuffed these useless artifacts into the compactor. Again and again, I was ambushed by the outgrown things we'd kept by accident, things that, simply by proving the passage of time, became freighted with emotion.

Now Marinda goes through the sweet ritual to which she occasionally treats me: naming all the things she misses, my abducted daughter—though Harkney is no Hades. From afar, he seems to be a good husband, and he makes a good living. He's the CFO for a series of wind farms off the Pacific coast. Marinda is as secure as I could wish. She lives far enough from the fire zones, far enough from the nearest city, and she works from home—though probably now she'll devote herself to the baby. I suspect Harkney would want her to be a fully dedicated mother. He's probably a closet member of the Backlash. Never mind. Better than a loony Timer, which is what Deeanne appears to have become. *Modesta.* Jesus.

As usual, Marinda ends her list with "Most of all, you. I miss *you,* Dad. You need to come visit! I keep telling you, you have to see this new aquarium. The reef is phenomenal. Even you couldn't tell it from the real thing, I'm sure."

I say, as usual, "We'll see, sweetie." The thought of a micromanaged reef—coral in captivity—drags me down, just a little. Living coral reefs—out in the natural world, where they belong—are like pandas, accessible only to those who can pay the price of admission. The transplants succeed in the short run, at great expense, but even the latest hybrids seem to be failing. It's a matter of temperature, pure and simple. We can fight to batten down and buttress our coastal margins, but we cannot cool the ocean.

"Dad? I'm sorry about being so mean when you called me that first time. I was furious you hadn't returned my calls. I already knew about the baby. I was just—"

"I know. Bad news upstaging the good. I know."

Before we say goodbye, I remember to ask if she can put Harkney on the phone.

Father and husband have a textbook exchange, brief and painless, of manly well-wishing. Did I have such a conversation with my father-in-law when Dee was pregnant with Egon? I hardly remember.

When I sleep the phone and lay it on the counter, I can't ignore the report I've printed out and brought home to review. As always, more cheery news: this time, the acid blooms in the Mediterranean, another wave of marine mammal die-offs—all those beautiful dolphins revered by the Greeks, so few of them left. Here, jellyfish cruise the beaches all summer long, and on a level the average beachgoer won't perceive, the vast banks of deep-rooted cordgrasses to the north—the muddy fortresses I think of as my little kingdom—are surrendering to the storms. Even at low tide, many of the twisting estuaries no longer reappear. The bay is now claiming the marsh.

I exert myself mightily toward hopeful thoughts of the world into which my granddaughter will emerge. The things she will and will never know. Stop, I tell myself. Is this the beginning of old age, this irrepressible pull of futility? My own father lapsed into a storm cloud of silence once he retired. It killed my mother, I'm sure of it.

I should probably get a scrip for something to lift my spirits. Is this another suggestion from the new voice I've acquired, my inner Margo?

I forgot to ask Marinda if she told her brother about the baby. Probably not. I should try to get them both to come for Christmas. Once the house sells, I'll be able to afford the outrageous airfares. I'll put Marinda and Harkney up at Twin Chimneys, camp out here with Egon. Could we bond as intergenerational bachelors? Or maybe Egon's found someone new. Not, I pray, another actor. The last one was disastrous, a dandy and a user. He stole half a dozen of Deeanne's antique trinkets, though I forbade her to mention it—especially once the dandy stormed out of Egon's life.

Christmas, then. I begin to dream up a menu. I imagine using my connections to get a whole salmon, a wild one, for less than a ransom. The fatted calf, I think; of course, a calf would cost a great deal less than a salmon. A crime in itself.

And then I realize that Marinda's baby will be only a few months old by Christmas, too young, too vulnerable, to risk the exposure of a trip cross-country. My resolve deflates, and here I am, once again, keeping intimate, unobstructed company with my anger and disappointment, my fruitlessly going backward in time to obsess over this or that incident, all the warning signs I clearly overlooked. Scientists are supposed to be smart about the details, aren't they? But if current science is any indication, we're better at hindsight than prophecy, the Sorcerer's Apprentice a more fitting patron saint than Nostradamus.

Could I trace the demise of my marriage to some specific evening on which I'd stayed home to pore over statistics rather than attend some YC membership reception or declined to watch Dee's favorite sitcom? Or how about the time, ten years ago, when the power company "updated" all our streetlights by installing new bulbs that, while far lower in energy usage, emitted an acrid light that turned Vigil Harbor, by night, into a movie set? Suddenly our bedroom, at the front of the house, was flooded with the blinding brilliance one associates with interrogations in old detective movies. I can sleep anywhere, but Deeanne, that first night, gasped when she turned off her lamp.

"What the hell is this?" she cried out, standing by the bed. She moved her arms up and down, jumping-jack style, to demonstrate the stark shadow cast by her body on the closet doors.

"The new lights," I said. We had read about the upgrade in the town paper, glad to know that our little power company cared about conservation.

"But this is insane! I feel like I'm at the airport!" She leaned close to the window, open to the summer air. "You can't even see the moon!"

"It does seem bright," I said. "But we'll adjust."

"Adjust? Adjust to *no night*? That's absurd, Mike! We have to protest!"

I pointed out that the town's money was spent, the deed done, that we were just unlucky in the proximity of our bedroom to the lamp. Perhaps we could install heavier curtains?

"And what? Seal ourselves off in some tomblike dark? No. Tomorrow you will call them and tell them it has to be fixed. Give them a piece of your mind. They know you, Mike, from your time on the seawall committee. They respect you."

"Deeanne, I promise you it's a done deal. They can't—"

"If you won't call them, I will. Why are you such a pessimist?"

"I'm not going to stage a tantrum, if that's what you mean."

"Did I ask you to stage a tantrum, Mike? Hardly. I asked you to make a civil request. Is that so challenging?"

At that, she bolted from our room, slammed the door, and went downstairs to sleep in the den. The next day, without mentioning the issue again, she made up the foldout sofa and, for a week, slept there. I knew she was waiting for me to bring it up, to cry uncle, but I didn't. The last thing I wanted was to go down to the power company and, if they were to laugh at my complaint, accidentally stage that tantrum.

And then, in all likelihood because braver residents spoke up, one day a utility truck parked in front of our house, raised its bucket lift, and a man in a yellow helmet attached a steel shade to the lamp, focusing its beam straight down toward the bushes at the base of the pole. Deeanne moved back to our room, again without comment. But a month went by before she let her body touch mine.

The thing is, I do have a temper. I try to lose it only in solitude. This resolution has been a moral credo of mine since well before my marriage. These days I am forced to wonder how well it's served me, to wonder if my, as Deeanne called it in some early attempt at a sparring match, *fucking placidity* made her regard me as somehow "less of a man." Because if there is one dominant trait in Tattersall, it's his blowhard alpha-dog nature, until recently on frequent display at the yacht club bar, down at the marina, and anywhere else he *knew* he was right or didn't get his way.

Well, he got his way with Deeanne.

I suffer, it would seem, not just from "placidity" but from emotional witlessness. I suspected not a thing until she announced, as she removed her pearl earrings after the First Hurrah, the dinner to launch the next sailing season, that she and Tom Tattersall would be moving away together. She made eye contact with me in her mother's antique mirror and said, after a few beats of my speechless staring, that she hoped I wouldn't fight it.

"Let's make it a clean break," she said, "for the children's sake." Had she calculated the rhyme? Why did that even enter my mind?

She and Tom, I learned through my virtual coma, had already purchased shares in a "small-footprint community" in northern Wisconsin.

"Wisconsin?" I managed. I have a gift for brilliant repartee.

"I promise to be out of your hair," she said as she brushed out her own. Quintessential Deeanne: ever the multitasking wonder. I had a fleeting memory of standing in the kitchen, years ago, as she labored over the stove, cooking up some complex French sauce for a dinner party while talking to our broker about rethinking our tech stocks. This was the wife I not only loved but admired. Whose fidelity, along with her knack for investments, I had taken for granted.

Through the surface of the mirror, I continued to stare at this same wife as she spoke rationally about her imminent departure while she unbuttoned her red silk blouse, baring a pink lace bra that I realized—stroke of insight!—she had purchased with another man in mind.

"We have to be calm about all this, Mike," she said, an order I seemed to be following already.

"Calm?"

"Oh Mike, when was the last time we had sex? I mean, *real* sex. Planned a vacation together, just us? Shared a dinner at home not in front of some screened entertainment? That is, when you're not running off to your sirens of the deep. It's no secret how lonely I've felt for years. Children do not a marriage make. Especially children who no longer live here."

Had she rehearsed this speech?

"'Sirens of the deep'?" I said, seizing on the detail least relevant to the crisis at hand. I felt the tears rising. Salt water: the essence, the crucible and crux, of my livelihood.

She crossed the room in her pink bra and long silver silk skirt—I had never taken such urgent notice of her garments before—and stood in front of me, close. Looking fearlessly up into my eyes, she placed her hands on my shoulders. "Mike, I know this is painful. I'm sorry about that. It's painful for me too! I know how much you depend on the routines of our married life—though let's be honest: haven't our lives been essentially separate for a while?" Her eyebrows rose. She had registered my tears. "Did you really not know? Not even see how absent I was? Oh Mike."

I wanted to strike back at her for mocking my work more than for demeaning our marriage (or my love of habit). Did that prove her right?

"Don't do this to—"

"The children? They're adults now. They understand that things change and that we outgrow so many decisions we made when we were younger, especially the big ones." She had removed her hands from my shoulders by then, and I couldn't help glancing at her left hand. When had she removed the ring I put on her finger in the Vigil Harbor Unitarian Church thirty-two years ago? "I'll sleep in Marinda's room tonight, and we'll talk about the rest of it tomorrow," she said. "The house is yours, of course."

Without a word, I watched her take her robe from the hook inside her closet, her toothbrush from our bathroom. When she closed the door behind her, I stood in the same spot on the bedroom rug where I had been standing when she launched her grenade.

Not until the next afternoon, following a "conversation" comprising a list of practical "next steps" delivered by Deeanne across our kitchen table, did it dawn on me exactly where she had been all those afternoons she claimed to be taking archery lessons and warrior yoga. Ironically, she wasn't lying; she had taken up these perplexing forms of recreation alongside Tattersall, "training" for their planned retreat from civilization. Their cue to make a run for it had been the offer of an honest-to-God full-time job issued to Tom's youngest daughter, the last of five children on both sides of the affair, leaving our respective nests empty. Whereupon it became searingly obvious to me that they'd been carrying on for years.

Who else had known? Had our *children* known? What had she said to me about the children? Not *They will understand* . . . but *They understand* . . .

When this eviscerating thought struck home, not long after Deeanne left to "do some errands and give you a little space," I went into my den, closed the door, and slammed my palms again and again on the surface of my desk until they were bright with pain, red as raw meat. Had I been my father, I would have destroyed something: a chair, a lamp, a row of family photographs on a shelf. And he chose inanimate objects only when he was alone in the house. My mother or I might return to discover a closet door kicked in, a stack of bowls shattered on the floor. Such a sight would bring us relief, though we never said so; we had missed the storm. In my own house, I ought to have welcomed such destruction. It was a house my wife had chosen and filled with useless ornaments, now apparently all mine to do with as I pleased.

Less than twenty-four hours after keel-hauling my ego, Deeanne left the house with two small suitcases. Apparently, she and Tom had a short-term rental a few towns closer to Boston. They would be driving west in a few days. "But until then, you are welcome to contact me with any questions," she said.

"Questions?" I laughed. "Aren't we going to hire gladiator lawyers and go at each other's throats?"

"I've hired a new lawyer who'll be in touch with Teddy," she said. "You will use Teddy, won't you?"

"Teddy isn't a divorce lawyer." I cursed myself for being logical.

"You won't really need one. There's nothing to fight over. I've left you just about everything except for the nest egg I had from my mother's estate."

"Tattersall is, what, 'treating you' to this runaway bride scenario?"

"Mike," she said. That she hadn't set down the suitcases told me most of what I needed to know.

"Go," I said quietly. "Just go."

The next week felt like a scuba dive into a shipwreck strewn with crusty, twisted metalwork and the skewered skeletons of trapped sailors, through which I kept on breathing, though I couldn't envision returning to the surface.

Another man might have found consolation in his work, the boisterous camaraderie of colleagues, but my job is largely solitary and has become disheartening, simply because the bottom-line numbers—from carbon levels in the rhizosphere to seabird reproductive rates—are increasingly dismal. If you meet me at a cocktail party and ask me what I do for a living, I'm likely to tell you that I study the health of the Atlantic coastline, with a focus on its diminishing liminal zones. I started out, thirty years ago, working for the organization that monitored the cod-fishing industry in New England, work that was—because I'd been such a head-in-the-numbers nerd in grad school—shockingly, upsettingly contentious. I couldn't take the politics. Living in a town where fishing as an income was still relevant if marginal, I would run into fishermen who kept an FBI-style most-wanted list of the top-tier employees of Marine Fisheries, otherwise known as the Quota Nazis. Their trucks bore stickers that openly accused us of destroying their homes and families. One summer day, while I was down on the town landing, preparing to take the children out on the boat, a lobster trap tossed through the air came shockingly close to my head ("Hey, didn't see you, man!" But who could miss that menacing leer?). Next day, I put in my notice. Now I'm with ORCA, the far more academic, idealistic Ocean Rescue Coalition Agency. In a way, I'm back to being a wonk, head in the clouds, which suits me fine. Except that the figures I compile from the samples we gather refuse to sugarcoat the truth. It's turning out that I study not so much the health of ocean life as its descent into terminal illness. I'm in marine hospice.

So after Dee left, I went through the motions at the lab by day and paced the house by night, ignoring calls, even from my children. She meant what she said: she had organized her entire defection, leaving me such "generous" portions of our once-communal funds and assets that there was indeed nothing to fight for, nothing to disentangle, no material revenge to be had (though I do not think of myself as vengeful). She told me that a volunteer for the church-sponsored shelter would call me to empty her closet! I took petty pleasure in wondering which of the calls I ignored was from said volunteer, probably a prurient member of the YC who would put on a faux-sympathetic act, hoping to siphon from me whatever grisly details she could for the local gossip mill.

I drank too much, bourbon my poison of choice, and ate very little. One night I emptied a jar of almonds, almost literally pouring them down my gullet, as I thought with grim, illogical glee of how much that jar had cost, trying to recall precisely when almonds had become a gastronomic luxury comparable to caviar, caviar now all but unobtainable, no matter how much money you care to spend. So many curiously random foods a thing of the past. Passionfruit. Vanilla beans. Certain kinds of tea. Never mind cod.

I tried not to imagine Dee and that absurdly giraffish man fucking in the tiger maple four-poster bed she had bought on our honeymoon in Nantucket. Failing to shut out those images, I took to sleeping down the hall in the twin bed once occupied by Egon. Every night, when I turned out the lamp, I found myself drunkenly astonished that those plastic stars and planets I had affixed to the ceiling still, decades later, glowed so resolutely in the dark. I awoke every morning to behold, through my jackhammer headache, a time-warped poster of some ambisexual movie star playing Macbeth, reminder of yet further anxiety: a child well past childhood who wants to be an actor (or *is* an actor when he can be); worse, a child living in New York City.

Unlike the phony constellations on the ceiling, New York has lost a good deal of its glow. Or, rather, its glow is now as much a reflection of danger as of glamour. No malicious attack has matched the scale of 9/11, and for a moment after the global death harvest of the first viral surges, I was among the gullible optimists who thought that calculated acts of violence might just—like passionfruit—be a thing of the past. But political rage is resilient, and after the "patriot" sacking of Congress, misfits and radicals and gun-happy yahoos from hither and yon all got back to work: the kidnapping of that attorney general, the explosion at Cannes, the gunman at the ski resort in Jackson—and then, a year and a half ago, the Union Square car bomb. Sure, the violence can emerge anywhere at all, but I still see New York, always, as the most tempting target.

I knew it was unsustainable, my gloomy retreat, and I knew I would have to move, sell the house. I would have to ask Egon and Marinda to come home, one final time, and sort through their childhood relics. I would also have to start answering my phone—or at least looking to see exactly whom I was ignoring. Egon and Marinda were the callers I dreaded the most, and I wondered if, had they lived closer, one or both of them would have materialized at the door on a mission of mercy.

As if my wondering had summoned it, on day eight of my self-exile, the second Sunday, the front door knocker sounded: vigorously, leading me to assume it was a man (though it was too vigorous to signal the arrival of my gentle son).

Deluded has become my middle name.

"Please tell me you are taking that whore for everything she's fucking worth."

Standing on my granite stoop was Margo Tattersall, whom I had last seen at the YC dinner—the final hours of my evidently willful ignorance: possibly hers as well (our Last Conjugal Supper).

When I failed to answer her challenge, she asked if she could come in. Could I say no? Why didn't I *want* to say no?

Knowing our house as well as anyone who'd attended our cocktail parties and Fourth of July cookouts, who'd dropped off and picked up children from playdates in happier if more chaotic days, Margo marched through the front hall and the dining room, landing on a stool at the kitchen counter. (Briefly, I registered my gratitude that the early friendships among our kids hadn't lasted.)

Casting an eye over the teetering stacks of cereal bowls and highball glasses, she said, "Another woman would sigh with compassion and put this place back in order." She stared at me fiercely. But then she did sigh with compassion, and her tone softened. "I know it's noon, but I know we need a drink. And I see from the contents of the sink that you have not been shirking in that department. Let me guess: a diet of cornflakes washed down with Manhattans?"

She lifted a glass from the sink and sniffed it. "Am I a genius or what," she said, and from a canvas shoulder bag she pulled out a bottle of . . . yes, bourbon. She ordered me to find or clean two glasses.

As I obeyed, Margo said, "So what did *you* do to drive the spouse away?"

"Are you blaming this on me?" The first words out of my mouth since her arrival.

"Of course not. But the general assumption around town was that you and that whore led a peaceful coexistence, probably spiced up with torrid sex. The absentminded science guy being the male version of the smoking-hot librarian. I mean, you were just about the only couple who never fell into a boozy squabble at one of the club dinners. 'Oh they're so simpatico, and he's so smaaaart,' " she drawled.

"I don't know who would say that. Most people there found me a crashing bore." Hearing myself assess my reputation at the club in the past tense, I realized that I would resign. This felt like a glimmer of good news. I loved the sailing, but I hadn't raced in years. I also recalled how much vicious pleasure I had taken, not long before, in cornering Vince, the insufferably vain vice commodore, and forcing him to listen as I described in detail watching an aquatic vet perform a necropsy on a minke whale that had washed up on a Gloucester beach. A parasite afflicting the inner ear was spreading like wildfire: alarming news in my parochial world, and I wanted to discuss it, though I'm usually well-mannered enough to respect the particular company I'm in. That night, however, I'd been in a spiteful mood. Had I sensed, but refused to acknowledge, that I was the club cuckold?

"Who knew?" I asked. "About them."

"Not me," said Margo. "I'd have had your wife's head on a platter, Salome-style. If others knew, I will find out, and I'll decapitate them promptly. Impale their heads on the tallest masts in the harbor."

This did not sound like a woman with a broken heart. A wounded ego, sure. Yet Margo was one of the club wives I had always vaguely enjoyed. She never hid her opinions, she was an accomplished solo sailor, and it was hard not to notice what a sexy dancer she was at the banquets. A little overweight by social standards, she wore dresses that told the world she liked her shapely shape.

"Do your children know?" I asked.

"I told Tom I'd slit his throat if he didn't let me break the news. I do wonder if Cynthia knew already. Her outrage sounded a little synthetic. She's his favorite. But I forgive her." Cynthia was their youngest, the one whose recent employment coup had green-lighted this fiasco.

She asked about Egon and Marinda. When I admitted I hadn't spoken with them yet, she took a slug of her bourbon and actually whistled. "Because . . . ?"

"I've been answering calls . . . selectively."

"Oh Mike. Jesus, Mike. You're a good man, but you are kind of a coward, aren't you?"

Perhaps my not feeling offended by Margo's remark only proved her right. "In answer to your first question, she's left me with practically everything."

"Ouch. Now that's emasculating, isn't it?"

Almost stunning, the sound of my own laughter.

"So let's get you out of this house." She picked up a pepper mill shaped like a Balinese dancer. "Away from all her tacky bourgeois shit. That is step one of your rehabilitation."

"Who asked you to rehabilitate me?"

"I need a new hobby. I've chosen you." Margo set her empty glass beside the sink. "And I'm the only one of your friends with the balls to take you on. You need a good shake-up, you know that?"

Did she plan to haul me off to my own bed, some post-equality take on the old caveman trope?

"Oh no," she said, reading my mind, "I have no plans to fuck you. And look, now you're free to traipse around with twenty-somethings. Girlfriends your daughter's age!"

"Margo," I said, "is this some form of shock therapy?"

"Yes, Einstein. Yes."

"So what is step two?"

"Wait. We haven't completed step one. Tomorrow, at noon, my pal Babette is picking you up. She'll find you a decent place to land. Only decision: rent or buy."

"If I want help of that kind, I should call Daphne. We always . . ." As I spoke, it occurred to me that Daphne, Deeanne's doubles partner every year at the YC tennis tournament, might even be awaiting my call.

"We? Mike, you're not a *we* anymore. I am not a *we* anymore. Christ, our fucking *country* is not a *we* anymore. You just haven't begun to admire the silver lining of your woe shirt. We are talking silk. We are talking kimono silk."

I had a flashback of Margo when she was the English teacher at the high school that all ambitious parents in Vigil Harbor wanted for their children—and that every child hoped to avoid. Against type, it was my daughter, not my son, who struggled under the iron hand of Mrs. T. Egon, my teenage hermit, my almost-but-not-quite-out-of-the-closet fragile adolescent, blossomed in her AP English class: had his first taste of Tennessee Williams, fell in love with Margaret Atwood and *Moby-Dick*. At the soliloquy recital that was a rite of passage for every one of Margo's pupils, Egon, a stunningly hilarious Malvolio, was the star.

I would always be grateful to Margo because she was the teacher who'd helped him find a direction, even if it was one that often distresses me now.

Margo looked at her old-fashioned watch. It was a large man's watch, with smaller dials inset, famous among her students as the timepiece by which she clocked the recitations that most of them dreaded. "I have to run. I've managed to nail an appointment with Kepner."

"You're building something?"

"Upscaling my second floor. Exorcising the demon husband. I am plowing through the money he claimed he was saving for a bigger boat. Looks like he decided on a woman with bigger breasts instead. Which I am pretty damn sure she wasn't born with. Don't answer that."

Reading my face, she said, "Don't be a softie, Mike. You will now have your choice of breasts. A four-star tasting menu."

"You are so vulgar," I said.

"Only in the company of allies and friends." She picked up her drink—mine sat beside it, untouched—toasted me, and took a small slug. "Twenty years in a classroom minding your mouth and you get to make up for lost time." And then she did something startling: she stood up and hugged me. I hadn't felt comfortable sitting, so she had to cross the room to do it. She held me tight with her soft yet muscular arms, the arms of a genuine sailor, and she made a low growling sound that might have meant frustration or affection. Or both. When she released me, she stepped back and smiled warmly. "Whether or not we were friends before, we fucking well are now," she said. "Agreed?"

"Sure," I managed.

She went back to the counter but did not sit. She picked up her drained glass and rattled the ice with gusto. "Okay!" She returned to me yet again and hooked her right arm through my left. "Your assignment today," she said as she guided me to my front door, "is to call your children. On this one, I'll give you a pass/fail grade. Shouldn't be hard."

"And future assignments?"

"Time will tell," said Margo. "As it always does, the fucker."

My call to Marinda, an hour later, after a cup of strong coffee, felt like the hardest of my life.

"Dad, what is going *on*? Where have you *been*?"

At hearing the fear in her voice, I was ashamed of myself.

"I'm sorry. I've been . . . a little in shock."

"What is going on?" she said again.

"What did your mother tell you?"

"That she's moved out. That she's starting a new life, like moving *out of state,* but I have to talk to you first before she tells me the 'whole story.' "

Maybe I ought to have wished that Dee had told them everything already.

"She did tell you it's her idea. Her doing. Did she?"

"That *what* is her idea? Dad?"

I had wanted to speak with Egon first, but as usual, I had reached only his virtual self. Whether he was tending bar, doing some sort of online wordwork, or lucky enough to be in a rehearsal, doing what he deemed "real work," he was hardly ever in a position to answer his phone. Egon and Marinda are still close, despite choosing lives on separate coasts, and had I been able to reach him, I might have asked him to call her before I did, to "feel her out," to scout ahead. (Yes, Margo, I am more than a bit of a coward.)

"Your mother hasn't been happy," I said. "For a long time, it turns out."

"You knew this? You must have."

I hesitated. Lie or tell her the truth, I'd look like an idiot.

"I should have. It doesn't matter. She made up her mind."

"But what—where did she go?"

"She's moving away . . . with Mr. Tattersall."

I suppose the long pause was predictable. And the explosion.

"Becca's father? What are you talking about, Dad? Mom is running away with *Becca's father*?" Becca Tattersall, the middle daughter, had been Marinda's date to the junior prom. Whether they were just friends or, as one used to say, an "item" was never clear to her mother or me, and since pregnancy wasn't a risk, we never broached the subject with Marinda. "Where are they going? I don't get this at all!"

"I don't get it, either, honey."

"And you, like, had no idea?"

"If you want to yell at me, go ahead, but I'd rather you yelled at Mom."

"So this wasn't mutual? I mean, is it because you both—oh God, don't answer that." She started to cry.

"Honey? Is Harkney there?"

"I am not falling apart, Dad. I am just furious that it's taken you a whole week to even call me back. And please stop acting like my husband is some kind of manager who needs to protect me from reality when it sucks."

"I'm sorry."

"Is that what you told Mom? Did you just *let her go?*"

I knew what she was driving at, yet I was appalled that my own daughter would corner me with the accusation that I didn't know how to fight for my marriage.

And that's when it hit me, like a pebble from a slingshot, or that airborne lobster trap if it had found its mark: I didn't even want to fight for my marriage. Perhaps Margo knew this and her visit was a noble effort at yanking me free from the carapace of delusion that had enclosed me for . . . years?

"Marinda," I said, "you need to talk to your mother. I don't want to talk any more about all this until you hear her version. You should also hear about her plans."

"Plans?"

"Sweetie, I can't speak for her."

Was her silence stubborn or frightened? "Dad," she finally said, "are you okay?"

"I will be."

When I got off the phone, I looked around the kitchen and saw it differently. I saw it as a sum of belongings to be sorted, packed, and disposed of. Margo was right. How had I come to live with a pepper mill shaped like a Balinese dancer? Where the hell had the object come from, and why? Never mind that the pepper it produced was pink.

Now only a select few of those belongings lurk in the stacked boxes that dominate my new living room (floor in need of refinishing, hideous ceiling fixture overdue for replacing, windows begging to be washed). If I unpack the box labeled KITCHEN, I can at least contemplate feeding myself, rather than going out to collide with people I know but wish I didn't. I realize that I now live within staggering distance of The Jetty, our one anachronistic dive bar. Except that certain members of the YC love to slum it at the pool table there, it might be a tempting refuge.

Why don't I just up and leave town? I could move north, closer to the lab. It's not as if I grew up in Vigil Harbor. Somewhat haphazardly, I landed here in grad school when my recently widowed thesis advisor offered me a room so I wouldn't have to mix drinks or wash cars to pay rent in some marginal precinct of overpriced Boston—and, he claimed, so he wouldn't pity himself into a lonely alcoholic stupor. He also groomed me to crew on his J/24 in the yacht club's Wednesday night races. For a time, I fell in love with sailing, with the precise yet whimsical dictates of wind, but that wasn't what seduced me. No, it was the casual privilege I misread as wholesome, old-fashioned trust. A few months after I'd moved here, on the day of a local election my mentor deemed important, I was swimming off the town dock when I realized that the polls were about to close. Wrapping my towel around my swim trunks, I sprinted to the town hall, wondering if I'd be turned away without an ID. In the lofty vestibule, a man and a woman, both with hair the same gray as the local granite, greeted my sodden self without so much as a raised eyebrow. *Name and address, young man?* I gave them eagerly and was about to apologize for arriving without a wallet when the woman simply handed me a ballot and pointed to a cluster of school desks set up for the occasion beneath the patriarchal gaze of Vigil Harbor's seventeenth-century founder, immortalized in bronze.

As droplets of water from my hair puckered the printed names of candidates for various offices, I decided I'd found the place to grow old. Not two weeks later, among sailors gathered after a race in which her uncle's boat beat my mentor's, I met Deeanne.

I'm once again walking the perimeter of the apartment, still learning the light switches, the water gauges, the various faucets, valves, and circuits, when the news alert sounds on my phone. In fact, I hear it sound both on my phone and on whatever device is being carried by a pedestrian passing beneath the window that looks onto the park.

It is only because of my grown children that I do not block the alert feature, the way I've refused so many other newfangled connections and conveniences. So when I pick up the phone, I'm alarmed to see that the news is indeed about New York, and of course it's bad, and of course it's sudden: not the creep of contagion but the shock of detonation. The boat basin at Battery Park, explosions from both water and land, destroying a dozen luxury sailboats, gutting the first floor of the nearest office building, killing or injuring an undetermined number of people on the walled promenade between. Casualties yet to be tallied. I watch less than a minute of the coverage, the sirens sounding tinny and mosquito-like in the palm of my hand, before my thumb finds Egon's name. While I listen, heart racing, to the voicemail I know all too well, his pleasant but businesslike tone aimed at agents and casting directors, I reluctantly switch on the wallscreen, submitting myself to full-scale mayhem, the specter of smoke and fire, shredded metal and trees become torches, while wondering, desperately, what other ways there might be to reach my son. Why don't I know any of his friends? What kind of father is this unconnected from his only son's life? I pick up my phone again and type on its tiny keypad, *Please come home. Answer me.* I meant to type *call home*—and does he even think of it as "home," the place that now resembles a high-end showroom of casual elegance, the stars peeled and scrubbed from his ceiling, his posters rolled into a cylinder now consigned to a storage pod in another town?

Political arrogance is highly contagious. There is no place for humility, much less modesty, in contests of power where egos cast the longest shadows—longer than those cast by childish or unethical behavior. Some people like to see their advocates act like children, because children often get what they want even when it isn't deserved. But what about violence as a means of getting what you want?

Terrorism has been around forever, often as the last resort. The citizen militia of Vigil Harbor, its gun-bearing fishermen, blockmakers, cordwainers, coopers, and masons, became terrorists when other options failed. What they wanted was in keeping with what their wealthier neighbors wanted: the freedom to fish, trade, make and sell goods, however and wherever they wished. It was a war about commerce and taxation, pursuit of prosperity as much as happiness. Prosperity enables *happiness (well, in theory). In the end, all stood a chance to profit, to raise their bottom line—all who were not indentured or enslaved.*

But what about fighting for abstract gains on behalf of others, maybe on behalf of people not yet born? What about remotely crafted, even symbolic acts of violence? Violence in pursuit of virtue? You know that to aim at your target, you will have to inflict innocent casualties—bystanders killed who weren't engaged in your war, possibly including allies—and you might even regard it as tragic, but when you weigh the collateral damage against the power of a catastrophically full-throated statement made in more than mere words, you'll come out in favor of whatever gets you the most attention. Why plan a stealthy assassination when you can set a bomb—or two—or, go ahead and make no bones about it, three. Three is a number with folkloric resonance. Maybe the collateral damage is a bonus.

Do not sacrifice yourself, however. Delegate the detonations—and run for the hills to plan your next strike. Feel just how powerful you are in the ease of your escape. You are no mere soldier. You are a general, back behind the lines to plan your virtuous violence anew. You are a patriot to progress.

Local historians in Vigil Harbor like to point out how many soldiers the town has sent forth in every generation. There were two or three generals in the furthest reaches of its history, but in modern wars, it has tended to produce fighters of less elite ranks. Seventeen young men and one young woman who grew up in Vigil Harbor were killed in the long wars waged in Iraq and Afghanistan—a fraction of those who died in the fight against the Crown—and of these eighteen lives, five were taken by insurgent bombs, outside the so-called theater of combat.

The last of them was Staff Sergeant Caleb McKenna, who died in the later years of that conflict, well after its intended target, a single man, was blown away. McKenna's funeral shut down the town's roads, along with many of its businesses, for one long blistering day in an exceptionally hot and thirsty August. By the end of the year, the select board had voted to rename the paved entrance to the high school—the dropoff-and-pickup traffic loop—S.Sgt. Caleb McKenna Circle. The dogwood tree planted in his honor, next to the flagpole, has grown to a surprising height of thirty feet. Every June, as the school year comes to a close, its large muslin-colored heart-shaped petals flutter down onto the bike rack and the bus shelter and the idling cars like a harmless late-season flurry of snow.

Connie

Today the children study science and math with Caitlin and Elio, so I am, as Trina, our onetime dancer, would say, flexing my soul in the wings. What that looks like, however, is pretty mundane. I make sandwiches and fruit salad, I do an inventory of art supplies, and I vext the education coordinator at our local historical museum to confirm next week's field trip. This leaves me time to sit down and join the children as they watch a film on plate tectonics. What keeps them riveted are the earthquakes and volcanic eruptions, of course, the lava in its spooky-silent red-hot ooze, the archival photos and shaky you-are-there videos of after-quake destruction in cities like San Francisco, Seattle, and Kyoto—all reassuringly distant in the eyes of our beloved little students.

We, the teachers, are also the parents. Most of the children are onlies, each eight or nine years old, though there are two sets of twins. Our families found one another when we were all in the same birth class, with the same midwife, at the hospital over in Knowles. We stayed in touch, and after sending our toddlers to various podlike preschools, we knew we didn't want to send them to the collection of public schools that some of us disdainfully call The Mill—our locked-down, test-focused, digitally driven educational system—and what others, like me, worry could once again subject our children to the next, possibly more lethal outbreak.

At first I questioned the fear behind my motivation. Was I simply afraid of letting my child go out into the risky world? And it's always been risky; how obvious is that? But when we decided that the parents who volunteered their home as the school base would be paid for it, I knew I was in. Our house is the smallest, but everyone agreed that when it came to play, our yard would be large enough, and it's fenced in. Besides which, no one has anything to rival our tree house. I gave up my part-time job at a local salon to teach art and manage the school's licensing and logistics. I'm the closest thing we've got to a principal—not that anyone gets sent to me for a scolding.

Because Caitlin insisted that seeing the world in living, animated color is crucial to studying science, we suspend our screen-free policy two days a week. Elio also persuaded the other parents to let our children use an online math tutorial, especially those who are precocious enough to gallop ahead of the rest. You would be right in guessing that the screen allowance makes science and math far more popular than they were when I was in grade school.

But the film's relentless disasters only remind me of last night's news: a bombing in lower Manhattan, all but destroying a walled riverside plaza and an adjacent pier where billionaires moor their yachts. Most of the boats were damaged beyond repair, a steel sculpture in the park was blown to jagged bits, and the first-floor façade of the nearest office tower shattered in a storm of glass pebbles. Nineteen people are dead—most of them wealthy guests at a party on one of the yachts—and dozens more injured. The explosion took place at the hour most office jobs let out, when financiers cut through this plaza to catch a ferry across the Hudson River.

Celestino and I have no close family or friends in the city, but we know people who do, and he lived there for a few years in his twenties, long before we met.

"Did you know that place?" I asked him last night. "That park?"

He shook his head. He lived in places far uptown, tough places that have since been gentrified, not that he's ever been back. The only thing the city gave him that mattered was the work he found after stumbling, sheer luck, into a bottom-rung job at a large, elegant public garden, where he learned to care for plants and trees. He also learned that it was in his nature to care for them—that he had an affinity for keeping things healthy and green. He used to say he would take me there someday, show me around the grounds, but I don't think it's something we'll ever do now. It just doesn't seem worth the risks. Our marriage is legitimate, sound, and nine years strong, but Celestino does not like crossing borders of any kind. He still worries about the student visa he violated when he was a teenager, about being punished for old crimes. He tells me we live in unforgiving times, old sins lurking just around a corner, waiting to ruin the lives of the people who've moved well beyond them. When I tell him that overstaying a visa nearly forty years ago would hardly get someone in trouble, he tells me I might be right—but also naive. I can never understand how careful he must be. And the harder it becomes to move here from almost any other country, the harder certain people will look at those for whom they think it was far too easy.

So he says, my husband, and I have decided it isn't my place to argue. He's also fifteen years older than I am, and he's seen how quickly the winds change direction for those who weren't born here.

I am upstairs folding laundry, listening to Raul give a presentation on his "life map" assignment (Caitlin is a fan of good old-fashioned geography), when I hear the front-door knocker sound. Because of the school, we get a lot of deliveries—and somehow they always arrive when I'm on the second floor. I shout down the stairs that I'm coming and abandon the basket.

On the other side of the door stands a middle-aged stranger who is not in the uniform of a courier. He wears black jeans, a black T-shirt and denim jacket, and he holds no packages. His skin is a gleaming dark brown, and his hair—as black as his clothing—is shorn close to his skull, gray advancing from his temples. He's wearing a backpack and, in one ear, a tiny red jewel.

"Connie," he says right away, his smile so bright it seems invincible. "You're Connie."

"I am," I say, aware of the heat in my face. Door-to-door salesmen are forbidden in Vigil Harbor; a sign at the town line states the large fine for scofflaws. I'm fairly certain I've never seen this man before, but he said my name with such familiarity. "Have we met?"

"I feel as if we should have. Celestino . . ." Now he's the one to blush. "I'm so sorry. I am Ernesto Soltera." He presses his palms together and bows slightly. I notice the tease of a colorful tattoo protruding from a sleeve.

I can see that he's poised to enter the house. Trained to see every stranger through my husband's eyes, I question whether he might be some sort of enforcer. Hardly—and, through my own eyes, I remind myself that there is nothing to enforce.

"Celestino and I are old friends from New York," he continues. "We've been out of touch these last few years. Which is ridiculous."

Suddenly, the idea of a renewed friendship for Celestino delights me. I beckon him in, though I also put a finger to my lips and say, "There's a class going on"—at which an outburst of laughter rises from the back of the house—"but come in, please. Celestino's out at work, I'm afraid."

"Yes, I expected so," he says. I notice, once we're together in the living room, that my surprise guest is unnervingly handsome. He has the large, shining eyes of someone eager and happy, clear youthful skin, and the broad shoulders of someone who cultivates his strength.

"Did you . . . work together in New York?"

"Yes, yes. At Wave Hill," he says. "I was in the office, an intern. Administrative nonsense. We were both essentially grunts—my shirt and tie were meaningless!—and we discovered that we both came from Guatemala, though we are from very different parts. In all honesty, hard as I work these days, I came from wealth." His smile conveys a playful apology. "Wealth, I should say, that's a thing of the past."

Perhaps he detects my surprise at his having no accent, because he adds, "And if you split hairs, I grew up mostly in Chicago, with my mother. We moved there when I was ten, after my father died. But I would travel to visit his family, my half siblings, almost every summer. In my heart, that's my home, my father's hacienda. It is—I think it still must be—a very beautiful place, though it's out of my family now. But I visit in my dreams."

He laughs self-consciously. Maybe he's thinking he shared too much—people don't generally talk about their dreams within minutes of meeting someone new—but I'm charmed by his eloquence. Now he's looking around my living room, taking in its practical, child-friendly furnishings. "I love these old American houses," he says. "You can feel the long chain of lives—not ghosts but guardians . . . of their future." He goes up to the one large picture hung in this room: a framed black and white photograph of a wind-sculpted forest on a cliff. I saw it displayed at our town's Fourth of July art festival and bought it as an anniversary present for Celestino.

"Where is this?" he asks.

"I don't know. I just thought it was . . . a beautiful place. Like your home. And my husband loves unusual trees."

"Ireland? Or possibly Norway." His face is close to the glass.

I almost give him my usual line—that to me, it's straight out of a fairy tale; I don't think of it as a real place, don't even want it to be—but I realize that I have no idea where he's come from or what, if anything in particular, has brought him to our doorstep. People do not search out old acquaintances in person without notice, and people do not pass through Vigil Harbor. It's a destination—or a place to leave.

"Are you visiting someone else in town?"

Ernesto turns away from the picture. He winces and holds out his hands. "As it happens, I'm a little stranded. I was supposed to meet a travel companion in the next town, in Knowles, but he's been delayed. Weather—always weather, isn't it?" He laughs. "But I realized, what luck! Here I am just a stone's throw from my old friend Celestino, and I thought—I know it must seem rude just showing up, but I thought we could reconnect. I'd like that. And I'd get to meet his family. You."

He holds my eyes for a moment, then glances again at the photograph. "You know," he says, more softly, "Celestino was an inspiration to me."

"He was?"

"His complete lack of bitterness for . . . things he'd gone through. As I'm sure you know. To lose so much but not to be angry. To work so hard and just—to find your talent and go from there. I understood how lucky I was. How I had nothing whatsoever to complain about."

He is turning his gaze to me again, and I am taking in his words—not surprised at all, because this is exactly who Celestino is, yet I'm moved to hear it from a stranger—when suddenly here is

Raul, pulling at my sleeve and telling me that I must come see how tall his seedlings have grown.

He pays no attention to the visitor until Ernesto says, "*Hola,* little man."

Raul looks briefly startled, then says, "*Hola, señor.*"

Only because it is the one foreign language some of the parents know from their own school days, our children are learning Spanish. If they were in the public school, we would probably have opted for Mandarin.

Celestino's first language was Quiché, the ancestral language of his parents, but even in his remote village, the children grew up speaking Spanish as well. Still, he likes to avoid it now that he lives comfortably in English, so Raul has no advantage over his classmates. Yet now, Raul and Ernesto have a brief conversation, in which the only words I catch are those meaning "eight"—Raul's age—and "father."

I hear Caitlin call Raul back to the classroom, and without another word, he pinballs down the hall. Raul's energy drains me at times, but he is a good student, hungry to learn almost anything new. "Come see!" he calls to me from the kitchen, on his way outside.

"Where are you staying?" I ask Ernesto. "Celestino can call you when he gets home."

He sighs. "That's the awkward thing. I'm not staying anywhere. I was expecting to head straight out with my friend, once we met up. We're going to Maine. I saw the inn down the street. . . ."

"Very expensive," I say. "For tourists who want a taste of the distant past."

"Footloose but penniless, what can I say? I know I'm too old to be living this way, but it's where I am. Who I am. I expect Celestino to tell me all over again that I just don't know how to settle down."

"Well," I say, "not like it came to *him* so naturally." I ask if he needs a place to park his car, and he tells me that he took a train, then used his hitch card from Boston. He laughs at my expression. "I know. They're for youngsters. What can I say?"

He's right: the recent program of sanctioned registration that's revived the antique practice of hitchhiking is popular mostly with the

Zero Footprint crusaders, but it makes sense, especially for anyone who'd describe himself as "footloose."

I tell him to have a seat in the living room. Can I bring him coffee or tea? I explain that the kitchen, as well as the sunporch-classroom, belongs to the children while school is in session.

"Just water." He thanks me and tells me not to worry about him. He takes out his phone and tells me he has work to keep him busy, so I leave him alone.

As I'm going to the kitchen for his water, he says, "Some town you live in here. Like a shrine to a bygone era."

"To visitors. Those tourists who stay at the inn. But if you grew up here, it's just a town like any other." I say that because it's the easiest thing to say.

I was never going to stay here, never going to return once I fled. I was never going to have children. I was certainly never going to live in a house overrun by other people's children five days a week.

Maybe "never" is misleading. I did not have such strong convictions until my brother was killed on some senseless raid in Afghanistan, a month after our father died of lung cancer. I was twenty-three, he was—had been, would never be more than—twenty-five. No mystery, the rage I felt. The relentless fanfare aimed at me and my mother by this obsessively patriotic town felt like an assault, and all I wanted to do was hide—or run. To hell with all the half-masted flags, the swoons of purple bunting, the dirge of bagpipes from two competing bands, the firefighters and a local group of Guinness-swilling Celtomaniacs who called themselves the Sons of Cork. And dear God, the endless condolences at the grocery store, the post office, the bowling alley . . . Everyone knew us, and nowhere was safe from their awkward sympathy or, at times, voyeuristic pity.

The sight of my frail, wrenlike mother accepting the bundled flag from his coffin was the last straw. For an instant, she might have been holding a baby in her arms, though she looked down on the object with terror, not tenderness. I scanned the mourners and saw in some of their faces a weirdly cruel pride on Mom's behalf, as if they were in fact at a christening, not a funeral. I half wondered if they would applaud after the deafening gun salute. Equally repugnant and surreal to me were the Vigil Harbor colonial reenactors, our self-appointed "regiment"—seven of them, uninvited—who, at the start of the ceremony, staged a salute of their own, their ridiculous muskets aimed at the clouds. The smell of gunpowder, intensified by August heat, made me retch.

Afterward, as people walked to their cars, Reverend Chalmers stopped me and put a hand on my shoulder. He said, "Caleb gave his life for our country, and he rests now in the strong arms of a loving God."

I shrugged off the unwelcome hand and said, "He did not give his life. His life was taken." I saw my mother being helped into someone else's car by two friends who, like her, had been recently widowed.

I skipped the reception at the VFW. I drove to the big, bland sports bar in Knowles, where I knew that the afternoon regulars, intent on the Sox, would give me a wide berth. On the way out of town, only by happenstance, I drove most of the route Caleb and I walked together for the two years we overlapped at the High. The route takes you right past Memorial Park, a shady green lawn where slabs of marble and granite bear the names of boys cut down by the endless scythings of war. I never fully understood why Caleb enlisted (never mind re-enlisted), and as I drove past the park, I wondered if the statues and plinths and their conspiratorial message of manhood and duty and sacrifice had wormed its way into my brother's heart as he passed by twice a day going to and from school, a place he had longed to escape.

From the bar, I called my best friend from college. While I had frittered away the two years after graduation by working for a gig agency in Boston (trying to figure out what to do with my art-psych major) and cutting hair—a self-taught skill with which I'd earned pocket money since high school—Harold had found a bona fide job as the production manager of a newspaper in Traverse City, Michigan. When he moved there, it was nothing more to him than a thumbtack on a map, but he was willing to take his chances. And he loved it. *Cherries, beaches, picturesque wildlife, violin prodigies, cute Midwestern guys of all persuasions . . . what's not to like?* he'd written me on a postcard a month after he got there.

"Hi. It's me. I feel like I'm going to slit my wrists," I said when he answered. "Dad and Caleb are side by side, six feet under, and life is screaming that I have no choice but to be the good daughter and take care of Mom. Who has basically nothing to live for."

"So, um, let's see, there's you," said Harold.

"I'm not a good investment these days."

"I'd buy shares."

"Even with insider info? That would be a big mistake."

"Where are you? I hear stadium sound effects."

"Sports bar."

"What's on draft? How soon can I get there?"

"Oh Harold." Predictably, I cried. "Everything's so awful. I don't even have a job, or a boyfriend, or a fucking dog, nothing to lose myself in. Except taking care of Mom. And this bar is as cold as a meat locker and I don't have a sweater. It was ninety-five degrees at the graveyard."

"You know what? Just hang up right now, my good friend. Go home, polish off the neighbors' casseroles with your mom, wash and return the chafing dishes, and then pack a bag and get your mournful ass out here. Visit . . . or stay . . . or head on up to Canada. Dodge the draft! Oh God—sorry. Listen. We'll figure it out."

"But Mom."

"Okay, so give her two weeks, during which you enlist her friends. She's a nice lady. She'll have good friends. Am I right?"

He was right.

"And she can spare you for a few months."

That was in August of 2019. I flew out in October, planning on a six-month "hiatus." Those who remember what happened that winter will understand how six months turned into five years.

I was lucky. As a place to find yourself marooned, Traverse City wasn't bad: land of cherry orchards, cheap concerts, nice upstanding citizens, and sand dunes tumbling toward a lake so immense that it looked like an ocean. Coming from a town beside a real ocean, I found the size of that lake preposterous, heart-stopping. A lake had no right to be so big. A lake could not stretch beyond the horizon; surely that was against some natural law. All the lakes I had known until then were lassoed tight by New England woods, every shore mirrored by an opposing stretch of green, where cabins and docks and boats, distant yet visible, winked alluringly in the sun. Maybe the distance was too far to swim, but it was a distance you could guess at by eye.

My adopted town was a gentle place, even in darkest winter, and gentle was what I needed. It was cheap enough that I could support myself by walking dogs and, once again, cutting people's hair. This time, through a deep dive on YouTube, I taught myself to color and perm and straighten and braid. Clients liked saving money by coming to my kitchen. Even through the lockdown, I had customers. Sometimes I cut their hair on a chair in the hall outside my apartment or, when the weather warmed, at a picnic table in a nearby park. When the prevailing fear dimmed and I invited them into my kitchen again, I made them tea and fed them banana bread or cherry scones. I was good at baking, too. I wouldn't call myself a people person, but now that the small talk didn't involve my hometown or my "loss," I was fine with it in limited doses. Just as we might step near intimate disclosures, the roar of the hair dryer would cut us off. And the people who came to me went away feeling happy, even if the same could not quite be said of me.

I lived in a large one-room apartment above a bookstore. A row of tall, steel-framed industrial windows pulled in vast skeins of morning sun and gave me a view of the town's main street below. Harold welcomed me into his small circle of friends, most of them other gay men he'd met through his job or his gym. We regarded ourselves as free agents in different though parallel markets. Harold, however, was the only one of us hungry for lasting love. "I didn't move to Wholesometown in order to cruise," he'd say. Me, I wanted peace before love. The second would come along in its own good time, and I was in no rush. I had no wish to bring children into this catastrophic world—or, as I thought of it back then, the world beyond the dunes, the orchards, and that yawning blue, blue lake. That was before the Timers started claiming the northern woods and waterways, before the severe fluctuations in winter weather turned from flukish to familiar, when you could suddenly count on the false early spring that coaxed the trees into premature blossom, then covered them in snow, all that embryonic fruit stillborn in flower. No cherries, no plums, no peaches. Or precious few. But that was later.

I spoke to my mother nearly every night, and gradually, maybe after two or three months, she could talk to me without tears. She did not blame me one bit for getting out of Dodge. She started volunteering at the soup kitchen in Knowles, where she said that the people in the lines were no longer just older, soul-stripped homeless people and addicts. There were a few young, single-parent families, and then a few more, refugees from an Ebola epidemic in Congo. They had been sponsored by a local church and were on their way up, not down. Or that's how Mom saw it. My mother was a good Christian woman in the hard-core sense, and I'm glad she didn't live to see the recent rash of deportations, which hit hardest in the poorer towns outside Boston, even Knowles, after another epidemic of our own. It was no coincidence, I knew, that as the local population became literally more colorful, new and stricter laws chased many of them away.

I was twenty-eight by the time I came to feel that this middle-of-the-country place might be a place I could stay (were my vowels broadening just a little?). It was the place where I'd observed three birthdays Caleb had never reached, each one renewing my sorrow but reminding me that my onliness was now a permanent thing, not a state of limbo. It was also the place where I stood beside Harold as his Best Person when he married Jerry, the new (and independently wealthy) owner of the bookstore beneath my apartment. Harold, I realized as I stood beside him in an orchard on a merciless August afternoon, trying not to sweat through my pale silk dress, was a different kind of brother—one I endured the heat to celebrate, not bury. Almost immediately, however, my mother was diagnosed with her own cancer and asked if I could return, just to help her through the worst of her treatments. "But then, please," she said, "go back to your wonderful life."

It was kind of her to call it wonderful—something I'd never have called it myself—when I'd probably broken her heart by refusing to strive for a marriage, a "best person" of my own. She had long since stopped asking me if I'd met anyone special. (Once, when she asked, I joked that Harold was special. I realized when I hung up how callous that must have sounded to her.)

Or did she somehow know that, returning to my first home to help her through her chemotherapy—just as she had helped Dad through his—I would end up meeting that best person, right in Vigil Harbor?

On Fridays, the children stay after lessons to play in our yard for a couple of hours, weather permitting. They're old enough by now to climb into the tree house as well, and up they go, nearly all of them. When Celestino built it, he put good, solid rails on all the platforms, and he makes frequent inspections.

Parents show up around five and linger for a drink to celebrate the end of the school week. Except at night, our door is unlocked, so they enter without knocking, sidling their way along the cluttered hallway from front to back, a long line of wall hooks buried under piles of jackets and hoodies, lunch bags, fold-up scooters slung on straps, negotiating the pool of shoes and backpacks that mine the floor. Today there are whispered reminders not to discuss the news, the stories unfurling from yesterday's events in New York, not within earshot of our children. They will know more than we wish they did, but we do our best to minimize the most violent news. We try not to show how much it weighs on our hearts.

But today we have the welcome distraction of Ernesto, now seated with a beer at the kitchen table. In the hours since his arrival, he has spoken Spanish with the children, poured them all glasses of water, admired the tree house and asked Raul to give him a tour. From the highest level, higher than the roofline of our house, he waved to me and called down, "This is no town like any other, are you mad? I see the whole world from here!"

Ernesto insisted on putting out the snacks, too, arranging the fruit and wafers artfully on the trays. In the midst of the gleeful chaos, I invited him to stay overnight with us, if necessary, since he had yet to hear from his friend. He tells me he's an excellent cook and will make us an "unforgettable" meal tomorrow night if he has to ask the favor of staying over Saturday as well. (This he volunteered casually, and I said nothing. He has made himself helpful, I'll say that.)

By six-thirty, three mothers remain at the small kitchen table, drinking wine, enthralled as Ernesto describes the coffee plantation where he spent his early years. He tells us what a paradise it was—and profitable—until the cartels muscled in, not long after his older brothers took on the business when their father died. Five children are still out back, playing flashlight tag in the looming dark, and I am getting the pot of stew out of the refrigerator to place on the stove (a hint that it's time for others to go home) when I hear Ernesto interrupt himself loudly with "*Hola, amigo!* A very long time, old friend!"

I turn from the stove to see Ernesto on his feet, facing Celestino, who stands in the doorway. I did not hear the front door, and perhaps because I'm on my second glass of wine, it takes me a moment to remember that the visitor is a complete surprise to my husband.

"Baby," I say, crossing the room to kiss him, "surprise."

Celestino is always beat when he comes home, and on Fridays he expects (and deserves) to collapse. I never insist that he socialize with the parents who monopolize our kitchen, but I do not kick them out, either. Often he simply smiles and waves to the room at large, and after throwing his soiled work jacket into the closet with the washer, he goes upstairs; a minute later, I will hear the hiss of the shower.

But tonight is different, of course, and even if he's startled beyond words, I'm confused by his expression, which seems fraught with what might be alarm or gloom. I wonder if he's been listening to the news while driving home—and if it's grown worse; sometimes these attacks come in pairs.

Or what if he simply doesn't remember this man? Wave Hill was decades ago. I realize I should have called him earlier, to let him know. But then, he tends to leave his phone in the truck, and I've learned to call only if something feels urgent.

Ernesto moves toward Celestino, arms outstretched. "I was telling Connie about how we met in New York," he says. "How many years ago was that? More than ten? Oh—way more than ten! Can you believe it? But here we are, both of us still spinning around on this planet together!"

I realize now that Brecht is standing behind Celestino. I urge them both into the room.

Caitlin stands up, saying it's time to get home, offering Brecht her chair. I bring out another beer. When the truck needs to be unloaded after a workday, Brecht ends up here. He never accepts my offer of a meal, but sometimes he'll stay for a single beer, then walk the eight or ten blocks to his house. He, not Celestino, is the one who introduces himself to Ernesto.

My eyes are drawn to the flashlight bobbing and winking on the lawn. As I watch, it shines straight into the house and, for an instant, into my eyes, as if accusing me. The remaining mothers have gone outside, and as it becomes clear to their children that the game must end, a relay of protests overrules any talking in the kitchen. *Nooo! We just started! I haven't been It yet! It's not totally dark! I'm not hungry!*

I leave the three men to themselves, turning to the task of the daily exodus, though most of the children have already left. The last ones are both amped up and wiped out, acting half their age—even Raul, who doesn't have to leave. The mothers' voices rise over loud pleas to stay, spend more time with their friends. "Focus, Dwight!" "Where are your shoes, Candace? You were outdoors barefoot? Ticks, honey!" "Coat! Lunch bag! Homework!" "Do not forget your hat this time, please!"

Before going out the door, each child reaches into the basket on the floor to retrieve the precious pocketronic, the limited-access phone that all of us agreed on as a healthy compromise. No commerce, no bait for hackers, no news alerts. Yet this is the one thing none of them would leave behind, and if I listen as they step onto the street, I'll hear the ping of all the devices as they are switched on, restoring their reach toward a much wider world—though a world cleansed and censored.

When I return to the kitchen, Celestino is still standing and has not helped himself to a drink of any kind, not even a glass of water. Raul is at the table with Brecht, showing him a book of antique maps.

As much as I have worried about Brecht, his state of mind, he works hard for Celestino, and Raul runs to him like a faithful dog every time he's here. I have to believe it's good for Brecht, too, the innocent boy-crush my son has on this young man whose life appears to have stalled.

Ernesto nods to the backyard and says to Celestino, "That tree house, *amigo—es espléndido.* Connie says you built it yourself."

"I had help," says Celestino.

"She says you have built others—one at a children's museum. I'd love to see pictures."

I go to the refrigerator, get out a beer, and just about force it into my husband's hand. "Guess what?" I say. "Ernesto actually got the kids to practice speaking their Spanish this afternoon." I turn to our guest. "Now, if a certain husband of mine, a fluent speaker, were willing to play tutor . . ." I feel a twinge of guilt, knowing that language itself—engaging the world through speech—is of no particular joy to Celestino, but I am saved by Raul.

"Dad would be a crazy-strict teacher," he says. "But sometimes we build something with him."

"Like what?" asks Ernesto. "Are you an apprentice to the tree house master?"

"He doesn't do that anymore." Raul beckons Ernesto onto the sunporch, which is furnished with shelves and wooden cupboards built by his father. "You have to come here," he says. "Brecht, did you see?"

When the two men join him, Raul points toward the back of the yard. Standing on tall posts tucked into the fringes of a neighbor's wall of arbor vitae are seven colorful wooden birdhouses. "He showed us how to make those."

"Very cool," says Ernesto.

"Skilling," says Brecht.

Ernesto asks, "And do they have tenants?"

Raul stares at him for a moment. "Tenants?"

"Did any birds move in?"

"Well, maybe in two of them," Raul says quietly. And I know what he's feeling: that the dearth of songbirds in our yard is somehow the fault of the children who built the houses inviting them in. The kids were already midway through the project when Caitlin suggested that perhaps birdhouses weren't the best choice for a carpentry project. "How many birds have you seen at your feeders the past few years?" she said to Elio, who, before fatherhood, used to lead far-flung birdwatching tours. "I don't think I'm ready to go into the subject of mass extinctions, not yet anyway."

Elio suggested that it wasn't our job to protect them from local "realities." And why be so pessimistic? Shouldn't we engage them in projects associated with hope? "Why would we have had children if we didn't feel hopeful?"

"Maybe I feel differently than I did nine years ago," said Caitlin.

"Then go be a prepper," said Elio. "Be a Timer! Move to North Dakota. Me, I'll fight the good fight, and so will Jack and Bonnie." I notice sometimes that the parents of our twins grow the most defensive whenever such tensions erupt. Their stakes in the future are twice as high.

Celestino, if he is around at those moments, will quietly disappear. When I met him, I thought he was shy, but as I got to know him, I understood that his reserve is more like a collage of watchfulness, fear, forbearance, and the knowledge that in almost any room—at least in this town, where he landed almost by accident—he is the most "other." He is the foreigner, more than ever now that borders of all kinds feel as if they've been redrawn on maps with darker, thicker markings. I try to tell him that he is far more American than he realizes—maybe more than he even wants to be—but I hear how flat-footed I sound. And I know that Raul's brown skin, no lighter than his father's, also sets him a little apart.

Which is why I am surprised to see Celestino so reserved around this gregarious friend from his past, this man who shares his birthplace. Does he feel outshone, upstaged? Or is it my overeager hospitality toward someone I hardly know? Do I look as if I'm flirting? I set my wineglass in the sink.

As if my gesture was a cue, Brecht takes his own glass to the sink. "Gotta run." He waves at Raul and nods to Celestino. "Tomorrow?"

"I'll let you know later," Celestino answers. "Good work today. Thank you."

"Like always, man, I thank you too," says Brecht, and he is gone.

Handing him a bucket, I tell Raul to take our guest out back to fetch water from the cistern for washing dishes. "And bring in the flashlight. I'll bet you guys left it out there."

As soon as they are out the door, I say, "What's with you? Something going on at work?"

"How long has he been here?" Celestino's gaze is aimed at the darkened lawn, invisible now behind our reflections in the porch windows.

"He knocked on the door this afternoon. He told me about your time together at Wave Hill. And he's . . . stranded. He'll explain."

"Stranded?"

"You want me to turn him away? I told him he could have our couch for the night. Did I have to check with you first? Or are you going to tell me he's some kind of serial killer? What is *with* you? This is a man who admires you!"

My husband seems to be thinking hard about something—not that this kind of stubborn silence is rare with him—but I also notice that he's set down his beer without taking a sip. "He told you he admires me?"

"Oh God." I stand close to Celestino and lean my forehead against his. We are exactly the same height, and it gives me pleasure that we can stand shoulder to shoulder, hip to hip, look each other level in the eye. "Look, just let him explain over dinner."

Just then, Celestino pulls away from me and lunges toward the back door. I turn around and see the flashlight beam, looping drunkenly out in the darkness, making brief snapshots of the tree limbs, of the paving-stone path, cameos of stockade fence. When Celestino opens the door, I hear laughter—Raul's and Ernesto's—and Ernesto calls out, "Dude, give me a break! I'm totally new to this game!"

Celestino freezes in the open door, and I say, "You know what? Go upstairs and take your shower. Untie the day's knots. Stew's ready, but Raul had a snack. I'll throw together some biscuits." I put my hands on his tensed shoulders. "Relax. Please."

Paying little attention to our guest—whose novelty must have worn off—and less to his manners (about which I won't bother to nag), Raul eats half a bowl of white bean stew and four hot biscuits in a matter of minutes, then asks to be excused from the table. Predictably, he gallops upstairs, and almost immediately I hear the sound of bombing, a game of conquest, from his room above my head. Every time it starts up, I feel the same dismay at having caved, but as even the most retro of the parents in our school will say, what choice do we have? All we can do is ration the violence.

As if we might set an example for the world around us. Maybe a rationing of violence would have spared my brother.

And it's me, of all people, who cannot resist checking on the news as soon as Raul leaves the room. "I'm sorry," I say as I retrieve my phone from the counter and bring it to the table. "I'll just scan the update."

Celestino goes to the stove and helps himself to a second bowl of stew. I notice that he doesn't offer to serve Ernesto, but then, our guest is now also checking his device. (I remember when I railed against living like this, on hits of news or other outside contact as if we are deep-sea divers dependent on pulses of air from our tanks.)

"They say none of the perpetrators were killed in the bombing, and they have a lead, but they're not sharing it," I say.

Ernesto smirks. " 'They' of the police state?"

Celestino looks up from his bowl. "This is not a police state."

"You don't think so?"

"You and I, we know what a police state is," says Celestino, "or perhaps your life was never touched by the war. Not even your father's, I think."

"You're right. I saw all that from afar. It was news, not my life," says Ernesto. "Unlike you. Your father, I know . . ."

Ernesto looks gravely at Celestino, whose expression is unreadable, even to me. I know, from his guarded telling of it, that his village seemed to escape the notice of marauding government troops through the worst of the massacres—but then an archaeological dig drew attention to it, brought in a band of soldiers who burned homes and took random prisoners.

"But your mother and sisters—they got to the city, didn't they?"

"Good memory," says Celestino. It doesn't sound like a compliment.

"Are they still there?"

"My mother is dead."

Ernesto reaches across the table and touches his arm. "I'm sorry. *Lo siento mucho.*"

Celestino sets his spoon in the empty bowl and withdraws his arm. And this I understand. His mother's death, of poor health without decent care, without her son anywhere near, is the least of it.

"He lost touch with his sisters a couple of years ago, after it became too hard to send them money," I say, trying to fend off further questions. The truth is, his sisters never forgave him for not returning to see his mother when she was dying. They accepted his money, and when it stopped, they let him know how angry they were at his defection. Had he tried to bring them north? Of course he had. But they didn't believe he had tried all that hard. He can't help blaming himself, so of course he shares none of this with anyone.

Celestino looks at me and sighs. I cannot tell through his reflexive sorrow if he is grateful or not, but he says to Ernesto, "This is history. Nothing to be done," and it's not the first time I'm left wondering what parts of that history, the parts that happened before I knew him, he's left out.

"I have dessert," I say, "so let's enjoy it, and let's talk about something else." I take away the soup bowls and pull a container of vanilla ice cream out of the freezer. From the rhubarb in our farmshare, I've made a compote. A year ago, our school group joined in creating a local Tiny Farm Lot. It's another responsibility—planting, weeding, hoeing, carrying produce to other towns in carts attached to our bikes (cars, even electrics, are frowned upon by the TFL founders)—but how could I not agree that it's part of the example we have to set for our children?

In the silence that keeps me company as I fill three dishes, I listen with minor, unavoidable spite to the virtual warfare over my head. No dessert, I decide, for those who cannot curb such habits.

"Ernesto," I say when we are seated again, "tell us about this trip you're taking."

He smiles. "Well, if my friend ever shows up to join me, our plan is to head to Maine, as I mentioned. We're doing research on some of the northern lakes, interviewing residents about the changes they've seen in recent years. So it's work—but who would complain about doing work in such a beautiful place? Threatened though it is. By too many things."

Before Celestino returned from work, Ernesto had explained to the lingering mothers that he was, broadly speaking, a climate scientist. He studied the change in wildlife populations—and migration patterns—affecting the lake ecosystems of northern New England. His colleague was a photographer.

"Scientist? You're now a scientist?" says Celestino.

"It's been a long time, *amigo.* I've become much more serious about what I do."

"You were serious, I remember that."

"I was serious, but now you could say I'm passionate."

"Passionate." Celestino's tone is neutral.

"Which I'm guessing," I say nervously, "is why you've never settled down. Like you said."

"I'm a compulsive nomad. I don't think a family's in the cards. I fly solo, as is my destiny. Which I accept!" He leans across the table and, once again, touches Celestino's arm. "You have a terrific wife. And son. You lucked out. And this, keeping an eye on them, keeping them *safe,* that should be what drives you. Your passion. Am I right?"

Celestino smiles tersely, as if something secret has occurred to him. "Yes."

"And you and I, newly minted citizens or legitimate visitors—whatever our so-called status may be—we must be careful all the time. We know that, don't we?"

Celestino glances at me, perhaps to underscore the confirmation of his own anxieties. He gestures at Ernesto's phone, which lies on the table. "Your friend—your photographer—has he been in touch?"

"Oh—his flight's still delayed. He's coming from out west, and that line of thunderstorms won't quit." He sighs. "He's thinking possibly not until Monday." He addresses me directly. "Would it be an imposition . . . ?"

I look at Celestino. He says, "There is an inn down the street."

"I actually just checked," says Ernesto, "but they're full up. I promise to take care of myself."

Celestino's expression is opaque, and I can't stand the silence. "Monday's fine by me," I say, "but school starts early and you'll have to make yourself scarce."

"I'm excellent at scarce."

Celestino says, "Tomorrow I have a nursery run."

I realize that I'm busy, too: a shift at the farm. We can all go on about our days. Perhaps Raul can go over to one of the other children's houses.

"Or I can watch him," Ernesto offers. "And don't forget I am cooking tomorrow night. Is he handy with a skillet?"

"Raul will go with me," says Celestino. "And we may be back late."

I give Ernesto sheets for the living room couch. Once we started the school, our third bedroom became a storage room. It's practically impassable now.

By the time I go upstairs, Celestino is in bed. I go into Raul's room and make him turn out the light, even though he is reading a book. I feel vainly comforted that he stopped playing the war game on his own.

In bed at last, I whisper, "What gives? What's with the bad-host act? Is this someone you only pretended to like? He's a big fan of yours, that's obvious."

"Is it?" He frowns. "But you did not think to call me."

"Of course I did. Would you have picked up? I doubt it. And you know what? I like him. So does Raul."

"I am very tired, Connie."

"Don't tell me you're jealous."

He sighs. "Of what?"

"His . . . well, it's obvious he went on to get a lot more education, after you knew him." I don't mean to be cruel, but I'm remembering Celestino's tone when he said, *You're now a scientist?*

Again, he tells me he's tired.

I warn myself not to pick a fight, but I do tell him I don't think he should take Raul along in the morning. "He'll be bored."

"Brecht is coming. He is never bored with Brecht."

This is true. "All right," I say, and, more softly, "All right." Once I give in to my husband's guarded self, he turns toward me and wraps his thick smooth arms around me, gently pushes one of his legs between mine.

"Shhh," I say, smiling in the dark. "Shhh."

People who live in small houses know how to bring stealth to passion.

After Harold met Celestino, he told me that we made an inspired but completely illogical couple—not because of our different cultural origins but because of our different temperaments.

I admitted that Celestino was restrained by nature, that sometimes it frustrated me. "The thing is," I said, "he's genuinely shy. And he's not affectionate in public—it's like he has this kind of old-fashioned dignity—but in private he's . . ."

When I hesitated, wondering if I ought to clam up out of respect for that very dignity, Harold growled. "La Bamba?"

"Yikes, Harold. I'll pretend I didn't hear that."

"What, do I offend?"

"You mean, in general? Of course you do."

By habit, we laugh at each other easily and often, and sometimes I'd wonder if that kind of banter, so different from the closeness I felt with Celestino, was something I'd need to find in a marriage as well. But Harold assured me otherwise.

"The two of you," he said, "are like one of those bentwood chairs. Those curly-backed chairs you used to see all the time in cafés. Do you know what kind of baroque technology goes into shaping the wood like that? But the end result is brilliant and strong! If you married someone like me, you'd kill each other!"

Harold, more than anyone else, rejoiced openly that I'd found a mate despite myself. I wouldn't have found him, however, without my mother's cancer, which, though it took longer than my father's, ultimately put her in the ground next to Dad and Caleb. At least she lived long enough to hear Raul give her a name and run toward her embrace.

On the worst winter days in Michigan, Harold would stay overnight in my apartment. Because he loved to garden, he rented a small house with a large plot of land just outside the city's suburban fringe, and he worried that if the mercury dropped too low, his car would refuse to start in the morning and he wouldn't make it into town. Meanwhile, my apartment was two blocks from his office. So whenever the forecast alarmed him, he'd call me in the early afternoon and say not his usual "Hey, you" but "Sleepover?"

Harold was an owl. For as long as I'd known him, he had thrived on being wide awake till two or three in the morning—a habit that suited his vocation. He was also, by nature, a social creature who no doubt loved any excuse to "den up," as he put it, with good friends. Nor did he seem to have a daily quota on gossiping, musing, philosophizing, raging at the plagues and evils of the world, all of which he was eager to share after showing up from work at nine or ten o'clock. I could tolerate the lost sleep, and sometimes I was content just to listen to Harold's soliloquies (I told him, time and again, that he should do local theater), but there were nights when I'd ask if we could just watch a movie, or I'd tell him I was reading a book too good to neglect for a single night. Sometimes I'd had one too many chatty clients that day.

"Okay, okay, it's quiet time. I get it," he'd say. "Time for Motormouth Man to shut it." I would agree.

Harold knew me through and through, especially since the months of our sharing lockdown in the first surge. So he knew that I craved silence at the end of my days the way some people crave a piece of cake or a glass of brandy or a TV host bellowing cynical jokes right in your face.

"We need to find you a quiet fella. The strong, silent type," he said on one bone-chilling night when he was simply unable to shut up. We were each wrapped in a quilt, our hands protruding only to grasp our mugs of tea.

I told him I didn't need or necessarily even want a man, though it would have been a lie to say I wasn't lonely or filled at times with a sexual longing I wasn't willing to complicate by letting someone know me a little too well.

"When," he said, "are you going to snap out of your mourning? Even your mom seems to have come through a little. Just because Caleb can't go on living doesn't mean you go on sympathy strike. Sorry if I'm being blunt."

Caleb had been dead for over three years, and by then, my mother had immersed herself in useful, social distractions. She practically ran the Knowles soup kitchen, and she was circulating petitions to get her church's basement rec room designated a pass-through shelter for Syrian refugees en route to Halifax. The satisfaction she found in these activities was like a mortar that held together the pieces of her shattered heart, however poorly.

"I am not in mourning," I told Harold. "I will always miss Caleb, always wonder why the hell he thought the army was a good idea, but this is my own life I'm living. Are you calling it pathetic?"

"Not pathetic," Harold said. "Of course not! For one thing, here you are with me! But if you don't mind my saying so, it's . . . narrow. Straitened."

"Straightened? Like I should get kinky somehow?"

"No. *Strait* as in . . . okay, don't get me wrong, but as in *straitjacket.*"

I remember marveling at the thick skin of glittering frost adhering that night to every pane of the long bank of windows I loved. My wide view of Front Street was totally obscured.

"Harold," I said, "last I heard, it's ten below out there, not even factoring windchill."

"You wouldn't be so merciless."

" 'As in *straitjacket*'? Really? Fuck you."

"I didn't mean it that way."

"Harold, not everyone wants a life of bonhomie and international travel."

He crossed from his armchair (my armchair) to my place on the couch and hugged me. " 'Bonhomie'? Where did that gem of a word arise from?"

I looked at the wall clock in my kitchen alcove. "It arose from a deep cavern in my brain accessible only when I have been awake for twenty hours straight."

"Oh honey, how I long to be kept awake for twenty hours straight—with the right man, if you'll forgive me."

And this was how—through the gaiety of Harold's gay humor—we generally sidestepped talking, close as we were, about what was obviously my severely prolonged if highly functional case of depression. So that when Harold did, at last, find the mate he'd been searching for, and he told me about their engagement before anyone else, and he hugged me tight and said, "I really, really want this for you, I don't care what you say," my answer was "What, in-laws, a queer trousseau, and a long list of compromises?"

I could be cruel when defending my muted despair.

But my muted despair took a backseat to my mother's far more justifiable despair at her diagnosis later that year. I had been back to Vigil Harbor several times during my years away, for holidays with Mom and a couple of weddings, though never a school reunion, and never, ever a Fourth of July. I would suffer no piety over blood lost to wars without end.

This time it was early fall, a warm azure afternoon, and as my mother drove me up the coast from the airport, she filled me in on town news, studiously avoiding any mention of the reason I'd arrived with such a large suitcase. I heard about how a movie had been shot in Vigil Harbor that summer—a picaresque comedy based loosely on *A Midsummer Night's Dream* in which B-list movie stars were seen chasing one another at all hours of the day and night through the town's narrow streets, along the rocky shore, through the leaning headstones of the burial ground. Crowds had gathered to watch body doubles rappelling down the face of Harrow Point. "The ice-cream shop had to fill daily orders for a hundred milkshakes," Mom told me, keeping up the small talk. "They had to rent five more of those twirling machines. If you had a yen for a simple cone, good luck getting anywhere near the counter!"

She filled me in on the scandalous firing of the school superintendent (embezzlement), the tax override to heighten the walls on the causeway (a nasty feud at Town Meeting over rigged bidding on contracts), the upgrades at The Drome (new bowling shoes for rent; much better onion rings). By the time we'd reached the town line, she seemed almost happy, caught up in the spirit of petty human skirmishes far from the vortex of mortality.

And then we passed the high school. Involuntarily, I gazed up the sloping drive toward the entrance, and I noticed right away. There was the flag, and there was the stone with the plaque lauding my brother's so-called service; but where was the tree we had watched the nurseryman plant in the circle and cushion with mulch? It was a coral-bark Japanese maple, almost exactly my height when it went in the ground.

"Mom, where's Caleb's tree?"

Why did I have to ask her just then? But it was too late.

Mom kept right on driving, but her face almost literally drooped. She passed two side streets before she said, in an even tone, "Well, honey, it died."

"Just . . . died? Like no one took care of it?"

"Oh, they took care of it, but it just didn't . . . thrive. Nothing they could do. I know they tried."

"So they need to replace it. How long ago was this?" My last visit had been a fly-by Thanksgiving; had I even looked up that way?

"It seems the kind of tree we chose is more fragile than we were told. Or, well, I don't know. Maybe the wind up there. The exposure."

"Then replace it with something stronger. But replace it!"

Mom glanced at me. "I have plenty to do, Connie, without adding that task to my plate. I think it's for the high school to figure out."

With great effort, I said nothing, and we were silent until, five minutes later, we pulled into the driveway of my childhood home. I grew up on one of the least grand of the original village streets, the houses small and leaning one against the next, backyards long and narrow, space for cars at a premium. None of the houses had changed much over the years—there was no room for growth, no allowance for knocking anything down—but each time I came back, there were signs of more money, more privilege: upgraded windows, new granite steps, a glimpse of well-groomed garden through a glossy white trellis draped in budding vines.

My mother took a nap, and we sat down to a dinner she had prepared before my arrival. We talked, finally, about the schedule of treatment she had just started. For the next few weeks, I would be her driver, her home nurse, her sentinel for unexpected crises. While we talked, I noticed how little she ate.

We said good night in a long, quiet hug at the foot of the stairs. My mother now slept in a twin bed in the tiny first-floor room that my father had used as a study, surrounded by his books. She claimed it was a matter of comfort—arthritis in her hips made stairs a chore—but I knew it was a matter of memory: steering clear of empty beds.

I woke to that same old rhomboid of slantwise sun on the wallpapered wall above the desk where I'd labored over twelve years of homework, written college applications, then overdue or slipshod papers, only to decide that the thing I did best wasn't the least bit scholarly. I was good at making people look their best, smile at themselves in a mirror, even marvel at the transformation. I readied girls for their first proms, widows for funerals, young men for job interviews. I wondered sometimes, once I started doing it seriously, whether my acquired talent was a benign form of defiance. Dad was an English professor, my mother his onetime favorite student. He never complained, and he was no less loving toward us than the young father who'd regarded Frost and Sarton and Hughes (both Langston and Ted) as if their words were a Catholic grace, reading them aloud at dinner, but surely he wondered at how his children grew up to become a hairdresser and a soldier. I sensed that he regarded our choices with resignation yet gratitude. After all, they were choices we had made—not choices made for us by others. My father was a man with a generous outlook on the world, and as fiercely as I raged at the cosmos after Caleb died, I was thankful that Dad died first.

But Mom: poor Mom.

I rose from my bed and walked to the window admitting the sun, and there I was reminded of what had once seemed like a shocking change in our resolutely change-averse town.

Two yards away from ours stood the same glorious tree I'd grown up to expect against my personal sky, the one framed by my east-facing window. Dad once declared it "bombastic," pointing out that but for that tree, we'd have a view of the harbor, and our house would be worth more money. "Would you sell our house if we had that view?" I asked him anxiously. I was sixteen; to move would have been a tragedy worthy of opera. "Don't be silly," he said. "But someday one of us will have to sell it. Maybe even want to sell it. No one can predict the future, bee."

Sometime in my early teens, when I was paying little if any attention to trees—or, for that matter, anything having to do with my neighborhood, since the older boy I was hopelessly obsessed with lived on the other side of town—the tree sprouted a tree house. Not overnight (and only later did I contemplate what a complex project it must have been), but one morning, probably a Sunday, I woke up and suddenly saw it; *beheld* it, as one of Dad's beloved poets might. Was this an optical illusion? Had some faraway house blown off its foundation, Ozzed its way through the sky, and impaled itself, all skewed and fractured, deep in the branches of the tree? (It looked, I remember thinking in my heightened adolescent state, as if the tree were having sex with a house.)

By the time of that return to care for my mother, you'd think it would have been just another part of the local landscape, yet because I came home so seldom, it startled me anew each time. Yes, there it still was, that crazy, crooked, convoluted tree house. A motherfuckin' *massive* tree house, Harold would have said. Bombastic squared.

This time, however, looking at that tree renewed the fury that had kept me up for too long the night before: I thought of Caleb's tree. I understood my mother's weary acceptance of its loss, but how dare the town officials, the smug surviving soldiers drinking cheap beer at the VFW, not replace that tree? I would replace it if I had to dig the damn hole myself.

Mom sat at the kitchen table, dressed for the challenging day ahead, drinking a cup of something hot with an unfamiliar, barnlike scent. Seeing my face, she said, "Don't worry, there's coffee for you. This is an herbal potion one of my nurses recommends. Did I just say 'my' nurses? Dear God. And you know what?" She held out the mug, as if to inspect it for cracks. "It tastes like carpentry. If that makes sense."

"Smells like that guinea pig we had," I said. "Maybe the shavings."

"I can see you're going to be helpful," said Mom. She wore a determined smile.

"I'll do my Girl Scout best."

"You refused to join the Girl Scouts. Remember? You refused to wear the dress. Margo Tattersall told me it was a sign that you might be gay. Thank you, Margo."

"Oh God, Mrs. T." I laughed. "She still around?"

"Honey, of course she is. Everyone over forty isn't one foot in the grave." Her words hit us both like a door slammed in our faces.

Mom stood up and poured the rest of her guinea-pig tea in the sink. She rinsed out the mug and filled it with some of the coffee she'd made for me. After she returned to the table, we sipped quietly for a few minutes.

I said, "That tree house. It gave me a heart attack all over again."

"Oh, all that fuss died down ages ago."

"Fuss?"

"The historical hysterics. All the purists wanting to take it down."

"What? Because there's no such thing as a colonial tree house? Fishermen never had fun? It's beautiful. Don't you think?"

My mother gave me a theatrically skeptical look.

In virtual unison, we said, "Eye of the beholder." What Dad would have said.

"But he's nice, the young man who lives there. By himself now, I think. I don't know what became of the old man who lived there with him."

These details meant nothing to me. I no longer kept track of who moved in and out of the neighborhood. I'd made a point of not caring.

"He has a gardening business," Mom said. "Works hard and keeps to himself."

"Mom, you sound like one of those witnesses describing the mystery neighbor who all of a sudden turns psycho."

Her expression was a scold. "What a thing to say."

"Sorry."

"Oh Connie." She put down her mug and closed her eyes. "I just found myself thinking how funny it is that the one thing you do so well will be pointless here. I lose my hair, all of it, nineteen to twenty-one days from my first treatment. From today. According to *my* nurses. They think it's comforting to know. Me? I'd rather be surprised. Have it sneak up on me. Have nineteen days to think I'll be the exception."

I pulled my chair next to hers. "We'll get you a killer wig," I said, immediately regretting the adjective I chose. "There is so little I know in life, but, Mom, I know from wigs. I have clients who bring me their wigs to care for, just like a real head of hair. Isn't that wild?"

An hour later, I drove her into Boston for her first round of chemo. The next day, while she took a long, battle-weary nap, I found my old bike in the back shed, dug up the pump to put air in its tires, and went on a difficult mission of my own.

I started in the front office of the high school. The principal was out, the vice principal "in meetings all afternoon."

The receptionist was unmoved by my telling her that the tree, the one that had died, had been planted in memory of My Brother the War Hero. "I don't know who's in charge of that," she said. "I don't think we had anything to do with planting that tree in the first place." Then she answered a call and spent several minutes conversing with a parent calling to excuse a child's absence. After hanging up, she seemed baffled that I was still standing at the Plexiglas partition shielding her airspace.

"Try the town manager. Public Works." She was done with me.

I returned to the circle of grass enclosing the stone with the plaque, the flagpole, and the slender stump. Someone had chopped down the dead tree—if it had in fact died. Who had done that?

My heart sank at the thought of phoning town bureaucrats. My mother had mentioned the new town manager, who was, in her words, a lazybones and a dimwit. She'd had to deal with him in her failed efforts to turn her church's basement into a shelter. Public Works was in charge of plowing snow and paving roads, not the planting of ornamental trees. I knew that much.

I rode my old bike back to my old house. As I dismounted out front, I saw a pickup truck turn into the driveway that went with the tree house. I walked down the block and stood at the mouth of the driveway until the driver got out of the cab. At first he just froze, staring at me. I realized I was the one who should speak first.

"Hi," I said. "I'm your neighbor. Or my mom is your neighbor." I pointed to my right. "A few houses down. Mary McKenna?"

I half expected him to thank me for my brother's service, but all he said was "Yes?" I had noticed that he was dark-skinned—inescapably surprising in a town where, as Caleb used to say, diversity equals brunettes. The man was compact, almost bearlike, and he wore a sturdy uniform, deep green with a tree stitched on a white triangle over his heart. Mom had called him a "young man," but he had at least a decade on me. "Does your mother need help?"

"No. It's me who . . . I just—I have a question." I didn't want to walk down his driveway, but he didn't walk out toward me, either. We stood about twenty feet apart. "My mother says you're a gardener. So the thing is, I'm looking for someone who knows trees?" My voice might have quavered.

"I have a landscaping business, yes." He crossed his arms.

His attitude wasn't encouraging, but I was desperate. I walked closer, made an awkward waving gesture, and told him my name. He paused before telling me his. He sounded only a fraction friendlier when he said, "What do you need to know about trees?"

"Actually, I need a tree. But a good tree. A tree that won't die on me." I told him my story, trying to keep it from becoming my brother's story, which would have made me cry. "So I just want to see the old tree replaced. I don't know who's in charge of it, and I don't want to go through a lot of bureaucratic bullshit"—I winced, too late, at my language—"and I'm only going to be here for a month or two, and I doubt—"

"I know that tree," he said. "It was the wrong tree to plant. I was surprised to see how long it survived."

I thought for a moment. "So what if I asked you to help me find the right tree?"

"I can do that."

"I'd pay, obviously, even just for your advice."

"The town is who should pay."

"Yeah. But you know what? I'd rather just do it myself. I mean, what's going to happen if I go ahead, take a shovel, bring a tree, and put it in? Are they going to arrest me? Pull out the tree?"

This is when he smiled. His teeth were crooked, but his face glowed with the day's perspiration, and the lines framing his eyes reassured me somehow.

"I will plant your tree," he said.

Two nights later, once my mother felt well enough to have a stranger in the house, Celestino came over after dinner with a large tree book, a kind of directory, filled with charts and pictures captioned with Latin names. The pages, some torn and taped back together, were marred by fingerprints traced with soil. You could tell the book was like a Bible to this man.

Mom insisted he have a beer, and I had a glass of wine. She had a mug of regular, non-guinea-pig tea. The three of us sat together, Mom and I to either side of our guest as he paged through the book and showed us the trees he recommended. I noticed that some of the trees had been X'd out in red marker, others in black.

He spoke about a dozen species that he was confident would flourish in the only place where anyone outside my family would be reminded that Caleb had led a life, that his life had been taken.

"Can we have a flowering tree?" I asked. "I want flowers this time."

"Yes," he said. I'd noticed by then that he never said more than necessary, never overspent his words. Once I understood this was his nature, not a sign of disdain or superstition, I liked him for it.

I told him I wanted to go to the nursery with him. I wanted not just to agree on a type of tree but to pick out the exact, individual tree, and he told me that was fine, but I would have to wait till the weekend.

I rode with him in his truck an hour north of Vigil Harbor, to the nursery where he said the stock was the hardiest we'd find. On the way, we rode mostly in silence—no radio, no awkward attempt at conversation for its own sake—although he did ask me about my mother, how serious her cancer was, and he asked me where I had come from.

"Come from?"

"Where you live now. It isn't near."

When I paused, he said, "I see you're a good daughter, so if you lived near, I would recognize you. Remember you." He turned to give me one of his rare smiles, then looked back at the road. I wanted more of those smiles.

I told him about Michigan. I thought he might like to hear about the cherry orchards. I told him about the festivals, to celebrate first the blossoms, later the fruit. I told him I'd learned to make the world's best cherry pie. "Just like in that corny old song," I said. "Charming Billy."

Suddenly I was mortified at the reference, but whether or not he knew the song, he said, "I'd like to taste it."

"Okay," I said. "Deal." I was glad he had his eyes on the road and couldn't see my face, red as the filling in one of my pies.

For the last half hour of driving, we were quiet. I marveled at how comfortable I felt, maybe because it was clear he'd grown comfortable, too.

Two weeks from the day I'd met Celestino in his driveway, I stood with him in front of the high school while he dug out the old stump and prepared a new hole with compost and peat and stronger soil. The hole he dug—he laughed at my offer of help, but he thanked me—seemed far larger than necessary to me. He drove the shovel more than three feet down, into bitter rocky earth, then used a pitchfork to remove the largest rocks. When he'd made a hole that seemed to me the size of a grave, he made sure the bottom was loosened and well soaked. He unbound and teased out the roots of the tall kousa dogwood we'd picked out together, and then he placed it in the hole. He turned it this way and that, standing back to look at it from different angles.

"This reminds me of putting up a Christmas tree," I said.

"You want the boughs to grow harmonious to the line of the sun." I could tell he'd said that often. He reached into the air and made a sweeping arc with his right arm. "I see which way it faced at the nursery. I will face it a different way here, to balance the next growth."

"Oh," I said, though I didn't fully understand. It was a brisk day, early October now, and when the shadow of the school suddenly hooded the place where we stood, I was cold, even in my fleece jacket. "It's not too late in the year to plant a tree?"

He looked at me appraisingly, and I must have blushed. What did I know?

"This is the perfect time."

We had made sure to arrive there after classes let out, though children with after-school obligations were being dropped off and picked up, or grabbing their bikes from the rack and gliding past us. No one paid any attention to us, and no one came out of the front office to ask what we thought we were doing. Having mixed new earth in with the old, Celestino was left with a large pile of useless soil and stones. He shoveled it onto a tarp in the bed of his truck. Carefully, he had reserved swatches of the green turf he'd removed to dig the hole; just as carefully, he replaced them, pressing them into the ground with the toe of his boot. I was mesmerized by the entire procedure. I wanted to remember it.

After he spread a layer of mulch in a loose, shallow collar around the trunk of my brother's new tree, Celestino said, "These next weeks, someone must come to water."

Immediately, I volunteered. But the school did not appear to have an outside hose—and no way would I deal with that receptionist again. In the bed of the truck was a water tank with a coil of hose, and Celestino said he would do it.

"But I want to," I said.

He looked at the plaque with Caleb's name and his dates, perhaps reading it for the first time. "Some days," he said, "in the evenings, I can lend you the truck."

That's when I cried. For which I apologized.

"He was your brother," said Celestino. He did not move to comfort me, not physically, but he said, "I see how you loved him. I see how angry you must be. I have two sisters, and I haven't seen them in many years. I worry about them."

And then I really, really cried.

He helped me into the truck, as if we were on an old-fashioned date, he in the role of perfect gentleman, and when we arrived in front of my house, he said, "I think you should not go in to your mother like this. You will upset her."

He drove those few dozen yards farther along the street and pulled into his driveway. "Come in and have something to drink," he said.

His kitchen—now mine, all these years later—was clean and gave me my first direct full view of the tree house, from the bottom up. "I need to know the story," I said. "Will you tell it to me?"

I watched him open a cupboard, which was generously stocked with plates, bowls, and glasses of several kinds (why should this have surprised me?), and once I'd told him what I wanted to drink—yes, please just water—and once he'd filled our two glasses at the sink, we sat at his table and he said, "It's a long story, the tree house. It's almost my entire story. If you want to hear it, let me cook you dinner. Not tonight, because your mother needs you. But soon."

"I'd really like that," I said. "Hey, I'll bring a pie. Like I promised."

That earned me one of his smiles.

When I did go over for dinner, and after I heard his long, strange story—requiring more words from him than I have probably ever again heard from him in one sitting—I was the one to make the moves; to, as Harold would say, ravage the man's spectacular bones. His bedroom was as plain and clean as his kitchen, and I knew he hadn't expected this from me—or not so soon. Both his body and the way he treated mine were unlike anything I'd known before, and when I left that bed the following morning, before we even spoke or ate breakfast together, I had a feeling that, just like Caleb's new tree, I had been turned a different way from where I'd been rooted thus far. Time to face the sun from a different angle.

Margo

I'm finding 4:30 unbearable. Four-fucking-thirty is un-fucking-bearable. A.m. or p.m., take your pick, and there I am in a metaphorical dinghy without oars. I can see the shore—cocktail hour or morning light, your choice again!—but I cannot GET there without jumping overboard. The meager distance between me and that pathetically Pavlovian destination is torture in and of itself, shallow water infested with sharks on the early patrol, man-o'-war jellies come *fin du jour.*

Mornings, I get up, make coffee, stare out the kitchen window, and dare the sky not to pale toward that deceptively coy pink of which it is so pompously and perpetually proud. I feel like torching every treacly ode to dawn I ever taught. (Where is Sylvia Plath when you need her the most? Dawn the perfect rose of bathwater sluicing blood from a lacerated vein. Overkill? Purple prose? Well, I was the teacher, never the poet. Mine the job of exposition, extrapolation—yet keeping the pupil awake with sudden swerves.)

Afternoons, at least I can strategize. Today: the first grocery safari I've made since, as I've come to call it, The Decamping. It felt, paradoxically, like one of the countless masked-and-gloved expeditions I'd make back in Early Pandemic, when, shopping for five yet striving to forage enough to feed us for at least a solid week, I learned to engineer a pyramid of produce rising from one of those behemoth carts. This time I was shopping for one, but McCoy's Grocery felt like just as much of a minefield, contact with other people a source of dread all over again.

When I make it back through the kitchen door, just before five, I realize the tile guy is still working in the bathroom—either that or a large rodent has moved in, complete with ghastly soundtrack. I told Bucky, everybody's favorite contractor, I'd pay extra for Saturdays; just get it done. (I would never confess that I dread the silence of the empty house.) "Just me!" I call up the stairs, however absurdly.

I am a living redundancy, I realize: the wife not so much replaced as deleted, just as I might take my green pen—never red; how trite would that be?—and blithely score through a student's unnecessary adverb when the verb can stand on its philandering own.

I set my sacks on the kitchen table and head upstairs. Yes, there he is, down on his knees—a position in which I like to see any man these days—hard at work on the floor of what will be my double shower, a gesture of futility or hope. I wave at him when he looks up, we exchange faux-casual heys, and back downstairs I go.

To hell with smaller quantities, I decided, with shopping like a spinster sparrow. One of our guilty, extravagant pleasures (and a blessing during times of plague) was always the basement freezer, the sort of wattage-guzzling colossus used by modern frontiersmen to store an entire elk or by mass murderers to hoard and preserve the remains of missing teenagers. (I can tell you this: Tom is going to pine for my gritty sense of humor, the chief side effect of having to police my own mouth all day, five days a week, in a public school with eyes and ears in every room, temperature sensors at the entrance, and bulletproof glass in the windows. Tom said he could always tell when I'd spent the day teaching Dickinson or Wordsworth or Billy Fucking Lanyard Collins, because my language was spicier and my taste in movies crude. Not that we don't all revere the curiously immortal Miss Emily, at least in moderate doses.)

I realize, as I hit the switch to the basement light, that I haven't been down there, either, since being here alone. Like all the dungeons that pass as cellars in these ancient houses, it's a creepy, hazardous place, rocks protruding like tumors run amok through the earthen floor, but ours, unlike many others, never floods, so the walls are lined with raw timber shelves, which Tom installed twenty years ago. The furnace, long defunct, still hovers at the back, a rusting heffalump, its removal too messy to face.

When I lift the freezer's heavy lid, the cold smoky light of its interior greets me like a spirit medium. Inside are three tubs of ice cream, a gift box of fancy chocolates with boozy centers, a package of that horrible synthetic crabmeat that Tom liked to buy on his cheapskate days, last summer's strawberries (frostbitten to the core by now), and a bag of ice for the picnic cooler, also a relic of summer. Or maybe it's left over from our Christmas party—apparently our last. Which makes me flash on Deeanne, that vile cunt, who was probably fucking my husband right on this freezer, red dress rucked up past her tits, while directly above their sweaty heads I served cups of fizzy punch to the revelers, jolly as a matron in Regency Bath, scheming to pair off one of the young bucks with one of my daughters. And actually, yes, all three of my daughters were home for that party for the first time in years, along with several of their local friends. "Hallooo, you're back from the wars!" Tom would bellow as he greeted members of the younger generation returned for a holiday or family occasion. "Not funny," I'd tell him in a whisper, not in a world broken out, like a virulent rash, in wars too many to count.

I add to the freezer packages of prefab burritos, soups, and soy sausages, a carton of juice concentrate, a mega freezpak of squid ravioli, a tube of calcium paste. The freezer is still more than half empty, and I think of the wasted amps with defiance, not remorse. I should unplug it and transfer the useful items to the kitchen fridge, but then what if I need a place to stash a body? Tell me, Sherlock, what then?

Before I go upstairs, I check the margins of the cold dusty floor for signs of vermin. Now it occurs to me why Tom went through that cleaning frenzy last month. "Time to play Keep or Throw, the deluxe edition!" he crowed pompously, dragging recyc bags from the transfer station down through the bulkhead. Should I look at this deed retroactively as some kind of favor? I will not.

Most of the shelves, once stuffed with beach, boating, and sports paraphernalia, are now bare, but a number of perennials remain: a picnic cooler, a pile of lumpen life jackets, two beach umbrellas, and a stack of moving blankets. A toolbox. And it looks as if Tom left his scuba gear—which I could sell, though it's probably outmoded. He gave up diving a decade ago. After the last trip for which he lugged all this crap along, a conference in the Bahamas, he declared that scuba diving was for people who liked to wallow in doom. "It's a moonscape down there, a death watch," he said. "I'll stick to sailing, thanks. Call me superficial."

Next to the gear, pushed back into a shadowy corner, is a sleek black box, the size of a briefcase, one that looks entirely foreign until I reach for the handle and pull it toward me. The moment its dense weight surprises me is the moment I recall, stunned, exactly what the fuck it is.

Yet again, fragments of memory coalesce, and whether I like it or not, here I am rereading another past chapter, one that seemed so tediously insignificant at the time. My inner time warden flips back through the calendar pages, struggling for certainty. Three or four years ago—fall? spring? wait; there was snow on that range—and yes, that's right: it was my birthday, for God's sake. November. Tom came home that evening with a voracious grin on his face, mixed us each a drink, and proposed a toast. "To the law," he said, perplexing me entirely since his professional life is the law, "and to our skirting its margins with the utmost respect."

I touched my martini to his scotch, took a sip, and laughed nervously. "Whatever you say, Tomcat."

"To vigilance"—he thrust his glass upward again, sloshing a little—"and doesn't our Yankee Doodle town oblige us to partake?"

"Partake?" Sometimes—and here is something I will not miss about Tom—he spoke with a pompous obscurity that made me feel like a bonehead. Maybe it was competitive. We'd met, after all, in a college seminar on Pynchon, after which he abandoned the English major—but not, for better and worse, me.

"Hold that thought," he said. He set down his scotch and bolted out the kitchen door. Through its windowed upper half, I watched him go to his car and open the trunk. He returned carrying two small identical suitcases. A surprise romantic getaway? He set them on the kitchen counter, where they crowded the processor and the toaster.

"Speechlocks! State of the art. Let's reprogram yours," Tom was saying as he laid his hands on the top of one case. He leaned down and spoke to the lock: "Bunting tosser one two three." He grinned at me. "Temporary. You'll choose your own."

I'd heard of these locks, but I owned nothing requiring such security measures, and it felt as if my husband had lost his mind and believed that, at the enunciation of an antique nautical term, a genie would emerge from the box he seemed to be caressing while confiding to it in code.

As he lifted the lid, I stood behind him and saw, settled snugly, smugly, in its bed of slate-colored foam, a gun. A gun, after all, looks not a thing like anything else. I recoiled, striking the table with my butt, toppling my glass and sending the saltshaker rolling off the edge to hit the floor with a crack.

Tom turned around, holding the gun in both hands.

"What the *hell,*" I said, my heart attempting escape from my chest. I felt as if my body had caught fire. "Tom?"

"Babe, relax!" he said. "Margo?" For an instant, he looked concerned, but then he laughed.

"Not funny," I managed. "Not . . . one bit. I have no idea what—"

"*Relax.* God, I knew you'd be surprised, but not horrified. I'm not suggesting we rob a bank! These are for us to . . . hey, kill two birds with one stone. Ha! One bullet? But seriously. It's something new for us to learn together. And the times we live in?"

"You bought these how? Last time I looked, no one asked me to fill anything out, showed up to take my prints."

"All taken care of," he said. "I pulled some strings, and we'll get you down to the precinct this week. Captain Sullivan has my back." A wink. "All we have to do now is sync your voice with the system. Choose a password."

I asked if he could please put the gun back in its case. My heart now mimicked a bongo drum. "This is your idea of a birthday present?"

Tom gave me a strange look, as if I were the one disappointing him on his own birthday—not that we were one of those couples who used our birthdays to prove who loved whom the most.

"I'm taking you out," he said after locking the case, "so fancy up."

When I came back downstairs after changing, the gun cases had vanished, and he didn't mention them again that evening. Perhaps, I hoped, he had replaced them in the trunk (though did that mean we'd be driving around with them?) and would return them to whatever shady establishment had procured them in the first place. You do not buy guns on a lark in our state. Getting a gun here is like applying to college. (Other states? Sam Colt, bar the door.) So we talked mostly about the girls—two of them called me en route to the restaurant—and about the Seattle quake and about the upcoming New Year's ball at the YC, when the next Regina Maris would be crowned and dance with the Commodore Elect. When we got home, we fucked in a bland but decisively satisfactory way. Our third daughter had left me a vid-mail. Except for the "gift," not a bad birthday.

But the next day, after breakfast, Tom went to the basement and returned with those satanic cases, and before I could object, he said, "One lesson. Indulge me. I scheduled us for noon, at a shooting range in Gloucester. I thought we could stop at that craft place you like, look at the jewelry."

"You want to bribe me with jewelry to take shooting lessons?"

"Call it negotiation." That dashing grin of his: the one I fell for. I used to tell my daughters, only half in jest, that I married their father for his teeth and his vocabulary.

I went through with it—and I did not buy so much as a toe ring at the craft shop, did not even allow him to stop—and as if to fully justify my disapproval, I indulged him in two more lessons, on the next two weekends, before I told him that was it for me. Three, I told him, is the charm—or it's not. In my case, not. I was aware that he took at least a few more lessons, but once the weather warmed and we were both out of the house so often, I ceased to care. I didn't even ask if he had kept my half of the his 'n' hers arsenal he'd seen as a celebratory gesture.

But maybe that refusal foretold our doom. Maybe Deeanne is turned on by weapons. Did he leave the gun behind as a grand fuck-you? Did he think I believed it was mine, no matter what? (Legally, God help me, it *is* mine.) I know how to open it—creepy how I can still recite my "personal words" and set of numbers to open the case—but fire the nefarious thing? Not on your life. Not on anyone's life.

I lug it upstairs to the kitchen now. I want it out of the house, but how? You can't exactly resell a gun, and I'm too stingy just to hand it over to the police. As I lay it on the kitchen table, I am startled nearly out of my skin by the tile guy, who comes down the back stairs at just that moment.

"One more day!" he announces cheerfully. "How's that for fast?"

"Fast. Yes. Thanks!" I babble.

I see him glance at the case on the table; does he know a gun case by sight, this sixty-something man whose inherited cod-fishing business collapsed? What if some terrible crime is committed tonight and he remembers seeing me all nervous, body-blocking a firearm?

"Have a very good night!" I chirp.

"Saturday night," he says. "Always good by me."

And out he goes.

I look at the clock: almost five-thirty. I open a bottle of wine. I decide on an omelet and green beans. Early dinner, a movie—in the den, not the bedroom—then up to bed and a good wholesome book. The bedroom smells like sawdust and caulk, but I don't mind. It's the scent of renewal.

I could, if I felt both brave and masochistic, gussy up and head to the YC for Lee Shore Happy Hour—refuse to embrace the shameful retreat of the ditched wife—but I am not in the mood for another numbing conversation in which yet another female friend gives me unsolicited advice.

What you need is a new hobby. Volunteer at the Senior Media Center! Join the Knitting Renaissance, the Village Cinephiles, the Compost Co-op. Make preserves! Make feature films! Make eco-friendly découpage lamps! Make love to a younger man!

Or how about . . . *Make bombs. Make dirty bombs. Smart bombs. Gifted bombs! Genius bombs! Deploy them! KABOOM! Summa cum laude KABOOM!*

I will scream operatically if I hear one more suggestion about how to fill up the purportedly painful and yawning void left by Tom's departure. Maybe it's quite the opposite: maybe it's more like good old-fashioned liposuction. What's been taken from me is exactly what's been weighing me down, a part of me I never realized I'd be so glad to strip away.

But just because I do not miss him doesn't mean I am immune to the hot rage that engulfs me like a cloud of napalm five or six or thirteen times a day, every time I am reminded that while I was perfectly aware, for the past year, that Tom was fucking somebody else (poor Mike hadn't a clue), I was dead wrong about *whom* he was fucking. I was certain the bitch in question had to be that "warrior yoga" teacher. The woman—what was her name? Katera? Cuntara?—couldn't have fought her way out of a folding chair, and while she had the kind of hot-wired body any man would love to find under his Christmas tree, she had the frazzled hair and boxy nose (and probably the brains) of an inbred Airedale. Fine, I thought. Let him boff the bimbo. I actually felt sorry for Tom, almost to the point of sympathy. He would slink home late, clearly thinking I couldn't hear the latch on the kitchen door; and meanwhile, without his horndog pestering, I got more sleep.

So when he announced, oh so mournfully-nervously, that he was moving out and—this was the worst part—I said to him, as calmly as I could, "I know who it is. You don't need to tell me. You're honestly running away with *her*?" I was baffled by his answer ("Christ, did you say anything to Mike?") and only compounded my idiocy by retorting, "Mike who?" Which left me thoroughly undone by Tom's hyena-like laughter.

"What do you mean, Mike who? I admit he's a pretty inconspicuous guy, but ouch. You know, he's the one I feel bad for."

It took me a minute to think of Mike from the YC; Mike with the slouchy cargo trousers whose pockets actually served a purpose; Mike with the sun-speckled, probably precancerous skin; Mike with the sweet, genuine smile (always the last to break open after some off-color joke at the bar).

So I exploded, "DeeANNE? The fucking queen of smug? You are leaving me for HER?"

"She isn't smug," said Tom, all at once the cool one. "She's insecure. And who wouldn't be, in this town of spoiled prigs? We're done with Vigil Harbor and its Fall of Suburban Rome pretensions. We are facing the future."

"She didn't seem so 'done' with all those pretensions when she vamped around as Regina Maris, crocked on those cumbertinis she practically gulped from the punch bowl."

"Margo, I get that you're hurt," he said. "Of course you are. I really am sorry. There's no way to do this kindly."

"Hurt? Sorry? I'm . . . Jesus, of all the women you could have . . ." But what was the sense of finishing such a thought? Was I implying that Tom could have had his pick? He was tall, sure (why on earth does "tall" give a man so much advantage as a mate? In terms of evolution, doesn't it mean he makes a better target for the enemy's poison-tipped arrows?), but despite the unsightly rack of weights he'd kept in our bedroom, he sagged nearly everywhere. Well, maybe Dee-anne did, too. Depending how much she spent at the cosmetologist. Just based on the woman's face, that budget looked to be pretty hefty. Well, no cosmetologists out at Rancho Apocalypse, I'll bet!

"Wait until the girls hear," I said. "Christ, Tom, you are still a *father*."

"We meant to make this happen more gradually," he said, "but we got to the top of the wait list much faster—"

"*Wait list?* What, for some game show?" I remember turning away from him, feeling the tears betray me, despite my best efforts. I cried in part because of the shame I felt; at that moment, I wasn't really thinking about our three daughters, who all—thank heaven—had lives of their own: two married (God help them), all three with real jobs, jobs they liked. I was thinking about the yacht club. I was wondering how many people had already guessed, even known.

"The membership stays with me," I said.

"Of course," said Tom. "Dee and I are moving away. You get the house, the car, the boat. Okay? And I've already told the girls. They're not happy about it, obviously, but they're adults and understand about necessary sacrifices, being true to oneself. Not being in denial. I wanted them to be ready to catch you."

That next surge of fury nearly knocked me to the floor. Out of pure reactive instinct, I punched my husband at the base of his rib cage, at the soft summit of his nascent belly. He gasped. "Catch me?" I said. "*Catch* me? I am not one to fall, you bastard. I am one to fly. Without you, I am going to *soar*."

I kicked him out of the house right then. I saw him exactly three more times. I gave him an afternoon in which to pack. I met him, without speaking to him, at his lawyer's (his fucking partner's) office—even though I didn't have to—to make a dry-eyed show of signing the agreement. And I caught sight of him, from my car, in the parking lot of the old-fashioned outdoor supply store in Knowles, where Vigilites buy things that are practical, not pretty. He was with Deeanne and they were laughing, hoisting bundles into the bed of an unfamiliar pickup truck. Their love-buggy.

"Ha ha fucking HA," I shouted at the rearview mirror, driving on.

Fine, I thought. Dandy. Let them hunt and gather, split their own wood, live in a log cabin with a compost toilet, a root cellar, and beverages brewed from burdock and thorns. Let them spend their days groveling through poison ivy in search of mushrooms and their nights dodging deadly mosquitoes. Oh, what wouldn't I give to see Deeanne Iliescu—and I flashed on how she treated me like a *pal* when we served on the committee boat during last summer's Point Penitence regatta—after a year of disemboweling innocent does, freezing her bony butt off in lustproof thermals eight months of the year, eating carrots fertilized with her own shit. Her hair, undyed, would settle toward possum gray.

Working this fantasy as I drove home, it's a wonder I didn't veer into a tree.

I don't know why we continue to think ourselves exempt from the madness of the world around us. Clearly I did. The lazy logic is to blame it all on Kip Kittredge and the backdraft of his progressive showboating. So maybe it will turn out to be true that he was the "Last Hope for Global Salvation"—if survival of the human race depends most urgently on reducing carbon dioxide emissions, declaring a permanent ban on fracking, and planting forests of leviathan turbines in sight of every civilized shore. But when it came down to ballots, few people felt he could handle the wily moral evasions of

Russia and China or stem the tide of jihadists who've begun to pop up like prairie dogs in places as far-flung as Aix-en-Provence and Jackson Hole. Nor did he pretend that he had a knack for the game of diplomacy, a disconsolate hybrid of Captain May I? and Truth or Dare. He declared loudly that the ecosystem had to come first or nothing else would matter; that if he were placing all of mankind's eggs in the wrong basket, then Noah had booked his zoo on the wrong ship. (I voted for him, though if you ask me, the guy's got a Noah complex.)

In the end, the basket everyone favored, like we always do, was the security basket. What did it matter that no single terror attack had yet to approach 9/11, the mother of them all?

So now where are we? Kittredge's party has fractured into a pair of doomsday cults—mocked by those who dismiss their apocalyptic views as the Good-Timers and the Bad-Timers. The Good-Timers will go out in a blaze of glory, flouting all shortages, reserves, and economies. They pay the penaltax to drive vintage gas guzzlers adorned with cartats reading, PLANET EARTH WILL ROCK ON WITHOUT US and EXTINCTION = MERCY. They hold opulent luaus, air-condition the bejesus out of their houses, and vacation their way around the globe, bribing customs officials as necessary. Leave it to my husband and his concubine to opt for the Bad-Timers, aka the New Shakers. They take the sackcloth approach: to the bitter, whimpering end, they will lead exemplary, carbon-neutral lives, the roofs of their tiny dwellings solar paneled, their foods homegrown, their clothing and furniture secondhand, their gray water cycled to their vegetable gardens and fruit trees. Good luck, I think, throwing your lot in with the freegans and vegans, reclaimists and redeemers. At least they're not having many babies.

Oh God.

Whatever else I do from now on, I think as I crack eggs into a bowl, I have to lose this rage. After all, I do not miss him. I do not, and I will not.

So yes, I have to find something to "do" with myself. This much is true. And like it or not, I may have to make money again. I think of the time, ten years ago, when, out of sheer boredom, I thought I might leave Tom—and this sanctimonious town where he grew up. (What might I have deduced from that?) I could probably have landed a teaching job in another district, but I was growing bored with that, too. The second-best skill I had was crewing a sailboat. That season, our boat, *Travertina,* was undefeated for a third consecutive season in her class. Well then, I thought, why not join the navy? In my teens, I was a lifeguard at the national seashore; I could ace any swim test in handcuffs. Excellent benefits, I'd be able to support the girls, and back then I was fit enough to look fetching in a white uniform.

I'd gone so far as to make some sneaky searches, but it turned out I was too old. Would I have gone through with it? Maybe I ought to have looked into the Coast Guard. I hear they're not so picky, especially these days. What with the new mandate to *secure our maritime borders,* it's a far more dangerous beat than it once was.

Now, though, I have little appetite for the open sea, and I'd look about as shapely as a tugboat in head-to-toe whites. As I close in on sixty, I like being indoors after dark or when it's pouring rain. In fact, it's obvious I'll sell the damn boat and probably, though not before I've sashayed defiantly through a few more parties, drop my membership at the club.

I am furiously whisking my eggs when someone knocks on the kitchen door. I assume it's Tile Guy, having left behind some tool of his trade, but the face behind the window is not his—and not one I know. Yet this is Vigil Harbor, town of unlocked doors, of cars parked in summer with windows ajar, and I open up with a friendly "Yes?"

"Hello! I am staying with neighbors of yours, and they mentioned that you are redoing your bathroom. I saw the workman's truck pull away. . . ."

Christ, I think, try clipping your nails in this town without reading about it in next week's paper.

"Well," I say, "that's correct." I haven't let him in yet, but he could barge right past me, flatten me to the floor, and bludgeon me with the schooner-shaped iron doorstop next to the fridge.

"Oh, I'm sorry," he says. "It's Connie and Celestino I'm staying with. And I told them I'm actually restoring an old house myself—in New Hampshire—and I'd love to get ideas on how to do something that isn't jarringly inharmonious for a master bathroom. The architect you used is Celestino's boss?"

Two things make me let him in, neither reasonable, one shameful. First, *jarringly inharmonious*. Burglars and scam peddlers don't talk like that, do they? Second, the revelation that this dark-skinned man is staying with Celestino, which answers the doubts hovering over how "different" he is from the normal random passerby.

I invite him in. "It's still in progress," I say, "but almost done."

He looks around the kitchen. "I love the exposed beams."

"Corny and, technically, all wrong for the period," I say, "but we enjoy our illusions."

He takes in everything, as if he's some sort of inspector.

"I'm Margo," I say pointedly.

He spins gracefully around to face me. "I am so rude. Ernesto Soltera. Forgive me." A slight bow.

"How do you know Celestino?"

"Old friend. New York days." He looks toward the living room. "I know I'm being intrusive, but could I . . . ?"

New York days. Though we've been neighbors for years, I know almost nothing of Celestino's history except that he came to this country as a teenager. But it's interesting to me that this "old friend," unlike Celestino, radiates none of the signs that he is an immigrant. Why I notice this fills me, again, with secret shame. Why do I assume he comes from another country? Why shouldn't he seem perfectly American? What century do I live in?

"Oh sure," I say, waving him through the door ahead of me. What else do I have to do with my land mine of a cocktail hour? Maybe I should offer him a drink.

He comments on everything from the mantel to the painted paneling. I find myself reassured that the resale value of this house is strong, what with all its noble-peasant touches of history. But I'm in no mood to show him the dining room, den, or downstairs loo, so I lead the way upstairs.

We spend some fifteen minutes in my almost-finished, practically palatial bathroom. Ironically, I realize that, Kepner's good taste aside, it is the very definition of *jarringly inharmonious*—but if Ernesto thinks so, he doesn't show it. He runs his hands over the Italian tile, the nickel fixtures, even fingers the fine pores of the two facing showerheads. (Now, there's redundancy for you!)

"So," I say at last, "not to kick you out, but I was just starting my dinner."

"I am so rude. Again!" He starts for the stairs. Back in the kitchen, he thanks me.

"But I'm curious," I say, "about your meeting Celestino. In New York. I had no idea he lived there. He's been here for more than twenty years."

"We worked at Wave Hill—the estate in the Bronx, do you know it? I think it's still open. But you won't hear him talk much about that time. He was—well, so many of us were—living there under the radar. Not so easy to do that now."

"No," I say. "Not even here."

The man is looking around the kitchen again, and I say, "Any other questions?"

"No, no. You have a lovely house. A house with character. I thank you for letting me intrude."

"Well, if you really like it," I say, "it might just be on the market soon. Though my daughters would kill me."

"And your husband?"

Insolent? Naive? Where did that question come from? But I say, "Decamped. Way of the world."

And why doesn't this man look embarrassed? That's when my own gaze, flitting from his handsome face, alights on the gun case. The goddamn gun. Had I really already forgotten its existence?

"I hope that was helpful," I say, leading him to the door.

"It was."

"Enjoy your time with Celestino. That household is never dull, from the look of it."

He thanks me again, outside the door, and he takes a minute to turn and leave. Is he appraising my neglected garden?

I return to my bowl of eggs, then visit the refrigerator to hunt for some herbs. As I close the fridge, I catch the flash of a passing car through the window: Celestino's truck, in fact—headed away from his house. Brecht, Kepner's poor addled kid, sits in the passenger seat. Brecht was in my classroom twice over his years at the High, and I remember encouraging his esoteric poetry—some of which was inexplicably beautiful—but there was something distant about him. Not school-shooter distant, thank God, or suicidal distant; he just seemed like a boy who didn't mind that he'd never belong. No anger, just acceptance. At least I can thank my ambivalent stars for dodging that parental challenge. My daughters are extroverts who party as hard as they work. Tom and I may have parted ways, but our genes cohabit with verve and good sense in our daughters.

But catching a glimpse of Celestino after talking about him feels . . . what, ominous? Charged with meaning? Seeing him always makes my heart clench, just a little. I remember watching the tree house go up, through an attenuated autumn, that October a seemingly endless succession of kind sunny days, like a flight of canaries. The house where Celestino lives is almost directly across the street, so I had a good view of its construction.

What was that, fifteen years ago? Twenty? It was the nadir of my life as a mother: three girls all careening toward their teens, already misbehaving (though in petty and callow, not criminal, ways: a tattoo here, a piercing there). Tom worked absurdly long hours in the city. The high school had begun to institute various crackdown security measures, running drills for all conceivable catastrophes—which seemed to alienate our children even more. They couldn't be persuaded that the lockdowns and the mock evacuations were reactions to our fears of the outside world, not of their rebel nature. Yet who could blame them when there we were reading *Things Fall Apart* as things appeared to be doing just that, when a student's shaky recitation of "When You Are Old" could be cut short so rudely by the blare of a fire alarm or the principal's voice ordering us to "shelter in place"?

I'd come home in those beleaguered days to an empty house and a dog too arthritic to take on long walks anymore. Except as a cook and changer of sheets, no one at home really needed me. (And just about no one, let's be honest, *needs* an English teacher!)

Late afternoons, I found excuses to cross the street and linger at the stockade fence enclosing the yard, peering over the pointed slats. Celestino (though I'd yet to learn his name) perched up in the branches, working alongside a younger companion; my guess was that they were at opposite ends of their twenties. They had only recently moved into the house, along with a much older man. What an odd trio they made when they were all there together.

One day, as I stood outside the fence watching the tree house grow, its trajectories stretching high and wide, I was startled to hear, "Would you like to come up and see the view?" The speaker was shielded from sight by a tenacious cluster of crimsoned leaves. Our quiet back street was empty, however, and there was no one he could have been addressing other than me.

He climbed down a spiraling set of footholds that sprang, like porcupine quills, out of the rugged trunk. "You like watching us work," he said when he came over to the fence. "Now it is secure enough to ask you in." After I just stood there, mortified at how obvious my stalking had been, he said, "Yes, come."

What choice did I have? I was the Peeping Tomasina caught on a ladder at the sill of a bedroom window. "I haven't meant to be nosy," I said.

He ignored my flimsy apology. "Let yourself in." He pointed to a gate.

"Celestino," he said, offering his hand.

"Margo," I answered. Meeting his gaze, I realized that he must have been one of the rare people in town who didn't know me from Willa Cather. I wasn't Strict Old Mrs. Tattersall to him. Mrs. T the Terminatrix, assigner of max-long term papers and like, OMFG, *memorization*? Normally, my reputation does more than precede me; it surrounds me like a force field.

He gestured at the ladder leading up the trunk. He went up behind me, a hand on the small of my back; oddly thrilling, that hand.

I rose through a trapdoor in a platform made from paint-splotched boards.

"One more," my guide instructed, and I took a sharply angled set of stairs to another platform, this one cantilevered from the main trunk. It was circular, enclosed by a driftwood banister, sheltered by a vaulted roof woven through the branches overhead.

As we stood together on the high platform, I realized that he was shorter than me—and I am not tall—but solid in a reassuring way. (Okay, so I'm a cavewoman. Shoot me.) His face was a deep terra-cotta from living so much in the sun, and his nose was wide, as if pressed against a window, his black hair almost impossibly thick. Christ, was I staring at him? But then I took in the view.

The panorama of the harbor was a shock, as all unfamiliar views of familiar places will be. I could actually spot *Travertina* at her mooring, one of the few boats outlasting the season (Tom was a die-hard frostbiter, sailing on into winter). "My God," I said.

"If you have one, now he is closer," said Celestino. He smiled at me.

I felt intensely awkward, disoriented in several ways. To fill the silence, I said, "What will you . . . I mean, is there a purpose? To this place?" What a knuckleheaded question! Did something so fanciful as a tree house need a purpose? Wasn't its purposelessness the purpose?

"It is advertising," said Celestino.

"For . . . ?"

"For others. For anyone who wants us to build them a tree house."

"Oh. Well. Of course." I thought about the *us,* the curious trio of men who lived in the house below. "You have . . . partners."

"One," he said. "You have seen Robert. He builds with me. His grandfather—I think you have noticed him, too—is the one who thinks we can make this a business."

If he was making a dig at my nosy nature, I deserved it.

"Well, count me a dependable reference. This is better than Disney World." Scanning the streets below, I saw a school bus heading up a hill several blocks away and realized that my youngest daughter would soon be home from her soccer game, in need of corralling toward homework before she could bolt to "hang" with her equally insouciant friends at the war memorial or The Drome.

Celestino guided me down to earth again, this time preceding me. "Come back when you like." He offered me a hand for the last step down.

But I never did go back up the tree, and my afternoons became overstuffed with more than reading papers on the weary works of Faulkner, Fitzgerald, and Steinbeck (that law firm of dead drunken white guys, recently laid to rest by my successors at the High). I was recruited to join the YC membership committee, and when Doro started singing in an a cappella troupe, I was guilted into running a fundraiser for Got Stage?, the entertainment arm of the PTO. But for much of that fall, I conducted an aching flirtation, sometimes leading to feverish sex, with Celestino—restricted to my somnolent life, I admit, yet I would awake so explosive with heat, the sheets on my half of the bed so tangled and damp, that if I had found his footprints leading from my bed to the nearest window, I wouldn't have been the least bit surprised. Sometimes I went to bed longing for these dreams, as if I might have private access to a bespoke pornography channel. Whenever Tom turned to me—caressing, hard, the implicit marital concession—I would yield simultaneously to my towering husband and to the fantasy of a much more compact, muscular man with a wide crooked smile and thick raven hair. My own pulpy bodice-ripper, to hell with Emily D and the three dead drunks!

That winter I stopped to admire the finished tree house only once or twice a week: fully exposed once the leaves had finished falling, then layered in luminous snow, attracting a good deal of attention. There were windows comprising mosaics of bottle shards, roofs shingled with old license plates, and tiles fashioned from shattered flowerpots. At Christmas, strung with colored bulbs, it was photographed for the front page of a local arts magazine. I read in the article that an architect had commissioned a tree house for some snug think tank he was building on an old estate in Concord. Celestino and Robert, his young partner, drove off early most mornings and did not return until dark.

A year or two later, I realized that the youngest of the three oddball roommates—Robert—must have gone away. Only Celestino and the older man—the grandfather—remained in the house across the street, and the following summer, I began to see Celestino driving around town in a pickup truck loaded with gardening gear and swaddled shrubs.

To this day, whenever I see his truck, his name now stenciled on the cab doors, I am, to my amazement, still stung by a jolt of desire, even if Celestino himself isn't driving the truck. He still lives in the house, though at some point the older man vanished, as quietly as the young partner had. One summer I no longer heard televised basketball or male repartee through the open windows. Instead, I heard a woman's voice; not long after, a baby's lament. The tree house has prevailed through every major storm, sometimes requiring a buttress or an alteration. And lately, in the past couple of years, a platoon of children clamber about, voices lilting and echoing off the rooftops. Homeschooling no longer seems that eccentric or antisocial to me, and I no longer need to see it as an insult or threat to the work I did in the classroom.

Now there, in an ideal world, is the younger man to douse my chronic rage, but he's a family man now, and there is one kind of mayhem that I will not be perpetrating any time soon. Detonate those dirty bombs, no problem, but infidelity, on anyone's part, is something I won't be messing with.

Once in a while, we wave to each other, I and the hero of that bodice-ripper nightlife I led in simpler times.

Brecht

So everybody's trying to keep the news away from me: stooge, of course, since I'm not sure you could avoid the news even if you were stoked on leaf, adrift on one of those stealth trawlers cruising the horizon. News of the Now is O_2. You breathe it in through every duct and pore; it's like we've evolved these special gills. Newsgills. If it's Big News, it's headed your way like a heat-seeking missile, the bullet that tunnels for bone. Storms, strikes, assassinations, pathogens, bombs, quakes, suicide pacts, door to door in a flash. Then there's Slow News: extinctions, famines, shrinking glaciers, creeping shortages, refinery leaks. . . . So this latest New York thing, explosives taking out a sculpture park and a bunch of yachts (I guess that hits home here in briny old Vigil), is it anything new? Nineteen dead, it looks like. Small-time! Noam and I said it in unison the minute we heard: *More of fucking same.*

Today's distraction was a tree consult at the nursery we visit when Austin says money's no object. I like the tree consults. I like watching Celestino peer close at the leaves, the bark, the soils, all with his horticultural X-ray vision. And Raul was along. He's a puppy when he's with me; in the truck, he was basically on my lap most of the time. Actually, he's good company. For one thing, he talks a lot more than his dad. We sang along to the songs on his tronic, we ate the stuff his dad buys that his mom would nix. Plus, Celestino drove like he was curled up inside his head today, even forgot to look amused by his kid's hijinks—didn't even have one of those cinnamon buns we buy on the way out of town; didn't tell us to watch the sugar we were spilling all over the seat.

"So who's that dude staying at your house?" I asked him.

"No one."

"No one?" Okay: none of my business.

"Someone I knew a long time ago—and I would be happy not to see again."

"Pretty friendly, though."

"It is not sincere."

Raul spoke up. "What do you mean, Dad? Ernesto's cool."

Celestino kept his eyes on the road. After a pause, he said to Raul, "I am glad he's nice to you." But glad was not how he sounded. And then he told me to take the job log out of the glove compartment. He's got everything online, but then, in an actual notebook, like my word book, he keeps a written record of purchases and work hours related to every job. He tells me to open up to the Tyrone job and remind him of the plantings we need to fulfill.

The list of jobs for the next month is fierce—and there looks to be a week of rain starting tomorrow. Finn will have to pull it together or Celestino will need to hire someone else. We need busy hands this spring, he says. Planting season could be short, like last year, which was rain, more rain, and then, slam, weeks of blazing heat. May was mud, and then, in a snap, July just up and swallowed June.

At the nursery, we had an appointment with Gil. Gil's like seventy or eighty, in max demand because he knows everything about what used to grow where and now doesn't, what works to replace the old classics, what's been re-biologized to stand the wildest weather or newest blights. GURU GIL, reads a hokey sign someone put on the wall over his desk. Today he got a little mournful, woolly eyebrows practically converging when Celestino asked about the birches we saw in the back lot. Five or six of them, root balls bagged, twelve feet tall, a harem of beauties huddled up sharing their secrets. Their bark was a priest-collar white, scored with inky strokes like slashes of night, peeling away in tiny scrolls to show its silky underskin. I can see my old self turning that bark into a poem. Noam would tell me, So do it now.

Celestino looks at trees with this chivalrous awe, and it's contagious. We stood there in that awe together. I shot a picture of the trees, for Noam.

Celestino hates it when we have to take down a tree, even one that's dying or took a lightning bolt. I know he's not religious, but every time we set up for a removal, I see him pause for what looks like some kind of private prayer before he swings the ax or revs up the saw. Last fall we had to take out a huge, totally healthy oak tree, all because the new property owner wanted a greener lawn; and oh, also, he didn't like the acorns falling on his fancy car. Celestino bid high, hoping he'd lose out. When I asked why he didn't just refuse it, he said that someone would take the job, make that money, so it might as well be him. But he was under a cloud for days.

Raul did circular sprints, looping up and down the rows of brooms and laurels and spring vines hungry for something to seize and climb. But me and Celestino, we just worshipped those birches for a while.

Gil shook his head. "Disease resistant, for now. But they don't like salt. Better bet inland. Not for that big job of Kepner's, up on the cliff."

Celestino smiled. "He call you?"

The guru shook his head again. "Your rival was up here Thursday, took all my hollies."

"I wouldn't plant holly."

"He's stubborn. And who knows? Sometimes you get lucky."

Celestino stroked the trunk of the nearest birch like it was a girl's arm, tender and wishful.

"Not worth the gamble," Gil warned. "Let me show you the new hornbeams."

Raul had dashed around the back of the greenhouse. I went to reel him in. That's part of why I was along, and I didn't mind.

By the time I caught up with the two men, they'd moved on to lilacs, viburnums. Celestino was frowning at the logbook.

"We taking stuff back?" I asked.

"A few bushes. But mostly I will place orders." He followed Gil toward the hut that holds his tiny office.

Raul pulled at my arm. "The fountain."

This is a ritual. So we went to the corner of the nursery where an old fountain runs out of a rock face. It's a relic of the formal garden this place used to be. The bottom of the pool is lined with worthless coins, and when he was smaller, Raul liked to count them.

"Wasting water," he said as he leaned over now, making faces at his reflection.

"Not so much. Recycles through a pipe."

"Every drop matters."

"Well, yeah. Sure."

"We are learning about hydroponics," he said.

"Excellent," I said.

"And rivers. The damage we've *done* to the rivers." He walked around the rim of the pool, balancing on the short wall. I thought of asking what rivers and how could he include himself among the damage-doers, but it's easy to guess that the ducklings are learning all the cautionary history: Arizona, the SoCal fruit fiasco, the lost aquifers. Agricultural Folly 101. It's the kind of thing those moms would teach in their homemade school, but I don't see the point. Hunker down or go forward, leave the past where it is, graveyard of greed. Let those sleeping dogs sleep, dream their dreams to kingdom come.

Celestino found us there. He had remembered to bring an old coin for Raul, pulled it from his pocket. Raul ran way back from the fountain, then turned for the throw. We ducked, pretending fear. Celestino laughed for the first time today.

We loaded six rhodies in the truck bed, washed our hands in the greenhouse, aimed for the highway. But first we stopped at the sandwich place we like. Celestino told Raul to go in and order for us. We'd follow.

"Growing up fast," I said.

"Too fast." Celestino looked at me. "I need a favor. I will pay you."

He asked me to take Raul home with me, let him sleep over. We'd done this a couple times before. The first time was when my mother offered, insisted, saying Celestino and Connie should have a night to themselves. Raul has this squirrel energy, but once he spends it, he sleeps like that same squirrel tucked in a high nest.

When we were back in the truck, lunch on our laps, Celestino told Raul the plan, and he whooped with approval.

So here we are up in my room, Noam across the floor in his, door shut, and just like we've done before, I set Raul up on the stool at the drafting table. He's crazy for drawing. Once in a while I join him, drawing on a pad, down on the floor or perched on my bed. I admit it gets to be relaxing. Since working with Celestino, I draw trees; today, I remember those birches and steal a look at the photos I took, though it feels like cheating. Besides which, my memory needs exercise.

Raul sets to work on his trademark aliens, half old-style robot, half iguana. He's got a thing for lizards.

Austin's office stuff, from what he calls the "everything-on-paper days"—days he mourns—is stashed up here, under the sloping roof at the edge of my room: two flat files and the drafting table. In the top drawer of one file, there's blank fancy paper, thick and soft, and boxes of these Swiss pencils in every color you could imagine. Raul is like a purring cat when I let him at this stuff. He could sit on that stool, curled over that paper, for hours. I ask him what music he wants, and I cue the speakers.

I get out my word book. In the truck on the way back, Celestino silent, Raul dozing off his sandwich against my arm, I did a mental spin on what I'm calling the City Words and their fickle ways. Because, just think about it, if atrocious people practice atrocity, and ferocious people ferocity, why aren't those with a happy nature felicious or truthful people veracious? And wouldn't it be skilling if speedy people could call themselves velocious? And good food praised for its delicity?

Oh, for the delicity of fresh figs with goat cheese.

Sitting on the floor, I get stiff after a while. I set my book aside and go check on Noam. He's napping, a book about to slip to the floor. I take it away, quietly, close it, put it on the stack of books by his bed. *Ocean of Stars,* it's called. More of his antique nautical stuff: a book on celestial navigation. He is out cold.

Coming back, I pass the stairs and hear a different voice from below. Mom was in the kitchen, alone, when we came in. Austin was off at a site, she wasn't sure where. So I go down, at least partway, to listen, find out who's with her.

Right: it's that woman, the grapefruit heiress. That accent. Mom's telling her she must stay for dinner, she must! The heiress is putting up the fake resistance that comes right before you say yes.

"Surely Austin won't want my nosy self lurking around on his Saturday night."

"Austin doesn't know Saturday from Monday," says Mom. "And I've told him to invite you. Tonight is perfect, Petra."

"I shouldn't have been snooping. But here I was, wandering the streets, and I realized I was *here*. He pointed it out—your house—on that drive-around we did."

"Of course you should snoop." Mom laughed. "You're a journalist."

"No, no. Just plain old writer-for-hire. No headlines or bylines for me."

"I've made soup. Very simple. Bread and greens."

"You are too kind. And I mean that."

Mom offers her a glass of wine, and she is oh-why-not-whyever-not?

Under my feet, their voices migrate back toward the kitchen, Petra asking about the photos on the screen, the sculpture on the table, the lithograph over the fireplace . . . the carefully curated surface of my stepfather's life.

"Austin came here from New York, I know that. But what about you, Miriam? What about *you*? I love those earrings, by the way. They complement your beautiful hair."

I could go down, but I stay on the second floor, leaning over the banister, listening to the chitchat, mostly a bore, but Petra's tone is different with Mom than when she was in the office with Austin. Like she's on a date. Giving out signals as much as words.

Mom's telling her about how, yes, she was in New York, too; that's where they met. How she'd been determined to stay after making it through the worst of the pandemic lockdowns—but then she just ran out of steam. (She leaves out the part about losing my dad.) And she had this kid, of course, who was making the place they lived in seem smaller and smaller—and didn't he deserve good schools, fresh air, open space, trees to climb? Bourgeois, yes, but . . . and then she tells the How We Met story: how, one day on her lunch break, in an art gallery, she struck up a conversation with a man she basically collided with in the middle of a colossal sculpture. Literally in the middle.

"Richard Serra," she says. "Do you remember his torqued steel pieces? I was walking along, on the street, and all of a sudden it began to rain. Hard, in an instant, the way it does only in the summer. Or used to. So I ducked into a gallery, thinking it would end as fast as it started, and the attendant, this boy at the desk, looked at me—as if he'd been expecting me—and told me to go right in. I just stared at him and he said, 'Into the sculpture. You have to hear the rain from in there.' "

"Goodness," says Petra.

"The thing is," Mom says—and of course I've heard this story a bazillion times, but I like hearing it, because she's always so happy telling it—"I'm kind of a compliant person. I was always a good student; with doctors, I'm the good patient . . . so I follow the boy's directions and enter what looks like a narrow tunnel between two walls of thick rusted steel, and it takes me on a curving path that makes me lean sideways, that takes me to this tall chamber—and it's all open at the top. The roof of the gallery is thick glass, the rain falling on it incredibly loud. And I nearly have a heart attack, because there's this man, just standing there, looking up at the glass roof, and I guess because he's so carefully dressed, I'm not afraid. But it's only the two of us. He looks at me and says, 'Here comes the thunder,' and he puts a finger to his mouth to keep me from answering."

My mother laughs, like she does every time when she gets to this part of her story. "So the first thing my husband did when I met him was to silence me."

Petra laughs, too. "And was he right? Did it thunder?"

"Oh God yes. The heavens split open. The sound of it filled the steel walls around us. I felt like I was inside the rumbling belly of a giant."

"Love at first sight?"

"No. But it was unforgettable. And I found out, after the storm passed, after ten or fifteen minutes alone with him in there, a small eternity because we were so silent, I found out that Austin kept a close eye on the weather forecast the whole time that show was up, and he'd drop everything just to be inside that space with the storm. That was his third time, he told me. His office was two blocks away."

"Brecht?"

Raul is standing at the top of the attic stairs, looking down at me.

"Hey," I say, "everything cool up there?"

"I found something."

"Found something?"

"You have to see it."

He sounds more worried than excited, and I hope he hasn't been poking around in Noam's room.

I go back up, and at first I'm disoriented, because my room, or my bed, which basically takes up the room, is a max-bright sea of color, like someone's thrown open a huge crazy-quilt. For a minute I think it *is* a quilt.

"I had to see it," says Raul, and I can tell he thinks he's in trouble. "I can't fold it up again. I don't know how."

The sea of color is a humongoid painting. I'm wondering where in the world it came from, but I see the open drawer in the flat file (not the one with the drawing paper, and I have a hunch Raul knew this). I lean over the picture and see that it's painted on some kind of thin fabric, maybe silk, and it's worn and cracking a little on the seams where it's been folded. Open like this, it's maybe six feet square, drooping way over the mattress.

And it's glorious. That's the actual word in my head when I give it my full attention. No. GLORY. It's just GLORY. Like in the church hymn sense of the word.

"Jesus," I say.

"I'm sorry. I was just . . ."

"Yeah, well, I get curious, too," I say, though I've never more than peeked into those other drawers, which are mainly full of old blueprints and anal renderings of suburban chalets and garages and swimming pool cabanas.

It's a picture of life underwater: reefs and fishes and weird creatures, all intricately made with colored ink and washes and pencil . . .

and no way did Austin do something like this, something so . . . insanely passionate. It reminds me of a stained-glass window but also of that famous Dutch artist who painted hell—and also of a space-agey Japanese mural I saw once on the side of a building in New York.

"We have to put it back," says Raul.

"Hang on, amigo. Let's get a good look at it first. What's a thing like this if not for looking at, right?"

Raul nods, his serious face a mimic of his dad's. "But please don't—"

"Relax," I say. "Relax." I could wake Noam up and get him in here, but first I have to figure out if I can ask Austin about it. Or more like, figure out *how* I ask him. The files are up here, and it's not like anybody told me to stay out. Nothing's locked. No big deal, right? But why does my radar tell me maybe it is?

Downstairs, Clio barks her Austin bark. Mom makes her futile attempt to calm the dog down. So Raul and I stop to take in the commotion of dog, voices, doors, Austin's surprise at the unexpected guest. Politeness all around (except Clio).

Next, Mom's footsteps on the stairs. I rush down, meet her halfway on the second floor.

"Dinner's in half an hour," she says. "How's Raul?"

"Making his art."

"Are you reading?"

She's always asking me that, like reading will return me to who I once was, or take me to a higher plane of existence. (Which reading can do, in a sense; ask Noam.)

"Hanging with Raul, that's all."

"Not driving you crazy, I hope." She looks at me with that mom-look of hers, a clustering of love, worry, the misery of ultimate ignorance: not knowing whether where I am is fine or if I'm on the verge of basic mental catastrophe. I would say I'm fine, but I also know how stuff can sneak up on you, how panic can take you hostage. She knows it, too.

"We have another guest," she says. "This woman who's writing about Austin for that film."

I tell Mom about meeting her at the office. She doesn't ask me to set the table or do any kitchen stuff, so she goes back down, and I go back up.

Raul is trying to fold up the painting.

"Stop!" I say, then apologize for scaring him. "Let's be careful," I explain.

"There's writing on the back," he says.

Getting down on my knees, I lift a corner and peer at the back side. It's in shadow, but he's right. You'd have to flip the whole thing like a pancake to read the words, and it would take a few people to do that without risking some level of damage. "Let's figure it out after dinner," I say.

I tell him we're having soup, and he tells me tomato's his favorite; I tell him I like Mom's stew with the oysters, but lately she's riffing on seaweed. She's obsessed with this Japanese chef.

"So let's wash our hands," I say. "Let's go get fed. And this"—I point to the bed—"we keep to ourselves. For now."

Noam, as usual, will fend for himself later. His hunger follows its own peculiar clock. Just as well, since Austin will be doing his Master Builder act for the grapefruit heiress. He doesn't know when he's doing it; his laugh is what changes the most. It takes on this opera singer vibe.

Mom's setting the table for five. Sometimes, I don't know why, I'm surprised to be included with the grown-ups: like what, Raul and I would be seated at some kiddie table, our food arranged on our plates like happy faces? I joked about this to Mom a couple months ago, and she didn't think it was funny. It clearly made her sad.

"Hello there, Brecht!" Petra exclaims. "And who have we here?"

Raul introduces himself.

"I take it your daddy's the gardening genius," she says. Which, predictably, clams Raul right up.

"He's an arborist," I say.

"A genius at all things green," says Austin. "I'll show you what he has planned for the Tyrone place when we drive up there this week. The site calls for a major windbreak. Wind, in these parts, is serious wind."

"I imagine it is," she says as he refills her wineglass.

I go into the kitchen to help Mom. Raul, my shadow, tails me.

Mom tells Raul she has just the job for him; would he break the bread into pieces and wrap them in a napkin to keep them warm, put them in the basket?

To me she assigns the ladling of soup. Beside me, she makes a salad.

"Intense, this woman," she murmurs.

"She make you uncomfortable?"

"No. But I feel like she looks awfully close at everything around her. Like she's taking some kind of inventory."

"So that's rude."

"No. No. . . . Just thorough. But what I realize is that she may write about us—or me. Or even about you. Oh God. Maybe this film is more than academic."

"Would you care? I wouldn't." I wonder for a moment why, if she's working on a film, there's no camera. But this is not my concern.

Mom hands me a cloth, to wipe clean the lips of the bowls where I've dribbled soup. Austin's sense of the immaculate was the first bug she caught from him, after we moved in together.

She shrugs. "People get paranoid so easily these days. Me too, I guess. Never mind." She pulls a tray down from a high rack. It's decorated with this baroque octopus, tentacles curlicued like ribbons on a gift box. Which reminds me of that . . . painting?—more than painting—sprawling its glory across my bed. Yeah, there's something erotic about it. There is.

Or even about you. Oh God. Why not about me? Because I'm something she's ashamed of? But I say, "You ask me, she seems lonely. That's all. Didn't Austin say she lost her husband?"

"Here to carry whatever needs to be carried," says Austin, who's come in to get another bottle of wine. Behind him, I see Petra paging through a large book. The book of coastal houses that includes a few by Austin.

When we settle at the table, soups steaming, waters poured, napkins in our laps, Petra leans toward Mom and says, "How perfect! I am so grateful!" And clasps her hands. Like we've thrown her a surprise party. "Now, first thing, I need to know about this whale."

She means the sculpture in the middle of the table. It's made of polished black stone, a whale breaching, aimed like a rocket for the sky. It seems to be connected to its plain flat marble base (the ocean's surface) by hardly a whisker. So it's as much a subversion of gravity as the act it depicts. You're sure it's got to fall sideways or break off the base. Austin says it's secure because of a perfectly placed thin steel rod at the core, but that doesn't bring the amazement factor down.

Austin starts to give his spiel about the sculptor, this Indigenous Canadian guy who—

Petra interrupts. "Oh but where did you get it? Do you know him?"

"No," says Austin, and maybe only Mom and I can tell he's startled at being cut off. He speaks softly by nature, rarely raises his voice, but that voice is always the alpha in the room, the one people lean toward, like he's a prophet. "I suppose it's the first 'significant' piece of art I bought. Back in New York. But it's still my favorite."

"Doesn't it make you sad?"

"When I look at it, I think of life, not extinction."

"Well, yes." She laughs nervously. "Life."

"Not all whales are extinct," says Raul.

"That's true, honey," says Petra. "And I didn't mean to go all gloomy."

"Some things are more sobering than sad," says Austin, "but for me it's just about the beauty. Is that tone-deaf? Is that above-it-all?"

"Above what-all?" says Raul.

"Above conscience," says Austin. And here's something I genuinely love about my stepfather: he never talks down. I know you might say it's because he's never been a father to a little guy like Raul, doesn't get how to simplify the moral stuff, but I think it's just that he's all about treating people as equals. Maybe he thinks he's brilliant, but he never condescends.

"Conscience is knowing right from wrong," Raul declares.

Petra looks stunned. "On the nose," she says. "My goodness."

"Except," says Austin, "here we are talking about action, taking a stand, versus doing not a damn thing to make a difference. Right?" He's addressing Raul.

Raul nods. He takes this stuff seriously, because of the way he's being schooled. Everything they learn in his house is tied to some kind of "issue," the big choices we make that are easy to fuck up. The choices already fucked up to the max.

Sure enough, he says, "Dr. Iliescu came for science and talked to us about the deepest part of the ocean, how even way down, *miles* down, it's affected by what we do to the air. Seven miles! That's how deep the deepest part of the ocean is."

Mom is beaming at Raul. Austin says to Petra, "I'm doing a job for Iliescu, in fact. Just a kitchen, but I make it a point to keep the firm working at every scale, micro to macro."

She doesn't follow up on this, ask about the project. She's still looking at the whale. "I notice you seem to collect marine art." She points to a wall where Austin's hung four pictures of the sea. Just the sea: waves, horizon, a storm. Two watercolors, a drawing, a painting in a gold frame that's two hundred years old. Different artists, different styles.

Austin shrugs. "Predictable, what can I say?"

"You started in New York? Collecting, I mean."

"In an accidental way. I wouldn't call myself a collector. I don't focus on particular artists. I don't care about art as investment."

"But it's all . . . art about the sea. Not so much nautical but . . . oceanic? Not ships, for instance."

"I live by the sea because I love the sea," Austin says. "So it makes sense, right? That I should buy pictures of the sea. Sea creatures"—he gestures toward the whale—"or scenes of sand and sky. As I said, predictable." He sounds a little annoyed, but he smiles. I'm finding this whole conversation weird.

"Sea creatures," says Petra, and she's staring at Austin as if what she's said is in code, as if it means something else. Creepy.

Mom's clearing the bowls, and I realize she's said not a single thing. She can be quiet, but this is extreme. I follow her into the kitchen. She tries to stop me, but I say, "Let me help."

"It's just a salad," she says. "And I found some good cheese in the back of the fridge. Is there any bread left?"

I reach across her and point to the half loaf I set aside.

"What would I do without you?" She touches my arm.

Any answer to that will get me in deep water. *Seven miles!* I remember, and I feel bad for Raul being stuck with adults unaccustomed to talking with children. But Mom is the one I may need to rescue from the social weirdness, so I take time to give her a one-armed hug. She leans in, grateful.

This kitchen is pure Austin—it's the one thing he changed about the house—and his theories about what he calls "the spatial sublime" might as well be decked in party banners across the perfectly accessible, silently hinged, indigo-patina cupboards. When I'm alone here with Mom, I get these memory pangs. My body, though it's much bigger now, remembers how the two of us moved around our tiny city kitchen together, when it was just me and her, locked down together for months after Dad died from the virus. She makes a joke of it now when people talk about where and how they made it through that time: "Poor Brecht's one and only playdate, for what I'm sure felt like an eternity to him, was his desperately sad widowed mother." She'll tell you food was how she fought her grief; she'll even apologize for how unoriginal that is—but what did I care about original? Every day, she'd take me into our shoebox of a kitchen, set me up on a stool, and teach me specific skills, which fit into making nearly every meal we shared. Chop and sauté onions. Wash and dry lettuce. Peel carrots. Grate cheese; grate ginger. Watch for the oil to shimmer in the skillet. Frost a cake, roast and peel peppers, make the best mashed potatoes in the world. Treat flour with respect. All these things I learned to do: with her, because of her—and, I knew even then, for her.

It was, corny as it sounds, a dance we did. Meal after meal after meal. Gradually, it made Mom happy, or gave her a source of satisfaction.

We don't have those rhythms here, in Austin's kitchen. We get out of sync, we sometimes collide. She has to remind me which tasks are mine when I help.

"You're being quiet out there," I say. "Like what, she'll quote you saying something stupid?"

"No. It's just that I still can't get over how . . ."

"Yeah, I know. The whole privilege thing. Like here we are discussing art when—"

"No," she says again, firmly.

"Then you can't get over what?"

Mom looks at me. "How afraid I am of what happens next."

I can't believe she's said this in front of me, even if I'm glad she has. Because who isn't afraid of that? Unless you are stooge to the ends of the earth.

And then she catches herself. "Oh Brecht. How could I say that to you?"

"Like you think, what, you're protecting me from something? The latest headlines?"

Now she gets that panicky look.

I put a clumsy hand on her back. "Turns out there was no suicide this time. Remote detonation. Maybe by drone." Before she can get emotional, I spin around and say, "The salad thing. Let's do it."

And we do it, the salad thing, the more-bread thing, the cheese thing.

Back at the table, Raul is standing, leaning in, stroking the stone whale with one tentative finger.

"Don't worry. It won't fall over," Austin's saying. "Isn't it amazing?"

"I know an artist whose work you'd love," Petra says. "Well, knew her. We lost touch. She painted seascapes. They were remarkable. Exquisite."

"Does she show?" Austin says. Mom's passing out salads, and he touches her vaguely as she puts his plate before him. Austin's affections are stealthy, like a cat's. I rarely see him kiss my mother; instead, he'll brush past her, a hand across her lower back, a gentle elbow jutting into hers.

"I don't know, but she lived in New York," says Petra. "It would have been—I mean when I knew her—when you were still there. You could have seen her work." And here it is again, the same X-ray look she gave me back at the office, but she's aiming it at Austin.

He's looking at his salad, digging in. He glances up and says to Raul, "You like kelp?"

"Mom says it's the new kale. It's okay." He makes a face.

Austin laughs and makes an exaggerated show of chewing, chewing, chewing (that's the thing about kelp). He doesn't look up until he's swallowed. He takes a swig of wine and turns briefly to Petra. "As I said, I'm no collector. If I stumble onto something, and if it appeals, I let it follow me home."

Raul giggles. "Like a dog. Is that how you got Clio? Did she follow you home?"

Petra's face is strange, like robo-blank for a minute. "I am just *certain* you would have loved her work," she's saying, but Austin is answering Raul.

"Yes, as a matter of fact she did! Clio was a storm refugee."

Clio was one of the dogs flung to the gutter by Cunégonde. People from a local humane society drove around catching stray pets. Some had chips, some had licenses, but even some of those had nowhere to go. Austin happened to drive past the place the dogs were corralled, over in Knowles. She followed him through our door that night, a surprise.

So now Clio hears her name and comes to the table, tail flapping, nose raised. Raul leans down to lavish her with boy-love. "I wish I could have a dog," he says.

But what's going on with Petra? Am I the only one who sees the tears? So of course she excuses herself, asks Mom where the bathroom is. And then Raul's tronic hums—Connie checking in—and then we're clearing the salad dishes and the two moms are speaking, mine praising Raul's good behavior, and then she's putting out her brown-sugar cake and telling Raul he can take a piece to the den, the room with the super-huge screen. Austin watches vintage movies there; before New York, I used it for gaming. Mom says it gives her vertigo, seeing images so large and so close at the same time.

I say to Raul, "Hey. Let's grab our cake and go back upstairs. Work on our drawings."

We're halfway up the stairs when I hear the kitchen screen, the urgent banter of the news. Last I checked, the bombing in New York was claimed by Oceloti, the rain forest defense group that usually does much tamer things—sabotage logging vehicles, stage protests at government agencies, mostly in tropical countries. They're all about foiling deforestation and mining. They haven't had much luck.

Looks like they just started playing hardball. The biggest of the yachts belonged to the CEO of a company stripping forests in Southeast Asia. Forget about lumber or oils harvested from the actual trees; they just need to clear the way for digging up some mineral essential to the manufacture of computing chips. According to what I saw this morning, Oceloti's main target was that CEO, though they had to know there'd be "collateral damage." The target was hosting a soirée on his big boat, raising money for some charity to distract from his business-as-usual pillage-and-burn, but he wasn't there yet. He was late to his own party. A dozen people, the early birds, were blown sky-high. Regrettable, but that's what you get for partying with the pillagers. What maybe they didn't mean to do was take out the random dog walkers and pedestrians on the promenade nearby.

But they sent a message of no regrets, declared themselves done with "simple sabotage." Mom had been watching in the kitchen early this morning; coming downstairs, I heard the gist of it. The declaration they made, claiming the blowup, was scrolling on the screen. Mom snapped it off as I came in.

And yeah, just like she suspects, I think about Union Square. What I saw and didn't see. What Noam saw. Or no, I remind myself, don't get confused. Because the more time that passes, the more I wonder how much I've forgotten. Which is surprising, because no way would such memories be anything but shockingly vivid, right? When I overhear people saying I was there, I don't correct them. People tend to exaggerate. I was nearby, but not *there*. Near is not the same as *there*. And I do remember my view, from a safe distance: all that smoke, rising forever into the sky.

Raul's rushed upstairs ahead of me, carrying his cake. I have to pick up his fork when it clatters off the plate and lands on the stair ahead of me. "Slow down, amigo," I say, and it's only when I get back up to my room that I remember the painting.

"What do we do? We don't have to tell anyone, do we?" Raul is standing at the foot of the bed, and he looks a little frantic. I should reassure him again that he's not in trouble, but I'm transfixed. It's more crazy beautiful than I remember, glistening in the dusky light from the window until I turn on the lamp. Then it just glows. It fucking *glows*.

I realize Austin put it away for a reason. To hide it. Why hide something so totally made of glory? Because that word is still in my head. Why isn't it framed, up on a wall? Though I realize we don't have a wall that big.

"Well, let's see," I say slowly. "Maybe for now we very, very carefully fold it up again. I'll do that."

"And we don't have to tell anyone?" I think he's disappointed now: more willing to get in trouble if it means finding out the story behind this, what, treasure? Buried treasure. Filed-away-in-paper-oblivion treasure.

"For now, we keep it under the radar," I say. Like the night trawlers. Like terrorists who get away with it, who live to set another bomb.

I concentrate on figuring out the folds in the silky fabric that holds the painting, the order of the folds. First, in half. Next, in quarters. I'm holding my breath. Not until it's folded completely, down to the size of a very large book, do I see the writing that Raul mentioned. It's small, confined to a corner of the fully folded painting. I lean in to decipher the spidery writing, the letters miserly and sharp.

Desecrators.
Murderers.
Fools.
Face your fate.
Don't tell us you'll change.
Guess what? It's too late.
Our city sank, but we go on.
Yours will sink, too,
But you will be gone.

Christ, a poem: a poem and a curse in one. The voltage that hits me is massive.

Noam comes in then, sneaking up behind me, giving me a second scare. I point at the message. Raul's looking, too. He says it frightens him. Noam tells him not to worry; it's a message from out of the past, from someone deranged who may well be dead by now. I study the handwriting, to see if I think it's male or female. Who knows?

"Hey." I make my voice extra cheerful. "Let's get this thing back where it belongs and finish our drawings. And eat your cake, little man, or I will. I forgot to bring mine along."

Raul laughs and grabs his plate off the table beside my bed, as if I might really steal it. This is one of those moments when I remember that he's the same age I was when Dad died.

Downstairs, I hear the front door, the indecipherable goodbyes. I go through Noam's room to the window overlooking the street and watch Petra Coyle walk away, her brown coat rippling in the night breeze off the harbor. What made her so sad at the dinner table? Something eerie about her, something maybe I'm the only one to notice. Maybe there's a sadness we share.

What would Austin Kepner say about why he left New York? Whatever he feels the truth to be all these years later, he would probably not say that he fled. He might say that he evolved. He might say that he needed to settle somewhere better aligned with his ambitions. But at gatherings where people trade their ambivalent memories of the city—many in Vigil Harbor love to mention a *phase*, a *stretch*, or even (tongue in cheek) a *tour of duty* spent in New York—he speaks about his time there only when asked, and he speaks about it in almost purely professional terms: the endless hours he worked, the projects he shared, the colleagues he shared them with. Because he left and returned there so often on business, he'll say, each trip reinforced that this city was his *home*. He got to see a lot of the wider world, but none of the buildings he helped build gave him any lasting, tangible sense of pride. Was he selfish to want that?

There is more to his story, though possibly he's pushed it as deep into the recesses of his past life as the painting he stored away, a long time ago, in his personal archives. Perhaps the confusion and guilt (and fear?) have faded into genuine oblivion.

This is far from true for the woman who calls herself Petra Coyle.

Issa is the kind of girl some will describe, dismiss, as a siren or seductress; others would appraise her type as naive, fragile, a delicate *scrim through which the jaded among us claim to see disingenuous motives. Or she* was *that kind of girl. Is or was? It depends on what you believe possible. It depends on whether you are Austin or Petra.*

Austin Kepner and Petra Anderssen met her, separately, during the same week in an exceptionally beautiful October when the air seemed notably cleaner and clearer, constantly stirred by temperate winds, the views across rivers and parks more crisp in detail. It was the time of year when people who live in the city renew their vows to stay.

To Austin, she was the Girl on Display. To Petra, she was the Woman on the Pier. Austin met her when he took a life drawing class, a gesture to save his sanity from crumbling under pressure in his eighty-hour workweek; Petra when she was walking along the Hudson River, a sanity-saving gesture of a more casual, spontaneous kind.

Petra met her first, on the Monday. She was walking into the wind (always stronger on the west rim of the island), desperate to push against something, numb with rage at the latest cad who'd pummeled her heart with declarations unfulfilled. Yes, she ought to have known. Yes, she chose the wrong men. But wasn't it fair to ask why the wrong men chose her? What did that mean? Didn't it work both ways? She knew she should go into therapy (yes, again), but where would she get the money? She was living on less than a shoestring; she was living on a filament of fishing line.

She laughed bitterly to herself, at herself, leaning forward into the gusts that swept in from the harbor and glanced off the hard, glinting surface of the river. Today the wind seemed colder (or was that her mood?), and she had just doubled her shawl around her throat when she noticed the figure standing on the stone bench, a girl, or no, a girlish young woman, wearing a raincoat but barelegged from her knees down—even her feet were naked—just standing there, up on the bench, looking out at the river. Petra saw her in perfect profile. Long hair, brassy in the sharp lateral sunlight, blew back from the girl's face, and for an instant she resembled a figurehead on the prow of some vintage sailing craft. Yet though she was pretty, her bare feet told Petra that she might be just another of the too many loonies who occupied the pocket parks along this fringe of the city, sleeping on vents at the PATH power station near Christopher Street, begging for change along the paved promenades (like this one) where most of the strollers and cyclists were the guilty, overfunded bohos of the suddenly unaffordable West Village.

Petra readied herself to steer wide of the bench just as the girlish woman turned toward her and said, plain and friendly, "Hello." And smiled—not the smile of someone unmoored or manic but a kind, familiar smile, as if they knew each other; as if the woman had been waiting for her there; as if Petra had simply forgotten their planned meeting.

Petra stopped and looked up, shading her eyes. "Well," she said, "hi."

The woman stepped down from the bench. "Look." She turned back toward the river and pointed.

Petra squinted; the water shimmered, but she spotted a small dark shape, moving steadily along. "Is that a seal?" she said.

"Mm," said the woman.

"I've never heard of seals in the river. Is that normal?" Petra felt odd in the woman's presence, but she had no urge to escape. "Should we call someone? Do you think it's lost—disoriented?" The creature was swimming north, upriver, away from the harbor.

"No. She's fine. She knows where she's going." The woman offered Petra her open smile again. "Sit."

Petra, who had lately begun to wonder if she ought to say yes more often (though not to all those wrong men), joined the other woman on the bench.

Now what? Petra felt unsettled but intrigued. Was this some sort of New Age encounter to which she should "open herself up wide," as the master teacher at her current studio was always urging her to do? She was too uptight, she knew that, but she also believed (contrary to her teacher's philosophy) that you could use that kind of coiled, self-conscious tension to inhabit a role all the more powerfully, deliberately. That month they were workshopping the play Ondine*; Petra had been cast as Bertha, the darker of the* *two women, the lesser role. She didn't have the dance chops for Ondine. Dance lessons: another expense for which she'd need to scrimp, sacrifice eggs or decent cheese. (She'd already given up meat, pretending the choice was political.)*

When the woman put her hand on Petra's knee and said, "I've seen you here," Petra very nearly cried out. She tried not to show her shock.

"I live nearby," Petra said cautiously. "It's nice along here. The sunsets. I have zero views from my apartment."

The woman's manner was confusing; she neither looked nor smelled homeless. Her coat, a greenish pale gray trench, looked clean and glossy, even new. "I come for the sunsets, too."

Petra introduced herself. What the hell.

"Issa," said the woman. "I'm Issa."

"I love that name," said Petra. "I've never heard it before—or is it short for Theresa? Clarissa?" She was prattling.

Issa shook her head. "Ee-sa," she pronounced carefully.

"My name means 'rock,'" Petra barged on. "I guess you could say it signifies solidity, but I'd rather be graceful than solid." She felt again the disappointment at being passed over for Ondine. "And it's the name of an archaeological site in Jordan. Carved out of a giant cliff. You haven't been there, have you? I hear you have to go in on horseback." Petra had a habit of filling silences, as if her words were water flowing toward a valley. Acting, to Petra, put her verbal compulsion to use, other people's words tumbling forth from her soul. She loved becoming the vessel.

Whether Issa absorbed or recognized Petra's small speech about her name wasn't clear. Petra said then, "Can I ask why you're barefoot? Aren't you cold?"

Issa looked at her feet and pulled them up onto the bench so that she sat cross-legged, her right knee in Petra's lap. And then she did something so startling that, looking back on it later that evening, Petra couldn't believe she hadn't fled.

Issa took Petra's left hand and placed it on her nearest foot. "Feel."

The foot was warm, the skin remarkably soft, uncallused—and glancing at the toes, Petra noticed how perfect the nails were: not polished, but unscuffed, as if this woman had never *worn shoes.*

She pulled her hand away—gently, as though it were imperative not to hurt Issa's feelings. "Well, you're lucky," said Petra. "My feet, and my hands, are frigid eight months a year. Still"—she glanced at Issa's small, flawless feet—"I wouldn't want to risk all the germs. And I mean, you know, the broken glass and the . . . well, the needles. There's nasty stuff on the ground." Why did she sound as if she were speaking to a child? Issa might have been as young as twenty or as old as thirty. She was in the golden passage of mature youth, the one that some women were fortunate enough to inhabit for far longer—the one you had to prolong if you wanted lasting success as an actress. Petra, nearing thirty, could see that she was reaching the moment when looking young would become a concerted struggle.

Issa laughed. "Yes. Shoes."

Did this mean she actually owned no shoes? That shoes were absurd? Maybe she was *homeless—newly homeless. There had to be a critical moment when someone crossed over to that life—unless another person intervened. Maybe Petra should offer to give her a pair of shoes. "What size are you?" she said.*

"Let's go somewhere."

Go somewhere? Petra began to examine Issa more closely: her hair was clean, her teeth straight, her eyes clear, unmuddled by drugs. Everything about her had a childlike clarity. Just as furtively, Petra glanced around them—into the tall grasses separating promenade from highway, at the couple on a bench some distance away—but she saw no hidden cameras, no peering lurkers, no indication that she had been targeted for a prank, a crime, or some random creative happening. The two women had this ribbon of park nearly to themselves.

"We could get a cup of tea," said Petra. Anything to avoid being alone again in her apartment, replaying that Dear Jane message on her voicemail for the ninety-third time, listening for . . . what, some nuance implying he meant the opposite of what he was actually saying?

She started south on the paved path; after a last look at the river, Issa followed.

And so began Petra's enchantment. Even she, for years to come, would associate that word with her meeting Issa. That afternoon, they sipped green tea and ate biscotti for close to two hours at an Italian pastry shop on Barrow, and as Petra returned alone to her apartment, uncertain where Issa lived—in fact, knowing nothing much about her except that she modeled for drawing classes and seemed to take an interest in the wildlife of New York's waterways—she felt elated, fortunate, and pleased with herself for inadvertently, in a different context, following her acting teacher's advice to make herself "wide open." It was the same feeling she knew from winning a good role in a good play, from eating a delicious meal at a welcoming restaurant: a far safer feeling than what she knew as falling in love, so at first she failed to recognize what had happened. But already she had fallen—just as Austin, only a few days later, fell.

The class had been advertised on the bulletin board outside the firm's cafeteria: Pop-up studio: draw from a model and pay per class. Cash only. BYO easel! The class met two nights a week in a makeshift wooden building adjacent to the fortified edge of the Hudson River, a few blocks south of the Intrepid and the Circle Line kiosk. Austin remembered noticing the building when it appeared, almost overnight, as if it had been built from a kit, plywood and glue. For barely a year, it had been a lively restaurant—popular because of its waterfront perch—and then, in a blink, it became a warehouse for equipment belonging to the parks department. And now, apparently it was an atelier? Austin expected it to vanish one day as quickly as it had appeared.

The first time, he was one of only four people to show up—other than the young woman who collected the money and the young woman who posed. He was also the only one to bring an easel; the other three sat on the floor and drew on their laps, one in a blank book hardly larger than a pack of cigarettes. When the model slipped off her robe—a raincoat the color of overcooked peas—Austin felt the blood gather in his groin. He was surprised, since *he'd been to dozens of life drawing sessions back in college; had he been deprived of sex for so long that any glimpse of a naked body could turn him on? But the model held her body in a way both pure and erotic, the translucence of her pearly skin heightened by the harsh light from the crude building's open fixtures, each of her ribs cradled in a stroke of shadow.*

The one startling aspect of her otherwise perfect anatomy was her abdomen, which was (Austin looked quickly around the room, to see if anyone else showed similar astonishment) smooth. The model had no navel.

At the end of the session, the money-taker invited them to return two evenings later—and to tell their friends. "Same model," she said, perhaps knowing that this would give them (or one of them) greater incentive.

At his office the next morning, Austin asked one of his coworkers, a guy named Saul who bragged about his sexual escapades, whether he'd ever encountered a woman without a navel.

Saul laughed. "My man, you've led a sheltered life—or you're dating older than you need to. It's the new thing: getting your belly button cosmetically erased. Closed up. Makes for a fine tattoo canvas. Or maybe . . . maybe you could see it as the ultimate statement of independence. You are the product of parthenogenesis."

Austin did nothing to hide his confusion.

"No umbilical. Get it? No roots, no family baggage. Symbolically. Down deep? Fuck you, Mom."

At the second drawing session, ten people showed up, and this time most of them had easels. Austin had to set up behind an older woman who drew with confidence and flair, so it surprised him to notice that she sketched in a dimpled navel every time she drew the model in frontal view.

During the first break, most people stepped away to chat with others, check messages, or go outside for a smoke. The model pulled on her coat, stretched a little, and then she walked around the room, gazing earnestly at the various ways in which these strangers had rendered her body. Austin had remained at his easel, where he pretended to be occupied sharpening his pencils. This did not stop her from giving his drawing equal attention. Austin didn't mind; he had always been deft at drawing from life. More than one of his architecture instructors had told him that he might have had a successful career as a landscape or portrait painter, had he wished to work in two dimensions only.

"Oh!" exclaimed the model when she saw the most recent drawing on his pad. In it, she was standing, facing him, hands on her hips, head turned in profile.

Austin stepped back to let her look. He resisted the urge to make excuses about being rushed or how the raw light was so unflattering. When she lingered, he said, feeling absurd yet too self-conscious not to speak, "You're good at this."

She turned around and looked at him. "You're better."

She gave him such an open smile that he laughed—and compounded his own idiocy by saying, "Well, it's not my métier."

Had he actually said métier*?*

"I mean," he said, "I'm an architect. Playing hooky."

"An architect," she said, her smile undiminished.

Austin forced himself to look away from her large dark green eyes. "Just an underling at one of the big firms. We're bidding on, if you can believe it, another *addition to the Met. But me, I get to schlep all the way to Dubai. Putting in my Emirates time. No fancy museums for me. Not yet."*

How she took this in was unclear to Austin, but she seemed interested. He'd had a few short stretches of romance since moving to the city, but work and travel had become so voracious, cannibalizing his time and energy, that he hadn't bothered with sex in close to a year. And love? Impossible to contemplate. Saul, the colleague who'd enlightened him on the matter of sewn-up navels, had even suggested that on his next jaunt to the Middle East, he take a detour to Bangkok for a long weekend. "Do I have an address for you," said Saul. When Austin asked Saul to try and remember the last short *weekend they'd been granted, his colleague said, "Just think about it. All I'm saying." Since then, Austin couldn't* stop *thinking about it.*

Now, as the money-taker signaled the model that the break was over, she startled Austin by saying, "I'd like to go to a museum."

After the third session, Austin asked if she'd be interested in seeing an exhibit at the Guggenheim the following weekend. He would have to work nearly through the preceding night to clear an entire afternoon, but he would cheerfully have worked through two. He could hardly believe it: he would have her all to himself.

Petra, meanwhile, threw herself into the Giraudoux play with all the renewed passion she felt in her discovery that sexual desire—the fever, anticipation, and stoked fantasies of that particular euphoria—need not have a thing to do with men. Issa had said they would see each other, and she had gladly accepted the napkin with Petra's phone number, the ink bleeding gently (but still legibly) into the white fiber.

"Whatever you're having for breakfast, Miss Anderssen, keep it on the menu," said her teacher a few days later. The hours she toiled at her proofreading job passed as if they were a pleasure. When she left the law firm at nine in the morning, having been there since well before dawn, she would hurry home not to nap but to shower and change, downing tea and toast before hurrying out again to patrol the river.

On the fourth day, her faith was rewarded; she ran into Issa—actually, spotted her from a good distance—in the wide grassy park near the slip for the Hoboken ferry. How gratified she was when Issa acted entirely happy to see her (and not at all surprised).

"Fancy meeting you here," said Petra, though she grinned in a way that she hoped would reveal her every intention to do just that. Playing hard to get was a thing of the past. She was done with games of emotional dodgeball.

"Yes, fancy!" said Issa. "Come see something." She took Petra's arm and, with no further small talk, led her south, past the playground with the hippo sprinklers, into the World Financial Center. Inside the Winter Garden, Issa pointed up at the palm trees.

Petra said, "You haven't been here before?"

"No," said Issa.

"It's amazing, isn't it? We should come to one of the concerts. They're free." She didn't mention how appalled she had been to read about what it cost to restore this opulent space, with its alien, exotic trees, after the terrorist attacks.

She realized then that the curiously "simple" quality Issa projected to those around her, a quality that Petra had so uncharitably misread as a form of mental imbalance (was she that jaded?), was nothing more than the shameless, undisguised wonder of the newcomer. Maybe Issa had her eccentricities—though today, to Petra's relief, she wore a pair of black leggings beneath her raincoat; also a pair of flats on her feet—but she was an ingénue, in the sweetest sense of the word.

Petra reached down and curled her fingers into Issa's palm. Issa did not shy away. "You're lovely," whispered Petra, suddenly fearless.

"You're lovely, too," said Issa, but she moved away toward the glass doors beckoning them toward the marina, the sailboats rocking at their berths, their fastenings tinkling like ice in a cocktail.

"I'm hungry. Aren't you?" Issa pointed toward a pretzel vendor's cart.

"I could make us omelets at my apartment," said Petra. She still had two hours until rehearsal.

*"What a good idea," said Issa, and she let Petra lead the way east, until they found a cab heading uptown. Petra was more than happy to splurge, to hasten their being alone. (*Slow down!* she heard her formerly subjugated soul admonish her giddy, enlightened will.)*

But when they entered Petra's building and started up the stairs, Issa seemed hesitant. She climbed the stairs slowly, so that it took them a painfully long time to reach the fifth floor. "I hope you're not afraid of heights," Petra joked. "I do live in the nosebleed section. Makes a huge difference in the rent. And keeps me fit."

Issa took a deep breath at the top of the last flight. "I'm here," she said, and she looked back and forth between the two doors, the front apartment (with its no-doubt-staggering view of the rooftops and river, along with a staggering rent) and Petra's (with its soul-shrinking view of the sooty space between her building and the taller building just behind, ending below in the courtyard of a Mexican restaurant).

She unwound her scarf and pulled her sweater over her head, hanging them on the overburdened rack in her dark entry hall. In the kitchen, she took eggs, cheese, and butter from the fridge. She told Issa to take off her coat and have a seat at the table. From the fruit bowl, she palmed the avocado she'd splurged on two days before. That it was perfectly ripe seemed like an omen.

Out of habit, she went into the living room and cracked open the window. "The one thing I wish is that I had a cross breeze," she said when she returned. Issa had taken a seat at the table but still wore her coat. "Oh—are you cold?"

"I'm fine," said Issa.

Not that Petra could halt her own babbling. "And then what happens by January is that it's so absurdly overheated, I have to open all *the windows. What's crazy is how typical that is. People moan about climate change, but look around the city all winter long and what do you see? Half the windows wide open, fossil fuel steaming right up into the sky. Ridiculous."*

Issa was nodding, attentive yet quiet.

Petra took what felt like her first breath since entering her own apartment. "Want a glass of wine?"

"No," said Issa. "I'm just hungry." She did not offer to help, but Petra's kitchen wasn't made for helping. Two people could barely sit at the table against the living room wall; one could barely stand at the counter.

As she beat the eggs and grated the cheese, Petra talked about her workshop and the play, about being cast as the villainess. "I'm the reality that pulls the man away from his dream. The ball and chain." Her back was to Issa as she spoke, slicing the avocado, dividing it between two plates. She watched the eggs as they began to solidify in their moat of butter.

After she divided the omelet, slipping half onto one plate, half onto the other, now describing the character of her rival, Ondine, she finally turned. Issa was not in the kitchen.

Petra went into the living room. Issa stood by the window, looking out.

"Food's ready." Petra tried not to sound hurt at having been left alone, attempting to amuse a pan of eggs. Not that her voice wouldn't reach the farthest points in her tiny home.

Issa turned around. "Come look."

Reluctantly, Petra went to the window. Across the drab shaft, through the window opposite, a man lay slumped on a couch, watching television. Petra had seen him a thousand times. He wasn't even attractive. What was there to see?

"You mean Couch Potato Man? I think he's waiting for his superpower to materialize," said Petra.

"Is he like that all the time?"

"Well," said Petra, "the day I know the answer to that question is the day you can put me out of my misery. I'm hardly ever here."

"Your misery?" Issa looked worried.

"I'm kidding. I'm a perfectly happy camper," said Petra. Or I am with you here, she thought.

She marveled at Issa's lips and tenderly coiled ears. Had any man ever looked so reassuringly beautiful to her? Of course not; for one thing, beauty in a man was, by definition, the opposite of reassuring. Beautiful men were poison: a lesson hard-learned.

Once they were seated, Issa ate quickly, almost wolfishly, and complimented Petra on her cooking. Too much small talk, thought Petra. Maybe Issa was nervous about their being alone together. Another nod toward taking it slow.

"You cook a lot of eggs when you work in a diner," said Petra. "I've done just about everything your average underemployed actor can do for a buck. Sold hosiery at Bloomingdale's. Political polling. Now I proofread. Schizophrenia, here I come. Sorry—bad joke."

Issa appeared to take in everything she said with the same calm expression. "I'd like to see you act," she said.

"Well, that might be arranged. This workshop, we'll be doing a

couple of open performances. I'll let you know." Something occurred to Petra. "Your modeling: do you . . . does that support something else you'd rather be paid for?"

The pause was agonizing. Christ, maybe modeling was all Issa *wanted* to do. (Was there anything wrong with that? She was *made* to be a model.)

"I'm finding my feet," she said. "I'm not sure yet what else I might do. I do like drawing. I like drawing the water. Drawing the life of the water."

"Have you been to the aquarium? Coney Island? You'd like it there, I think."

"Let's go."

"All right. It's a plan," said Petra, pleased that Issa had (so to speak) taken the bait. Looking at the wall clock, she realized that she had to be at rehearsal in an hour. She had to compose herself, take a shower. Alone.

"So yeah. Let's do that. Like next weekend? I'm free on Sunday."

"Sunday," said Issa. "Yes, Sunday. I'll come here. You tell me when."

"Ten," said Petra, snatching an hour from thin air. "The downstairs door is usually open, but ring if it's not." They'd given up on asking the super to fix the lock.

When she let Issa out the door, Petra kissed her on one cheek. "Next Sunday," she said, and she made herself close the door before Issa went downstairs. *Another tease,* mocked her old self, weary with scorn. *No, not at all,* countered New Self. *Shy. Modest. That's what she is. It will take time to know her. Be patient. Like your mother used to say: worth the wait.*

So Issa spent her Saturday afternoon with Austin and her Sunday with Petra. Both of them were enraptured, mostly because—and neither of them was fool enough not to know this—they hadn't met anyone in a long time, or possibly ever, who radiated wonder the way Issa did, her naked delight in discovery, in seeing things she had apparently never seen before. Seeing was not so much believing;

seeing was being. Or discovering. Each new sight became a question. She had no fear of admitting that she didn't know about this or that painter (while drinking in the pictures with evident joy), and she listened alertly to Austin as he told her about the place the Guggenheim held in the history of modern architecture: how it marked both the end of a magnificent career and the beginning of a new aesthetic for the city. A *virginal moment,* he called it. When they emerged from the elevator at the top of the museum, she rushed ahead, to the nearest balustrade, and leaned so far over that Austin was afraid she might fall.

"Careful," he said.

"It's so deep," she said.

"Funny," he said after catching his breath. "I think of it as tall. So tall."

"But we are looking down," she reasoned, and he had to agree. There was nothing profound in her observation, not really, and yet as they descended, looping into and out of the cavelike galleries, he imagined the entire structure filling slowly, silently, with water.

At the aquarium, Issa seemed more comfortable with Petra than she'd been before. And what Petra had suspected was true: she had a genuine interest in aquatic life—or at least a fascination. While she peered at length into the various habitats, Petra savored the neon colors mirrored on Issa's already luminous face.

Here and there, in what Petra now recognized as her signature exclamation, Issa would say, "Come look!" The object of her scrutiny might be a blue lobster or a starfish the size of a platter. It became increasingly easy to share Issa's enthusiastic attention to the world around her. It was rejuvenating, a form of flattery.

At the circular tank in which the belugas swam endlessly round and round, Issa laid both of her palms on the glass and leaned in till her nose and brow touched the surface as well. "Oh no."

"I know," said Petra. "This is the depressing part. A big activist group wants to free them, do away with this . . . *exhibit.* What a word, right? But the smaller fish, the seahorses . . . they're protected here."

"No fish are protected," Issa said.

Well, who is? Petra wanted to say, but why did she have to be so cynical? Part of Issa's appeal was that her wide-eyed nature reminded Petra, admonished her, that it was all too easy to assume a skeptical stance whenever fortune failed to smile on you. Wasn't that the stance of a coward—or an adolescent? Gratefully, she took Issa's hand and led her to a railing over which they could simply gaze at the horizon.

On Monday, Austin flew to Dubai for another marathon of meetings in an overchilled high-rise hotel that ought to have collapsed under the weight of all the marble floors and walls. Even the surface of his desk was marble. His room overlooked the swimming pool, and through a sashay of palm fronds directly before his window, he spied on a hairy middle-aged man frolicking in the water with his small wiry son, the reedlike boy brandishing a large orange water pistol. The father wore an obscenely tight black swimsuit, his orb of a belly exaggerated by the immodesty of the garment; the boy a loose pair of trunks revealing the cleft of his buttocks. Yet there was the mother, shrouded head to ankle in black, lying on a chaise longue, doing nothing to hide her boredom, no doubt hot as hell. As the boy aimed a jet of water in her direction, she raised a single hand in half-hearted defense. The scene depressed and enraged him, yet Austin could not stop staring.

When, a moment later, the woman rose from the chaise and walked away, her shoes flashed in the sun each time they broached the hem of her billowing robe. Austin realized that beneath her stifling costume and its metaphoric allegations of chastity and fidelity, she wore a pair of gilt stiletto heels. She carried a large purse to match, its brazen buckle—visible from four stories overhead—the logo of an American designer. Was he wrong to see the cacophony of her getup as offensive?

He felt the gut-wrenching disgust at his judgment of a culture he would never understand, alongside the vague nausea resulting from the consumption of too much pita bread with too many pureed roasted vegetables and charred meats.

Suddenly he sensed the onset of an existential futility so extreme that it seemed to stronghand him back onto his king-size bed and its crush of tasseled cushions. Every color in the room was a variation on sand or dust. Out the window, beyond the acid-blue pool and the pewter-colored palms, the city resembled a convention of cranes and digging equipment, its hundreds of construction sites like distant parties of robots, a dystopia of dinosaurish machines at play among the phallic skyscrapers lining the gulf.

He was homesick, that was all. But what was home, for Austin? Was it that equally vast if greener, more feminine city? Was it the apartment he rarely saw, with its "peek" of the Hudson River, high ceilings, and Greek-key parquet floors? Or was it the house his parents had sold in Toms River so they could make the sensible move to a retirement community? Did he have a home to be sick for?

He went to the bathroom (its shower walled entirely in glass so that, if he declined to close the beaded blind, people down at the pool could look up and watch him soap his armpits and penis) and rummaged through his kit for a handful of Tums.

He had another meeting—a presentation to give—in ten minutes. "Pull your pitiful self together," he told his mirrored twin. "Don't be a sissy."

In the elevator down to the floor where conference room after conference room bustled with sly tycoons and bureaucratic dweebs from all over the planet, he whispered her name: Issa. It sounded like a wave, gently claiming then retreating from a smooth stretch of sand. That, really, was what he longed for: the beauty and simplicity of a companion who looked at the world and saw its better nature. Had he ever met a girl like that before? No, he had not.

After the meeting, he returned immediately to his room, intent on finding—and there it was, tucked in his planner—the museum postcard (Magritte's soulful Empire of Light*) on which he had written the number she gave him as they left the museum. No, it was the middle of the night in New York. He mustn't seem like a madman. He ordered an immorally overpriced steak frites, with half a bottle of Bordeaux. He turned off the ringer on his hotel phone and rented* A Fistful of Dollars*. Clint Eastwood never felt sorry for himself. But* oh God, Austin had managed to choose a movie set in another place that was nothing but sand and dust. And what was Clint wearing, an old blanket? He fell asleep without turning off the lamps, taking off his clothes, or pulling back the sheets.

In the morning, he called Issa's number. It rang twenty, thirty, forty times—no voicemail. He felt irrationally jealous, unnerved.

He decided that when he got back to the city—only two days more of this Vegas wannabe, this camel market jacked up on Viagra—he would call her first thing. Silent and sure as Clint Eastwood, he would claim her. And maybe he would threaten to leave the firm unless they let him work closer to home, gave him the time off that surely he had earned by now.

Good God, he thought, I *am* a madman. And laughed as he straightened his tie.

Back in the city, in Austin's absence, Petra and Issa were, once again, sitting beside the Hudson River. They ate ice cream, though it was no longer ice-cream weather. Sugar-courage, thought Petra, vowing that she would make her passionate intentions clear to Issa that afternoon.

And then Issa said, "I'm going away for a little."

"Away? For how little?" asked Petra.

"Oh, just a little little. Few days," said Issa.

"Family?" Petra knew only that Issa came from a big family, and when she'd asked where home was, Issa had answered, "Too many places. Coastal places." It was clear she didn't want to say more, and Petra wondered if she was an army brat. Or a navy brat. She pictured a crew-cut father, stern in his blinding uniform, a cruel disciplinarian. She thought of Captain Bligh as played by Trevor Howard.

"No. Just a little trip. I want to look at some things. I'm going out to the beach. Montauk, I think."

"Montauk's spectacular," said Petra, itching to invite herself along (forget that she had rehearsals nearly every day that week).

"Mm," said Issa in her characteristically dreamy way.

"When are you leaving?"

"Today." Issa was still eating her ice cream. She would take a spoonful and lick it carefully, almost pensively, with her coral-colored tongue.

Petra had finished her own ice cream and tossed the cup in a nearby garbage bin. "Look." She took Issa's cup away from her, very gently, and set it on the bench beside her. "I've got to do this. Sink or swim. Do or die."

She leaned toward Issa and pulled her by her shoulders so that they were face-to-face. She pressed her mouth to Issa's, just praying.

This was not what Issa had expected. "Oh. Oh!" she cried, and though she did not pull entirely away, her eyes widened. What she did next was to embrace Petra tightly, so that their chins were forced over each other's respective shoulders, and when, after a moment, she separated herself from Petra—gently, holding Petra's arms—she was smiling.

"I wasn't thinking this," she said. "Or I wasn't thinking this now."

Petra laughed, too bitterly perhaps. "I could ask for clarification: like, if not now, then maybe later? Oh Christ, forget I said that."

"I'm going away for a little. Just a little little, like I said. I'll see you after."

"But are you saying—" Petra put a hand up, to stop herself. "No. Never mind. I'm completely mortified." She groped to her right and, well, one thing hadn't been upended; she picked up the cup of ice cream and handed it back to Issa.

Issa resumed eating her ice cream, but the look she gave Petra over the cup was warm, possibly apologetic. "I need to see some things first," she said.

Seeing; looking. Issa was forever observing—or was she searching? Was it some kind of restlessness that attracted Petra, the quality that made women fall head over heels with sailors, mountain climbers, Iditarod mushers, the world's most patently unavailable men? Was it just another version of that? Would she never learn?

But when Issa finished her ice cream, she leaned toward Petra and said, "There will be more. There will be."

If he could muscle his way through Immigration and Customs fast enough, and if the Midtown Tunnel wasn't clogged with traffic, he could make it to the drawing class before it was over. Would he look absurd with his suitcase—without his easel and drawing pad? Did he care?

And as if there were indeed some benevolent God, Austin seemed to sail through the various stages of his mission, and for once he didn't mind that his driver took the LIE like a fugitive being tailed by the law. The cab dropped him in front of the Intrepid *an hour into the class, and as luck would have it, one of those freelance flower vendors was working the downtown lanes of the West Side Highway, dashing in and out of traffic with a compound bucket of yellow roses clamped in one arm.*

Austin waved him over to the curb. "The whole thing," he said. "I'll give you a hundred bucks."

He spent the next ten minutes bent over beside a garbage can, removing the roses from their plastic sleeves and stacking them gently on the ground. The southbound traffic sped heedlessly by, just a few feet behind him. When he was done, he unfastened a flight tag from his suitcase and, using his teeth, tore it from the loop of elastic string. With the loop, he bound the roses together, thorns be damned.

He found a bench near the building where the class was held, and he waited. It was chilly, but he was warmed by his resolve; his heart beat far too fast. He used an airline napkin from his pocket to clean up the wounds on his fingers.

As the artist-customers streamed out into the night, backlit by the fluorescent lamps that would have lit up Issa's nakedness, revealing not a single flaw, he rose to his feet and waited. She would be one of the last to leave. After ten minutes, he saw the light dim as the lamps were switched off. He moved closer; at the door, the money-taker was locking up.

Austin had no choice but to ask. All that came out was "Issa? Is she . . ."

"She was off tonight." The woman eyed the roses, which Austin could hardly hide. She failed to repress a smile; embarrassed, amused. "Oh my. Well. Sorry."

"Never mind," said Austin, but what now?

He was half-tempted to thrust the roses upon the money-taker woman and flee.

"Sorry," she said again. "Have a nice night." She hesitated, then walked off. Worse, she turned and waved—as if worried he might follow her like the crazy he had just become.

Austin returned to the bench and fumbled in his pockets for his phone. He tried Issa's number. Again, it rang into oblivion. "You are a fucking fool," he said as he put the phone away. He took a cab home and stuffed the roses, which teased him with their ditzy Marilyn glow, into three of the five vases he owned (which, he knew, would brand him as gay in some circles). He thought, I have been decidedly unmanned. *Unmanned?* Since when did he think in such terms? Maybe it was better, after all, to throw himself into work whole hog, forget about the humiliations of love. Sex? Saul's offer of that address, halfway around the world, mocked his celibacy.

That night he dreamed of Bangkok, a place to which he had never traveled but whose architecture he had seen in magazines. In the dream, he wandered its streets, taking pictures of the buildings, old and new alike, while beautiful naked women passed him by. He understood, in the dream, that he was invisible. He felt powerful, immune to the distractions of women.

And then, the next day, just as he began to feel free of the previous week's self-centered delusions, he walked out of his office building at lunch and there, right on the sidewalk, stood Issa. Right there. She faced the revolving door, her still presence parting the swarms of suited workers as they spilled into the cool autumn sunlight.

She was waiting.

"How did you know where to find me?" he said.

"You pointed to the top of your building. When we were walking, after the museum."

Then, right there on a midday-rush-hour Manhattan sidewalk

(not that many people would be easily diverted from their mission of hunting down the desired bagel, burger, or bento box), she did something startling. Issa took Austin's right hand in both of hers and guided it gently beneath the baggy sweater she wore under her ubiquitous raincoat. She pressed it palm-side against her supernaturally smooth belly. She held it there for several seconds, gazing into his eyes. When she let go, he retrieved his hand, reluctantly.

"I like how you really see me. Your drawings show it," she said. "I've been thinking about it, and I believe we're made for each other. I think you believe that, too. Do you?"

Austin laughed hysterically. "I'm happy to find out."

They spent every night for the next two weeks in Austin's bed, and every spare daytime hour he could wrest from his schedule walking around the city, dazed yet energized, as if they were tourists from far away. "Look," she would say, pointing at a bridge or a bird or a stroller holding twins, and each sight, to Austin, was miraculously, enigmatically fresh, even if he had seen it a million times. A pigeon was a miracle. Her body mesmerized him completely—he had no desire to ask about why she'd had her navel erased or why she had no body hair—and he was delighted when her verbal reserve gave way to a new expressiveness. She would ask for full accounts of his day—joyously, not jealously—and she began to show him drawings she did at the drafting table in his apartment while he was away. He did not mind (no, he loved it) that after a long, ardent sex-soaked night, she stayed in his bed while he showered and dressed, that she told him she would see him in the very same spot whenever he came home.

She had found a blank drawing pad in the top of his closet and the drawer in which he kept a supply of colored pencils, chalks, watercolors, and gouache, most of which he hadn't touched since school days. And with Issa in his bed, he could hardly continue attending the evening classes for which she posed. Let her be the artist now. (Without their discussing it, she had essentially moved in with him. He didn't even want to discuss it—to jinx it.)

She began to fill the pages of one pad, and then another, with *drawings of sea creatures, watery patterns, intricately curlicued webs of fins, tentacles, shells, eels, reeflike fortresses bedecked with anemones, seaweeds, and fantastically floral outgrowths. He began to buy her bigger and more expensive pads of paper.*

"These are outrageous. I mean, outrageously good," Austin told her. "You need to show them to someone."

"You're someone," she said. "I'm showing them to you."

"I mean, you know, a gallery someone, somebody who might put you in a show," he said (although Austin knew he was ignorant when it came to the city's sophisticated, eccentric, perhaps impenetrably elitist art scene). Maybe her work was essentially conventional, but there was no denying its beauty and cunning sense of composition. At the very least, she should have been a successful illustrator, yet her only source of income, or all that he knew of, was her modeling job.

"Can I take a few of these and show them to someone at my office?" he asked.

"No. No, they are not for anyone else. Just you."

Austin would have been an idiot not to puzzle at Issa's laserlike devotion to him, to them, and he knew that the depth of his sexual gratification half-blinded him, but there was a reassuring simplicity to her unencumbered life. She was new to this place, and he was the lucky guy to find her first, and if she seemed almost suspiciously free of the usual phobias and emotional calluses that women brought to "relationships," so what? Did all intelligent, creative people need to be tangled up in thickets of neurosis, their psyches riddled with the stigmata of previous heartache?

This is what he knew: Issa made him happier than he could remember ever having been before. He wanted her—and he couldn't help feeling he deserved her.

If she had parents and siblings, clearly she wasn't close to them. He knew that she had been born in France but wasn't French. She'd been born in a town destroyed by the sea—which would explain her obsession with images of the sea, wouldn't it?—and after that, she'd lived "all over." Did it matter, anyway, what passport she carried?

The world was a place whose borders grew only more porous as time went on—or so it seemed back then.

One month from the day she had waited for him outside his building, he called his parents and said, "I'm going to ask someone to marry me. And if she says yes, I'm bringing her out there to meet you." His mother was speechless, but Austin knew that, more than anything, she wanted grandchildren, so she did not tell him he was rash or impulsive or ought to bide his time. Not that she could have changed his mind.

"Man, you are bewitched," said Saul. "I hope it's not just that you were so damn horny."

"Bewitched or not, sometimes you just know," said Austin. "Sometimes you strike gold."

"Or get struck by lightning," said Saul.

And so, decided Petra, her stodgy, stonewalling old self was right. She had moved too fast. How absurd to think that women didn't need teasing, courting, the playing of all those wearisome games. Why had she never found out where Issa lived? Why had she been so passive? *Oh you were hardly passive,* scoffed her old self. *Anything but.*

The worst part of this painful aftermath was the way in which her sexual self had been turned on its head. Had she really been meant, all these years, to search for her soul mate or true love or romantic destiny (whatever!) in a woman? Petra was a card-carrying believer in the importance of *knowing oneself,* so what did this mean? She took a retrospective tour of the women she'd felt close to—in truth, not many—in New York and, before that, during her college years in Maine (fun, but wasted; if she'd been braver, she'd have insisted on attending a conservatory, and maybe *there* she would have known herself better).

She burrowed deep into the role of Bertha, pouring into it all her bitterness and bewilderment, the sense of abandonment she felt at Issa's vanishing. Her teacher was impressed and promised her a *prime role in the annual Shakespeare production. Maybe Rosalind. Maybe Kate. Time for a comedy, he said. (And how, thought Petra.)*

Her gig at the law firm ended. She found a waitressing job in a tavern on Bank Street. The tips were huge, the owner humane. She landed a commercial for a painkiller aimed at menstrual cramps. (She played tennis in whites! She romped with a poodle, also white! She danced in a sleek gown! She sailed! A sporty life lived in less than thirty seconds.) And, as promised, she nailed the lead in Shrew. *Cosmic compensation. To hell with love.*

In January, on one of the coldest days that winter, she approached a table with a newly seated couple. The woman sat with her back toward Petra, turning her head just as Petra offered the menus.

Issa smiled at her, without a hint of guilt or even surprise, and said, "Hello." Nothing more. But it was obvious (wasn't it?) that she recognized Petra.

"How've you been?" said Petra, rummaging frantically among her stage skills for a tone that would sound light, impersonal, even mockingly servile.

"Happy," said Issa, glancing at her companion.

Petra couldn't help appraising him. Handsome enough—dark hair, blue eyes, an earnest, close-shaven jaw—and stylish in an oh-so-artful way. His shirt was Rose of Sharon purple, his dense glossy hair cut so that it looked both tended and tousled.

"Good to hear," said Petra. She watched the companion smile awkwardly at Issa; did he expect an introduction? Or maybe this was just a first date—somehow Petra knew it was a date, maybe more than a date—and then she saw the glint on Issa's left hand as she opened the menu.

"Let me tell you the specials," said Petra. Never had the words halibut *and* heirloom *and* loin *felt so heavy on her tongue. She made herself as busy as possible for the next hour and a half, even taking an extra table off the hands of a swamped colleague.*

Just when she was sure it wouldn't happen, Issa came up to her—from behind, touching her at the small of her back, as Petra waited for a tray of drinks at the bar—and said, "I miss you."

Petra turned sharply, wanting to snap, *Really? Oh bullshit.* But she wasn't in a position to make a scene. She glanced pointedly at Issa's hand. "So you're what, engaged?" She looked toward Issa's table. The stylish man wasn't there; he was standing by another table, having a jovial chat with its occupants.

"Yes," said Issa. She still had that foursquare purity about her, and there wasn't a mote of guile in her voice.

"So, congratulations, I guess."

"It happened just after I saw you."

Petra couldn't help laughing. "What was that, three months ago? Did he show up from your past?" Why was she bothering to ask for these details? Walk away, she told herself. Let the pretty-boy fiancé stiff her on the tip.

"No. . . . But he . . . has a kind of power."

"Power?" Who *was* this bitch? "Really."

Issa clearly didn't hear the sarcasm. She was looking straight into Petra's eyes, her green gaze unfaltering. "I need someone who's seen the world, who knows it," she said. "But I missed you. I still do."

"I'm not the one who disappeared, honey. You knew where to find me."

Issa just looked at her. "I'll find you another time."

The strangest thing was, Petra believed her—even, God help her, wanted it to be true. What could possibly make this thoughtless drifter seem remotely trustworthy at this point? What evidence was there of conscience or heart?

Later, much later, the dissonance of Petra's emotions would become entirely clear to her, even if, in the end, it would lead to a mystery greater than any that either of them—Petra, driven unabashedly by her passions, and Austin, whose view of life demanded rational explanations for everything and precluded all regrets—had ever faced before.

Miriam

In secret, when Austin's not around—and certainly not Brecht—I obsess over the news from New York. Nineteen people are confirmed dead, seven are wounded (two in critical care), and two are missing. There are divers in the river off the marina, searching for remains as well as evidence. Talking heads speculate about the escalation of tactics by this group, Oceloti, the self-proclaimed "jaguar warriors" who emerged a dozen years ago, when Brazil's leaders refused to put a stop to the outlaw fires clearing the jungle for grazing land. Before this week, you would see their acts of defiance in the second or third tier of news. They poured acid into the fuel tanks of expensive mining equipment, crippled bridges (so they do have a history of using explosives), mined logging roads with blades strong enough to shred tires, dumped toxic sludge into the swimming pools of corporate executives. They were good at dismantling security systems, good at being heard without being caught, but they weren't in the business of killing. They would claim credit from afar, over the internet, taunting their targets in videos that blurred their faces.

I don't really care about who or what is behind the act. They aren't jihadists, and their spite and fury have seemed rational, even noble, to me in the past—but I draw the line at mowing down hapless bystanders. I look at the pictures of the dead and the surviving—posed portraits of these people in the before, always smiling; how can we know our fates?—and if they are young, I think about their parents. The youngest victim of this bombing is eighteen. He was a political science major at NYU. Well, he intersected with politics at its most vengeful.

So I think about vengeance, and I think about righteousness, and I think about people for whom success is measured in body count. This bombing was an assassination attempt, or so they claim, yet having missed their principal target, they do not apologize. No: they tell the world that you reap what you sow. Lie down with dogs and you stand up with fleas. Greed will make you pay. Do terrorists understand that they deal in clichés? That clichés may be true yet do not go to the heart of the matter, no matter what the matter is?

You're only as happy as your unhappiest child. Another cliché. Every mother has heard it—or every mother who thinks of herself as a good mother. Like all its fellow clichés, it is true, but so what? And when you have just one child, your happiness follows a firmly inked graph . . . unless you can no longer read your child's so-called happiness factor the way you could in the first few years of his life. Of course, you read in the wisest of the baby books that it's a mistake to think that your job is to prevent a child from knowing grief, pain, anxiety, the everyday blues of a dark rainy day. Sometimes the child just has to have a good long cry, has to travel through a long tunnel, has to know that despair can be endured.

All this I took for granted, rarely examined, before Brecht went away to college. When he was eight, we suffered Andrew's sudden death together—though very differently. Sometimes I think all the talking I had to do, all the explaining, the comforting, the reassuring (which felt false at the time), is what kept me on my feet and in the world. It is strange to me that Brecht now remembers so little of that time, certainly none of our intense conversations, all my euphemizing—because we weren't religious—about where his father had "gone," all my ultimately dishonest avoidance of *never*. Of course, time was molasses in the cold months that bracketed that very long year; time was monotony. When all days are the same, memory caves in on itself.

And really, what do I remember of when I was eight? I have a mental album of snapshots, most of them blurry: my favorite red shoes worn over white tights, our generic grassy backyard with its swing set and slide, a favorite teacher and the voices she used to read the Narnia books, the stuffed horse I still kept on my bed (palomino!). Most memories of that time in my life are static.

As for my own private grieving, I had to do my best to contain it until Brecht was in bed, well asleep, because all day long, for months, the two of us were cooped up together. I had everything delivered, even Andrew's ashes. Brecht had spent a scant five months in a new school, and I hadn't yet cemented those "mom bonds" everyone had spoken of so glowingly when we toured the building. In occasional e-blasts the principal would send out during the lockdown, she'd sign off, *Stay at home, stay healthy, stay sane . . . and be kind to yourselves!* The first one came when Andrew was still alive and healthy (he read it aloud in a pitch-perfect twee impersonation of the woman), the next while he was in the ICU, the third just after he died. My mother wanted Brecht and me to flee to Idaho, where she had moved after my father's death the year before, but no way were we going to get on a plane.

At the firm, I am regarded as the keeper of order. I am always being told that without me, the business would fall apart. "Austin knows how to make a house stand through like basically anything," Filene said last week, "but you keep us on our toes, pointed in the right direction."

So there is this widespread notion that Austin is the "creative" in the house (how I hate that adjective as noun), the sun around which we orbit, and I am . . . what, the timekeeper? The warden? Back in New York, I'd be compared to a super: the one to fix the pipes, sort the recycling, vanquish the vermin. And yes, I'm good. Organization is a talent of mine, and it doesn't insult me that this is one of the qualities Austin loved in me, early on. The first time he came over for dinner (with Brecht as well as me), he looked around our pocket kitchen and told me it resembled a sonnet. He held up a wooden spoon and a water glass. "Look how they rhyme!" he said. I had no idea what he meant, but I was unavoidably charmed. Brecht, eleven at the time, told me the man was nice but clearly nuts. (Funny, perhaps, that Brecht grew into writing sonnets himself, at least for those two years in high school.)

But now, while my kitchen (compact yet luxurious) might be seen as a place of harmony and cadence, beneath all the poetry runs a subterranean cave that threatens to destabilize the floors, to bring down everything else I do in sudden collapse.

It is one thing for my twenty-two-year-old son to have shaky memories of losing his father when he was eight; it is quite another for him not to remember being caught in the crosshairs of a cataclysm, less than two years ago, that killed the companion with whom he was walking the neighborhood. I don't care if the doctors see this amnesia as "a natural defense of the nervous system" or think I'm reassured that my child is suffering from "treatable" PTS. What can they predict?

I was frantic after the news that day and tried to reach him. No luck; not even voicemail. The bombing took place on a sunny Saturday, early afternoon, the Union Square farmers' market teeming with shoppers. After two hours of futile messaging, I told Austin I was getting in the car and driving down. Austin pointed out that the bridges and tunnels might be blocked. Instead, he phoned Steve, a former colleague with whom he stays in touch. He asked Steve, who lives in the Village, if he could go to Brecht's dorm.

An hour later, he called us. After I pulled Austin's phone from his hand, Steve told me, "He's with me, and he'll be fine. But I'm taking him to the hospital."

"What?" I demanded. "What for?"

"He's a little stunned, but he'll be fine, I'm sure."

When I asked to speak to Brecht, Steve said, "I'll have him call you later. I think he needs . . . maybe just a quick look by a doctor."

"I want to hear his voice!" I shouted, as if Steve were holding him for ransom.

Faintly, I heard Steve tell Brecht that his mom was on the phone. Tears leaked from my eyes as I waited.

"It's me, Mom," said Brecht. He sounded as if he had a cold.

Before I could do more than tell him I loved him, Steve came on again. "I think his hearing is off. Let me get him looked at. I promise to call you once we're in the queue. Because I am sure we'll have to wait. But it's going to be okay. It is."

"What do you mean, his hearing is off?" I was sobbing.

"We'll figure it out. Please try not to worry. I'll bring him back home with me after," said Steve, very gently.

Austin was standing so close behind me that our bodies were nearly spooned. I let him take the phone back to thank his friend.

Only after he hung up did I think of Noam Fletcher. Noam was a boy from Vigil Harbor who had taken time off after high school and was thinking of applying to college. He wasn't a friend of Brecht's, but I remembered seeing his tall figure loping around town. In his senior year, he'd become famous as the point guard who had finally broken Knowles's dominance over our town on the basketball court. I was the one who suggested to his mother, while chatting in the produce aisle of the grocery store, that if Noam wanted to look at schools in New York City, Brecht would be happy to let him crash on his floor. And he was. So Noam went down. That week.

But probably Noam had his own agenda; perhaps he'd been looking at another school in Manhattan—or in another borough altogether. And wouldn't his mother have messaged me if she was worried? Noam must have called her from wherever he was at the time.

My idea, was all I could think when I found out, two days later, and not from Brecht, that the boys had been together. Noam had cammed his mother half an hour before the bombing, just to say that everything was skilling, and hey, New York was great, he was having a blast, but maybe it wasn't the place for him. Joan Fletcher saw my son, bobbing in and out of the video margins, as she spoke to hers. Noam's father told me this.

What do I really want now? What should I want? How could it be a relief to send Brecht back to New York, to resume his classes as if he'd taken time off for a case of mono, for a stint of community work to earn a cut in tuition? He never had a career in mind. He was taking history and literature classes alongside the school's famous CCT "core": climate, computer, and trade. In a way, the work he's doing now seems to center him—the way running once did—unless it's a form of psychological camouflage, a mere distraction from panic.

He had been home two weeks when it looked as if, at least physically, he had recovered. Where fine shrapnel had struck the left side of his face—his body unblemished, shielded by Noam's—he still bore a patch of small scars, like a scattering of chrysanthemum petals. He told me they itched a little, but the nerve pain was fading. He would go out on short runs, and I would do nothing but fret until he returned. He would go up to his room, and if I stood at the foot of the stairs, listening as hard as I could, I heard nothing. He could have been listening to music on his earphones or reading a book or playing games on mute or, and this is what I feared, just staring into space.

Of course, I still had work to do at the firm. I could do it when I wanted, much of it from home, but there were times I had to go in, leaving Brecht to himself.

"I am fine, Mom," he'd say calmly. But he wasn't fine—because what was his day-to-day purpose? Was it just to appreciate surviving—or, on the dark obverse side, to feel guilt over Noam's death? I had no idea if, in fact, he felt the guilt I did. I made him see a therapist for a few months, but I couldn't ask what they discussed.

Noam's funeral, which Austin and I attended less than a week after Brecht came home, was horrifying. Joan held nothing against me, but she was a visible wreck. How could she not be? And she, unlike me, had another child, a daughter. I was now terrified of taking my eyes off Brecht.

One night, Austin insisted on taking me out to dinner. "And Brecht stays home," he said.

At dinner, he told me that Brecht should work. Work hard. "The summer I worked for a mason," said Austin, "was the summer I figured it out."

"Figured out what?" I said defiantly.

"That I would do anything not to lay bricks for the rest of my life."

"So you think, what, he should work for a mason? That will solve everything?" I had become prickly and argumentative. Nearly everything my husband said irritated me, even when he was trying to help me figure out my son—because suddenly Brecht was *my* son. I hated my petty possessiveness, but I couldn't help it.

Austin ignored my sarcasm. "Not a mason," he said, "but close." He had already spoken to Celestino, who had one full-time employee but would, with the demands of Austin's new clients, need at least one more. "I can tell he's not thrilled," said Austin, "but I told him just to try it. If Brecht flames out, no hard feelings. And either way, I'll owe him big. My prediction? Two months of digging and planting, he'll miss the classroom."

"So you're a mental health expert all of a sudden?"

Austin smiled sadly at me. "Of course not. But I am the guardian of a young man who needs distraction from his sorrows. And something to make him sleep soundly. What else do I have to offer?"

I was ashamed of myself when Brecht said that he liked the idea.

After the first day, he came back with dirt wedged under his nails, thin scratches along the backs of his hands, and dried gray sweat glazing his arms and neck. It was a warm day in late fall. "We planted a row of trees," he told me. "A windbreak next to The Drome." He asked when we had last been to the bowling alley. "Maybe we should go sometime," he said.

After a week, during which Brecht never once complained, I had a chance to speak with Celestino, when he stopped by the firm.

"He is a good worker," said Celestino. "He does not tire and learns fast. Maybe to ignore what happened, just go forward, is the best strength for him now. And maybe forward does not mean back to school."

"Maybe for now," I said.

Celestino smiled. "I am happy to have him however long he stays."

And this is where we are, a year and a half later. Am I a snob, that I think Brecht shouldn't be content to do the work he's doing? And shouldn't I want him to move out of my third floor? Am I impatient? But really, how could he not be lonely? How could he not want a life on his own?

Austin asks me to meet Petra at the office, to show her some of his past work. "Take her to the YC for lunch," he says. "A shame it's too wet for the porch."

It looks as if it will be too wet for much of any outdoor anything this week, but even so, and even though it's Sunday, Austin's agreed to meet Thaddy Tyrone for another site visit, mud be damned. Tyrone's become convinced he needs a bomb shelter and wants to show Austin exactly where to build it. Austin will pretend to listen, then talk him out of it. Or that's the plan. As Austin says in a video on the firm's site, "I consider myself an architect for the future, not the apocalypse." He's joked to me that he wishes we could move to the Netherlands, where encroaching water is something the citizens have grappled with, inventively, for hundreds of years. He's itching for a commission to build a house over a flood canal in one of the coastal cities that made the cut in the federal triage. (Houston yes, Galveston no. Charleston made it; Gloucester, to everyone's shock, did not.)

She arrives, promptly at ten, wearing yet another outfit in her trademark shade of fawn. I find it odd that a woman with such an exuberant personality dresses in such subdued colors, but I wouldn't be surprised if it's an aesthetic irony she cultivated long ago. Not that she strikes me as scheming. In general, I've never warmed to Southern women, but I like Petra Coyle's directness.

When I open the door, she's shaking out a large umbrella in the hallway. She leans it against the wall, doubles over, and—first raising a hand to acknowledge that I'm there—delicately removes a pair of shapely galoshes. As I watch her go through these motions, then right herself quickly, I wonder if she was once an athlete. Not the slightest bit breathless after climbing three long flights of stairs, she greets me by grasping my shoulders and says, "So! He told me you're to take me on a guided tour of his history! I want to go back to his very roots."

Stepping in, she looks around eagerly. "We have the place to ourselves?"

"We do," I say.

"And when the cat's away . . ." She winks.

She walks the perimeter of the central meeting space, looking at the framed drawings and photographs of the firm's most impressive projects. Outside, the rain clamors at the harborside windows in Austin's office. His door is open, as usual, and when I glance through, the large sheet of glass looks like marble, completely opaque, veined with twisting ribbons of rushing water.

"I love this one," says Petra, calling my attention away from the weather.

I join her. The Knickerson Cove cottage, one of Austin's first commissions after opening the firm. "I loved it, too. Sad to say it's gone."

"But who would destroy such a lovely little house?"

"You mean what," I say. "Remember Ciaran? Five years ago, I think." Maybe Texas was spared that time.

But Petra nods. "Oh, Chincoteague."

And I know we're both thinking, unavoidably, of the photograph that dominated newsfeeds the day after the storm: all those ponies, washed up, on the Virginia shore, the sort of image you want to banish from your retinas the minute you see it—and just the sort that wins awards and won't leave you alone.

"He built it for a songwriter, up on Cape Ann. That house—well, after it was destroyed—is the one that made him rethink his building materials. He went to a conference in Japan. Though even if that house had stood, I don't think it would have made sense to live there much longer. The cove is more or less gone. No beach left."

Petra continues to take in the photograph. "It's the kind of house you dream of as a child, one you can tuck yourself into at night like a nest, all alone with the stars and the sea."

She moves along the wall, looking at other houses, floor plans, pencil sketches; murmuring, pointing, nodding.

"You know," I say, "you can tour most of them. In virtual. Did Austin show you?"

"Show me?" She shifts her gaze to me. (Is it ever anything but piercing?)

I point out the door in a back corner that looks as if it might lead to a closet. And it does—or did. In the early years of the firm, we kept all our supplies in there—until Austin went to yet another conference and came back followed by a large box that he unpacked to reveal a compact set of equipment. "Just wait," he said when the rest of us asked what it was. Hap, a veteran gamer, recognized the headset and put it on, miming gunfire. The rest of us were clueless.

"Very funny," said Austin as he took the headset back. He led Hap and Filene to the closet, opened the door, and said, "Rip out all the shelves. Most of these supplies we don't use much. Pare down and find another place to store them."

Now, in the shell of the former supply closet, there is little more than a comfortable armchair resting on a stretch of plain wall-to-wall carpet. The overhead light is rarely turned on.

I go to the large desktop in a neighboring alcove and scroll through the choices till I find it. I ready the headset for Petra. "You can still tour the cottage, even though it's long gone." I bring her into the Vroom. "I try to resist being superstitious."

"Superstitious?" She follows my gesture to sit in the chair.

"It feels a little like calling a spirit from the grave. An architectural séance."

"Ooh," she says. "I'll take my chances."

She reaches for the headset; she knows the technology. This is typical of people under forty, but I never assume that clients my age and older have had this experience. I tell her to get her bearings in the chair, and then, if she likes, I'll get her to her feet and stand with her while she moves through the house. This is how we get clients to fall in love with the houses we have yet to build them. Filene does the imaginary furnishing, according to the results of a questionnaire on the clients' tastes. Often, they'll ask to purchase this couch or that painting, even a set of illusory saucepans suspended over an equally illusory kitchen counter.

Petra leans raptly forward in the chair. She is headed down the steps, carved into the preexisting granite, that lead from the parking area to the cove. Those steps are the one feature of Austin's design that weren't destroyed in the storm.

I still know this house by heart, and I can tell from the slight gasp she emits exactly when, having passed through the front door, her gaze is drawn to the right, to the bright expanse of water just beyond the large, arched row of windows that filled the wall facing the ocean and the grand piano at center stage. The entire first floor was a wide open space, a compact eight hundred square feet, yet it felt far larger by day in the brilliant, almost blinding light—and then, at night, cozy as a warren. Running beneath the windows enfolding the vista was a long, cushioned bench, which at one end formed the rear seating to the dining table. At a party, guests sitting there would face away from the drama of the water view—but they would see, through windows at the inland side of the house, a reach of wild, salt-hardy grasses that once skirted a gathering of boulders. Even some of the boulders were washed away.

"Oh my," Petra exclaims as she rises from the chair. I touch her elbow lightly, to let her know I'm there to spot her, but she is sure on her feet, moving forward and back as if dancing, her head moving left and right, owlish. I imagine she must be exploring the kitchen alcove with its pale pink quartz counters.

"I'm heading up these outrageously elegant stairs," she tells me.

The top floor of the house was also open, reached by a cherry-wood spiral staircase (in itself a master construction, trucked north as one piece from a cabinetmaker in Brooklyn, a craftsman who's since moved to Michigan, reportedly to outfit a series of high-end Timer cabins). Its ocean wall, recessed from the wall below, opened to a balcony with a retractable awning.

But the upstairs bathroom was Austin's favorite feature of the small house. Hidden behind the built-in bed (which faced the ocean), it bowed out like a half moon, the windows above the sink and curved stone counter looking down over the wild grasses, the boulders resembling islands in a golden sea. The large shower stall, off to one side, was walled on three sides by one-way glass, giving its occupant a tripartite view: inland, down the coast, out to sea. Overhead, a tempered glass scuttle cranked open to the sky, releasing the steam, admitting the salty air.

The owner of the house enjoyed its jewel-box pleasures for two and a half years before it was destroyed. Newer clients have asked for that shower, and though Austin will tell them he no longer trusts those materials, he's told me that that particular location, that private cove, was too perfect to re-create.

I can tell when Petra's reached the shower by the way she swivels her head almost frantically. "Am I looking . . . oh lord, is this—" Not surprisingly, she becomes disoriented and teeters, but still I'm unprepared when I have to catch her.

She is tall, and when her body collides with mine, it's not roughly enough to knock me over, though for an instant I panic. We both reach for each other at the same time, but her arms are the ones to encircle me.

For a moment, before she pulls up the headset, she holds me close, and I realize that what made me panic was how much her stature reminded me of my first husband.

She removes the headset completely. "Well. That was a trip. My goodness. Can I tour other houses like that?"

"Yes," I say, though I hear how hesitant I sound.

"Not now." She strokes my sleeve with her free hand. "I need a good dose of boring old gravity first. And maybe I'll say yes to that tea you offered when I came in."

While I work on the tea, she asks if she can take a peek at Austin's office, and I tell her to help herself.

I listen to the rain, its relentless battering, and I resist the temptation to check on the news. If he were here alone, Austin would have it running in the background, low-volume but merciless, that river of rarely reassuring information from the world beyond. On my way here, stopping at the store for milk, I overheard that there's video footage, that the police and the Feds are circulating images of three suspects.

"That is some splendid view." She startles me, framed in Austin's office doorway.

"When it's not a sheet of water," I say.

"Cruel, isn't it?" In the pause she allows, I'm confused. "That so many people are dying of thirst, and here we are up to our chins. Or you are," she adds. "Heaven knows what's in store for Texas this summer. I suppose I'll find out!"

I ask if she wants milk or sugar. She takes both.

"What's interesting here—and surprises me," she says as we sit, "is that there's no evidence of his ever having worked in the city."

"It was very different work. Not his own. Institutions. Buildings measured in tens of thousands of square feet. Hundreds."

"So he started over when you came here. Architectural witness protection?"

I laugh. "Not exactly. He did do a couple of residential projects back then. In New Jersey, for friends of his parents. And here, he started with another firm."

"But you knew him in New York. What was he like then? Very ambitious, no doubt. That firm he worked for—not for the faint of heart. Or scant of education!"

"The hours were ridiculous. Even now when he works seven days, there's no comparison."

"And now he comes home to a wife and son."

"Brecht lost his father very young," I say—as if it's important for her to understand that he's my son, not Austin's. "Though he's known Austin for half his life."

"No children of his own?"

"No."

"He was never married before?"

I look at the wall clock. "You know what? We should head over to the yacht club. Aren't you hungry?"

Petra is peering at me with a faint smile on her face. "I am indeed hungry."

The day we met inside the Richard Serra, after the odd intimacy of sharing that thunderstorm as if we were alone inside the storm itself, Austin asked me a number of questions. Did I work in the neighborhood? Was I in the art business? Did I love or hate the city in the summer? "It's one extreme or the other," he said. "No one's neutral." We walked out of the gallery together, and I liked his courteous attention, his comfortable banter.

When, at the corner of Eighth Avenue, we had to part ways, he said, "We should meet there again, don't you think? Before it closes? We could see the exhibit without the histrionics."

I am what some people call "slow on the uptake," and the collision of his suggestion with that word, *histrionics,* left me confused.

"The weather, I meant." He held his phone in one hand, and I realized that he had brought it out because he assumed I would give him my number.

I did think he was attractive. I did not want to be disappointed.

"Maybe I could bring my son next time." Did my voice shake?

"How old?" Not a beat of hesitation.

"Eleven." Already I was sorry. Had I just asked for a first date with my child along, recklessly suggesting that I wanted Brecht to meet a man who, in all likelihood, would have no lasting presence in our lives?

"Mmm," Austin said, as if savoring that number, as if eleven had a special meaning.

I waited. If I had blown it, there was nothing to be done.

"Of course you should," he said. "So when's he free? That's a very busy age."

I still have pictures, somewhere in the digital depths of my life, showing Brecht as he explores the creosote-colored steel tunnels. It was a sunny Saturday afternoon, and Austin joined us there. He was friendly to Brecht but did not accost him with flattery or patronizing questions. The first thing he said to Brecht, after introducing himself, was "You like art?" "Sometimes," said Brecht. "Lots of art is boring, that's the truth," said Austin, and then we roamed the hangarlike gallery, Brecht staying as far from us as he could. I felt strange, silenced by the imbalance of my knowing one of them so well, the other not at all. None of us spoke for quite a while until Austin said quietly, just to me, "What do you think of clams? How about sweet potato fries?"

In the cab, I took the middle. At our first stop, Austin waited in a large, chilly lobby while I escorted Brecht up in the elevator to the apartment of a school friend for a planned overnight. There would be no overnighting with Austin, I knew that, but there was a long ride on the L train, during which we told each other some of our history in voices raised over the rattletrap rush and the conductor's announcements, and there was a plain but lovely dinner (clams in red plastic baskets, at a picnic table in a sandy Rockaway parking lot next to a beach), and I understood something, though he never said it in so many words: This man was ready, even longing, to settle down, to claim his own metaphorical picnic table. He was in his forties, and like so many men his age who work too hard at something demanding their every humming synapse, he had forgotten about making time to make a home. Or so I sensed.

I told him about losing Andrew, but I made it a fact, not a story. And then, because I didn't want him to ask any questions, to make me fall apart, I said, "Can I ask if you were ever married?"

"Can you?" he teased. "You just did."

For an instant, I realized he might have an ex-wife and three children. Or three ex-wives and no children. Or, for all I knew, a current wife. My heart lurched. I'm not good at rooting out lies.

"Almost," he said. "I almost got married. But the truth is, for a long time I was married to my job." He laughed. "You've never heard that before, have you? I will say this: Because of the job, I've traveled a lot. Enough for a lifetime. I wouldn't mind never using my passport again. And really, who wants to these days?"

We covered the topics you always do on the first date, though he didn't ask me about Brecht. Was this a symptom of respect or avoidance? We learned that we'd lost three of our four parents and that we grew up half an hour away from each other in New Jersey. Also, that we both felt our time in New York ticking to an end.

"I've come to think that the city is for young people and for old people," said Austin. "Not so much the in-betweeners."

"Old people?" I thought of crowded subways and Times Square on any stifling summer night; how the pandemic had been cruelest of all to them.

"Old people who've planned well," he said. "You know. The ones who go in groups to movie retrospectives and the ballet and know which restaurants have which specials when. They live in doorman buildings with elevators, go to elder-yoga classes at the Y, hire tattooed dog walkers who make them feel better about their grandchildren's choices. They have earned their years of cultured leisure."

I actually recalled a dog walker whom Brecht and I passed frequently on our street in the Village. Wherever he went, he turned heads. His hair was an explosion of thick ropy braids dyed like spumoni, and an arc of piercings on the left side of his face swooped from upper lip to eyebrow. Over time we grew accustomed to nodding and smiling at one another as he corralled his canine gang to one side of the pavement. One day Brecht commented, "That's a lot of dogs. His apartment must be giant." I explained that the dogs weren't all his. "That's his job," I said. Brecht turned to look at the receding tails, all waving with delight, and said, "Cool job." I opened my mouth to contradict him—but who said it wasn't the coolest job ever? Did I feel sorry for the guy, assume he had little education? He probably made more money than I did. I pictured a grown Brecht, tall and graceful like his dad, ushering his own pack down our street. (Though please, I thought, no piercings.)

By chain association, suddenly I was summoning Andrew, trying not to get tearful, when the check arrived on our picnic table. I was relieved when we split the cost without a fuss, and I assumed we'd walk back to the subway. I didn't want the evening to end with memories of my dead husband.

But Austin steered us down to the water. "There used to be a line of summer cottages along here," he told me. "Not a sign of them anymore. They were demolished after Sandy. No insurance company would touch them. But you know, what I've always wanted is to build houses by the shore. The coast. Do you think there's anything more restful than looking at the line where the ocean cuts off the sky?"

I thought of looking at a father sleep beside his infant son, but I hedged. "Maybe not."

It was dark by then, and we watched the line of blinking lights tilted toward the horizon: planes waiting to land at JFK. Austin said, almost sadly, "So many travelers," and then, after a long moment, his voice brightened. "Let's go find a milkshake. I have a few ideas where. Depends if you like malteds."

Getting ready for bed that night, I realized that I'd learned nothing about his almost-marriage. More important, though, were the things he'd made clear about the future he had in mind.

Now, over lunch at the YC, I find myself telling the story of our courtship to Petra. To my relief, she isn't taking notes—but then I realize she hasn't been taking notes at all, not even back at the office.

Is she recording our conversation? I suppose it wouldn't be rude to ask, but there's nothing risky here. This is not a deposition.

"He did tell me he was almost married once," I'm saying.

"Let me guess. Another architect. That would be doomed from the start. Two spatial perfectionists? Conflagration!" Her hands rise wildly over her plate, gesturing explosion.

I shake my head. "I'm not sure she was . . . grounded in a profession. He said she was one of those young women who's so powerfully magnetic that you blind yourself to the illness until it's too late."

Petra's hands settle to her lap. "Illness?"

"Instability."

"Mental instability?"

"Yes. A kind of mania. A brilliant mania—he said she made pictures, drawings. Compulsively. But she was also . . ." *Delusional* was Austin's word. Which has nothing to do with his work.

Petra leans forward, her beige silk blouse nearly touching her salad.

"Ancient history," I say.

"But you were saying that she was also . . . ?"

"Very young. Too young."

Petra pauses. "You never met her."

"Oh no. She was long gone from Austin's life. No pictures, nothing."

"They just . . . split up?"

As he clears the adjacent table, the server catches my eye. My sandwich is gone, Petra's salad hardly touched. To let him take my plate would be rude, but I'm wishing that something, anything, would derail Petra's interrogation.

"Austin isn't one to dwell on the past," I say, and it's true. "Are you unhappy with your food? I'm sorry if I steered you wrong."

"Oh no, my dear. It's delicious. I'm just so very distractible!" Petra plunges her fork into the greens and takes two bites in close succession.

I glance out the window, which is frosted over with moisture. The rain has lapsed into a thick fog that sits on the harbor like a massive pillow. Few pleasure boats are in the water yet, but I spot the crimson hull of Carl Unger's lobster boat, which rests at its mooring year-round. He hasn't used it for lobstering in years, but he takes it out on the water a few times each summer, and he tells anyone who asks that he keeps it there through the winter in case he needs to make a quick escape from terra not-so-firma.

"Austin told me to take you to visit one of his favorite finished projects after lunch," I say. "A living space over a boathouse. The owners are expecting us in half an hour, though I can call them to say we'll be a little late. Would you like dessert?"

"Oh no, this is just the ticket," says Petra, working on her salad as if it's only now occurred to her that she is ravenous.

With the weather so gloomy and the sailing season yet to begin, the dining room is nearly empty, but out of habit, I look around for familiar faces. I'm instantly sorry, because there's Margo Tattersall. She is eating alone, and she waves cheerfully. To my shameful relief, she does not get up but goes back to eating her meal and reading her book. Well, good for her, I suppose, refusing to hide beneath a rock. And why do I even think she should? Her husband is the fool.

I happen to know it wasn't a clean split, the breakup between Austin and the woman he almost married. What I told Petra is true: Austin shrugs off the past as something that, once learned from, can only interfere with forward momentum. But when I asked him about this woman—*girl,* he insisted, in terms of her maturity, and that was part of his mistake—I could tell that whatever had happened between them wasn't so easily dismissed. He told me that he had never before understood how it's possible to fall for someone so mentally off balance; maybe it happened when you talked yourself into believing that the imbalance was simply a kind of balance you'd never seen before.

"You think, Oh, I had it all wrong. I was such a square! You think that this new intensity is the truth about love that's been evading you all along. It's like being swept along on a warm current before you're rolled under. Well, I was rolled all right."

He told me all this the third time we saw each other. He was walking me home from a movie. We were still a few dates from sleeping together, or I might have asked him if it was the sex; was that the power she held over him? But I didn't want to go anywhere near the place I hoped we were headed ourselves. So all I asked, thinking it was an easy way to help him end the story, was "Whatever happened to her? Do you . . . keep track of each other?"

"No," he said forcefully. He let go of my hand. "She killed herself. She left my apartment in hysterics one night, and I followed her, but not fast enough. And she dove off a pier into the Hudson River."

"Dove?" I asked.

"Dove. Jumped. It was night, and I was too far behind her."

"Did you—" I stopped myself, but he finished for me, his tone fierce.

"Dive in after her? No. But it was March, and I'm no lifeguard. I did the cowardly thing. I called the police."

"And they came?"

"Of course they came. Not in a split second, but pretty fast."

We were standing still on a sidewalk, people passing us, glancing at us quickly, maybe wondering if they were witnessing a breakup. Austin's voice was agitated, and he was gesturing broadly.

"I'm sorry," I said.

Austin stood there, just looking at the pavement between us. "It would have been easier," he said, "if at least they'd found her."

Mike

One thing I can most certainly assure you," says Margo, who's alternating her energies between unpacking a box of my belongings and drinking a large limeless gin and tonic, "is that there is no way on earth my next husband—or boy toy or gigolo or who knows what form of mate—will be from this burb."

It takes me a moment to feel vaguely disappointed. Is she "assuring" me that we would never make a viable couple? Is this a veiled insult? She's been at my place for an hour and already I've had too much to drink. The tonic I unpacked is a shade flat, but the gin is good and strong. And fancy. A legacy of Deeanne: nothing but the best brands of everything. (How's that working for you now, Modesta?)

"Mike, we're going to find you a new wife. A so-much-better wife that you are going to regret wasting the last twenty-thirty-whatever years of your life. I'd encourage you to make hay with a gleeful vengeance, but I'm getting the vibe that you are the wife type." She peels a long strip of tape off a box, pauses to give me a wry look, then wads up the tape and tosses it toward the wastebasket I set in a corner. (She doesn't miss.) "You know what your problem is, Mike? You didn't get the message, back whenever, that geeks rule the world. That science can be—*can* be—sexy. But you gotta leverage it." She pulls a handful of paperbacks out of the box. "Wow, you still read books on paper? I thought I was the only one."

"Not much. But sometimes. Yes."

"Books." She sighs. Almost tenderly, she lines them up on a shelf, patting their spines for good measure. "I knew I was one foot out the door when the High went over to screens for everything, no exceptions. *Moby-Digital.* Ugh." She reaches deeper into the open box and pulls out my photoshow, a dark screen in a black frame. "Oh boy," she says. "Will this need revising?"

I nod.

"I could do that for you."

"Margo, you don't need to protect me from her. She's already beginning to fade. Your influence, I think."

Margo looks pleased with herself. "I knew our alliance would be productive."

"For me."

She sits on the edge of the couch. "Mike, you will never know." She shakes her head. "You are giving me the welcome feeling that your ex made a very stupid choice. A couple of stupid choices, but the first one was *my* ex. Whose choices have been visibly stupid for a while now."

I feel my phone vibrate. "Sorry."

"Dad? Any word?"

"No, honey." My heart sinks all over again.

"It's only been a day."

"Two, Marinda. How can he not call—at least call you—just to say he's all right?"

"He's just . . . wrapped up in himself. You know how he gets." Marinda is silent for a moment. "Dad, is that music?"

She knows me; I've never been one to listen to music on my own. "I have company."

"I'm glad. Who?"

I hesitate, but why not? "Mrs. Tattersall. Margo."

"Dad? You're joking."

"Not at all. She's having a good influence on me."

"Dad—"

"Marinda. It's fine. Don't worry. In fact, stop worrying—about me."

Margo, catching the drift, starts to laugh. She says loudly, "Marinda, honey, I am unworthy of your fabulous dad. I am just helping him get his life in material order."

"Dad, are you guys drinking?"

"We are. We have to. I have to." I feel my composure cracking. "I think I have to get off. We'll call each other the minute we hear anything." I shouldn't say it, but I do: "Has your mother been in touch?"

"No," she says coldly. "Aren't they willfully out of touch with the world? Fingers in their ears, eyes squeezed shut? Like those three monkeys."

"I'm going to concentrate on your baby," I say. "You think about her, too. We'll . . . somehow."

"I'll tell you a secret. We have a name," she says.

"A name," I say, at first confused.

"Eden. We're going to call her Eden, Dad."

"Eden." What a hopeful name. Somehow a line from an old song worms its way into my head: *And we've got to get ourselves back to the ga-a-a-AR-den.* A song from my mother's youth that always brought tears to her eyes.

"It's going to be okay, Dad."

Or not. I know about not. But I tell her I love her and say goodbye.

I have gone weeks at a time—two, maybe three—without hearing from my son. Ever since he graduated from Wesleyan and moved to New York eight years ago, he has been absurdly difficult to reach; and not, he claims, because he's wanted to avoid his mother or me. He takes whatever jobs he can get, from tending bar to unloading trucks to spur-of-the-moment babysitting for friends who land auditions. All to allow space for his own auditions, which lead to enough work that he still hangs on to that dream. Not "stardom," he'll insist, but life as a so-called working actor, the goal a modest but steady income, union benefits. Egon turned thirty last year, and I seesaw back and forth between pride and despair at his perseverance.

What I hate right now is how angry I am at him. It's been more than forty-eight hours since the bombing, and even if the chances of his being among the dead or wounded are next to nil, why can't he imagine my anxiety? Isn't empathy the actor's stock-in-trade?

It was Margo's idea to come over and force me to unpack, just to keep me busy on another unmoored Sunday. I see her eyeing another box.

"I'm done for now," I say. "Thank you."

She goes to the kitchen and refills our glasses. "That is one antiquated fridge," she says. "No more ice."

"State of the planet. But you don't need a glacier for a cocktail, do you?"

She nods. "Overkill." She hands me my replenished drink, the last of the carbonation rising toward oblivion.

We sit down on separate pieces of furniture, both facing the window that frames the park of slowly dying maples. Only some of the branches are, as they should be, putting out their spring finery. Others are clearly barren. A few years ago, scraping together more funds for the seawall, our town laid off the tree warden. Dead limbs go unpruned, while trees growing up to block rich people's views go unprotected from the ax.

"Can I tell you something weird?" she says.

I raise my glass. "Whatever you tell me, it's all bets off whether I remember it tomorrow." I turn to her expectantly and have a flashback of sitting across a desk from Margo at a meeting about Marinda, about my daughter's lackluster English grades in her sophomore year of high school. Could I ever, *ever* have envisioned this change of scenery? "Go on," I say. "Your weirdness is safe with me."

"Well, it's not *my* weirdness," she says. "Me, I could use a little weirdness. No. It's just this . . . man staying in my neighborhood. At Celestino's house. You know Celestino, right? The tree house."

I nod. The tree wizard. I wonder, in fact, if I could hire him to look at those dying maples, even though they're not mine. Maybe, like souls only marginally lost, they can be saved, reclaimed.

"So I guess this guy is a friend of his, and he's staying with them, but all day today he's been pacing along the street, up toward the point and back, and he's always on his phone. I tried eavesdropping from an upstairs window, but I'm not even sure he was speaking English."

I smile at her. "And this is weird?"

"Okay, it doesn't sound weird, maybe, but it is. The thing is, last night he came by asking to see my bathroom."

I laugh. "Now that is weird. Your bathroom?"

"The one I'm renovating. He says he's looking for 'ideas.' "

"You let him in?"

Margo shrugs. "Sure. He's a guest in the neighborhood. And he was nice. . . ." She laughs. "Smarmy, really! But after he left, I just thought—well, weird. That's what I thought. Weird."

"I think we've had a lot of gin."

"I know we have."

I raise my hand like a student. "So let me tell you something weird."

"Good. Your turn."

What the hell. "You know how much of my work is out on the water. Taking samples. Temperatures. Visiting the probe stations in the marshes. Acidity, salinity, biocounts."

"Chemistry." She sighs. "Formulas."

"Chemistry." I nod. "Practiced mostly alone. If I'm heading out from the lab, sometimes I take an Ensign that my boss's son keeps at the wharf. Just so I can sail. Think. I like the quiet."

"Mmm," says Margo, sinking into my new couch. Is she falling asleep? Maybe I don't need her to hear. Maybe that's better.

"Last week I am out north of Halibut Point, a decent ways offshore, when the wind practically quits on me. I'm coming about when I see someone in the water. Like I said, I'm pretty far offshore. I figure it must be a diver, and I look around for another boat—nothing. So I call out, ask if they need my help. I mean, of course they do, unless they're crazy or, God forbid, ending it all. And the swimmer stops. Turns toward me. Head and shoulders out of the water. I go to start the motor, but when I turn back, the head is gone. So I motor over, I call and call, I circle wide. Nothing. But I wasn't seeing things."

"So," Margo interrupts, though she pauses to yawn, "a seal. Always turns out to be a seal. Asshole and I had experiences like that when we used to go cruising. Especially in the fog."

I shake my head. "Not a seal. Unless it was . . . an albino seal. Or an Arctic seal a long way from home. The coloration wasn't right. Too pale for a gray or harbor seal."

"Oh Mikey, you need a vacation. Or a transfer. Dry land. The mountains."

Margo sets her glass on the table. "I am now toasted," she says, "but I swore to you that boy would call, that favorite student of mine, and I am not leaving till he does. What if I stay here, right here on this couch? Fully clothed."

"You don't need to do that."

She lies back against a pillow and pulls her feet up. "In point of fact, I do. I don't think I can walk straight, and neither can you. I'd fall right down those ramshackle stairs my friend Babette probably described as 'charming.' Or 'authentic.' " She faces the ceiling and closes her eyes. "Words. Do you have favorite words? Mine change. I like *calumny. Vivisect. Rigmarole.* Rig-a-ma-role. Isn't that a great one? I say it with four syllables. It's the password to my gun. Did you know I own a gun, Mike?"

"No, Margo, I did not," I say quietly. I wonder if she's going to pass out. I go to my bedroom and bring back a pillow and blanket.

"Probably you have a gun, too," she murmurs. "Probably everyone does."

"No. No gun here."

Now she is stretched out full length, shoes kicked off. "You are a classy, undervalued man. I wish my ex hadn't run off with yours." She fumbles the pillow under her head. "I wish I'd run off with you first."

I bend over her and tuck the blanket in. "If I say, 'The same to you,' we might be in trouble, so I won't." I switch off the lamp beside the couch. I go into my bedroom with my phone and sit on my cold, well-made bed. I do not want to be "classy," forget about "undervalued." Did she think that was a compliment?

I clutch the phone in both hands. *Just call. Just please one word from you and nothing else will matter.* The jilted lover's plea.

I may be drunk, but I am hopelessly alert. I go back out into the living room, the woebegone corner kitchen. I switch on the stove light, then glance across the open space toward the couch. Margo is out cold, snoring in a soft, soothing way.

Here sits the last box marked KITCHEN. Margo had gone as far as to remove the tape. I reach in and lift out a stack of plates, padded with dish towels. I remember packing them hastily, half hoping they'd break in the move. The "everyday" dishes Deeanne chose to "revitalize" our table last year, they are white ceramic, each glazed with a pale blue sea creature at the center: starfish, seahorse, lobster, crab, stippled urchin. Had she stopped to think that the fate of these creatures is my work and that their future, long term—Christ, even near term—doesn't look terribly rosy?

Now the anger rises from my gut to my temples, the urge to lift the stack high in the air and simply drop them on the floor. Perhaps only Margo's presence prevents me from following through. Instead, I take them, one by one, and line them up in the dishwasher behind the plastic plates that Margo brought along for our takeout. In the bottom of the box, I see a tangle of miscellaneous utensils: a spatula, salad tongs, a peeler, and a clutch of lobster crackers. At least I tossed the Christmas stocking novelties (gizmos to pit cherries, salt the rims of cocktail glasses, turn carrots into rosebuds). Looking around, I wonder which drawer will become That Drawer—the one with the hodgepodge of intermeshed metallic tools—and then remember that all these drawers and cupboards are about to be taken away. All this unpacking, then, was an exercise in futility.

But what is the object wrapped in a cloth napkin?

The ceramic spoon rest. Egon, second grade. It's glazed with a primitive daisylike flower. Bright pink. When Egon presented it to his mother, he looked sad. "Pink is a girl color, they said."

"Who said?" Dee asked.

"Boys in art class."

"Well, I'm a girl. And it's for me!"

"But I made it," he said mournfully. "I picked the color."

His mother then demanded to know which pint-size philistine had made fun of Egon's color choice, and Egon went silent. No amount of torture would have pulled that name from him. Grade school omertà.

I thought I understood what it was like to be a Different Boy; I was the classic science nerd who'd rather study the ants colonizing his driveway than join in pickup basketball. So it pained me, but it didn't upset me, as I watched Egon grow up outside the hormonal mainstream: singing instead of soccer, books instead of ball games. On summer evenings, when the neighborhood boys convened at the burial ground for games of manhunt that lasted till well after dark, Egon played online Scrabble or practiced guitar. He did sail—though every able-bodied child in this town has sailed at some point—and briefly, too briefly, he excelled at a sport. Gymnastics is hardly football, but it demands a level of physical discipline that people (or those not brainwashed by football) respect. When Egon hurled himself through space in lofty, convoluted trajectories, his body a gyre of muscle and grace, nobody laughed. Nobody told him it was a "girl sport." He was perfect.

That he had to stop was my fault, and I still agonize over the accident. Once Egon made it past the worst of his pain, the excruciating physical therapy, and knew that he would walk normally again, he insisted that he was, truthfully, glad to be freed from the obligation to fulfill that gift. "Not like I was headed for the Olympics, Dad." Later he would say that the accident helped him find his way to the stage that much sooner. ("*This* is the way I was meant to use my body in space," he said to his mother and me the summer he played Ariel at a Shakespeare festival in the Hudson Valley.)

He was two weeks shy of starting high school. The week before, he had sailed on the yacht club's team in the juniors regatta, and they'd beaten Duxbury, their archrival, bringing the cup back to the trophy case in the Galleon Lounge. The summer heat at its zenith, he slept late and lay about in the den, finally facing the assigned readings for freshman honors English.

Marinda was back from lacrosse camp, catching up with the girls she'd left behind; they hung around in her air-conditioned bedroom, varnishing one another's toenails or, lying facedown on the bed, three abreast, watching YouTube videos of whatever current movie star incited their swooning.

I made a snap decision and marched through the house calling out, "Turn off the AC! Get your suits! Time for the last fishnic!" Groans and protests—too tired; too behind on *Gatsby;* ever hear of sunstroke, Dad?—but I clapped my hands and issued orders: gather fishing gear, fill cooler, pack layers, and why not bring *Gatsby* along? Jay, I told Egon, would fit right in. Marinda asked if her friend Fran could join us. Sure, I said, she could be Gatsby's date. Laughter, eye-rolling. Fran joked, "I'm like sort of taken, Mr. I. But Mare is free." The girls poked each other, laughing harder.

Deeanne drove off to buy wine, charcoal, and deli salads; she'd meet us at the dock. She wore an aqua beach sheath with silver sequins winking alongside the glimpse it gave of her breasts (which were, contrary to gossip, entirely authentic). Her legs looked longer than usual and gleamed with fragrant lotion. A long day in the sun, I knew, always made my wife amorous.

All these years gone by, and I still remember so many details of the morning, and then the long day, because I replayed them, beginning to end, over and over, while I waited alone, shivering, in the ER some twelve hours later.

We had the big Mako then, a twenty-three-footer; it was back when everyday citizen fishing seemed innocent, unclouded by politics or science. I loved going out for stripers—still plentiful then—and on the way back, I would check my traps off Doe Island. If we were lucky, we could have lobsters for lunch the next day (after I'd slept late with my sun-stoked bride). This, to me, was the perfect weekend.

Perfect it was, until it wasn't. Marinda and Egon, separately occupied, did not argue once. Fran took a genuine interest in the fishing, especially because the fishing was good. I enjoyed being a teacher, and she was a quick study. When it came time to go ashore, we were near one of our favorite coves on Cape Ann, a sandy stretch of protected dunes that was hard to reach by land—unless you owned one of the old shingle shacks grandfathered into the park.

The tide was inbound, so we anchored close. One other boat had anchored already; a couple lay reading on the beach, probably perturbed by our arrival. While the children swam in the placid waves, Deeanne stayed on board, cleaning the fish. (On our very first waterborne outing together, her cheerful deftness at cleaning fish was one of the things that gave me, however absurdly, an inkling that she might be the one I should marry.) I ferried the rest of the food, the towels, and the grill setup to shore. The smooth sand of the tidal shallows made it easy to wade, holding everything aloft.

And I was right about the couple; less than half an hour after the kids staked their claim with towels, umbrellas, and soft drinks, the two readers gathered their gear and, without a word of casual kinship, motored away in their launch.

I scooped a basin in the sand to hold the grill pan and made the girls hunt for rocks to form a perimeter. I had this down to a science; I had even packed a jar of marinade for the fillets. Before lighting the coals, Deeanne and I shared a small thermos of chilled vodka, poured over ice in plastic tumblers.

"Mr. I, you are a damn good provider," she murmured, removing the sheath that covered her swimsuit. The fabric, like the fine quartz sand, twinkled in the sun.

Overcome with a sense of great fortune, I felt briefly teary. "We are a team," I said.

Deeanne rolled toward me and, changing her drink from one hand to the other, laid a cold palm on my inner thigh. "I'll show you teamsmanship," she said. "Anon."

She had a knack for igniting my passion, my boyish desire to please this woman who was prettier than I once thought I "deserved," with a single, suggestively off-kilter word. *Anon.* Was I pathetic? Who cared? I was grateful.

By the time we'd had our fill of grilled fish, carrot and potato salads, and store-bought cupcakes (and emptied a bottle of pinot gris), the sun was closer to the horizon than ideal. We could certainly make it home safely in the dark, but a perfect day cruise ended with a sunset return. And Fran's never-ending exclamations of praise and wonder ("This beach is like the end of the world, like it's totally ours!" "Oh my God, where did these awesome cupcakes come from?") had secretly inflamed some tacky Tarzan pride in me, so that I wanted to give her that experience of the salt air in her face as the water around her bloomed crimson and pink, a gossamer hint of moon in the east.

The three teenagers were playing Frisbee, triangulating over and over along the smooth expanse of sand, and I decided that the fastest way to get our little camp packed up was to do it myself, rather than go through the tedium of delegating. Deeanne swam out to the boat, to bring it closer in (the tide now at its highest point). I stuffed paper plates and plastic cups in a cooler, scraping uneaten food into the bakery box (no leftovers there!).

And then, reversing the rituals of our arrival, I hoisted the gear, wading it out to the boat in three trips (the towels, now soaked, a heavier load), Deeanne leaning down to pull it on board. We worked silently, contentedly, our bodies and minds lulled by the potency of sun mixed with spirits.

Last of all was the grill. I always brought along a pair of silvery fire mitts, the ones that lived by the hearth all winter, and—wearing my water shoes, taking care to be careful—I carried the pan to the water, wading in up to my waist and leaning well out before slowly pouring the coals into the surf. They sizzled angrily as they sank, their orange glow resistant, a few seconds longer, to their dousing. And then, careful to move away from the submerged coals, I slipped the pan itself beneath the surface, swishing it back and forth till it stopped hissing. It was a ritual I loved, the last step before we set off again, along the coast toward home. Normally, Deeanne and the children would be aboard already, slipping into robes and hoodies, pleasantly chilled.

But I hadn't yet called them away from their game; I enjoyed the sound of their voices, the teasing and yelping. With my back turned, it took a moment for me to realize that what I'd been hearing for a few seconds was an agonized keening, the sound of desperate pain. Looking over my shoulder, I saw Egon lying on the sand, screaming and clutching a calf, as the girls, terrified, stood near him, Fran holding the Frisbee.

"Dad?" I heard, and the high-pitched fear in my daughter's voice was as terrible as the confusing vision of Egon in the sand.

I threw the pan out over the water and ran back through the shallows.

Now Egon was crawling toward the water, sobbing.

Marinda had run to me in a panic. "He was backwards, he was going backwards to catch it, and he stepped . . . but it was still . . ." She, too, was sobbing.

I understood right away what had happened: running backward to catch the goddamn Frisbee, Egon had stepped inside the cautionary stone perimeter where the grill had sat, his bare foot making contact with the sand that still held the ovenlike heat from the metal pan. My last task, not yet accomplished, was to cool and bury the scorching sand.

I reached Egon as he was thrusting his foot into the water, screaming even louder. When I leaned over him to examine his foot, he shrieked, "Don't touch it, Dad, don't touch it, don't touch it please!"

I waded around Egon's legs to see the damage. To my horror, I could see the live blistering of the sole, as the burn ravaged the skin and soft tissue, changing in places from red to black. The transformation resembled the fierce cooling of the coals as they'd fallen through the water a minute before. On the outside of my son's foot, the damage rose toward the ankle, where it had clearly sunken sideways into the searing sand before he yanked it free.

Everything that happened next—the black comedy of cell phones in a pocket of disconnection (how nice it had felt, just moments before, to be "away from it all"); the pitched, half-drunken argument with Deeanne over whether to somehow get Egon to the boat or run for the nearest cottage; the vision of the two girls crouched together, whimpering, shivering—lives on as a carefully staged play curated by my memory as if through some accidental act of reverence.

As it turned out, the gamble to run for one of the cottages paid off. An older man was drinking on the porch—he, too, anticipating a fine sunset—and he let me use his landline.

The ambulance made its way to the beach twenty minutes later, wheels spinning as it drove along the sandy track that petered out beyond the cottage's driveway. Exerting my will over Deeanne's with a bullying force I had never used—my father's temper manifest—I announced that I would be going with our son to the ER; she was to take the boat back with the girls. I couldn't look Marinda or Fran in the eye, and they seemed drained of words as they watched the crude, nasty exchange between the adults while the EMTs strapped Egon onto a board at the water's edge. ("You are fucking telling me, after *you* fucked up, that I am not—" "Yes, I am fucking telling you exactly that, Deeanne. And I will call you from the hospital. And if you want to drive up to wherever—" "I goddamn will drive up, and you may just have to take a taxi home." "Fine, go. Yes—yes, I'm the boy's father. I'm coming. I'm sorry.")

An ER physician who spent long hours at the YC bar had once told a group of us that the worst pain is a third-degree burn. It was one of those idiotic muscle-flexing conversations in which some overpaid summons-pushing attorney couldn't resist asking the airline pilot or the round-the-globe sailor about the hardest or scariest aspects of his job. The ER doc told us about a little girl who'd spilled a pot of boiling spaghetti down the front of her body. "It was touch-and-go for weeks, and she survived, but Christ," he said, "there were times when we kind of wished she wouldn't. Her mom asked us, the ones who'd been there when she came in, to visit her up in the BU. Christ." Someone ordered him another stinger, asked for another story.

Not that there was any danger of Egon's not surviving, but the pain—that part was horrific. By the time the salves and the morphine had separated Egon from the desperate newscast of the nerves in his cauterized foot, he had cried so hard that his eyes were swollen shut. Mercifully, I was permitted to spend the night on a chair in his room. At sunrise, when his mother arrived, she refused to speak with me.

Egon insists that, but for negligible numbness, his foot is normal—except that he did lose the smallest toe, and those that remain, along with the outer edge of the foot, look waxy, always stubbornly pale even in the summer. I can't help glancing at it every time I see my son barefoot; the surface reminds me of pottery glazed and fired in a kiln.

Over the years since, whenever Dee and I argued about whether some course of action, practical or financial, was wise, more often than not she would pull out the Burnt Foot card. Was it fair that she refused to see herself as equally oblivious to the lapse in safety? Or that she recast the medical situation as one in which Egon might have been an amputee? It didn't matter. "You think so? And this from Mr. Oh-Don't-Worry-It's-Only-a-Foot?" or any variant accusation would silence me every time.

Looking back on that day yet again, the experiences, the physical components, I am struck by how much of it is gone. Never mind Deeanne, whose desertion is beginning to feel preordained. But Marinda now lives on the far side of the country—and her friend Fran? She was a bridesmaid at Marinda's wedding, but she's spun off to some distant corner of the world as well (World Bank? Global FoodBanking Network? Something both financial and political, last I heard). The Mako I sold a dozen years ago, when Egon went off to college; the fishing equipment I gave away. The abundance of striped bass is long over—and even the pristine sand has been stripped from that once-idyllic beach. I pass it sometimes on my routine rounds for samples; it's nothing but a narrow swath of pebbles. And Egon: where is Egon right now?

Egon

Pearl leans against me as we walk along. The rain falls, then doesn't fall, then falls again. We no longer care. We are somnambulists. Drenched-to-the-bone somnambulists. My right arm, clamped around her shoulders, is numb, but it's there to keep her going. "Almost there, we really are," I say every so often.

"Dearie, what a lousy liar you are," she tells me the third or fourth time. But on we soldier.

Since the last dropoff, we've been walking for maybe an hour, maybe three, shoes leaking, minds fogged. It's good I know the back roads for the last stretch, since we're without a GPS. I'm relieved when we pass the stone posts that mark the entrance to my long-ago summer day camp, though the sign is gone.

We left Jersey while it was still light out, and at first we got lucky on rides, especially considering everyone's so jumpy, knowing the bombers are on the lam, though surely they've fled the country by now, the jaguars back in their jungle. Pearl and I both have hitch cards, and they seem to be reassuring enough to the drivers who pull over. Almost always, they're listening to the news. In one car, we heard a broadcaster refer to the Oceloti as enviro-jihadists, which, even if it's hardly appropriate, I do find sort of catchy. The novelty of the attack has the city on high alert, and security beacons we passed on the thruway were all flashing red.

There are rumored threats of an "echo explosion," an "after-bombing." Manhattan's shut tight as a sphincter. After twenty-four hours of crashing with Pearl in her primitive squat, my phone stupidly forgotten in the city, I'd had it. I decided north was the way to go: get out, even take a break. I hadn't done that in I don't know how long. Maybe I'd figure out what the hell's going on with my parents, though my life isn't much connected to theirs. I've got no auditions lined up any time soon, and if I don't make it downtown to haul flats for the change of shows at Roach, they'll figure it out. The theater might go dark for the next week; nothing new there. But I'm clueless, and Pearl's ornery no-fi lifestyle only makes it worse. At least she has the hitch card—and carries an actual wallet. We're both old-fashioned that way.

I told her, as soon as we heard the news, that we ought to make sure everyone we knew was fine.

"The casualties are peanuts," she said, reserving the right, with her own grim history, to downplay the carnage.

"But don't you want to make sure?" I said.

"Who is fine? Who is not?" said Pearl as we stood in the PATH station with all the other anxious, thwarted travelers. "What does it mean to 'be fine' in the game of roulette the city's become? Though it's nothing like living in Baghdad, Beirut, Cairo, São Paulo. Come to think of it, hey! Ever notice how most of the bloody hotspots are, literally, hot spots? Why never Oslo, Anchorage, Gdansk?"

But all that banter was hours ago. We're out of words, so I don't bother telling her when we're actually, finally in Vigil Harbor, not till we're at our precise destination—or what I'm pretty sure is the place.

"Here," I say quietly, pausing at the stone steps. How odd that my father lives here now, in this random building I passed hundreds of times while growing up. It's a hulking old clapboard house, three stories, divided into apartments.

"No," says Pearl. "You are torturing me, right?"

"No, I mean yeah. Come on." I loop my arm through hers at the elbow, as if she is very young or very old, to guide her up. There are no buzzers to be seen, and then I realize the front door isn't locked. Even in my zombie state, I am jolted: the doors of the town where I grew up, still innocently open, keys often lost to locks out of use. How could this innocence prevail?

Inside, I peer close at the list of tenants. There are three, Dad's name sandwiched in the middle. "One more flight. A dozen steps and we are there. You can collapse. I promise. I'll do the talking."

In a wooden crate beside the door, I recognize Dad's rubber boots. His clammers, my sister and I called them when we were little. To Pearl they'd be Wellies.

I knock gently. The old clock on the meetinghouse (still running!) told me it's nearly four in the morning, which means we were on the road for nearly twelve hours. I wait a few beats before knocking again. Pearl has slumped to the floor, back against the wall, eyes closed.

When the door opens, I am dismayed. I apologize. A woman has answered, bleary-eyed, hair pressed flat to one side of her head, springing wildly from the other. Lit from behind, she looks familiar, yet perhaps it's generic; she might be any of several moms I knew as a child: pencil-thin, pink-loafered, cocktailing on the YC verandah whenever I climbed the gangway from the sailing lessons I never loved. Though this woman is neither pencil-thin nor even shod.

"I am so sorry. I'm looking for Mike . . ." And then, "Oh fuck," I say from the shock of recognition. "Mrs. Tattersall?"

"Mike!" she calls out, nearly in my face—and before I can retreat, she reaches out and pulls me in by my wrists, so that I stumble on the edge of a rug and nearly fall into her arms. But she lets go and leaves me there to regain my balance. Calling my father's name again, she crosses the room toward a closed door.

I am confused and slowly becoming enraged. Marinda swore that the break came from Mom, that Dad was not the one who'd strayed. But—Mrs. T, my English teacher? Isn't she the ex of the man who . . .

Suddenly here's Dad, hurtling across the dim room. He is sobbing and saying my name, over and over, then holding on to me as if one of us is drowning.

"Dad, wow, it's okay." His fingers press, painfully, into my shoulder blades. "Really. It's okay. Let go, Dad."

"Where have you *been*?"

"Dad."

"Why didn't you *call*?"

"Dad!"

Finally he lets me go, and I turn around to see Pearl, now up on her feet in the hallway. Her expression is blank, catatonic.

I coax her in. It's like hauling in a big fish, she's so inert.

"Dad, this is Pearl. Can we please talk later? We need to sleep."

"How did you get here?"

"Hitch card. Dad? Later. Please."

Mrs. Tattersall stands in the middle of the room, keeping her distance. "I'll go home," she says.

"No, Margo, no," Dad says. "Stay. I have . . . I have no idea where the sheets are, but there are twin beds in the other room." He nearly sprints into the room from which he emerged, returning with two pillows and a jumble of blankets.

He smiles apologetically at Pearl as he points us to another door. "Go. Sleep all you want. I'll be here. Here," he repeats, the word a sob. My dad: stoic until he's not, and then he's really not.

I look briefly around at the modest apartment he has chosen when surely he could (couldn't he?) opt for a whole house to himself. Has he lost his job? But I have no energy to consider this—or to wonder again why Mrs. T is lying on Dad's couch (the couch that was in his den at home—not home anymore, I remember).

Pearl and I take turns in the bathroom, then go into our appointed room and lie on the two naked mattresses, each of us wrapped in a quilt, head on a pillow. I recognize in the pillowcase against my face, still warm, the smell of my father's shaving soap, same and comforting as ever. Poor, deserted Dad.

My mind rebels against sleep. It begins to buzz like a hive, to worry its way backward to the place where I belong, where I'd be sleeping now if, by happenstance, I hadn't agreed to visit Pearl's class in Newark. I lie on my back and gaze out the unfamiliar window. The colorless sky, neither starry nor hinting at dawn, is all I can see. It's a void. As my eyes adjust, I take in the boundaries of the room: shapes on the wall, maybe flowers, a fretwork of pattern; wallpaper. No curtains, not even a shade, no pictures hung. But according to Marinda, Dad's been here less than a week.

What a fluke not to have been in the city that I so rarely leave. Pearl had asked if I'd take the PATH out to Newark and help her run an improv workshop for the afternoon drama program she directs in a public school. "Shake 'em up a little," she said. "New faces'll do that." She couldn't pay me but promised to take me out for a nice dinner.

Pearl's kids were a shock to me, mostly because I spend no time with children. Middle-schoolers, these guys, and from the grim, military look of the school—this part not a shock—they were from families with few if any luxuries. I took one look and braced myself for resistance, backtalk, willful indifference. But they loved Pearl, they glowed with it, and when I entered the room (a small, improvised gym with chipped gray linoleum, windows blurred with abrasion), two dozen faces, all brown or black, some as dark as Pearl's, turned toward me without a catcall or even a sneer. I wasn't used to being the only white face in the room.

"So my chum here," Pearl said to her pupils, "is a fancy actor from the city, which normally would mean"—she poked me in the side—"we'd eat him for snack time, eh?" The children laughed and nodded.

"But let me tell you something max cool. He can do a double backflip, this fella." Whereupon Pearl crossed her arms and gave me a dare-you look. "Make space, my friends and collaborators." The children all stood and backed up against the windowed wall, whispering, poking, giggling.

I smirked at Pearl. But she was right. I could do that. For two summers in high school, I'd made money by clowning at children's parties. And I was an acrobatic clown, not just your average balloon-animal-making, yuck-yuck goofball clown. As I removed my jacket, I whispered to Pearl, "Wasn't part of the deal."

"Spontaneity, dearie," she whispered back.

I gauged the space I had, the clearance—well, there were basketball hoops—and launched myself. My body knows certain extravagant moves by heart, even though I hardly have occasion to deploy them these days. In the studio where I met Pearl, the teacher sniffed out my physical talents and exposed them. He compared me with Cary Grant, who'd left school at thirteen to juggle and walk on stilts. Pearl never lets me hear the end of that one. When I'm not Dearie, I'm Archie.

After my feat, Pearl's workshop was a cinch. We began by asking the children to share their family labels. The Smart One. The Smart-ass. Hermit. Possum. "Too Hot to Handle," said a tall, sassy boy; the girls erupted in squealing. Taco Man. Splendy Girl. The Rock. Predictably, the labels got wilder as they went along. Some were no doubt invented. It didn't matter.

The last to speak, a wiry girl with large deep-set eyes, said to Pearl, "How about you? What label are you?"

Pearl paused and then said, "Me? Plague Orphan. As good a label as any for me." No one laughed. "But true!" Her smile was wicked. "I'm a survivor of an epidemic. Long time ago now. Happy ending for me. And my friend here, let's just call him Tumbler, shall we?"

That was Pearl: blunt as an anvil. She'd been an infant when both of her parents died in a vicious wave of Ebola that swept through Congo; a Kenyan woman from Doctors Without Borders adopted her, raised her in Nairobi, and sent her off to Oxford. "Used up all my luck right then and there," she likes to say about her early rescue. "Now I watch my back." Pearl has the most beautiful British Empire accent I've ever heard, and it's nailed her a number of commercials for upper-crust commodities and causes, won her roles in a couple of plays. But still, like me, she's a long way from a foothold in the world we both burn to conquer.

She divided the children into groups of three and gave each group a situation they were to tackle, according to their labels: washed up on a desert island, sitting together on a train, waiting in line at a grocery. . . . I worked with half of them, Pearl with the rest. The noise level rose, but they were eager to please us. They paid attention to one another. I understood, by the end, why Pearl did something so challenging for so little money.

She walked me to the PATH, and we were discussing whether I could find the time to return for another visit—"They're crushed on you, my girls, that's plain as peas"—when we saw the newsfeed outside the station.

All trains were canceled in both directions, indefinitely. The PATH ran right below the site of the bombing.

Suddenly, in this dark unfamiliar room—and it makes me jump—Pearl speaks.

"Know what I'm thinking?" Her voice is muffled by her pillow.

I sigh. "No clue."

"Restitution," she says.

"We should really try to sleep. Our brains are amped out."

"But I can't. I started thinking, on the way, maybe time for me to go back."

"Back?"

"Back where I was born. Not Nairobi. Some village in Congo."

"You're a lunatic."

"That news to you, dearie?" She chuckles quietly. I can hear that she's shifted onto her back. And though I don't want to talk, least of all about dangerous schemes like joining the Corps and going to a war zone or a place of drought and famine, I'm glad to recognize the Pearl I know: impish, contrarian, provocative. Through the last leg of our journey, she was almost entirely silent. (So that's where she'd gone.)

"Maybe I'll go with you."

"You think I'm ribbing you," she says. "Finish the semester with my kids, I'll do that. But then: go."

"Maybe I'm serious, too," I say, though of course I'm not. Am I? "The wandering minstrel, I."

"Oh poofterman," she says warmly. "You'd be toast, you. With Marmite."

"You're probably right about that. But I can't bear losing you." Did I let that slip out?

She raises herself on an elbow to look at me. "Are you proposing?" She laughs, reaches across the space between our beds to pat my arm, and whispers, "Silly you." I think Pearl loves me as much as anyone can. Then, at last, we're quiet.

As I gladly, finally surrender to my exhaustion, I hear the suppressed murmurings of my father and Mrs. Tattersall. Footsteps approach the door to the room. Is Dad listening for my breathing, the way he used to do when I was small, lying sick in bed? Sometimes he'd wake me like that, without meaning to, in the middle of the night. Dad was always the tender parent, also the worrier. Mom was the demonstrative one, gestures large, gifts extravagant; losses of cool extravagant, too. What the hell has become of Mom? She sent me a vext that made her sound like a cult member: the cult of Tom Fucking Tattersall (my first sailing instructor; no wonder I never loved it). But even this sickening turn of thought—my mother's new, remote, ridiculous life—cannot reel me in from the briny depths of sleep.

I wake to Pearl's face, inches from mine. "Wherever *are* we?" she whispers. "What is this *place*?"

Something is tickling my chin. When I sit up abruptly, nearly conking heads with her, I see that she's holding a tiny white feather, probably leaked from one of our ancient pillows. As I lean back against the wall, she hands me a cup of coffee. She's wearing my long heavy sweater over her clothes. Someone's clearly sent it through a dryer, because it's warm to the touch.

"Your dad is making pancakes," she says, still whispering. "He said he's skipping work. I don't know him, but he's looking . . . purposeful."

I ask her what time it is; ten, she tells me.

"Oh God, what now?" I say.

"Vacation, I suppose. Thanks to your dad, I've phoned in a family emergency that gives me a couple of days off from school, but yes, what *was* the plan? I can't recall for the life of me."

Now I smell the pancakes, and I realize I'm famished. I have to eat before I can think. I brought us here to escape, to run away, but from what, precisely? Not like I hadn't seen the place I chose to live sprout explosions before.

I get up and pull on my jeans, which have also been sent through the dryer. They feel wonderful, but the shirt I'm wearing is thin and I'm still cold. All I have—minus the sweater poached by Pearl—is one of the quilts, which I drape over my shoulders. Somewhere, I shed a rain shell.

Dad's apartment is surprisingly bright by day, even a gray day, which makes it more pleasant and yet, with its worn-out floors and details revealed, also drearier than it seemed in the middle of the night.

Mrs. T appears to have left, her blankets folded neatly on one arm of the couch. (Is my old English teacher now my father's confidante? This is a mind-bender.)

"You gave me such a scare, not calling," says Dad. He's flipping pancakes.

Excuses useless, I tell him I'm sorry, but he's smiling at Pearl now, urging her to sit down; no, no help required. Please! All he wants is to feed us, to get us whatever we need. Anything at all. I take a good look at him while he can't look back. He's lost weight—not a bad thing—but is he grayer, too?

Three placemats lie on the small table I recognize from our upstairs porch. I mourn a little at the loss of that view: over my mother's garden, the distant harbor, bright stripes between a neighbor's trees. I wonder if I care more about losing that view, that house, than I am willing to admit. Vigil Harbor is a town toward which I claim to feel no nostalgia, no pull. I've always sworn I will not be your typical hometown revenant. I'm gone for good.

Once the three of us are seated, my father says to Pearl, "I'm glad you came along. I miss meeting my son's friends."

"My sad-sack fellow *artistes,* he means."

"Speak for yourself," says Pearl. "Likes to feel sorry for himself, doesn't he?" Her sidelong smile at me is a tease. She pours a lake of syrup onto a tall pile of pancakes. Pearl is one of those women who eats heartily but stays ethereally thin. ("My orphan soul," she said the first time I mentioned it. "Insatiably hungry.")

I decide not to rise to her bait. "So, Dad, *Mrs. Tattersall*? Isn't that, like, fraternizing with the enemy?"

"Oh, but she's the enemy of the enemy, isn't she, dearie?" says Pearl.

I haven't told her many details about my parents' split, so I wonder just how wide a range of subjects she covered with Dad while I was asleep. I suspect there will be no fudging about my current lack of roles or scanty wages.

"She pulled me out of my hellhole of self-pity," Dad says. He starts to say more but interrupts himself. "Pearl, can you stay awhile? Here, with Egon? With me? I'll give you my room."

"Dad, we really can't stay. We've both ditched out on our jobs, and it's not even as if the current catastrophe—"

"As if it's 'serious'? Is that what you're going to say?" Dad lays his fork and knife on his plate. "I want you to stay. Not go back. What if I said I need you?"

"Need me to what?" I will myself to speak softly.

"He needs you to be the good son," Pearl says, never one to repress her opinions. "Do the male kinship thing. Align your forces. Why not? You're between gigs. I mean, mostly."

I glare at her. I look at Dad. "What would I do here, Dad? What do you envision? Work as a bartender at The Jetty? Serve beers to my yacht-bro classmates from the High when they show up to slum it at the dartboard?"

Dad looks wounded. "Go back to school," he says. "You could teach. No matter what happens to our world, there will always be teachers."

In front of Pearl, I wouldn't dare say anything about how teaching—I assume he means teaching drama, to kids—is a comedown to me, a surrender to mediocrity. Call me vain or grandiose. Never mind that there are precious few teaching jobs of any substance in the arts these days, and none of them go to white men. Or maybe, as someone who still really reads—reads books—I could train and certify to teach world lit. I could step into Mrs. Tattersall's shoes.

Now both of them, my father and my best friend, regard me as if I'm in a game show and the answer I give will determine if I set off the bullhorn, score the bonus.

And then Dad says, "Or," pausing a long moment, "you and I could go into business."

"Dad?"

"I hear The Drome is going on the market," he says.

"The bowling alley? You want to run a bowling alley, Dad?"

Pearl says, "I've never bowled! Is it still open? I'd love to go. Let's go, dearie!"

I'm in an eyelock with my father, wondering just how far around the bend he's gone. Or has he become a morning drinker?

"No, of course not a bowling alley," he says. "Margo thought, well, why not a dinner theater? Like a . . ."

"A *cabaret,* Dad?" If he's not drunk, he's officially lost it.

"Remember how much people loved the old Pocket Theatre? Remember when your mother was in that Sondheim revue?"

"Oh Dad." I direct a silent plea toward Pearl, but she is concentrating on her pancakes. "Dad, that place closed."

"Not because people didn't love it. The town needed new office space."

"So maybe you and Margo should do it, if you really think . . . But, Dad, you're a scientist!"

"And maybe I'm done with science. Maybe this entire"—he sweeps his arms toward the ceiling—"this whole *rearrangement* is a message from the blighted cosmos." He has a slightly desperate look on his face, and I think of the last real conversation I had with my mother, a couple of months ago, when she complained that it was obvious Dad had lost faith in his work. "Being with your father these days," she said, "is like keeping company with a big dark cloud. It's not fun. It is far from fun."

I wondered, was that what their marriage had been based on? Fun? After all those years together? I had no idea what to say. Nor do I now.

Pearl is staring at me, except that I can't read her eyes.

"Enterprising idea, Archie, wouldn't you say?"

"For someone else, sure." I take my plate to the sink. Off to one side, I see my father's phone. It's dark, probably out of power—Dad used to make a point of letting it die for days at a time—but I imagine it still contains dozens of images from my childhood here in this town to which, there's no denying, so many people rebound despite vows to make a life out in the larger, less protected world. The revenants.

"Not for me," I say.

I think, for no clear reason, of my freshman year at the High, how it started with my arriving on crutches, my foot thickly bandaged from the terrible burn I suffered at a family picnic. The girls I knew from eighth grade fussed over me, carrying my books, opening doors, holding the elevator. But that attention earned me another kind. "Hey, Oedipus, how's the clubfoot? Mommy picking you up today?" snickered some random upperclassman in the lobby one morning. I was baffled.

The girl escorting me, though equally baffled by his remark, told me he was the captain of the lacrosse team. Within a few days, I found out that he was a royal asshole who got away with homophobic abuse by disguising his insults. He clearly had my number (a number I was still desperate to keep to myself).

Pretty quickly, friends of Captain Asshole would greet me in falsetto: "Hey, Oedipus, how's it hanging? Been to see the Oracle lately?"

I knew the myth, but none of it made sense till I realized that they were all in Mrs. Tattersall's class, the one she started off with Sophocles. I've avoided that play ever since.

I've also done my best to avoid everyone I knew in those days, making my trips back to this town fraught with the risk of involuntary reunions.

Dad is staring at me now, and so is Pearl.

"Look," I say. "Dad. Do you really think I could move back here and be happy? Think about it. I might end up leaving New York, but if I do, it will be to go somewhere else completely. Somewhere new."

"It's just that I . . ." He shuts his mouth, censoring himself.

"Worry about me? I know that, Dad. I can't stop you, though I wish I could."

Pearl is now looking at my father with obvious sympathy. He turns to her and says, "Your parents—they must worry about you being there, in New York. Your accent—I mean, you clearly didn't grow up there."

"My mum," says Pearl, "lives halfway around the world, and she has a job that makes mine look like quality control in a pillow factory."

Dad looks predictably confused.

"Doctors Without Borders," I say. "Danger's a workaday thing."

Pearl pats Dad on the shoulder. "Think how much less insomnia there'd be if people didn't have kids."

Politely, Dad laughs. "A world without kids? No thanks."

Pearl looks at me. "Tell your dad about my kids. Tell him how you kept them on their toes. You haven't seen the last of them, you know."

Connie

Mondays, I am on. We are making collages, and the first floor of my house smells like glue. I keep boxes of old magazines that I've salvaged from the transfer station. They turn up whenever a new generation cleans out the home of a grandparent who hoarded *National Geographic*s, *New Yorker*s, *Vogue*s, and *Time* magazines back when people read them as actual magazines.

Create the house of your dreams, I told the children. They are now in the phase of deep concentration, scissors snip-snip-snipping, faces pinched with the tension of fine motor work. Except for brief noises of frustration as they labor to place the pieces *just so,* they are immersed in a brief harmonious silence, so I steal away. Half an hour ago, while I watched the children set up their tables, I heard a news ping from somewhere beyond our yard, probably through an open window in another house. Rain is still falling, but it's coming down straight and gently, and the air is warm, so I've opened our windows, too.

I go into the living room and do the forbidden thing: take out my phone. Confirming my fears, another bomb. But this time, and my stomach lurches, it's Cambridge, less than an hour's drive away. Without sound, I have to go by visuals alone. Through a drone's view, I recognize the Charles River and then, a few blocks inland from Memorial Drive, the dark locus of mayhem: plumed smoke, the gyrating orange and blue lights of emergency vehicles speeding in from all directions. I wish I could call Celestino, who left earlier than usual for the second day in a row. We had a fierce but muted argument last night, about Ernesto—whose real name, I learned, is Arturo. Celestino tells me the man is an elaborate liar, and he still doesn't know why he turned up on our doorstep. He is, as I might have realized the moment I saw my husband's face when he walked into our kitchen Friday night, anything but a friend. Yet Celestino could have told me this that first night, even found a way to get me alone before we so much as shared a meal. Instead, he turned inward out of knee-jerk fear—fear that somehow seems to overrule his trust in me, despite all our years together.

"Connie!" one of the children calls out. "I'm done!"

I return to the porch. There is a clear divide between the children who have cut large swatches of color and slapped together a blocky assemblage and those who, tongues poised between teeth, shoulders hunched, have approached the picture surgically, scissors working the glossy pages like scalpels, their imagined houses made of curlicues, thumbnails, slivers of paper in subtle variations of color whose original contexts are indecipherable.

I hand fresh sheets of paper to the two boys who've completed their houses (having cut out literal doors and windows from pictures of actual houses). "Now your dream garden," I say. "And don't just look for pictures of flowers and trees. Make your flowers out of . . . cars, boats, women's dresses. . . ." Make sunflowers from explosions, I think. Make lilacs from skies raining purple steel debris.

So I am marooned. But if the news is bad enough (is there such a thing as "sort of bad" news?), other parents will show up to retrieve their children and take them home . . . to, as the authorities like to say, shelter in place.

If the day proceeds as planned, Axel, who's teaching history after lunch, will arrive in an hour. Maybe he'll take me aside and fill me in. Sometimes I am comforted by the cocoon we maintain in this house. Other times I feel suffocated, terrified of what I'm missing, ashamed that I have been brainwashed by the urge for so-called *connectivity.* Are we hypocrites to think we can spare our children the high-tech compulsions we claim to despise—or, at best, postpone them? What good will it do them if they are "behind" their instinctively wired peers?

I visit each child and ask questions, ration out praise. Raul, who has stockpiled magazine pages dense with blues and greens, tells me he's making a jungle house. "A house made OF the jungle," he declares. "Dad's jungle. Like the walls are leaves."

Jungles were part of what we discussed on Saturday night, when Ernesto, as he promised, made us dinner: grilled leeks, peppers, and squashes with a rich chili sauce and brown rice with nuts. It was good, but too spicy for me. He told us that he hasn't eaten meat or fish in ten years, so he concentrates on his sauces. (Are we aware that if cattle were a country, they would constitute the third-largest emitter of greenhouse gases?)

The three of us stood around the fire in the yard. We often cook in a stone hearth that Celestino built at the back, beyond the tree. He built it with a chimney that captures the sparks and directs the smoke toward open sky.

"I have embraced the nomadic life my work demands," said Ernesto, over the sizzle of the grill, "but I must admit, this is a life anyone could sanely embrace. Your life."

"Sanely?" I laughed, though I felt his condescension.

"Not everyone can take the sane path," he said. "Or maybe what I mean is that there is another kind of sanity, which obligates you to take on all the *in*sanity. Confront it. Do battle." He brandished the spatula at Celestino as if it were a saber. His earring flashed in the firelight.

"What, like this group that bombed New York, the Oceloti?" I said. The escalation of the group's tactics was nearly the only topic in that day's news; how a quasi-covert operation known for demonstrations, for costly but nonlethal trespass and sabotage, had turned terrorist.

"Well, why not?" said Ernesto.

"Because killing people proves nothing, accomplishes nothing!" I said. "Extremism always leads to alienation. Violence to more violence. I don't care how 'worthy' the cause is."

"Extreme action is the only answer to extreme urgency, the urgency of survival. You have a child. Isn't that urgent to you?" He turned to the fire, using tongs to rearrange and flip the vegetables.

I did not know what to say, but when Ernesto's attention returned to me, he was smiling warmly. "And speaking of this child, where is our young man Raul?"

"Taking time off from our very sane life," said Celestino.

I was puzzled when he came home without Raul. He told me that when they returned to town and dropped Brecht at his house, Miriam invited Raul to stay.

"Did Brecht want that? He has better things to do than entertain a little boy—a little monkey—all night." I had grown to like and trust Brecht, though back when Celestino had agreed to hire him, a favor to Austin, I was unhappy. I knew his story. How could such trauma leave anyone capable of hard, dependable work? All I want is for Celestino to remain as admired and in demand as he has been for the past few years. *Above reproach.* Because even I sometimes worry that it could come to an end, his luck at having missed deportation before our marriage. He had a sponsor in the amnesty—the older man he cared for in this house, before I came—yet we've all read about marriages split by tightened rules of documentation. To become a citizen, Celestino must wait his turn in the ever-lengthening queue.

"So maybe the vanishing jungles seem too far away for you to see them as urgent," Ernesto said. "But the rising sea level, surely this concerns you. Of course, your little town is fortunate, up here on your cliffs. You buy an extra century, don't you? Before the waves lap at your doorstep."

"Everyone's concerns are our concerns," I said. "That's what we teach our children. It's not as if life stops at our borders. Our town line."

"But doesn't it? Please. You are a bubble within a bubble within a bubble. Your town, your state, your country—for now, here you are sitting pretty. You won the geopolitical lottery. And it's human nature to protect your winnings, whether you deserve them or not."

"Gloucester didn't win the lottery," I said, wondering if Ernesto would know this bit of bad news, issued just the month before.

"Coastal triage is one of the most sensible things your government's done. Facing reality. At a conference I attended last month, there was a talk called 'Listening to the Hurricane.' Standing room only."

"What do you mean, 'my' government? Yours, too, isn't it?"

"Touché," he said. "Yes. I am a citizen. Though as I said, the home of my heart is elsewhere. I am a spiritual expatriate wherever I go. But I have no right to complain." Every few minutes, I heard the subdued signaling of his phone in the back pocket of his jeans. Someone had been trying to reach him for half an hour or more.

I glanced at Celestino. He is never talkative, but he is not without strong opinions on matters related to the natural world. His arms were folded, his expression hard to read. I moved closer to him and ran a hand over his shoulder blades. He did not react. Suddenly, he said to Ernesto, "You leave tomorrow?"

Ernesto did not look up from the grill. "Would one more day be inconvenient? I'll stay out of the way, especially when school's in session." He gave me a quick smile. "I can't sing for my supper, but I can cook yours. And I could tutor!"

"It is not convenient, no. This is a demanding week for me," said Celestino. He added tersely, "Sorry."

"But it's supposed to rain nearly every day," I said. Why was I arguing? Was I enjoying the way in which this guest quietly insulted my life? Though that isn't how I saw it. I think I wanted to be asked to account for myself. I had been complicit in creating the smallest of the bubbles he was mocking.

Celestino frowned at me. "Rain doesn't bring my work to a stop."

Ernesto jumped in. "So then, put me to work. You know my talents."

"I do," Celestino said quietly.

Ernesto turned to me and said, "He knows how soft I've grown, and he's right." He held up his hands. "No calluses."

After the vegetables were cooked, Ernesto excused himself to answer some calls, walking around the side of the house toward the street. I carried the food to the kitchen and set the table. Celestino stayed outside, to extinguish the coals. It was dark, and he worked by the light of a portable lantern, but I stood at the windowed wall of the porch and watched him, his darting shadow.

My husband came to this country, as a young teenager, from a village in the Petén—now there is a place from his past I will definitely never see—but the way he arrived was unconventional. His father was the foreman at an archaeological excavation, and he made himself indispensable to the Harvard professor who supervised the work. This was more than forty years ago, when borders between countries, at least in this hemisphere, were easier to cross, so when the archaeologist offered to take Celestino for a school year in the States, his father was ecstatic.

Enrolled in a program for international students, Celestino was, I imagine (but would never say), a kind of trophy for the professor. This is not how Celestino sees it—the professor was a second father to him, and he remains only grateful—yet I envision this esteemed intellectual (a Frenchman, no less!) taking magnanimous, secretly egotistical pride at his dinner parties whenever he introduced to his fellow academics this boy from the jungle, one he had chosen to bring to his grand house off Brattle Street, to bestow with his privilege, endow with the chance of a far more civilized, prosperous life. And look how aware his own children would become of the world beyond their privet hedge! What was another mouth to feed, another set of books and shoes to buy?

Yet other than the few years of education he had, along with his good English (hardly trivial), a smattering of French is all that Celestino seems to have retained from the time he lived with that family. The professor died suddenly in the third year Celestino was staying in his home—and somehow, the boy did not return to the jungle, where his village had been overrun by brutal soldiers and his father had disappeared. After a conflict with the professor's widow—who could not cope with this extra child—Celestino panicked and fled to New York City, to relatives he hardly knew.

When Celestino told me this story—in his succinct, unembellished way—we were just coming to know each other, just emerging from a nearly wordless sexual fever that had possessed us both for a period of weeks, our middle-of-the-night meetings constrained, on his side, by the work he did all day, seven days a week, and, on my side, by caring for my mother as her chemotherapy intensified its attack on her body, its rogue side effects sending me with her to the ER at least once a week. My old friend Harold had called me, a month into my stay, to ask if I was in the witness protection program. I told him I didn't know when I'd return. I said nothing about Celestino. Could I say, in the midst of this life-outside-my-life, that I was falling in love? And was I?

Compared with the circumstances of my life until then—maybe with the exception of my losing a brother to a meaningless war—those of Celestino's life, or the ones he chose to share with me, were hazardous and shifting, at least until he'd found his way to Vigil Harbor. But it took my asking question after question to learn what I did, because Celestino is not a man who thinks that thorough knowledge of a person's history, much less his or her emotional "journey," equates with greater trust or deeper love. He does not dissect or dwell on feelings, so I find myself interpreting, filling in blanks—to the extent that sometimes I wonder if I've merely imagined parts of his past.

A few years ago, when I asked him questions about his mother that he was clearly reluctant to answer, he told me that he didn't start leading a life with true direction until the day we decided that we would become parents together. He had his business, but that, he said, was just his form of survival. Even his coming to this town was a matter of survival, not choice.

I thought that the years he'd told me the least about were the ones he spent in New York, after his rash flight from Cambridge. From his late teens to his early twenties, he'd lived with relatives and worked, at first, in the most menial jobs: janitor, busboy, plumber's assistant. His first job at Wave Hill did not pay well, but he'd lucked into a boss who became a mentor, the kind of boss who takes a shine to workers who want to learn. Going online, I had seen pictures of Wave Hill: its formal flower beds and vista of river, its trellised avenues of blossoming vines. Celestino told me that it was the happiest work he'd known before finding a way to work for himself.

On a gamble, however, he'd returned to Massachusetts, where he'd heard it was safer to live and work under the radar, taking jobs where documentation was beside the point, even unwanted. Qualifications were the ability to work hard and never complain when asked to keep long, unreasonable hours, not to care about luxuries like insurance and overtime pay. To see yourself as lucky and therefore grateful. He had settled into regular work on a landscaping crew in a wealthy suburb of Boston, making enough money to take night classes that trained him as an arborist. There, he also met the older man who bought our house and invited Celestino to live with and care for him—and to build the tree house I could see from my childhood bedroom.

I knew all this when I moved in with him, when he still rented this house from the daughter of the older man, who'd passed away. But about Ernesto—Arturo—I had heard nothing. That, as it turned out, was a chapter my husband had omitted from his story. Of course, very soon after I moved in, my accidental pregnancy turned our attention, in an instant, from the past to the future. As if someone had snapped up a window shade in a darkened room, we had to face what we were doing, our intentions as well as our feelings, in the full light of day. We had decisions to make, and the first—because I knew I'd keep that baby, no matter what—was to agree on what promises we were willing to risk.

Once we sat down to eat the meal Ernesto had cooked us, he turned his attention to me. He wanted to know about the years I'd spent in Michigan—a place where, growing up in Chicago, he'd gone two or three times for summer camp.

Yet again, however, as we discussed attractions like the Art Institute and the Chicago theater scene—though, he pointed out, who could ignore those record-breaking heat waves?—I was struck by the broad gulf between how the two men at the dinner table had spent their boyhoods. And when Ernesto alluded to having attended Harvard, I looked at my husband's face. Was this a connection somehow, beyond their time at Wave Hill? That Celestino had lived in the home of a Harvard professor? Had Ernesto been a student of the professor? No, of course not; the timing was all wrong. Ernesto was younger than Celestino and would have been a schoolboy himself.

He asked how we had founded our little school, and I told him about the perils of public school: the attrition of playtime and art, the scarcity of books, the extreme reliance on technology. More than reliance, immersion.

"Aha! You speak of your *own* rebellion against extremes."

"Yes, but that doesn't mean we plan on blowing up the elementary school."

"Fair enough. Schools, even inferior schools, should be sacred ground."

"They should." I thought of my brother's tree at the High. That ground was probably as sacred as any patch of turf could be to a heretic like me.

When Ernesto produced the flan he had made for dessert, Celestino announced that he had to turn in. He wanted to visit a site in the early morning, when the forecast promised a break in the rain. I learned long ago never to complain if he chose to work on Sundays. After all, we didn't go to church. Since Mom's memorial service, I hadn't set foot once in the place where she had been a faithful congregant and tried to do good deeds that, as Ernesto preached, embraced the urgent needs of the wider world. What would Mom say to Ernesto's radical sense of mission? I felt a surge of missing her, missing my parents' because-we-say-so certainties and liberal-side-of-the-picket-fence values. And then I thought of Caleb, and I felt a parallel surge of rage at what Ernesto saw as "my" government and its own increasingly paranoid certainties and principles, braided into law.

Left alone with Ernesto, I wished I could make my own excuses. I'd had a long day, putting in my hours at the farm, weeding in the mud, but how could I refuse to share the flan? It was soothing, the perfect end to a spicy meal, and I made small talk about the ingredients (his "secret stash" of vanilla beans, some of which he always carried with him). But at the first silence, he said, "I will leave Monday morning, and I thank you for putting up with me. Tomorrow I promise to make myself scarce."

"You're welcome," I said. I was tempted to apologize for Celestino's sullen behavior, but I had a feeling that's what he hoped for, and my enthusiasm for his charms had waned. Armchair anarchists come cheap.

He claimed my gaze, however, and said, "Your husband has mixed feelings about our past."

"He's been preoccupied with work. It's a busy time." I added, "Which is good."

"He should, and does, resent how much was given to me by the circumstances of fortune," Ernesto said emphatically. I wondered if it was a statement he routinely deployed as a shield. "But in my work, I offer dividends on that good fortune—to others."

"To Celestino?" I said before I could help myself.

"Oh, there was a time." He shifted in his chair. "Did he tell you we worked together on the first tree house he built? Before this one." A nod toward the window.

"No. Where was that? Wave Hill? You built one there?"

"No," he said. "Years later. In Matlock."

Matlock was the town outside Boston where Celestino had found safe if backbreaking work when he returned to Massachusetts, a town wealthy enough that its residents can afford to be progressive, pro-tax in their politics. Nowadays, they are the most idealistic of all the Timers, the ones who wrote eye-popping checks for Kittredge's presidential campaign.

"He knew you there, too?" I was confused; something didn't fit. Ernesto had never, I was sure, been a day laborer, standing by the side of the road, waiting to be picked up almost at random.

"It's a sore spot with him. Which is why I didn't bring it up."

All Celestino had said of his few years on that landscaping crew in Matlock was that it had been monotonous, exhausting, and lonelier than his years in New York, but the money had been better.

I knew he'd had a callous, racist boss. He'd felt powerless, sometimes angry. But being there had led him here, hadn't it?

"That wasn't a good time for him," I said to Ernesto.

"Certainly not. He nearly landed in jail."

Had I heard him correctly? But he was an enunciator, this man. "Jail?"

"I've said too much. That isn't my story to tell, and I'm not surprised if he's chosen to keep it to himself. But it's well in the past, and he is fine now!"

"*Jail?* What are you telling me?"

"Connie, I'm sorry. Sometimes I open my mouth and . . . out come things I should not share. I was foolish to think he'd be happy to see me. Unfortunate memories, I think, have eclipsed that earlier time when we felt like comrades."

I'd had only one glass of wine, or I might have been certain that my thinking, my perception, was warped by alcohol. "You told me that for a reason," I said. "You knew I didn't know."

"No, Connie, that is not the case. It's not. Forgive me."

I took my empty plate to the sink. What was happening? While I stood there, pretending to fuss over rinsing the dishes stacked in the sink, Ernesto came up beside me, reached around, and placed his dish on top of mine. His hand brushed my wrist.

I turned off the water and returned to the table, but I did not sit. "I don't know why you're here." My voice shook. "I think you should leave tomorrow. Find somewhere else to stay, even if your friend is still delayed."

"I'm so sorry. I didn't mean—"

"It doesn't matter what you meant. Or didn't. I'm . . ." I was about to say that I was confused, but I didn't want to admit uncertainty. All at once, Celestino's fears, which sometimes bled into his dreams—fears of losing his right to live here, of being "taken away," fears I tried to laugh off as kindly as I could—washed over me as well. I felt ashamed of being taken in by this man; were his good looks, eloquence, and flattery all it took to charm me? Did I, as a white woman with her safe countercultural ideals, see him as some kind of clever "model" for Raul, my brown son?

He was looking at me with what I now saw as a postured sorrow. Whatever his motives, he was a good actor. I tried to hold his eyes but found myself looking at his earring, the dark red stone I'd noticed when he showed up on my doorstep. It looked precisely like a drop of blood.

"So then," he said, "yes, I will go in the morning. I will be sorry not to have said goodbye to Raul."

Had he read my mind?

"I wish only the best for all of you," he said.

"Thank you," I said. "I am going to bed now. Please leave the dishes. Leave everything. If I hear the water running, I will come back down and stop you."

Without waiting for him to answer, I rushed up the stairs, so fast I nearly tripped. I felt myself blushing so violently that my face burned. Shame and anger together are potent. I sat on the bed, in the dark, next to Celestino. It took me a moment to realize he wasn't sleeping.

"Who is he?" I whispered. "Why did you leave me with him?"

"I'm sorry." Celestino sat up and put his arms around me.

"You're afraid of him." I switched on my reading lamp, to see his face. "You are, aren't you? Well, he's leaving in the morning. I told him to."

Celestino reached across me and turned the lamp off. "I will tell you everything after he is gone."

"About your almost going to jail?" I whispered sharply.

"Yes," he said. "Yes, that."

I wanted to shock him, but of course he'd been listening to every word I exchanged with the man who now had the first floor of my house to himself. There wasn't much he could destroy or steal. I had never felt so relieved that my child was elsewhere. Had he been here, I'd have had to leave the house myself, take him away.

Out the bedroom window, I saw the kitchen light, or its illumination of the great tree, switch off. I heard Ernesto's footsteps travel the hall to our living room.

To my surprise, I slept. We both did. And yesterday morning, when I went downstairs, he was gone. No note, nothing left behind. Only the dishes in the sink were proof of the night before. I rolled up the sleeves of my nightgown and washed them.

We are pinning the collages on the corkboard, standing back to admire them, when I hear a knock on the front door. Axel doesn't have to knock when he's showing up to teach, but perhaps he needs help carrying something. If by some chance it's "Ernesto" again, I will refuse to let him in.

It's Brecht. "Are the two of you back for lunch?" I ask. Celestino must be in the driveway.

"He didn't need me today. He's with Austin. Are you . . ." He peers around me. "You're busy with school."

"It's art day, so I'm on, but come in. You're wet."

Brecht is dressed in jeans and a plain dark blue T-shirt, no jacket to shield him from the rain. He's carrying a flat package wrapped in plastic, and he's shivering.

"Please come in now," I say when he hesitates. "Let me get you something dry to wear." I bring him into the kitchen, where Raul nearly pounces on him. I order Brecht to sit and Raul to return to the classroom.

"Everybody," I say to the children, "make sure all your houses are pinned to the board, and please clean up all your scraps from the floor. I mean *all* of them, even the teeny tiny ones." I tell Raul to get out the bin for paper, which we will pulp for a future art project. One of the school's stated objectives is to generate little to no waste. Food scraps go to compost, worn-out clothes to the Restitution Corps, broken pencils to the chipping machine at the transfer station, to be made into particleboard.

Upstairs, I take a clean T-shirt from my husband's dresser, a flannel shirt from our closet, a towel. Back in the kitchen, I hand them to Brecht, who looks frozen to the bone. I tell him to go into the bathroom and dry off his hair, warm his hands in the sink.

I hear Axel enter the house, calling out, "History's here, like it or not!" A few of the children issue mock groans. Axel is the most popular father, an exuberant bear of a man, towering and broad with dark rebellious hair, both tirelessly funny and impossibly patient. He is a manufacturing efficiency consultant who, according to his wife, does most of his work with distant clients in the middle of the night. She has learned to sleep through conferences during which her husband does nothing to suppress his brawling laughter.

Axel is teaching our children about the Renaissance in Europe—and, simultaneously, the colonization and brutal conquest of the New World. The Yin Yang of Western Civ, he calls it. In fact, he discusses the notion of civilization itself, what it means not just to be civilized but to be civil, to be a *good civilian.* Not the same thing, but they should be!

I realize that there will be no time for a side conversation about Axel's take on the news, especially with Brecht in the house.

As I oversee the cleanup, and as Axel takes books and maps from his satchel, I hear talking in the bathroom. I go to the door. I hear Brecht say, "Don't argue with me. She'll know what to do with it. She's an artist. Or she used to be."

"Brecht? Do you need anything?"

"I'm fine," he says.

A moment later, he emerges, Celestino's flannel shirt drooping on his bony frame. I resist my motherly urge to straighten the shoulders. He holds his damp T-shirt in one hand, the plastic package in the other. The towel I gave him is folded neatly and balanced on the lip of the sink; somehow, this reassures me.

"Axel, sandwiches are all made, in the fridge," I say. "Would you mind giving them lunch?"

"Go ahead, exploit me!" he proclaims, once again making the children laugh.

I take Brecht's T-shirt from him, spread it over the back of a kitchen chair, and tell him to follow me. "Take off your shoes. No, don't worry about the water. The children track everything everywhere when it rains. I just worry your feet will freeze."

He sits on the one unupholstered chair in the living room and does as I've told him. He sets his sneakers, which he's worn without socks, neatly paired on the floor beside him. His bare feet are rosy from the cold. He sits up straight, holding his package across his lap. He must have dried it off with the towel. At first, he just looks at me, as if I am about to interview him for a job.

"What do you have there?" I ask.

"This belongs to Austin, or I guess it does, and maybe I shouldn't take it from the house, but can I show it to you?"

"What is it?"

"Can we go upstairs?" he asks.

"Why upstairs?"

"It's big. I need to unfold it somewhere, not on the floor. Like, on a bed."

I hear Axel talking in his theatrical teacher voice. He is telling stories about Florence and the Borgias, about Leonardo da Vinci. I wonder briefly about the suitability of the Borgias for third graders, but our philosophy is not to think in terms of a conventional education. Another of our objectives: protect but never patronize.

Brecht stares at me, earnest, silent, expectant.

"Okay. Upstairs then."

I don't believe that stars influence our destiny, I'm not at all superstitious, yet as I think about the past few days, I'm uneasy. I feel as if something uncanny is brewing, the way some people feel an approaching storm in their joints.

I lead Brecht into my bedroom, glad that my husband turned me into someone who makes the bed every morning.

Brecht stands at the foot of the bed and stares at it.

"Brecht, are you sure you're all right?"

This, I realize, is a stupid question to ask someone who may, in general, be far from all right, but he seems to ignore my question, or maybe it reminds him to act. He sets his package on the quilt and gently removes one plastic bag from inside another. From that one he removes what looks like a thick pad of paint-stained linen. It looks like a used drop cloth. I stand back as he unfolds it, revealing, by increments, a wildly colorful painting.

It covers nearly the entire mattress. He stands back and looks at me.

"Brecht, where did this come from?"

"In my room. Old stuff. Defunct stuff. In a drawer."

Whatever he means, I don't probe. I lean over and examine the painting. It's a complicated, painstakingly rendered underwater landscape, ink and . . . gouache or tempera. The cloth backing is thick but unprimed, so the colors are held in the weave of the fabric, like dye. I spot lines of cracking here and there, but otherwise it's in fine shape. "Austin made this painting?"

"No," he says. "No, I think someone gave it to him. Someone who wanted to, like, haunt him."

"Why do you think that, Brecht?" I notice that he's faintly shaking. "Honey? I don't think you're okay. And I think you're cold." I go to the closet and pull an old sweatshirt off the shelf. When I turn around, Brecht sits cross-legged on the floor.

"I'm going to call your mother."

"Don't do that, please. She's working. It's her busy day. It's just me and Noam at home, and we're fine. What I just want is . . . is I want you to tell me if I'm right about this painting. That it's brilliant. Max genius, if you don't read the curse. Like, it should be in a museum."

I have no idea what he means about a curse, but in the long, hollow pause during which I pretend to be further admiring the painting, I do recognize the name of the Vigil Harbor boy who was killed in that bombing, the one that Brecht survived.

"But you're right I'm not totally fine," he says. "This one was too close."

Downstairs, laughter. Axel's voice raised; a phrase from Shakespeare?

I drape the sweatshirt over Brecht's shoulders. I get down on the floor and sit facing him. At least he's stopped shaking.

"Okay," I say calmly. "First, yes, this picture is *absolutely* brilliant. You're right. I don't know why it was stored away. Did you ask Austin?" I don't really care about the painting, but I have to get Brecht to let me call his mother.

But then he says, "Raul is the one who found it. He didn't mean to be nosy. And I'm glad he found it."

He sounds anything but glad. He sounds incapable of glad.

I wish Celestino were here, and I wonder where he's gone, why he didn't need Brecht today. I also wish I could be alone, just to think about what he told me about Arturo, our deceitful guest, about the heedless way in which he'd once put Celestino in danger. Others were caught in the fallout, too, but none of them stood to lose as much as Celestino. Everything feels skewed, shadowed, tinged with threat. I recall seeing on the calendar this morning that it's a full moon.

"How would Raul have found it?"

"When we were drawing," says Brecht. "Saturday night . . . but it doesn't matter. I mean, it's okay. Forget I told you that part. About Raul."

Again I look at the painting, as if it might help me out. It's hard, actually, to look away from it. It's really something. It has the primal, uninhibited verve of what used to be called "outsider art." Anti-institutional, some scholars called it. Renegade. As if making art outside the old-school traditions, outside a studio or an academy, was an act of defiance.

"Honey," I say, "I don't know what I can tell you about this except that you're right: it's brilliant. What do you want to do with it? How can I help you?"

We are still seated on the floor. Brecht's shoulders are caved forward, as if he might curl into a ball. He's looking into his lap, not at me. Celestino has made me comfortable with shared silences, but this one feels fraught.

"They're putting cops at the town line," he says. "Every town is."

I consider this. It doesn't seem out of the question. "Where did you hear that?"

"Mom. Mom was talking to Petra Coyle this morning."

I have no idea who he means, but I worry that asking him may fray his nerves further. Instead, I ask him if he's hungry and tell him I have extra sandwiches.

"I should go," he says.

"I think you should stay. And I'm getting you a sandwich. I'll bring it up. Just hang here." I try to think of a project for which I could ask his help. I know how much he looks up to my husband, and I suspect he'll do anything I ask.

But my true aim in going downstairs is to call Celestino. If there are cops at the town line, he will already know this—and he knows most of our cops by name—but I need to know where he is.

Typically, maddeningly, he doesn't answer. In the kitchen, I look into the classroom and wave at Axel before I put together a tray of food for Brecht. I remind myself that if anything worse has happened in the wider world, anything local, parents would have shown up.

Just as I begin to go upstairs, I feel my pocket vibrate. I duck into the living room; it's Harold. I text him that I can't talk but that we're all fine. Yes, it's terrible. It's beyond terrible. It occurs to me that I do know a few people who work in Cambridge.

In the bedroom, Brecht hasn't moved. I set the tray in front of him and decide that the best thing I can do is buy time. I say, "So Celestino texted me to say he'll need your help unloading the truck in a couple of hours. Why don't you just stick around? Tell your mom you'll be here for dinner."

He nods, and—this fills me with illogical relief—he reaches for the sandwich.

I turn to the painting. It reminds me of an exhibit I saw in Boston a long time ago—before Dad and Caleb were gone—of pictures made by a nun in Mississippi in the 1950s. They were townscapes, furious with detail, in saturated colors. You could hardly have counted the windows, doors, even individual bricks on the buildings, their outlines in spidery black ink that crisscrossed the scenes like complex math problems, formulas you'd see on blackboards in old movies about astronauts and scientists. The convent community, I read in one of the captions, unwittingly sheltered the nun from the worst effects of what was clearly—in hindsight—a consuming mental obsession. The art she made was the obsession reaching for a language. She lived into her eighties and made more than a thousand pictures, which the other sisters hung in their rooms. After the art-making nun died, someone pointed an art dealer toward the trove of strange, fabulous art treasured but sequestered in the convent. He "discovered" it and made a deal with the mother superior that reroofed the convent and pointed all its bricks.

Madness transformed, through art, into money in service of religion. Some would see that as a circle closing back on itself. No wonder the world is imploding.

Yesterday morning, in the kitchen, I finally got Celestino to talk. He had retrieved Raul from Brecht's house, and when they got home, we allowed Raul an hour of his noisy game to buy ourselves guaranteed privacy. As we spoke in low voices, we could hear him engaging in militaristic maneuvers, all virtual, over our heads. During our silences, which were frequent, we might hear him shout "Yes!" or "Target achieved, enemy disarmed and prisoners secured!" He often reads the endgame messages aloud from the screen.

"Just tell me that whatever happened back then wasn't violent and no one died," I said the minute we sat down. "This was in Matlock, right? When you worked for that bigoted asshole?"

"No one died. There was a fire that destroyed a house," Celestino said. "An accident. But I will get to this part later."

Celestino told me that Arturo had never, to his knowledge, been at Wave Hill, or they had not been there together. That part of the story was a blatant lie. I gasped. "What the hell? How could you—"

"But it is true that I knew him," Celestino said sharply.

He had met Arturo Cabrera thirty years ago, not in New York but when Celestino was on the landscaping crew in Matlock. They met when Arturo, a student at Harvard, was enlisted to build a tree house—ancestor to the one in our yard—along with a classmate. The classmate's grandfather owned the tree, and Celestino worked on the surrounding yards and gardens.

"So the liar did go to Harvard?" I laughed quietly. That part I'd have pegged as a certain lie.

Celestino's look warned me to listen. "Percy was the grandfather of Arturo's friend. Percy owned the tree. That is how I met Percy. I met them, Arturo and Percy, at the same time. Building that tree house." He sighed. "We were friendly, all of us. And yes, with Arturo, there was between us this shared . . . There was Guatemala."

"But wait. Percy?" This, too, was a shock. Percy was the man who'd brought Celestino here, to keep him company, before I entered the picture. Percy's dishes are the ones we eat from every day; some of his furnishings still occupy our rooms. By the time I met Celestino, Percy had gone to live with his daughter. My mother had met him, but I never did. After Mom died, I sold her house and bought this one from the daughter. We could have moved into the house where I grew up—but it was also where Caleb had grown up. And we couldn't have taken the tree house with us.

"Why didn't I know this? Any of this?" I said.

"No need."

"No need of what?"

"For you to know."

"But you—you could have had a criminal record, for—what? Reckless destruction of property? Arson? What *happened*?"

"Arturo and his friends were in a student group with a political message. They wanted to make a demonstration at a big party given by rich people, to shame them in a public way. It got out of hand."

"You mean they willfully wrecked people's lives, somebody's home, for some juvenile political cause."

"The cause wasn't childish," Celestino said.

I remembered, from my own time in college, all the flyers on the bulletin boards, all the demonstrations against fossil fuel investment, against new wars, against the revival of the KKK, against discrimination of so many kinds. All the righteous anger that boiled over and ultimately turned to vapor, either because it came to feel futile or because we were distracted by the pressures of becoming adults. I felt my own righteous anger that Celestino had been an unwitting accomplice to such youthful acting out.

Had Percy been drawn in, too? "Is that how you came to live with Percy? Because that house—his house in Matlock—burned down?"

Slowly, Celestino shook his head.

"Then what? Christ, can you give me an inch?"

"It wasn't his house, the one that burned down. But . . ." Celestino sat across from me at the table, and now he gazed at the ceiling.

"But what?"

"It was the house next door to his. I was trusted to take care of it while the owner was gone. Her plants and her cat. A house older than this one. A house like a museum." He paused. "Arturo tricked me into showing him the house, taking him inside. I was stupid."

"So Arturo burned the house down."

"Yes. But he did not mean to."

"And they didn't catch him?" As if the answer weren't obvious.

"He disappeared. Left the country." Celestino swept an arm abruptly through the air. "And Percy's grandson, Arturo's friend—we were both in trouble. Involved."

I could piece the story together now. But I laughed at the thought of some rich Harvard student being in serious trouble. No, my husband—the "undocumented immigrant," as the liberals in Matlock would have oh-so-correctly put it—would have been the one to take the fall.

But what I felt right then wasn't sympathy. "What else? What else have I missed?" I no longer bothered to lower my voice. "Or do you *in fact* have a criminal record out there, just waiting to be unearthed? Just what, *exactly,* brought you here?"

Was my husband a fugitive? Like a car without brakes, my mind veered wildly through a series of hysterical questions: Were Celestino's fears of losing this life of ours legitimate? Was the name I knew him by his actual name? What about Percy and his daughter? I'd never met her, either, though her name was on the documents transferring this house to my ownership. Maybe she wasn't the esteemed doctor Celestino had told me she was.

"Percy," Celestino said quietly. "Percy brought me here. With his grandson."

"Like he owned you?" Hearing my words, I said, "Oh God."

He glared at me the same way he'd glared at Arturo.

"Oh God," I said again, but this time it was because Raul stood in the doorway, probably drawn away from his game by my raised voice.

"I came down for my charger," he said. He had probably taken it to Brecht's, and it was in his pack on the coatrack in the hall.

Celestino walked past Raul, briefly laying a palm on his son's shoulder. "I must check something," he said, and he went out the front door.

Numbly, I watched Raul reach into his pack and shove things around until he found what he was looking for.

I was sure Celestino would be gone for hours, but he came back in five minutes.

"I had to check the cellar," he said. "Arturo hid in a cellar. In Matlock."

I just stared at him.

"He is gone. I hope for good." He returned my stare, but his look had softened. "Everything I told you is true. And most of what he said to you, not true."

"Why did he show up here?"

"I do not know," said Celestino. "But I did what I thought I had to do to keep him from hurting us. I am sorry if you don't agree."

He wasn't going to embrace me or tell me he loved me, and I knew that what had just happened in our house, my letting that man into our lives, was as much my fault as Celestino's. Maybe more. "I'm so sorry," I said, but Celestino was already leaving again.

It's while I help Axel and the children clean up the classroom and put away supplies that Brecht slips out of the house, because when I go back upstairs, where I left him on the small sofa by the window in my bedroom, he's no longer there. I see the tray on the floor, half of the sandwich untouched. The vast picture of life beneath the sea still blankets my bed, but Brecht, like Arturo, is gone. And where, oh where, is my husband?

Petra

This is risky. No. More like certifiably insane. But if the man chooses to hide his past from me—I even wonder if he's *onto* me, or at least onto my wholesale fakery—then it's time to act boldly. I hear Carly asking me just what exactly I hope to accomplish. She might question whether what I really want, more than anything else, is to confront and shame him, this coldhearted jackal—and would that satisfy me? But no, I tell Carly, her posthumous avatar, what I want is just to *find out.* Find out what really happened to her. Issa's story is part of mine, and I cannot stand stories without endings.

They do not lock their back door. Miriam actually mentioned this fact when I was with her in the kitchen after dinner and she let the dog out. "I don't think I've laid eyes on the key for years," she said. So trusting!

But the dog. I forgot about the dog.

I am standing in the middle of the sidewalk, my umbrella laughably inadequate, when I remember the damn dog. So, fine, if the dog barks, I'll flee. She's a nice creature, so I doubt she'll take a chomp of my ankles.

As I said, risky ground. Wet ground, too, with the water table clearly rising, though at least I am wearing my rain boots (a birthday present from Carly, inside each one a teeny box containing a pearl earring). At breakfast, looking out the window of the inn, I could see pools of moisture emerging from the lawn.

The trees and bushes in front of Austin's house stoop in surrender to this tiresome deluge. I pass the front door and find the side gate into the yard, flanked by lilac bushes that ladle cold water onto my head as I push through. Cautiously, I open the latch—and now the dog begins to bark.

"Clio, Clio, Clio sweetie," I croon, hoping to placate her.

Am I going through with this? I guess I am.

She is jumping at the inside of the kitchen door when I get there. It's a windowed door, so I can see her, and she can see me, and I note that her tail is wagging madly. "Good girl, good girl!" I murmur as I quickly close and drop my umbrella on the ground. I open the door and sidle through, in case the dog should choose to bolt.

She jumps up on my raincoat, then shoves her cold nose beneath the hem and starts licking my bare knees. I lean down and scratch her behind her ears. I realize I haven't taken the time to listen to the house. What will I say if I'm caught? But Miriam said, when she gave me that tour of the office yesterday morning, that Monday is her busiest day at the firm, the day she spends doing the books and setting Austin's calendar for the week, how much time he'll allot to each project, how he'll delegate smaller tasks to the minions. She told me she'd come straight from the office later on, to meet me for a glass of wine at the inn.

I have to wonder about the stepson, but he has a job. I can't quite figure him out, what he's doing living at home when he's clearly old enough to be out on his own. That seems to be more and more the norm these days. The more all such norms become skewed, the more relieved I am that I never had children. Carly broached the subject once, after we'd been together a year, but when I pointed out that her long hours plus my reluctance did not add up to the rosiest of parenting scenarios, she agreed. She would never step aside from her job.

Clio finally gives up on ravishing my knees. She wanders casually over to a plush red cushion against the far wall.

The kitchen, every surface of it, emits a subtle gleam in the cold light from the windows. The wallscreen is dark, the sink empty, the wineglasses lurking behind a glass-paned cabinet door. I look around: no cookbooks, no quaint bouquets of miscellaneous utensils, not even a pepper mill. No photos pinned to the fridge, no souvenir magnets. Clean and inviolate, this room.

I realize that I am dripping on the floor, so I take off my coat and boots. There is, of course, a set of wall hooks and a copper tray below for practical footwear. Does a cat burglar avail himself of such conveniences? Well, I do. Call me a lady burglar. Though burgling is not on my agenda. Knowledge is all I seek.

I take the three steps up to the dining room, careful not to slip in my socks. Austin and Miriam do not seem partial to rugs, though I recall noticing the small antique kilim in the living room.

And now I know why. Through the old plank flooring, I feel the subtle comfort of radiant heat. A sin to leave it on in an empty house. Unless you count the dog. But who am I to judge anyone for self-indulgent behavior?

I doubt I'll find anything useful in the dining room, but I can't resist running my hands up and down the whale in the center of the table, its polished stone skin. This is an object I'd covet if I had the slightest idea where my life will be lived after this mission is over. New York recedes further and further in the rearview mirror. The number of messages I'm ignoring dwindles daily. I know perfectly well that most of our friends were Carly's, really. My surviving her may be more socially awkward than I already assumed it would be.

Other than the quietly handsome furnishings (and the compelling seashore art that does not include anything by Issa), it's a dining room like any other. The tiger maple sideboard contains three sets of dishes—one a collection of brash, exotically painted plates from some colorful Mediterranean country—and a stack of serving platters and bowls. Napkins both modernist cotton and mother-country linen; a box of ivory candles; matches from a restaurant in Portland, Maine; a silver punch ladle . . . why am I bothering here?

I listen again—nothing but the sizzling onslaught of rain—and pass through the sparsely appointed living room without stopping. (Not a stick of furniture with shelves or drawers.) Upstairs is where I have the greatest chance of finding anything.

You'd think an architect would choose or build a large house for himself, no matter how small his family, but Austin Kepner seems to be a man of economy, for which I begrudge him minor admiration. On the second floor I find one large bedroom, one smaller room that appears to be an all-purpose study, and a bathroom—although the bathroom is disproportionately large for a house of this scale, containing a long, deep tub and a capacious shower tiled in a stone that looks like stormy skies with the sun breaking through between clouds.

It might be a good idea to pee while I have the chance. I lift my dress and sit on the toilet. The floor in this room is also warm.

I go to the sink and look at myself in the mirror. I smile my sunny Southern smile, noticing with dismay how the flesh beneath my jawbone rumples ever so slightly. I do not bother to investigate the contents of the medicine chest. I am not that sort of nosy. No desire to view your unguents or sample your methods of calibrating your mood.

The bedroom, then the study (if that's what it is; it doesn't look terribly worked in).

The bed is a queen. I'm guessing they still have sex. Sex. Carly, her nipples the color of those dark tomatoes you used to find at farmers' markets in the hottest days of August. Black Prince, I think. You could eat those tomatoes like apples. I resist the urge to sit on the bed. The eclectically patched quilt lies hotel-smooth across the mattress, the pillows symmetrical and high. Above the bed hangs the only artwork, a large black and white photograph of Venice in the fog.

His and hers bureaus, the first conventional antiques I've seen in this house, the sort one inherits and can't be bothered to sell.

I go to the one without the jewelry box. On it sits a shallow white dish edged in gold—a purloined soap dish from the Plaza Athénée; ha! I am not the only scofflaw here! It's the sort of dish that might once have been used for loose change mined from pockets at the end of the day, spare keys, vagrant safety pins. But this dish is empty. Next to it stands a framed photograph of Austin and Miriam, literally cheek to cheek, eyes squinting against a noonday sun. From the white and blue geometry in the background, I deduce that they are on a sailboat. They are a few years younger.

The top drawer.

Good grief, was this man in the marines? The contents are allocated across a grid of rectangular boxes: watches, tuxedo studs, cuff links, sunglasses, lip balm, a defunct passport, a big fat Swiss Army knife. Faded face masks, solid black. Pale gray handkerchieves! The well-accessorized gentleman architect, *bien sûr.* I open the passport, which spans the decade during which we knew Issa. Yes, that's the handsome man from the restaurant all right, the fiancé. And oh, the places he went! Back off, Dr. Seuss.

When I return the passport to its domain, I spot a tiny slip of paper pinned down by a watch. With two fingernails, I pull it loose. It's a Chinese cookie fortune.

Your dream life beginning now.

I put it back and close the drawer. I wonder when he got that fortune and why he saved it. Men do not save things like that, not men who live like this.

Is it far-fetched to think the fortune is a relic of Issa?

Since Carly's death, sinking into memories of Issa has gradually lost its aura of treachery.

Within a few weeks after waiting on the lovebirds that heartbreaking night, I had given up on her (I wasn't a *total* fool), yet I thought of her often. Every time I bundled up to walk along the Hudson River, I couldn't help looking for her, even as winter wrestled with spring. And then, one Sunday night, she just showed up. I had fallen into a mercifully solid sleep after a production of *Our Town* at a defrocked church space in Brooklyn Heights; I'd played Mrs. Gibbs in four performances over a second and final weekend. Close to half the pews had been empty, despite a splashy notice in *New York* magazine, and after declining a nightcap with a few of my castmates, I had to wait forever on the platform at Clark Street, dodging the drunken weavings of an old man muttering nonsense. King Lear awaiting the uptown express.

I awakened to knocking on my front door, light but staccato in its persistence. I almost ignored it; too often it was that sad, cranky woman from below me who wanted to shut down the restaurant on the ground floor. Though this was no time for petitions, I got up and peered through the peephole.

Issa, in fish-eye distortion.

Soaking wet and sobbing.

"Get in here," I said, closing the door and opening my arms.

She fell against me, crying harder. I pulled her raincoat from her shoulders and hung it on a hook. She was wearing a thin white nightgown and a pair of those translucent jelly sandals you could buy for a few bucks in Chinatown. It was early April, but hardly warm. I steered her to my sofa and pulled her down beside me, shushing her litany of sorrys.

"What is it?" I asked (not *Why the fuck are you here?*).

"Oh it's him, I'm sorry, it's just that he doesn't . . ." Sobs engulfed her words.

Well, of course it was him. And of course he "didn't." What woman runs into the New York streets in her nightie, weeping, unless it's because of "him"?

I made her tea, and I got her a blanket, and I listened to the ways in which this man did not understand her, refused to see her for who she was, to accept how "different" she was—that she didn't want to go to parties, didn't want to find work other than her modeling job (which now made him jealous; why should others continue to see her naked?).

I would have despised the man, no matter the level of his crimes, but nothing she said struck me as warranting this: running out into a cold late-winter rain and finding her way to me, of all people. Sure, I was certain there had been something between us, something in the way we locked eyes whenever we did, but that was months ago. Why did she think I'd be sympathetic now?

"I think of you so much," she said, as if to distract me from coming to my senses about this invasion.

Same here, I wanted to say, but no way would I do that. Hard as it was, I waited for her to say more. She leaned against me on the sofa, tucked beneath my left arm, so I did not have to look her in the eye.

"I've been painting and painting," she said. "I can tell he resents it. He doesn't believe I am painting what I know. He says he loves my pictures, but he thinks I need to 'see someone.' As if I do not know exactly who I am and where I come from. I do."

"I'm sure you do," I assured her.

I asked her who he was, and she told me his name. She told me about his job, the long hours he kept, the trips that took him away for days at a time.

"You must be lonely," I said. "You know, architects are crazy. I mean, I've read the profession has the highest divorce rate. That tells you something."

She frowned at me. "I'm not lonely. I just want him to understand what I am here to do. To say."

"To do?"

"To show how terrible it is, what we live with, how our lives, all the lives around us, are threatened. It's what happened to the place where I was born."

"What happened?" I said.

She shook her head, as if this were irrelevant. "The sea took it."

I thought of all the towns, along the Gulf Coast, abandoned after Cunégonde. Was that where she'd been born? Hadn't she said something about France? Or living "all over"?

"The world can look like a terrible place," I said, "but listen, late at night is the worst time to dwell on all this existential stuff. But this guy . . . I hate to say it, but he's sort of right about seeing someone. I mean, it couldn't hurt. Maybe see someone together?" How noble I was. Though I added, "And then, if you can't make it work, if you have to move out . . ."

Was she listening? I couldn't tell.

After a moment of silence, I asked her if she had a place of her own, somewhere else to go, other than his apartment. As I feared, she said no.

"Okay, well, let's see," I said, buying time to talk myself off that ledge. "I am totally wiped out. How about you sleep here and we figure it out in the morning? I don't have to be anywhere until noon."

She nodded but said nothing, not even thanking me. When I stood, she curled up on the sofa, under my blanket. I watched her for a moment, waiting, and when she still said nothing, when she closed her eyes, I went back to my room. I fell asleep quickly and woke to the pearling turn of the sky outside the window beside my bed. I realized that what had awakened me was the careful closing of the door to my apartment.

Blanket folded, no note.

"You cannot do this to me," I muttered. But she could, and she had.

Austin and Miriam's bedroom window looks across the back garden toward a one-story house and, beyond that house, the harbor. No people anywhere. A few boats rock fretfully on the rain-dimpled surface of the water. I feel a pang of loneliness so sharp that I want to cry. Where *will* I go from here? Even from this very spot in this bedroom where I do not belong?

But I make myself go to the closet. It's massive—obviously not an original feature to this old house; probably once a nursery—and in it, his clothes outnumber hers. Suits galore. Do they represent his former life in New York, or does he really wear them all in his small-town life? For a few intense moments, I'm carried back to the last job I had—the one I fell into through friends of ours, did well, and even sometimes enjoyed—after I gave up acting. I guided, even cajoled, wealthy men through the purchase of expensive clothing at a men's haberdashery club on a tree-lined cross street near the Met. I coaxed them to learn fabrics by hand (and now my hands riffle Austin's suits; sure enough, one of his jackets is high-end cashmere). My employer loved that I was a lesbian: no collateral fraternizing, no mutual stirrings when I measured inseams or ran my palms, all business, down a man's rib cage to smooth away folds from a chambray shirtfront. But how many hours had I wasted doing that work, work Carly told me I didn't have to do, though out of pride I insisted that I did?

Christ, I am falling into a vortex of self-pity.

I force my hands away from Austin's soft flannel shirts and look up. The shelves above the hanging clothes hold translucent boxes containing bed linens and blankets, summer hats.

I search in vain for a shoebox of secret mementos, a hidden cache of sketchbooks. The most interesting thing I discover is a large envelope containing photos of a much younger Miriam with a man who must be Brecht's father.

I wander into the hall and listen for a moment: only the rain.

In the study, I go for the drawers of the desk, where I find outdated letterhead stationery from Kepner's firm (different address), an orphaned computer keyboard, miscellaneous power cords, blank art cards showing Japanese landscapes, a candy tin stuffed with marijuana, rolling papers, more restaurant matches . . . nothing of interest, nothing even terribly personal beyond a packet of old letters that appear to be from Austin's mother in New Jersey, sent to his address in New York. (Christ: he lived within five blocks of me. Not so far for Issa to run.) A framed school portrait of the stepson, an adolescent in braces.

After cruising through the uninformative closet (this one tiny), I leave the study and take the steep stairs to the attic.

One peak-roofed room to either side, in each a bed, small table, small chest of drawers. The larger one is clearly where the stepson sleeps. It's not disorderly, but it has a lived-in smell—laundered clothing, wet leather, the feral tang of weed. A pair of workboots under a table stacked with books. When I enter, I see to the right, tucked under the pitch of the roof, a drafting table with gooseneck lamp, beneath it a flat file and stool. On the table are two drawings made by a child: aliens in front of their spaceship; a series of tall pine trees looming over a house (an alien spaceship in the sky).

One of the lower file drawers is wide open. An invitation, no?

From the drawer, I pull an old-fashioned artist's portfolio, a black folder tied with flimsy laces. I put it on the table. It holds a set of architectural plans for someone's kitchen. The work is Austin's, of course, but the date is what hastens my pulse. It's the year Issa turned away from him, however briefly, toward me.

I move the file to the bed and pull out another. This one enfolds drawings of a small, angular, well-windowed house. *Spring Lake, New Jersey,* the artful lettering tells me; and again, the year I am trying to pull from the past. One by one, I remove half a dozen folios from the drawer, all projects from within a two-year time frame, all modest in scale. So this, I realize, is when Austin was probably moonlighting, getting ready to break away from corporate work.

Nothing of Issa. I replace the portfolios in the drawer, close it, and open another. Drawing supplies: sketch pads; large sheets of fine toothy paper; colored pencils; a flat box containing tubes of gouache, rumpled with use, mostly hardened. The closed doors of a past life.

I sit on the bed (this one hastily made, no worry of Goldilocks leaving her imprint), surrounded by Austin Kepner's drawings as a fledgling architect and certified cad.

She showed up, again in the middle of the night, a few days after her first hysterical visit. I tried not to answer the door, but my resolve lasted less than a minute.

"You know," I said when I answered, "you can't show up in distress and then just vanish."

She threw her arms around me, crying. "I'm sorry, I'm sorry, I'm sorry." She was profligate with her sorrys; this I'd learned.

I let her cling to me for a few minutes, then led her inside.

"I have enough challenges, Issa. One more might do me in."

She sat on the couch, composing herself, catching her breath. "I don't want to do you in," she said in a sad, defeated voice.

I sat next to her. "I know that. So can you just be straight with me about what's going on?"

"He says it won't work. I have to move out. I have to go."

"So look, I'm just going to say it. Screw him. He's right. It won't work. But that's his problem," I said. "His loss."

"It would work if he would accept."

I paused but said what made sense. "Accept what?"

"Who I am. Which I need to tell you if I want to stay. If you let me stay."

Suddenly, she seemed calm. Her eyes were red from crying, but she gazed at me steadily. Her voice was level.

"Okay," I said. "I have sort of wondered. Who you are." I laughed, though now I was nervous. "So who are you?"

She continued to stare at me, as if making a decision. She shook her head and stood up, walking to the window on the air shaft. The restaurant had closed an hour before, so the night was relatively still. Lights were off in the apartment of Couch Potato Man. "I never should have wanted this," she said, still facing the blank view. "We're warned it's all wrong, it never works, but what can you do if you're given the chance to try a new life, breach the surface, go back toward the light we came from? Who says no to that? A coward!"

"Slow down," I said. "Say no to what?"

"Living on land." Again, that fierce stare of hers. "You don't believe me, either."

"I'm just confused, Issa." But I felt deflated. She was nuts. Wasn't she?

She stood and paced to and fro on the small rug. Her feet, in the city light from the window, were so beautiful.

"The place where I was born, you would have seen it on a map as Ys. What you call a hurricane wiped it away. Swept all of us under the ocean. Where we see everything now. We understand what's happening."

What's happening, I thought, is that now I'm losing my sanity, too. Because I wanted to believe her.

"Can I ask you something weird?" I said. "Are you telling me you're not human?"

My question seemed to make her happy. She stopped in front of me, faced me, and said, "I have been, and I am now. With you." And then came that seductive refrain of hers: "Come look."

She took my hands and pulled me up. She led me into my bedroom, pushed me gently down to sit on the bed. When I reached to turn on the lamp, she said, "No."

She closed the bedroom door, so that the only light came from the one small window. I could hear more than see her removing her coat and then whatever she wore that night beneath it.

So she was naked when she sat on the edge of the bed, but she was holding her coat, that same greenish trench she wore constantly, like some postmodern Mata Hari. For a moment, she just sat very still, holding it against her chest.

I knew I had more on my hands than a sad, disillusioned girl, a spurned lover, but in my life, curiosity has so often trumped good sense (and I might add that curiosity hasn't killed me yet).

"Here." She pivoted to sit beside me against the pillows. She spread the open raincoat, inside out, across our laps. In the dim nocturnal glow from the window, I wondered what I was supposed to be seeing other than the plain white lining of an imitation Burberry, a knockoff from T.J.Maxx.

"Just . . . feel it."

"The coat?"

Issa took my right hand and placed it flat on the coat's lining. What I felt wasn't the surface I believed I was seeing, and at first I pulled my hand away.

"No," said Issa, in a surprisingly forceful voice. *"Feel it."*

The fabric looked like silk, but beneath my hand it felt softer, not slick but almost furlike. And as I moved my hand, the sheen of the surface seemed to brighten, even phosphoresce, in its path. Was it a trick of the moonlight? There were nights when I awoke, startled to see a warped square of radiance, the shape of my window, projected across my body.

"It's mine," she said. "Who I used to be, in the water, and who I may be again."

I focused on the coat, avoiding her face until she reached beneath my chin and turned my head.

"I can trust you," she said, though she sounded doubtful.

"Of course you can," I said, because what else was there to say?

"He will never believe me." I saw the tears in her eyes.

Christ, him again. "Men don't tend to believe women," I said, "when we show them who we really are. Or they simply don't like what they see."

"Women," she said quietly. "But we know more, don't we?"

I could no longer avoid her eyes, and I didn't know if I wanted her to kiss me or not. I wasn't going to move.

"I want to become a woman who knows everything," she said, "who can say what she knows and who she is, and she will be believed."

I did not believe in otherworldly creatures—not vampires, not zombies, not changeling trolls or hobbits—yet maybe, I felt in that electric moment, maybe Issa was *not* a woman. Was she trans? Was I in the middle of a story involving sexual surprise? I thought of the play *M. Butterfly*. I thought of David Bowie in *The Man Who Fell to Earth*. Objectively, this scene could well play out as farce, but I found nothing to laugh at. Something about Issa was different, alien, other.

When my hand rested on the coat again, I felt it move—on its own, I was certain—rising, as if to caress me.

"This is crazy," I said.

"That is your common knowledge of the surface world speaking," said Issa. "You don't have to listen. Listen to me instead."

She pushed the coat to the foot of my bed, and she took hold of my nightgown and began to pull it over my head.

When we were both naked, Issa pressed against me, head to feet. Her entire body felt so smooth it was almost slippery, and I wrapped my arms tightly around her, to hold her fast. At first, she seemed to resist my kissing her, but when she gave in, I felt as if every nerve of every cell along the surface of my skin were engaged with every single cell of hers.

As we twisted and tangled, fitting ourselves together, I felt like a virgin all over again, unaccustomed to the way my limbs wrestled with hers, the way we met each other. My clumsiness surprised me. She said nothing, so I said nothing, and at some point I simply let her lead, like a dance partner who already knows the steps.

Her body was a woman's, but her profound silence and the feel of her skin were strange. How does someone so enthralled—and I knew she felt no less passion than I did—not gasp or whisper or sigh?

It felt as if we made love to each other for hours, yet it was still dark when she sat up and told me she had to go.

"Back to him?" I said. "Why?"

"I have errands," she said quietly. "Things to do. But I will be back. I promise you that."

I laughed. "Errands? What, like shopping in the middle of the night?"

Standing beside the bed, she reached down to touch my cheek. "Go to sleep."

I did sleep. Soundly. And dreamed vividly. I was by the river, with Issa, at the spot where we met. She invited me to swim with her, and I was delighted. We were in the water immediately; it was warm, even clear, and that seal, the one she'd pointed out to me, joined us. But all of a sudden, so did several of my fellow actors from the workshop, including the one who played Ondine, the one who'd played both Hans in *Ondine* and Petruchio opposite my Kate, and our teacher. I was distressed, but Issa didn't seem to notice them. Someone suggested playing a game; all I wanted was to be alone, naked in the water, with Issa and the seal.

I woke, sweat-soaked, the sheets twisted around my hips, to the sound of a garbage truck consuming the waste from the restaurant below. I got up to pee, and as I left the bathroom, I stopped to look at myself in the full-length mirror on the door. I expected to see bruises or at least some faint physical evidence of the night before, but if anything, my skin looked more unblemished than ever.

On my way back to bed, I saw a white garment draped over the back of my desk chair. Issa's nightgown. Impulsively, I slipped it over my head. The cold fabric against my skin made me shiver, so I took it off. I examined it closely, all the seams, the pleating at the yoke where the thin cotton ballooned toward the ankle-length hem. No labels; no signs of labels ripped or cut off. Perhaps she had made it.

In my mind, memory and dream coalesced, confusing me. She'd really been with me, I knew that, and hadn't she promised to return? If she wasn't quite human (could I actually believe this?), she was better than human: more loving, more transporting, more innocent and giving. If, for now, I had to share her, so be it.

First the dog barks, and then, immediately, a door slams open.

"Brecht? Brecht, are you here?"

Miriam. Miriam in a panic. Oh God, if only there were a fire escape. Where are the New York City fire codes when you need them?

If she is searching for Brecht—and I'm certain he's nowhere in the house—she will be headed for this very room. I contemplate, in a synaptic nanosecond, trying to hide in the smaller room opposite this one. Maybe it has a closet, and . . .

Rapid footsteps on the stairs. My only options are sitting and standing.

As I hear her approach (is she crying?), I raise my voice, as calmly as possible, and say her name.

She lets out a shriek when, entering the narrow door frame, she sees me standing beside the bed (which is strewn with Austin's portfolios).

"Miriam, I'm so sorry," I say. "I would say I can explain, and I can, but I see you're upset and looking for your son, and I—"

"Where is he? Where is Brecht?" she demands. It feels almost as if she rushed here expecting to confront me.

"I don't know," I say, still striving for calm.

"What the hell are you doing here? In my son's room?" She takes in the bed, the open file drawers, and immediately, she goes into the other room, looking frantically around. She then goes to the head of the stairs, between the two rooms, and calls down, "Brecht! Brecht!"

"He isn't here." I sit on the bed. "I've been here for an hour. I'm sure of it." This is when I realize that I am not speaking in my faux-Texan drawl. I wonder if Miriam, in the fever state of a mother who's misplaced her child, even notices. (I flash on Iphigenia's mother, after it's too late; yes, I played that role in a fairly bad one-act play at a festival staged in a converted Yonkers firehouse.)

Miriam takes perhaps five seconds to focus, silently, on my presence. "I don't have time to figure out why you've broken into my house. But you had better be telling me the truth. That you haven't seen him."

"I haven't," I say, feeling strangely relieved to have stripped myself of all the ridiculous pretense I concocted to accomplish . . . what? For a moment, I actually cannot remember why I am standing in this claustrophobic garret bedroom.

"Go downstairs now." And, when she sees me glance at the disarray I've made of her husband's archive, "Don't touch anything."

I start down the stairs, and she follows close behind. Though she could strike me dead with a heavy object or push me to certain injury on these steep, uncarpeted steps, I do not hurry. On the first floor, I start toward the kitchen, my coat and boots, but she orders me to stop.

"You are going to help me find him," she says. "There's no use calling the police, because he's a grown man. Besides which, their hands are full with the lockdown."

"Lockdown?"

"The bombing," she says impatiently. "The blockades."

It would be shameless for me to ask more, so I just wait for her to tell me what she needs—or, I'm hoping, change her mind and kick me out. When I can't meet her eyes, I find myself looking at the dog, who sits beside Miriam, its expression both worried and perplexed.

"You are going to stay here, in case he comes back." She registers my look of surprise. "I don't care if you've collected a bag of loot. You're what, a thief posing as a writer? Or some kind of private eye?" She attempts to laugh and fails. "Never mind. There isn't a thing in this house I would miss. Take the dog, for all I care."

As if understanding the insult, the dog cringes and retreats to its bed.

"Can you do that? Wait here and call me if he shows up? Or do you need to tuck tail and run?"

"Miriam, I can do that. I promise I won't leave. I'm not a thief, I—"

"I don't care if you're the anarchist who planted those fucking bombs." In the kitchen, she gathers her own rain gear (her coat having fallen from a chair to the floor) and goes out the back door, leaving me with the dog, who regards me with that look of mournful disappointment, the one that leads dog lovers to believe not only that these creatures understand everything we say, everything we do, but that they wish they could stop us from committing our many acts of folly.

"Clio," I say, shocked that I remember her name in the midst of this fiasco, "what I need from you is to be totally ignored."

And honest to God, just like that, she looks away, sighs, and turns her face toward the wall.

Now what? Will I go back upstairs and resume my aggressive meddling?

Of course not.

I sit at the dining room table, facing the stone whale, epitaph to its certain extinction, and I wait. I don't even bother taking out my phone.

The rain raises its stakes, and it's so loud, falling on streets and trees and cars and roofs, that I decide this is what justice sounds like when it makes one of its disgracefully rare appearances: righteous, unflinching, trailing in its thunderous wake consequences that echo for miles.

Once, for more than a hundred years, the skies over Vigil Harbor swarmed by day with loud, voracious seabirds, driven away from vast racks of drying codfish by boys with sticks. In the streets and pastures and graveyards, when they were not in lessons or doing chores, swarmed packs of children, loud and unruly as those seabirds. The harbor itself was as populous as the streets and the skies, a jigsaw maneuvering of vessels large and small, from skiffs and punts to dinghies and dories; schooners and sloops when fortunes were high and the catch was in. Masts creaked, sails and halyards snapped and clattered in the wind, fishermen and merchant mariners whistled and sang and cursed and bellowed orders. Barrels rolling toward shore along worm-eaten, dung-spackled wharves mimicked the rumble of an incoming squall.

Now, the skies are mostly vacant except for passing aircraft, the pastures are well-groomed lawns—though children still play there, the boys with sticks playing fetch with their dogs—and the streets, most but not all of them wider, carry cars and bicycles, sailboats on trailers. The harbor's traffic changes just as radically from season to season: engorged with pleasure and racing craft from May to October, nearly vacant by December but for the harbormaster's powerboat and the occasional Coast Guard patrol. Vigil Harbor falls equidistant between the two nearest Coast Guard stations, one up north near the border of New Hampshire, the other south of Boston. A few gulls and ducks skim the surface, searching for what scant sea life remains in the shallows. Even hermit crabs are rare, their shells no longer sturdy enough for shelter. The seals have learned to thrive on jellyfish and squid.

Several miles offshore, however, all year long, the Atlantic currents carry a stealthy nocturnal traffic. The crews who man these boats, tech-savvy privateers, outwit and outnumber the Coast Guard. They deal in cargo from cultural refugees to contraband pharmaceuticals, from black-market seafood to unlicensed weapons.

As evening, and still more rain, reaches toward Harrow Point, a cold, confused young man huddles, arms clamping knees to his chest, in the shelter of a magnificent house—or its unfinished but well-constructed skeleton—shivering in wet clothes that belong to someone else, knowing that he should go home but worried that where there are people, there may well be more explosions. And oh, there will be questions. He doesn't look at his phone and has turned off its signal. He is safe from the news, but he will also not receive messages from the two women wondering desperately where he is. He is aware of this, but they will have to keep wondering for now. He needs to be alone to work out his confusion. If he can do that, maybe he can find the sense of calm he had before he heard that explosion replayed in his mother's kitchen.

Because of the rain, the park on the headland is deserted. Only the young man will see one of the boats, in the late afternoon, draw close to shore, soundlessly, stopping at the foot of the cliffs when the tide is low and a small stretch of pebbled shore is bared. He will watch three men disembark, all wearing black, and wonder, hasn't he seen this before? But he has no one to ask, because his friend and most frequent companion—or the acquaintance who had just become a friend—has deserted him. Noam is dead, isn't he? Why did Brecht ever think otherwise?

He tries to talk himself into facing his mother, but he knows the reaction she'll have: her panic and grief and pity. Enough of all the pity. He could go back to Celestino's, but there are too many people there—and wait, he thinks as his pulse surges, he left the painting there, with Connie. No, he's not ready to face her, either.

In his mind, he's veering around town, as if on a bike, looking for a refuge drier and warmer than this one, and then he thinks of another woman, someone else he wouldn't have dreamed of searching out a year or two ago, but now—maybe now she's the one. Maybe she's someone with more answers than questions.

Margo

Already I'm worried that I didn't buy enough food: the two overpriced chickens (oh excuse me: *pullets*) from the farm depot look scrawny when I split and flatten them, and though the ramps overflow my largest colander, they'll probably shrivel fourfold in the skillet. Plenty of potatoes, however, and maybe I'll roast them with a few yams. A cheerful touch of orange to what I now realize looks like a meal fit for a Dickens poorhouse. But then, I bought a cake for dessert. Bought! No more Bakeoff Bessie for me. Let others grease the pans and cream the butter.

In that not-so-long-ago former life, I was rarely the anxious hostess—but accomplished and organized as I was in the kitchen, it made a difference to have my he-man cohost. We never did that he-grills-she-braises two-step; I've always been the everything chef, soup to soufflés. I stood over the meals cooked by fire. Whenever I fell behind or risked the quicksand of some fussy, byzantine recipe, Tom kept the drinks filled, the chitchat witty, the jokes sharp. And what for, really? (Unless you count the boozy double-jointed sex we often had at the end of the night, liking each other more because we'd just reaffirmed that others liked us, too.) During the two years he swanned about as YC commodore, I thought I'd have to join Canapés Anonymous. It felt as if any evening we weren't in the Galleon Lounge, at the buffet, or on that football field of a porch, I was tossing swordfish over hot coals, rolling out puff pastry, mincing shallots. The grumbling of the dishwasher after midnight foretold the grumbling (mine) to follow eight hours later: No, never again. Yet how to flout local customs? Braver souls than I had declined to do so.

To my amazement, Mike convinced Egon and his lady friend to come along. Or, to hear him tell it, the lady friend bullied Egon into "being a grown-up and just saying yes." I do sympathize: dinner with your old English teacher whose husband ran off with your mom isn't exactly anybody's ideal evening out. Mike promised we wouldn't talk about *them*.

I have the news running on the wall as I prepare; on days like this—all terror all the time—it's hard to look away. What's clear to the authorities, a day and a half after the explosions in Harvard Yard, is that it's an echo, an aftershock, of the boat basin bombing in New York last week and that the perpetrators are alive and well—they use that peculiar phrase "at large"—and that they include two ponytailed men who, captured in fleeting profile on video outside Harvard's art museum, are estimated to be under age thirty. No facial recogs matched. Oceloti has now owned up to both bombings on its satfeed. Running across the bottom of my screen is this excerpt: *Let the thinkers do more than think. Let them act. Make them act. Make them decapitate the corporate plunderers with whom they collaborate by their failure to resist. Turn your back and it will become the target.*

I find the decapitation metaphor unfortunate (though I appreciate that genteel *with whom*). Who can forget the spate of actual beheadings enacted and videotaped by earlier, more nihilistic (fanatically sadistic) terrorists? Our oldest was in preschool when I asked Tom to give up his breakfast NPR. "Enough with the beheading du jour," I told him. "It doesn't go well with waffles."

The property damage is superficial yet significant: the façade of Widener Library is ripped away, the charred interior exposed like a zombie dollhouse. Directly across from the library, the front of the university chapel is also toast. Hurtling chunks of masonry are responsible for a third of the casualties.

As night approaches, klieg lights once again blanch the scene, as if one of those Teatro Goth groups is about to descend and stage yet another of its soul-slashing dramas. (For a few seasons Doro was mad for their performances, which had sophomoric titles like *Intimate/Ultimate*

Demise, Cerberus Unchained, and *Auto Da Catastrofé.* She'd obsess over websites where pop-up tickets might appear at three a.m., selling out in a matter of minutes.) When I refused to take interest in these spectacles, Doro said to me, "Are you unwilling to face the future, Mom? To see what it will look like if we don't *do something*? They're showing us what it will look like if we're passive. The ways we are going to *go down*."

"Honey," I said, "I prefer to witness the self-destruction of our species unfold in real time."

Harsh, perhaps, but she was out in the world, living on her own, and I've never been the kind of mother who coddles her daughters (or her students) by wrapping the truth in blush-colored tulle.

I think of Egon in his final show at the High. He played the cuckolded husband in Pinter's *Betrayal,* and though the psychology of that play is laughably out of reach to an eighteen-year-old boy from a plush American suburb, Egon managed to mine some deep reserve of genuine sorrow that stunned me so profoundly, I saw all four performances—and shed tears every single time. Inescapably, there was a maternal tinge to the relationships I had with all my students, the "challenged" and the delinquent along with the fawners and the prodigies. But once in a blue moon, I had an "if I'd ever had a son" yearning toward a male student, a kind of nonerotic crush. Egon was one of those boys. Part of what drew me toward Mike after our mutual cataclysm, I admit, was his connection to Egon.

Seeing Egon emerge from the rain last night was eerie: for a moment, in the dim doorway, he was his father some thirty years ago. I'd never seen the resemblance, even though Mike was someone I saw in numerous contexts around town for years: not just at the club but at school functions, at sailing races, and, for a stretch of intense early-parenting years, at the bowling alley on weekends, when children's birthday parties overwhelmed the place with shrieking and spilled orange soda. I don't remember ever thinking twice about whether Mike was the type of husband to tempt a roving eye—but Egon's looks make sense for the aspiring actor: those intensely blue Chekhovian eyes, that prow of a chin—and, undeniably, his mother's dramatic chestnut hair.

Yams: I thought for certain I had yams. There are none in the wooden bowl, none in the fridge. The basement? I did stash some root vegetables from my profligate shopping spree down there.

I turn on the light and take the steep stairs slowly. I have a ghoulish vision of myself, ten years from now, less stable, catapulting head over heels into this dungeon, dying a lingering death without anyone around to find me. But then, I won't be here in ten years, will I? Not in this house, at least. I suddenly envy Mike his new if shabby bachelor pad, his "free to be me" austerity. I know perfectly well that my embracing the mandate to *cheer him up,* to make him *see the joy in his freedom,* to *stir his indignation* . . . that it's all about me and my own self-pity, my mousy paralysis.

Okay, stop (my numero uno commandment these days). And yes, here are the yams. On the table next to the freezer. I check the freezer, just in case there's something I want to ferry upstairs. Ice cream, to go with the cake?

Something tucked between the side of the freezer and the fieldstone wall catches my eye, a sliver of scarlet. I'm guessing it's a placard or poster. I set the yams back down and haul it out. Skeins of cobweb come with it, and I pause to cough.

"Christ," I say as I cross the cellar to the rag bin. I pull out an old pink T-shirt advertising one of Doro's a cappella concerts: the High Seas, her group was called. This T-shirt, one of a series, came from a regional singing competition called Voices With a View, held in a park overlooking the harbor. I lift it to my face, but it smells only of this dank basement, soil and incipient mildew.

I resist the pull of tears. Brusquely, I wipe off what turns out to be a cheaply framed poster for—to my shock—*Betrayal,* the production starring Egon. And then I remember that Becca designed the poster and worked on the crew. My life, or the portion of it that looms largest from this perspective, begins to look like the sum of my children's achievements. I doubt it feels that way to Tom.

Okay, stop.

Obviously, I must take this artifact upstairs and show it to Egon when he arrives. It will amuse his charming friend, who will tease him gleefully and make Mike blush. (Not like I failed to notice his knee-jerk reaction to that young woman's exhilarating beauty. Good lord, her hair alone: twisted into a hive of complex braids in a tapestry of reds and browns. Not hair our local salons are likely to see.)

Grasping the bag of yams in one hand, I manage to lift the poster in front of me and sidle up the stairs to the kitchen. Twice, I bang my chin on the top of the frame when the bottom strikes a higher step. I return to the kitchen cursing at my clumsiness, and, as I carefully lean the poster against the kitchen table, manage to drop the sack of yams on my foot. Now I am laughing, glad to have no witnesses, glad as well that I've distracted myself from getting all maudlin over that T-shirt, when I glance up and see that someone is standing at the back door.

I look at the clock: my guests aren't due for an hour.

The figure at the door knocks gently on one of the panes.

Wiping a hank of cobweb from my face, I lean over and pick up the yams before heading to the door.

It's Celestino's houseguest. He looks as if he's soaked to the skin. (What is it with men and their congenital aversion to umbrellas?)

"Good grief, come in!" I say as he apologizes, stamps his feet on my doormat, and tells me he's somehow misplaced the house key they gave him, that no one's home to let him in and of course he feels like a fool. A very wet fool.

He laughs sheepishly. "I came close to breaking in."

It does cross my mind that Celestino and Connie, with all the comings and goings of the home school, aren't likely to lock their doors. But times change, and trust erodes. The events of this week may be the tipping point.

"Let me get you a towel," I say, and I run upstairs.

"Really sorry to intrude," he calls after me. "I see you're in the middle of making dinner."

When I return, he's watching the news.

"God, let me turn that off," I say as I hand him the towel. "We get sucked in, don't we? Down the rabbit hole and in pursuit of what? Mayhem?"

"No, leave it on," he says. "This news is close enough to matter."

As I compromise by muting the sound, I'm struggling to remember his name; he reads my mind.

"Ernesto. And you are Margo."

"Yes. Well, I think I am! Sometimes I wonder."

I watch him dry his sleek head, rub at his wet shirt and pants. Am I supposed to offer him a change of clothes? Not that a stitch of Tom's clothing remains. I made sure of that.

"Do you know when they'll be back?" I say.

He apologizes yet again; we seem to have a duet going. "Really, I should go down to that café I saw on your main street—"

"Don't be ridiculous."

"You're kind," he says. His smile is a feature whose allure he fully understands, and that gem perched in his ear speaks volumes about his self-assurance—but then, I suppose I'm not feeling charitable in general toward most men these days.

I offer to make him the predictable cup of tea, and he accepts. As I'm going through the minor tasks of tea-making, I notice his assessment of my preparations for dinner. It must be obvious others will join me, and I wonder if I'm going to have to include him. Small talk, I admonish myself. Make small talk!

"Where are you visiting from?" I ask (though perhaps I asked him this when he dropped by to inspect my new bathroom).

"All over, in a way, but the simple answer is Chicago."

"Oh, I love your art museum," I say. "And that park with the outdoor concert hall. Though the last time I was in Chicago . . . well, I didn't have children back then. A very long time ago."

"I was raised there. Mostly. Now I'm . . . nomadic." He stands by the table, as if we're about to go somewhere together. He glances down at the poster but makes no comment.

"Please sit." I move the poster against the far cabinets. I take it in from a distance: the three young actors' headshots, black-and-white, expressions solemn and pained, superimposed over my daughter's painting of an unmade bed. The mussed coverlet is the splash of red that caught my eye in the basement. I hear the kettle start to purr. I offer up a modest choice of teas; he chooses mint, I find a mug. "Honey?"

He shakes his head. "You're so kind to let me hang out here."

"Kindness is not my cardinal virtue. Just ask my students. Even my A students. Especially my A students."

More polite laughter. He doesn't ask about my teaching. Over his head, through the window, I see that Celestino's driveway is empty.

"Excuse me if I do a little . . . chopping and such." I wave at the food.

"Ramps," he says. "Did you grow them?"

"No green thumbs here." I give him an accidental thumbs-up. "We . . . I belong to a co-op. Local farms—to the extent we have them."

And such. To the extent. As if I'm auditioning for *She Stoops to Conquer.*

"That's good. It's your job to keep them alive."

"In these parts, it's more about appearances." I give him his tea and watch him take the first sip. "I can't imagine our quaint little farms make much of a dent in corporate agriculture."

"Appearances are a place to begin," he says.

This seems like a peculiar remark to me. I decide not to ask, Begin what? Is he saying *Fake it till you make it?* Which hits a little close to home. As I cut up the potatoes and yams, my back to this unexpected visitor, something occurs to me. "So if you're a nomad, where are you renovating a bathroom?" Didn't he mention a house in New Hampshire? Maine? I must be shuffling my mental playing cards.

"Oh, that's for my mother. Didn't I say? She still lives in the apartment where I grew up. Things are . . . falling apart. I told her it's time to renovate. Especially if she wants to sell."

Yes, I think, that's the solution to falling part. Renovation! Easy-peasy.

"Kitchens and bathrooms still make all the difference to the sale price," he says. "Silly but true."

I glance out the window: driveway still empty. "Maybe you should call them," I say. "Connie or Celestino. Ask if they keep a key somewhere. You know. Under a flowerpot?"

"I did call. They won't be back till later. It can't be helped."

I fill a bowl with cold water, to keep the potatoes from browning.

Far more than raising your own teenagers, it's years of teaching other people's children, of forcing them to do work they disdain, that attunes you to their lies; no one lies as cleverly or creatively as a seventeen-year-old dodging a term paper on one of those dead drunks. Sometimes you forget that adults, too, are frequent fabricators.

I want to turn around, but I don't. I force myself to continue the task at hand. Already the water in the bowl grows cloudy from the starch leaching out from the potatoes. I'm wondering what to say next—whether to go along with this ruse, whatever it is—when I hear Ernesto's purposeful footsteps. I hear the door open: is he leaving, just like that? But when I turn around, my heartbeat spikes.

Here are three more guests, and they are not Mike, Egon, and Pearl.

Four men, including Ernesto, now stand in my kitchen. No: one is a woman. Last to enter, she closes the door behind her.

These new strangers turn their attention to Ernesto, not to me. In the few beats of silence we all share, what I feel more than anything else is shame. Why was I so slow to acknowledge my instincts? What made me so gullible, so glib?

"Margo," says Ernesto, his voice and smile as congenial as ever, though now the look on his intelligent face fills me with fear, "these are friends of mine."

The friends now do turn toward me. One of the two men—both much younger than Ernesto—also smiles at me, but his two companions exude the weariness of bureaucrats, faces like masks of studied ennui, emotional remove. When no introductions are made, I feel the threat of tears at the back of my sinuses. I also realize that I am holding a small knife, and the flash suspicion that I may have become a victim of some kind while peeling and cutting potatoes forces a noise from me that sounds like a snort of laughter.

And it is laughter—because that literary term *epiphany* crossed my brain. Will I be an English teacher to the literal, rock-bottom end? Oh, and will that end be now?

"Margo," my visitor-turned-captor says again, not a note of chill or danger in his voice, "we need to hang out here for a few hours, if you don't mind. We might have to help ourselves to some food and your phone, but otherwise we promise no disruption."

I somehow doubt my minding would matter, but I do not volunteer this opinion. And "no disruption"? Maybe they'd all like to pitch in: open the wine, choose music, set the table, light the candles. Many hands make light work!

The two younger men are watching the silent news on my kitchen wall. The woman is watching me. Not one of them has said a word.

"I should call my friends and cancel the dinner." My voice is flat but steady.

"That's not necessary." Ernesto's gaze wanders purposefully until it finds my phone, on the counter next to the dish of raw poultry. He picks it up.

I am still holding the knife. If I were in a movie, would I lunge?

Clairvoyant, Ernesto comes toward me and gently removes the knife from my hand, drops it in the sink beside me. "Let's go sit down," he says. He guides me graciously toward my living room, just the way Tom used to steer me toward a dance floor, the fingers of his right hand nested between my shoulder blades, as easily as they might rest on the tiller of our boat, pointing it toward the start of a race.

From the top of the neglected piano, my three daughters, separately and in a variety of social constellations (those including Tom already banished), regard me with oblivious cheer as I sit in one of the chairs flanking the fireplace. All promises from this lying, smooth-talking motherfucker clearly moot, I fixate on the Chinese deco carpet, its green pagodas and peacocks and (as my mother used to say) *Oriental poobahs,* and I wonder if it's the last piece of art I will ever see. (Tom's antique painting of a schooner at sea under stormy skies, formulaically mounted above our mantel, I banished as well.)

Ernesto cases the room, eyes resting on the door to the foyer, the main entrance to the house that almost nobody uses. He goes into the foyer and pushes the antique bolt at the top of the door into its hasp. When he returns, he says, "Honestly, you have nothing to worry about, Margo. Just sit tight. We're using you as a rest stop of sorts. Just consider us a group of wayfarers."

"Wayfarers?" My scorn, alas, is loud and clear. Oh good, I tell myself, piss the man off. Again, I'm in a movie: this time I'll be pistol-whipped into bloody silence.

But Ernesto no longer flatters me with his attention. "Pia!" he calls out suddenly.

The female sidekick comes in, and they have a brief conversation in clipped Spanish. "Pia will keep you company," he tells me.

Pia reminds me of a small dog bred to fight, perhaps a Boston terrier: strong, alert, with thick joints and a hard jaw immune to mirth. Her hair is cropped as short as Ernesto's. Vivid tendrils of some botanically inspired tattoo seem to be straining for sunlight at the wrists and neckline of her dark windbreaker.

"So, Margo," says Ernesto, "last time I was here, I noticed something on your kitchen counter, something I'm wondering about."

I stare at him, as defiantly as I dare.

"A black case. Where did it go?"

Oh why, I wonder, didn't I just take it to the police station? Why did I return it to the basement, as if putting it out of sight would put it out of mind, out of anybody's reach?

"It's in the basement," I say, because what's the point of trying to hide anything from this man? I understand that he will get whatever he wants, one way or another.

He doesn't ask me where the basement is. He's not one for expending extra energy; he's highly self-sufficient. "I'll bring it up," he says, "and you'll familiarize me with it. Thank you."

Only a few minutes go by—I hear his footsteps echoing down the stairs; silence; returning up the stairs—and then the heavy case is in my lap, and I'm speaking my password, ashamed of its careless whimsy, and the bad guy takes possession of the birthday present I ought to have simply refused all those years ago.

Ernesto, gun in hand, is almost out of the room when he turns and says, "Would you like a book?" He's no doubt taken in the bookcases, crowded with actual books, that occupy two walls of the room, and I can't help wondering if this question is a taunt.

"Really?" I say. "A book?"

He shrugs. "There's time to fill. Suit yourself."

Pia roams the room, the terrier on patrol. She looks out a window at the sky. She pages through a songbook on the piano, and for a moment I think she might sit down and play. She glances at me, coldly, then sits in the chair on the other side of the fireplace. We might resemble a couple of longtime spouses who've run out of repartee.

I wish there were a clock in this room.

I also wish, desperately, that Tom were here, and this wish, the raging humiliation of it, is what breaks me. But if I can't repress the tears, I can force myself to cry silently.

The terrier glances over when my hands go to my cheeks. She says nothing. If she were my guest, what would I ask her? Not who she is, because I know; it's obvious her two mute companions cut off their long hair. Not what she's doing, because that, too, is obvious: she's waiting. I don't want to know what for.

Slowly, so as not to startle my warden, I lift the hem of my shirt to my face and blow my nose. This time, she doesn't bother to look at me.

Tom's name almost escapes my lips: a plea, a scold, a curse. If he were here, however, we'd both be tied up, possibly to each other. He would be considered a hazard for his size alone. Without him, I am nothing to fear, am I? I am a pathetic divorcée destined for the boneyard.

Austin

It's a popular, clichéd assertion that architects have outsize egos, and I won't argue. Why shouldn't we? We put the roofs over your head: home roof, school roof, work roof. Dormer, cupola, belvedere, dome; mansard, atrium, vault. Birds build nests, bees build hives, and bears are skillful at finding secluded spots for crafting their dens. So roofs do not make us an exceptional species, do they? But roofs that rise in such a cunning yet frivolous range of shapes and styles? That artifice puts us, the practitioners, in a different, supra-instinctive order of being.

Another cliché: A man's home is his castle. The place he can most freely be himself, spread his limbs, exert his will . . . crank up the music and dance. A man's home is his night club. That one I like.

So I don't know what to make of this invasion, this . . . infiltration?

Miriam's voice, as soon as I heard it, before she had three words out, told me something was seriously wrong, something beyond the escalating worries she has, and which I share, though to a lesser extent, about Brecht. She said that Connie called her, alarmed. Brecht had come to her house in a strange, agitated state, and then he'd fled. He wasn't with Celestino.

She called me and said, "You have to go home," the way a bartender might kick you out after last call. I was at a potential job site, looking up at another defunct, decommissioned house of worship, this one destined for conversion to a single-family home. A nineteenth-century white-clapboard church, its two long flanks defined by rows of windows three feet wide, twenty feet tall. How to divide the place into rooms without violating all that reverent verticality: that's the nut I have to crack.

"Where are you?" I asked.

"Out looking," she said. "I need you to be at home. Now. I can't explain what's going on, but that writer woman of yours—Petra—I found her in the house when I went back to look for him."

"He let her in?"

"No. He's not there; just her. In the house. I told you: I can't explain. I have to go. Please go, just go. Go figure out what the hell is going on. I have to find Brecht." After a pause, she says, "You might not remember what day it is."

My mind lurches; have I forgotten a special occasion? April . . . "Andrew," I say. And I don't resent its weight on her, because of Brecht: it's the anniversary of his father's death.

My boots leave divots in the sodden church lawn as I return to my car.

I see her before she sees me. She stands in my kitchen, leaning forward against the long stretch of counter, hunched over and motionless, as if an anvil rests on her shoulders, pinning her in place.

I enter quietly, hoping to frighten her. I do.

"Oh God," she gasps. Frantically, she wipes her eyes.

I just stare at her for a moment, while Clio voices her rapture at my unexpected midday return. Sometimes she becomes so excited that her teeth chatter, and only a pair of human hands will soothe her. So before saying anything to Petra, I lean down and lavish my dog with caresses, attentive to her ears and, her omega pleasure zone, the base of her furry throat. "Good girl. Yes, good girl. You are. You know you are. Yes indeed."

I can hear Petra trying to control her breathing.

I take my time as I straighten up. "You had me fooled," I say as if it pleases me. "Mostly." Calm in the midst of a storm can be merciful or ruthless. She can take her pick.

For several seconds, I let her struggle for an answer, daring her to find one. She finally says, "I won't apologize. Not to you. Never to you."

I sit on one of the stools at the island. "So. Call me slow, but I realized your showing up has nothing to do with me. Or my work. All that talk about some woman who made brilliant, under-the-radar ocean art, back when I was in New York? You knew Issa. Funny. I didn't think anybody knew her except me. Or I had no idea who did. Ridiculous, right?" The painful truth is that Issa made me feel like the center of her universe—and that, as Brecht would put it, I zoned on that feeling. Yes: proof of my outsize ego.

I keep a hand on my phone, hoping for news from Miriam. She wants me here, in case Brecht shows up, but what I do about our suddenly unwelcome visitor is up to me. I could just say something on the order of *Leave town and never show your face again, you vixen,* but how can I not be curious, even if she's here only to stir up trouble?

When she doesn't answer my rhetorical question, I say, "What do you expect from me? Or was this all a scheme to, what, humiliate me? Make a fool of me because you think I made a fool of you—half a lifetime ago?"

"Maybe I expect, to begin with, a sign of remorse . . . regret. Sadness."

"Remorse for what? What she did was beyond my control. Obviously. But why is this even about me? Who are you?" Suddenly I realize: this could be a long-lost sister. This one, too, seems half deranged.

Petra is clearly struggling to maintain some kind of balance. I think I'm on top of this until she says, "Where is she? You let her go. Did you really just do that—let her go—without caring where she went?"

"How could you possibly know what I cared about then—or care about now? You know what? I mourned her for a long time."

I remember running after Issa when she fled the apartment following the last of our too many strange fights. "I'm done," she said that night, and there was something about her voice, deep and even, that worried me more than I'd worried when she was inconsolably weeping. So I chased her. And after that night, after the police (who, in the end, were clearly skeptical that I had seen anything like what I claimed to have seen), I waited for a long time—even months—for someone else who had known her to show up and make demands, even accusations. But she seemed to vanish into the void from which she had come. She had introduced me to no one, and I had believed her when she said she had no family—at least until she began to hint vaguely at a life she had lived at sea, a life she had left behind to become some kind of marine evangelist. She had chosen me to help her—to "sound the alarm" was how she put it. It didn't seem to matter to her that I had neither the time nor the inclination; somehow I had been "chosen."

"How exactly did you know her?" I say now.

"Just tell me what happened to her. Tell me."

"She killed herself," I say. "You didn't know that?" I try in vain not to sound angry. This isn't something I want to revisit. For a time, I went to a therapist to get me past the shock and confusion, the fear that I had spent those few intense months in thrall to a phantom.

"That's what the idiot cops concluded," Petra says angrily. "But no one found her body. I hired a detective."

"Her body was swept out to sea," I say. "I saw her go into that river. Do you know how cold that water had to be?"

"Did you even *listen* to her about where she came from?"

I open my mouth to counter with my therapist's theories about Issa's delusions, how it seemed so clear in hindsight that she'd been abused as a child and had rejected everything to do with her origins. Biologically, geographically, existentially, she had conjured a history for herself linked to a mythical city under the sea—and tried to draw me into it as her companion. What Petra says next confirms the wisdom of my keeping those ideas to myself.

"Well, I listened to her. I have no proof, and neither do you, that she didn't return to the sea. And if she did, there's no way she went back for good."

Forget the sister theory. Perhaps the two women were members of a cult before Issa came into my life. That would make sense. Accidentally, I make a sound that must come across as a laugh.

"She was right. You are every bit as cruel as she said."

What should I say to this insult, coming from a woman who is an imposter, possibly a psychopath, who broke into my house? Who, apparently, has been stalking me.

"I don't think she's the one we should be discussing," I say.

"I need a glass of water," she says.

I point to the cupboard that holds the glasses. "Help yourself. You've already made yourself at home. I'm sure you know where everything's kept."

Without taking a glass, she leans toward me and says, "You owe me answers."

"I don't see why or how I owe you anything—anything more than a call to the police, and I'd kick you out if I wasn't burning with curiosity about what drives somebody, after . . . how long, Petra? Is that even your name? After what, twenty, twenty-five years, you're here to dig up a tragic story about a woman who needed serious help and didn't get it—and sure, go ahead and blame me for not getting her the help she clearly needed. Okay, I didn't try hard enough to do that, I admit. But do you really believe she didn't die jumping into that frigid river? It's not as if she swam to New Jersey and hauled herself out to find a new identity, a new life." Though for the first time, it occurs to me that, considering what little I knew of her, perhaps that's exactly what happened. "Maybe," I say, "maybe she's an aging housewife, with grandkids and an almost-paid-off mortgage, living in Weehawken or Saddle River. Maybe she found bliss. She certainly wanted it. Whatever she wanted, it wasn't logical. So maybe you're right that she wasn't connected to the world as we know it, to reason or reality. But me, I'm long past the age of needing to believe in magic."

The silence filling my kitchen is broken by Clio's whining. She looks up at me, concerned, from her bed. She doesn't like my tone. I go over to her and reassure her, with my hands cradling her soft head, that she is fine, fine, everything is fine and she is a very, very, very good girl. I have the odd thought that this dog's love for me feels every bit as real as Issa's love was not.

"You are a monster," says Petra. "And you're right. I don't know why I came here, what I thought I would accomplish." Petra tries to move past me, but I hold up my hands to block her. I don't touch her, and yet she stops.

"How did you know her?" I say. "Because look, I can't deny it, she wasn't like any other woman I ever knew. And I did love her. I did."

Petra's face takes on a determined look, on the verge of rage. "I loved her more than you could possibly have. What *do* you know? You're a fucking man. She came to me when you turned a cold shoulder to her, when you refused to understand her. I guess you didn't have the imagination to see her, see that she came from another world. I do not mean that figuratively. I feel sorry for you, that magic is something you think we outgrow."

What do I say to that? I decide on "So. The whole Southern widow act, a total charade." I don't need to make this a question. Perhaps ten minutes ago, I noticed that she no longer has a Southern accent, not even a trace. "You had me, you know. My vanity, I guess. But you really—I mean, you really hunted me down after all these years? Why not then? Why now?"

"Because the cosmos reminded me of your existence. I wasn't brave enough back then. And you know what? Unlike you, I had a broken heart. I was paralyzed with grief."

"Well, I hope you got over it and led your life, because I did. That's what people do after something tragic they cannot change, right? Go on. Lead their lives."

She stares at me, as if I've just confessed to a capital crime.

"You could have changed things. You could have let her go when you should have let her go. She would have come to me. She came to me, you realize, when you hurt her the way you did. I was her refuge. But too late."

I suppose that if this woman had confronted me within months, even a year or two, of Issa's disappearance, this revelation (if true!) would have wounded me. But now it feels absurd, someone telling me that I have an incorrect memory about how some classic movie ends, a movie I haven't seen in decades. Do I tell her how deluded she was, try to convince her that Issa was obviously unhinged, possibly schizophrenic? But if it was so obvious, why did I keep hoping that she was simply eccentric, that it was somehow even a little charming? Was I that blinded by the physical attraction? And the art—that, too, seduced me. The crazy-complex drawings and paintings she made while I was away—for a long workday or a trip to the Middle East. Every time I returned, I came home to an apartment that looked as if a strong wind had blown it full of madly colored papers, on the floor and tables, across the bed where she had me bewitched. (Had she ever gone outside?) And there she'd be among it all, bent over a drawing of an octopus or a coelacanth or a watercolor vision of the trafficked surface of the sea as viewed from far below. She would look up at me when I came in the door, the planes of her lovely, unblemished face smudged in shades of cobalt, alizarin, ultramarine, and she'd greet me with her broad, warm, even yearning smile . . . and then her warm, yearning arms. If I told her she had to let me take her work to a gallery, she would look at me with dark dismay and tell me no, that wasn't the point of what she was making. She was preparing to take the beauty of her world as a weapon, take it to "the powers," show them what they stood to lose—what they needed to fully understand they were destroying.

"This is my sacrifice," she said to me finally. "This is why I am here. This is why I am with you. You will be my voice. You travel the world. You build important buildings. You know important people. I am . . . I'm not that."

"So what are you?" I said lightly, trying to calm her. "A mermaid? Am I that lucky—not even a sailor and that lucky?" Instantly, I was sorry I'd made a joke of it.

"Don't mock me," she answered, pulling away.

"I am not mocking you. I am just trying to understand what you're telling me. Can you see why I'm confused? Sometimes it feels like you're speaking in code."

"I thought I wouldn't need to tell you where I came from," she said. "I thought you would understand." She gestured angrily at her pictures.

"Issa, I'm a rational guy. I believe in physics, not folklore. You can't seriously be telling me that you—"

"I am not a fairy tale. 'Mermaid'?" She laughed coldly. "There is not a *word* for me, what I am or mean. I traveled a long way to find you—told you I would love you as long as you wish, and I will! But I need you to help me!" Her plea defused my fear. "You keep asking me who I am. I am a refugee of a city lost to the sea. To an angry, deafening, poisoned sea. And I carry that anger with me! I *am* that anger!"

I tried to embrace her again. She was on the stool, at my drafting table, on it a large drawing of seals on a shore of jumbled rocks. "I will help you," I said. "I will find you someone to talk to, someone who understands."

She pulled away, to look at my face. "Someone in power, someone who will listen?"

"Listen, yes," I said. "Listen to everything you have to say."

"Who?" she said. "Tell me who!"

I hesitated. "Someone who will help you understand where this amazing art comes from inside of you, how to talk about where you are really from. Because if we . . . if we are going forward . . ."

"This is useless," she said. She stood up violently, knocking a box of pastels to the floor, pushing me off balance. That was the first time she left the apartment and did not return until morning.

But she did come back, and when she did, she told me she had a plan: that I would find the names and addresses of the right people, the powerful people, and we would write a letter to each one, and send to each of them one of her pictures. This time I just let her talk.

We had been together five months when I began to realize how hasty I had been, how the wildness I'd fallen so hard for might be seen as the extrusion of an ingrown chaos. But before I had put that ring on her finger, I had taken her with me to a couple of parties—parties with colleagues, since the life I lived then allowed me no other space for socializing—and there she seemed perfectly ordinary to everyone (or so I observed), leading me to dispute the inner alarms that were beginning to sound, telling me that something about her "wasn't right." With others, including my parents, she was shy but in a warm, almost apologetic way, her head tilted down slightly to one side as she conversed with strangers—or, for the most part, listened to them talk. My mother told me, after the one dinner we shared, that she loved Issa's "modesty"; what a rare and undervalued virtue it was in the modern world. When Issa told me she owned nothing to wear to parties, it hardly worried me; I found her lack of concern for fashion charming, even frugal. I bought her a purple dress, short but long-sleeved, that turned male heads across the room as soon as we entered. (And yes, seeing that reaction gave me a foolish certainty as well.) One party, to celebrate the completion of a small art museum in Asheville, was at a restaurant on a barge, not far from the place where I'd taken that figure drawing class and met her. Saul took me aside after the speeches and murmured, "Now, there's a keeper—if she keeps you happy in the sack." Which, God knows, she did.

So she wasn't a product of my overtaxed, under-rested psyche. Even the police, after I showed them the blizzard of artwork in my apartment, the framed photo of us I'd placed on my dresser (Issa in that purple dress), the ring she'd tossed aside on a table before running away, agreed that it looked as if there was a someone to search for. And that damned raincoat of hers; the next morning they found it wrapped around the base of a wooden support beneath the pier from which I'd seen her jump.

"Where is all of her art?" Petra says. "If she killed herself, then she left it with you."

"She destroyed it," I say. "Tore it to shreds."

"I don't believe you."

"Then don't." I think of the one picture Issa left me—folded, slipped onto a shelf in my bedroom closet, so that I did not find it until that summer, when I went to store my blankets away for the season. On it she'd written a crude verse designed to shame me. That's when I knew I needed to talk to someone.

That painting, so opulently beautiful, so cruel, was my albatross. I have kept it with me all these years, and when I stop to think of it, it reminds me of one of those saint's bones you see in medieval churches, something weird but sacred that you'd never dare let go. Except that I do not display it. I keep it in a dark place. I can no more look at it than throw it away. I haven't opened it since the day I found it.

"Go to hell," Petra says, and she starts toward the door to my yard, though she stops when our phones simultaneously buzz, like a pair of angry bees. Neither of us will resist, because it's the sound of news that everyone is supposed to care about.

We stand still, like characters in a play, looking down at our gadgets, which tell us that three suspects in the Harvard Yard bombing have been spotted in video footage from a sidewalk security camera in Boston—and that two have been identified as recent Harvard students. They are at large and considered dangerous. The typically grainy photo is attached to the alert.

"At large," I say aloud. I wonder for the first time what the origin of this odd phrase might be. Could you be "at small"? Could you be "at enormous"? What if you were at infinitesimal?

"Go on," says Petra as she puts her phone back in her purse and pulls her own raincoat off my coatrack. "Go on leading your smug, protected life. Men like you—white, wealthy, married, employed—you get away with everything."

After she makes her dramatic exit, it takes me a few minutes to steady myself, not because of the insult (who would say she's wrong?) but because I am hopelessly enmeshed in a trance of memory. I take the three steps to the dining room and stare at the whale. I had owned that sculpture for about a month—it was a splurge after a small raise—when Issa came to my apartment for the first time. I kept it anchored on a side table in my living room (my dining room then just a nook of my kitchen), and when she entered, she made her way swiftly toward it, as if she'd expected to find it there. She wrapped her delicate hands around it and leaned down to press a cheek against the blunt prow of its nose. She looked so happy when she straightened up and looked around the room. "This is me," I said, making some awkward gesture. She nodded in obvious approval and said, "I'm glad it's you." Whatever she meant by that, I was glad, too.

As I stand here, knowing I should snap out of it and call Miriam, Clio comes to my side, as if to guard me. I lean down and tell her, because she can't hear it often enough, what a good girl she is.

Egon

Sooner or later, dearie," says Pearl, "the anarchists were bound to storm the ivory tower. From within makes it all the more seditious."

"Pearl," I say, "no one talks about ivory towers anymore. Harvard, Yale—your old bastion, Oxford—they've been vandalized, regendered, liberalized—"

"And now, apparently, weaponized." She pokes me in the arm and laughs.

"It isn't funny," I say.

"Mike," she says, appealing to my father, "is there room for humor in violence these days? Is there?"

"Yes," says Dad, but he sighs loudly.

We are walking to Mrs. Tattersall's for dinner, and we are trying to reason out how two Harvard students have joined, or at least enabled, this heightened crusade by Oceloti. "When Activists Turn to Terror" was the title of an editorial in this morning's news.

"Colonial guilt still looms over us all," says Pearl. She stops. "Case in point?"

"What do you mean?"

"Dearie, let's talk color lines. Those students are white. Oceloti is brown. They are trying to atone for their genetic sins by burning down the plantation. By blowing up the hand that raised them. Not complicated."

"Are you saying they're not genuine believers in a cause?" says Dad.

"No," says Pearl, "but identity will out."

"I guess it's come to this," I say. "That no source of righteous anger is immune to violence."

"Rightful anger, you mean," says Pearl.

We happen to have paused before the old First Congregational Church. The signboard on the façade is empty of homilies or meeting times, the door padlocked. I imagine it's destined to become another rich person's home, its footprint oblivious and greedy.

Pearl walks on, her long legs putting her out in front, as if she knows exactly where she's headed. One of the reasons I never tire of her company: her conviction is comforting, sometimes even catching.

Dad has said very little on our walk. That's not unusual—Mom was always the talker in their marriage, often needlessly talking *for* him—but now I realize he's doing more than listening; he's drinking us in. He's wishing that this could become a part of his new life: me, even maybe me and Pearl (though Dad has to know we'll never be a couple), staying here.

He's dropped the crazy subject of our starting a business—for now, at least—but I know he's scheming to hold me. We called Marinda together, after breakfast, and as Dad spoke with her, he'd glance at me with the happiest expression on his face, as if in fact all three of us were there, physically united in his new home, pulling out some antiquated board game.

I've told Dad that Pearl and I will stay two more nights, but then we're heading back to where we belong, to the obligations of the lives we've chosen. Forget colonial guilt; I'm feeling, while trying not to, filial guilt. I cannot give him what he wants most: my security on his terms—or, to be fair, on the terms of his generation—yet what a tease it is that here I am now, literally dressed as my father, wearing a clean shirt he loaned me for the evening.

Pearl ran her bright smock and jeans through Dad's washer and piled her braids into a regal sort of hive, making her seem intimidatingly tall. From the depths of her backpack, she pulled out a dark red lipstick, and now, as she speaks, her mouth glitters in the early evening light. Day in and day out, I've watched men fall in love with her, but she remains resolutely independent. I never ask why, simply grateful to claim so much of her as mine.

Mrs. Tattersall lives at the opposite side of the village from Dad's apartment. We won't pass our old house, not directly, but we could if we went a block out of our way. Even as I squabble with Pearl about the state of the world, my inner compass urges me to the right at the corner of Market and Gage.

This afternoon, while Pearl napped, I gave Dad the third degree about Margo Tattersall. They have an alliance, possibly even a friendship, he says, but nothing more. I want to tell him how much it would upset me if something were to "happen" between them, but I'm thirty-one years old, and it's none of my business. I also realized, as I watched him fight the urge to demonize my mother (and who could blame him?), that I've finally reached a point in my life at which nothing my parents do can embarrass me. So what does it matter if they swap spouses? If Dad falls in love with the English teacher who understood my adolescent agonies—and here's what's brilliant: made me understand that she understood, without ever saying a word—wouldn't that be an alignment of the stars, give me a taste of justice?

Among my queer friends of all persuasions, most would say mothers are the first to know. You may not know she knew first until you're free of all your home ties, open to yourself as well as those around you, but one day it'll come to you. Except that I'm pretty sure my mother was not the first to see that I was gay. To the bitter end of high school, Mom badgered and fussed about my lack of enthusiasm for the prom. There were always a number of girls who paired up for that particular form of misery, but I can remember only one pair of boys who went together as an actual couple (in twin tuxedos!). They had been lucky enough to find each other early on, and one of them was captain of the swim team. In our town, athletic prowess of any kind makes you bulletproof.

In my junior year, we lost our drama teacher to a high school in a neighboring town that cared more about arts than sports, and Mrs. T stepped in to direct the fall play. She chose *Pygmalion,* a play she taught every year in one of her classes, and to my panicked amazement, she cast me as Professor Higgins. Once we were off book, she met each of the principal actors to talk to us one-on-one about our characters. I'm sure I wasn't the only one a little nervous about meeting her alone in her classroom; in another context, we all knew, such a summons meant you were in trouble.

She sat not at her desk in front but in one of the cramped student desks. She'd pulled another one around to face her and urged me to sit. She told me she was pleased with my work so far and glad she'd cast me; it was my first lead, and she'd chosen me over Sven, the guy who'd been the pet of the departed drama teacher and played the male lead for three of the past four productions.

We talked about the play in general, about Shaw's social world versus ours. We talked about class and language and the necessity of performing it with the appropriate accents. And then she said, "So here's the most important question to ask yourself: Do you love Eliza? That is, are you, by the end, in love? If so, how do you know? If not, then why?"

I must have blushed horrendously. My first thought was whether she was asking me, Egon, whether I was in love with Marie, the beautiful redheaded senior she'd cast as Eliza. But of course, what a doltish thought. She was speaking to me as Professor Higgins. (In fact, I was miserably, hopelessly, mutely in love with Freddy Eynsford-Hill—in real life, Jesse Moore, a Black student who was bussed out from Boston and whose high jump had already won him a track scholarship at Yale.)

"No," I startled myself by saying. (Was I so certain? I took my role seriously and had given earnest thought to whether the professor was a misogynist or even, fundamentally, a misanthrope.)

"Good," said Mrs. Tattersall. "So then, why? Or why not?"

I was silent for a moment, during which she looked at me and I looked out the window, at the school tennis courts, their bright green surfaces drawn and quartered so clearly in white. "I don't think he likes women. Or like, well, I guess that's obvious."

"Doesn't 'like' them? That's a little broad."

"Isn't really comfortable with them?" I said, now less certain.

"Egon, do you think he's ever been in love?" She looked at me in a piercing but kind way.

"No," I said again.

"Do you think he ever will be?"

"No."

"Is he afraid of love, do you think?"

I honestly had no answer to this, but I also knew that Mrs. Tattersall wasn't going to accept any dithering, so I thought hard, contemplating those empty tennis courts yet again. Still she waited.

"I think he might be gay," I said.

"Might?"

"Okay, well, he is."

"Does he know that?" she said. "Or, sorry, that's a stupid question, isn't it? I mean, how afraid is he of being found out?"

"Well," I said, "I guess considering the era? I guess, probably very afraid. Like probably terrified."

"Interesting that if he lived in this era, here at least, things would be very different," she said. "Not that he'd ever feel completely safe. Especially in the beginning, when it's a secret, or at least unspoken. That's the hard part. You're figuring out whom you can trust. Even, maybe, whether you trust yourself." She said this so gently, and then she was quiet. I almost wanted her to do the inappropriate, totally-against-the-rules thing, just go ahead and ask me. Other guys were out and doing fine, so I had to wonder if she knew what a coward I thought I was.

She sat back and pressed both hands against the surface of the desk, getting ready to stand and end our conference. "So lean into it," she said. "Lean into that very vulnerable part of your character. It's where you'll find the greatest source of empathy, I think."

I nodded, unable to speak.

"You're doing such good work, Egon. I have a feeling I'm going to be very proud of this production. And I'm going to resent it when I have to go back to being just a boring old English teacher again!"

After I stood up, Mrs. Tattersall did something odd. She shook my hand. By then, almost nobody shook hands anymore, and we certainly never shook our teachers' hands. Had we just made a pact of some kind?

"Thanks," I said, and I rushed from the classroom. But in the hall I laughed. I was, in a way, finally out. Or the door had cracked open. Daylight poured in.

When we get to her house, Dad reminds me that the Tattersalls never use the front door. They are (or were) an enter-by-the-kitchen family. The back door is actually on the side of the house, and as we approach, I try to remember when I last entered that door: sometime in middle school, I'm thinking, when I was paired with Doro on a science project.

"You've got the wine, so why don't you go first," I say to Pearl, pushing her playfully ahead of me.

She knocks on one of the glass panes, and we wait for a moment. I see her peer in, free hand cupped against the side of her face.

After several seconds the door opens, and I hear a male voice invite us in. One by one we enter the kitchen, but the person who greets us isn't Mrs. T. He's a stranger, maybe in his forties, dressed all in black—more New York than Vigil Harbor. "Come right on in," he says, and he takes the bottle of wine from Pearl. His smile is comfortable and encouraging. "Margo asked me to welcome you."

The kitchen counters hold the early preparations for a meal—loose vegetables, some chopped, others waiting; chicken, seasoned but still raw, in a glass dish—and the wallscreen is on, tuned to a news show but muted. And, to my shock, leaning against a cabinet is the poster for *Betrayal,* the last production I was in before graduation. Clearly Mrs. T dug it up from somewhere as a surprise. I cross the room to see it up close, laughing. How gravely serious we were as teenagers playing roles absurdly far from our emotional reach! Now, in fact, I'd be twice as humbled to play the role of Robert.

I am about to call Pearl over when I hear the bolt being drawn on the door. Turning, I see another stranger, this one much younger, join us from the living room. He doesn't look unfriendly, but he holds a gun at his side. Plain as day, a gun.

"Dearie," whispers Pearl, and she takes my hand.

"I don't want you to worry. Really," says the man who let us in. He introduces himself as Ernesto. "I'm going to hold you here for a short while, and then I'll leave you in peace. Though I might need a favor." He looks at Dad. "You'd be Mike."

My father doesn't move, nor does he take his eyes off the man addressing him.

This doesn't seem to unnerve or offend Ernesto, who says, "So why don't you all join Margo in the living room."

Single file, me first, we obey. Mrs. Tattersall sits in a wing chair beside her fireplace. I can tell that she must have been crying, but she's stopped. Meeting my eyes, she begins crying again. "I'm sorry," she says.

I smile at her and shake my head. I don't dare speak, but of course I wouldn't blame her for whatever drama it is we've entered, whatever roles we'll be assigned. I find myself strangely unafraid. Pearl is still holding my hand, tight, and we sit on a small brocaded couch—a love seat. So we are a couple, for the moment, after all. And it could certainly be said that we love each other, Pearl and I.

"Mike," Ernesto says, "you come back to the kitchen with me."

I register now that we have a minder: a woman with short dark hair, who does not look the least bit friendly, blocking the way to the front door (probably stuck shut after years of disuse). And then the man with the gun—the very young man with the gun in one hand, hanging so easily at his side—comes in from the kitchen and gives her the weapon. He comes straight up to me and Pearl and holds out his hands. "We need your phones," he says, and he adds, "please," as if we might not otherwise comply.

"I don't have mine," I say, "and she doesn't own one."

His expression hardens.

"It's the truth," I say.

He tells me to stand up, to turn around, as he feels each of my pockets, even the pocket of Dad's shirt, beneath my sweater. I've had to release Pearl's hand.

When I sit back down, he makes Pearl stand and go through the same search, makes her turn full circle. When she sits again, she leans on me, and I can feel stray braids from her sumptuous tower of hair tickle the top of my right ear. She takes my hand again and squeezes it hard.

"Thank you," says the man who searched us. He goes to stand at the door to the kitchen and says, through it, "They don't have their phones."

I hear Ernesto reply that it doesn't matter, that they already have two phones they can use. "Mike," I hear him say, but after that he lowers his voice, and the words are unknowable. What I do know is that my father will do whatever he's asked, all because of me. Because I happen to be here.

I become acutely, consolingly aware of the places where Pearl's body and mine are touching, and I feel bad for Mrs. Tattersall, who sits alone in that posture-scolding antique chair. She is looking down at her hands, joined in her lap. We are all silent and very still, as if in a museum diorama or perhaps an absurdist play in which time moves like molasses.

In the studio where I met Pearl, we loved being paired for two-handers. We simply clicked. After a month or so of seeing our easy connection, our teacher kept us mostly apart, pairing us with other actors, to keep us challenged. Pearl and I took to leaving together, at the end of class, heading to a nearby bar on Rivington. We'd giggle as we left the building where our class met. "We narrowly escaped detention today," I might say, and Pearl might respond, "Write on the board one hundred times, *I will not lock eyes with Pearl Kinoro. I will not lock eyes with Pearl Kinoro. . . .*" Pearl has seen me, with grace if not a lack of judgment, through three disastrous relationships.

Ernesto reenters the room, without Dad. He starts to speak, and, forgetting my situation, I interrupt him. "Where's my father?"

"We'll be going on an errand," Ernesto says, very matter-of-fact. "We'll be back. I want you to know that nothing will happen to any of you. Very soon, you will all be free to go about your lives. I'm not in the habit—" He stops abruptly. He seems to be considering something. Then he turns toward Mrs. Tattersall. "I want you to know," he says, "this wasn't in my plans."

He doesn't seem to mind our staring at him, and now I understand exactly who he is, who his henchpeople are, and I feel a sharp spasm travel through my body, the revelation that I—and Pearl and my dad and my onetime English teacher—have, as some would say, intersected with history. We may become survivors of a political drama, or we may be casualties. We may raise the body count of Oceloti's radicalization.

Ernesto leaves the room. I hear the kitchen door open and close.

Again we are all silent, and in the silence, I hear a car pull into a nearby driveway, a door slam, and I wish I were brave enough to leap up and shout. But I want to save my skin, so I simply lean harder on Pearl. I wonder what it comes from, the particular scent of her hair. It's a familiar smell to me, a spice or perfume I've never bothered to parse, but I focus on it now, a mystery to ponder while I await news of my fate. And my father's.

Look down from the top of Celestino's tree house, days of rain soaked into the bark, new leaves scoured and dripping but holding firm, and you might see, beyond the rooftops, at the mouth of the harbor, the seals on Ruby Rock tucking themselves in, all accounted for, water still too cold for the sharks. Three of the seals are a much lighter gray than their podmates, a conspicuous mutation spreading through the mingled populations north of Boston. Farther out, if your vision were supernaturally sharp, you would spot an old fishing boat, no nets aboard, apparently uncertain on its course. But it's waiting, waiting for a signal to come in after dark, to pick up passengers and carry them onward, away from danger of their own making.

Closer in, on land, look to a high clearing near Harrow Point, where a brief chink of sunlight catches on something shiny in prismatic splinters and a single figure paces in circles and tangents: He remains fretful and confused, yet also in the process of willfully un-confusing himself, except that the clarity is frightening. He doesn't know what to do and cannot decide where to go. He knows that his mother will be worried, that he should simply go home, but he isn't ready for her to know what he knows. Except that of course she already knows it; what he can't figure out is how to face her with the knowledge that she protected his delusions. Should he be grateful or angry? Did some doctor tell her to "humor" him, to "protect" him from the truth? He isn't a child! So he is angry as well as fretful.

Except that he is a child, or he is hers. So she drives in relentless loops, down all the dead-end lanes, getting out and searching among the boats dry-docked in small fleets, waiting to be launched as spring warms to summer; following the paths of the single swath of undeveloped land in town, a thirty-acre wood where a few deer still manage to eke out a wild living and teens go to escape the cams they suspect may be hidden under the eaves of any building they pass. Not that they have serious crimes to hide. They just want to be left alone.

Most teens, this evening, are home, though many are still at the middle school or the High, in sports practice or mock trial or eco-initiative or play rehearsal. Teachers are packing up after a day they wish had been called off, because who could teach anyone anything when everyone knew that Vigil Harbor, like all other towns within a wide radius of Harvard Square, is on high alert?

From the tree house, you might notice, as a matter of fact, that all twelve VH community cruisers, as well as the fire chief's van, are roaming the town, though looping with less purpose than the car in which Miriam Kepner is looking for her son. Over at the town landing, Barry Unwin, the harbormaster, stands in his boat, talking by radio, on a protected frequency, with his buddy Walt at the CG station just south of Boston. Any reason to believe that the persons of interest will flee by water? No evidence so far, Walt tells him, but stay tuned.

All points bulletin: that's the antiquated term from classic movies in which criminals are on the run. The oldest members of local law enforcement in normally uneventful suburbs experience the secret swell of feeling more consequential, more *noticed,* than they have since the visa raids. Even the worst of the storms do not give them this degree of authority, this stature, this sense that for once, they make people feel grateful for their presence and protection.*

This you cannot see from the tree house, but June Smithson, in her post as select board chair, feels useful as she drives four trays of carrot muffins, warm from her oven, to the precinct. There, she lingers with today's dispatch officer, Mink Taylor, who recently crossed the line from male to female. No matter the social whiplash she feels, June wants to be in the thick of it, the first to hear if the perpetrators are captured, though she knows it won't be here. She's old enough to remember quite clearly the manhunt that followed the bombing at the Boston Marathon, those demon brothers, the murder, the carjacking, the citizen who noticed blood on the cover of the boat he kept in his driveway. That was Watertown, a town as law-abiding then as Vigil Harbor is today.

June's husband, who loves his role as revolutionary reenactor far more than his cleanware sales chief job, kept her company while the muffins were baking and remarked to her, as they watched the news, that this is what it must have felt like in 1775 when the town's insurgency went from clandestine meetings to open defiance, when all eyes were peeled on highways and harbors, waiting for the Crown to send out the torches, to burn Vigil Harbor to the ground.

June told him not to get carried away. This wasn't a revolution.

What was any revolution, countered her husband, if not terrorists having their way?

Immediately below the tree house, so close that the tree's own branches would hide the view, Celestino sits in his truck, in his driveway, suddenly knowing more than anyone else in town, because he's made a connection that no one else can. So: will he go inside, to Connie and Raul, and willfully, defensively pretend he doesn't know what he knows, or will he take his new, perilous knowledge and face the necessary risks to make sure, if he can (and he must), that he never crosses paths with that man again?

As quietly as he can, he puts the truck in reverse, backs into the street, and drives toward the commercial pocket of town. On Washington Street, he passes Miriam. They are so intent on their respective missions that they do not recognize each other.

Petra

To hell with *everyone*. EVERYONE. Myself included. But most recently, to hell with that woman at the desk downstairs, who informed me that the reason my car hasn't come, won't come, is that the cops have closed the town border to all but residents, who are readily identifiable by the stickers on their plates. Meaning that if I want to get to the airport or train station, either I will walk or I will have to steal a car. And then just imagine the security lines at any nearby transit hub.

I sit on my creaky four-poster bed, with the glass of local wine the innkeeper gave me by way of consolation, and I fume. I decide to postpone the anger I'm feeling at myself.

She tells me she'll charge me only half the room rate for the extra night's stay to which I am probably doomed. "And tomorrow, well, we'll see about tomorrow tomorrow," she said. Cheerfully!

I finish my free glass of bad wine quickly.

My suitcase, fully packed, sits next to the door. I will have to unpack at least some of it all over again. I go into the bathroom and look at my face in the mirror. It happens to be a flattering mirror, and I do what I sometimes do in solitary vanity: I extend my neck to its full length, turn my head slightly to the left, and smile in a way that's both seductive (or used to be) and jaw-tightening. I'm trying to re-create the headshot I sent out for nearly a decade, my puffed-up résumé on the reverse.

"Fuck," I say, observing what gravity's done to my jawline. Cosmetic surgery's a cinch these days, more about lasers than scalpels, but Carly and I made a pact that we would never succumb, that we would love each other no less for the accumulation of folds and creases and rogue pigmentation. Of course, that was after I'd given up the stage—and before she left me by dying. No, I remind myself, don't blame her. It wasn't even as if she had some looming, encroaching medical condition to which she gave the finger. A stroke is well named, because it comes unhinted-at, unbidden, like a truck running a red light, an avalanche loosened by stampeding elk, an armed drone descending through a cloud.

Do I believe Kepner that she destroyed all the art she made? The funny thing is, I saw only the contents of the small sketchbook she left propped against my door the day she came by and I wasn't there. It still doubles me over, to think of missing her that final time. To wonder if, had I been there and not at a stupid audition for a stupid commercial I didn't even get, things might have turned out differently.

This would have been her first visit by daylight, not counting the very first time, months before, when I'd brought her home with me and made her eggs. I did not wonder for an instant who'd left the sketchpad, and I held it close as I hurried the keys in the locks. Hungry with hope, I was deluded enough to think she might be waiting for me inside. Perhaps the otherworldliness I'd seen in her included the ability to walk through doors.

The pad contained a dozen pages of delicate colorful drawings: different species of fish so specifically rendered that I knew they were probably impeccable in their accuracy; an otter; seahorses; an extravagant jellyfish. Had she gone back to the aquarium without me, tried to recapture what we felt that afternoon? I remember sitting on the edge of my bed with the sketchpad, going through it again and again, longing to be able to see her that minute. I lay awake a long time that night, listening for a knock on my door. (This time, I would give her a set of keys.) If I had known I'd never see her again, I'd have gone mad.

Why, once I realized she was never coming back, once I'd hired that buffoon of an amateur detective, didn't I seek out Kepner and hold him to the fire then?

I have to get out of this room or I will torture myself into a human knot. At least they haven't barred pedestrians from the streets.

On with my coat and back downstairs. "Excuse me, but where," I ask the gloom-proof innkeeper, "do people around here go for a lively scene with drinks? Within walking distance."

"Lively?" She laughs like a glockenspiel. "I'd recommend two places: The Jetty, your basic faux dive bar—you know, rich people slumming it—and the bowling alley."

"Bowling alley?"

"The Drome. It doubles as a bar and a place you can get a decent falafel. Avoid the fake fish sticks."

I spare her my opinion that there is no such thing as a decent falafel. I ask for directions to both. One involves going left out the front door; the other one, right. I decide to go for the quirkier choice and head right.

The rain has stopped, at least for now, but still I'm the only person out and about. Cars pass me every so often, and I walk alongside houses from which I can hear, muffled but still discernible, newscasts yammering on as background to the suburban dinner hour. At one point, I hear a chopper speed past high above, heading out to sea. Choppers remind me of searches, and searches remind me of Brecht, that poor stunted young man, his mother desperately looking for him. I hold nothing against her and hope she's found him by now.

The murky sky admits streaks of dull orange, the sun sinking somewhere out of view. I follow the curve of Market Street, as instructed. It parallels Cove Road, the street that hugs the seawall and the boulders hemming the harbor, so I get occasional glimpses of water, but I am spared the bluster. I pass a couple of older schoolchildren, to whom I'm invisible, then a man in an overcoat carrying an old-fashioned briefcase. We greet each other primly before he crosses the street to give me the narrow sidewalk.

I hear my destination before I see it: the echo of bowling balls striking pins, gleeful shouting. My luck, I'll walk in on some birthday party for third graders, find myself hauled into a game of Pin the Tail on the Donkey. Do children play that anymore? The Drome is a long, squat cinder-block building separated from the shore by a large lot filled with sailboats that look as if they've been shrink-wrapped in blaring white plastic. I've arrived in a shockingly ugly pocket of this otherwise picturesque village.

I hesitate, as if once I've gone in, there's a chance I'll never get out. Or maybe it's just that I'm reminded of the days, starting a year after Issa vanished, after I gave up on finding her, when I summoned the nerve to walk alone into bars I'd learned were designated for women who prefer women. At first, it felt about as comfortable as walking into bars designated for burly, tattooed male bikers. I had to figure out if I had "a type," if I wanted to invite or be invited. The first woman I went home with was a jigsaw-puzzle addict, the second a devout early-morning practitioner of yoga. I never fully relaxed in these places, yet I went back again and again—until that night at the theater; until Carly.

Inside, the first thing I'm grateful for is the warmth; the second is the din. There is indeed a group of rowdy young teenagers at one lane, cheering, teasing, dancing to the piped-in soundtrack. But the long bar is populated by adults, standing two deep behind the stools, all focused on the wallscreens, which show not sports events but the progress (not much, I soon gather) being made on the pursuit of the men—and the woman—believed to have set the bombs in Cambridge and, before that, lower Manhattan.

No one pays me much mind; this is a crowd of people who mostly know one another, locals seeking other locals at a sensational moment when the spouse and kids don't provide enough friction to sustain the excitement.

I shoulder my way through the scrum and get myself a gin and tonic, safer than any wine they'd probably serve me. With no seats in the bar, I wander over to the lanes. There are seven, three occupied, so I look for a space as far from the action as possible and sit on a bench facing a row of marbled balls. I haven't thought of bowling, whether anyone does it anymore, in decades. So I'm now in a time capsule, hurtling back to those middle-school birthday parties: sleepovers, boy talk, limp cold pizza.

I should call my mother, break my silence. I pull my phone from my purse. Most New York friends have taken the hint and backed off. Am I going back there now? What *am* I doing with my life?

This is when I spot him, sitting even more aloof from the bustle than I am, in a small booth wedged into an odd alcove beside the lane farthest from the bar, no food or drink on the table before him. And my first reaction is, even though I'm not a mother, a lurch of relief in my chest: he's safe. Maybe he's hiding, but he's safe. I think for a moment of calling Austin. Ha. As if.

As I'm staring at Brecht, perhaps because I'm staring at him, he looks up and clearly recognizes me. The expression on his weary face, in his gentle eyes, is so stricken that I understand I have no choice but to join him. I pick up my drink and cross the shiny blond floor, passing two empty lanes. When I sit across from him, he doesn't smile, but he says, "I know some of those people at the bar, but no way would they even look at me."

"Well, you're my one familiar face," I say. "And also, did your mother find you?"

"No. She'd never think I'm here."

"So you're hiding."

"No." The word sounds more like a question than a protest.

I lean across the table. "Then why would you go somewhere you never go?"

His hands are spread flat before him, and he looks intently down, at the stretch of cracked blue Formica between them. "I don't know."

I stare at the top of his head, his damp dark hair, which falls in slim, untidy wings down over his cheeks. The part in his hair is deeply tanned.

The funky smells of this place—beer and grilled cheap meat vying with old sneaker—make me realize, perversely, that I am hungry. "Are you hungry?" I ask my mournful companion.

His mop of hair swings as he nods. Then he looks up. "The only really good thing here is the rings. The onion rings."

"Fair enough. We'll feast on rings." I tell him not to go anywhere, though as I wait in the short line to order, I keep glancing back, worrying that he might try to slip out. I laugh when I see him steal a sip of my drink. I decide to risk ordering him a beer. It's impossible, while I'm waiting, not to look at the news. Above the talking heads lurk three rectangular photographs. One shows a woman, her head and shoulders, seen from the typical spy-cam street view: mostly dark skullcap, but a fairly clear profile. She has been identified, a mugshot popping into place, as a known "lieutenant" of Oceloti. She is Brazilian, and she was jailed once, in Manaus, for destruction of public property.

The photos of the other two suspects show them posing, smiling cooperatively for the occasion: two young men, both around Brecht's age but wearing the patina of entitlement. One shot is clearly an excerpt from a sports team photo (the uniform; the flanking shoulders); the other could be a headshot from a yearbook. Good lord—that's right; they're actual Harvard students. "What the fuck," I mutter as I take the basket of onion rings and the tall glass of beer. Froth spills over the edge, drifting down onto my skirt.

"The world is doing what it does best: going to hell," I say as I set the glass and the basket on the table. Then I wonder just how much of an idiot I am to say this to a boy in obvious distress. As if I haven't already proven myself an Olympic-stature numbskull these past few days.

"Yeah," he says. "The basic truth."

He thanks me for his beer and takes a long draft.

"How about I call your mom?" I say, pulling out my phone.

He gives no indication that he heard my question, though he is staring at me. "Like, who are you? Why are you here?" His tone is respectful, as if he might somehow be in awe of me. Or maybe he's just trying to distract me.

"I came here out of heartbreak and rage," I tell him after a few beats of silence. During that silence someone has a strike (not to be confused with a stroke). Pink lights flash, a bell rings, and the shouting washes over us like a wave. "Which I'm beginning to see adds up to regret."

He nods, as if that's the answer he was expecting. "Yeah, regret," he says.

And yet I wasn't honest with him, was I? I came here wanting to get some sort of retroactive revenge, my pound of flesh. What made me think that I could do such a thing?

"I've despised your stepfather for thirty years, without actually knowing him," I say.

Another nod.

"Are you all right?" I ask.

Again, he stares at me before speaking. "I don't think so."

Oh terrific. And I know that it would be easy enough for me to get up, say I'm going to the restroom, then duck out of sight and alert Miriam.

"This is the day my father died."

"Oh, Brecht."

He rushes on, saving me from the predictable platitudes. "Not like I'm not used to it. We don't make a big deal of it, me and Mom. I mean, that would be max awkward with Austin. But we don't forget about it, either." He looks directly at me. "You don't have to say anything. Like, I just wanted to tell someone. Guess it's you."

He looks around the space, even up at the industrial ceiling, a fretwork of pipes and steel beams. "In World War Two," he says, "this was a munitions factory. Then it was empty for twenty years."

"Everything in this town has an important history, doesn't it?"

"This town is about war," says Brecht. "Like, everywhere you look."

"The world is about war," I say. "Or sometimes that's how it appears."

"No, I don't think so. Don't let people make you see it like that."

Is he crying? His head is lowered, his nose almost touching the rim of his glass. What would happen if I put a hand on his shoulder?

"I want my mind back," he says.

Now I'm paralyzed. Christ. My inner Carly is telling me this is what I get for my misbehavior. "Let's take you home." I gesture broadly, at the disaster junkies hugging the counter, at the three groups of people blithely bowling, defiantly having their fun. "Everybody, really, ought to go home."

"I can't," he says.

"Why?" I wonder if something abusive has taken place. Is Austin, after all, an evil stepfather?

"He won't be there anymore."

"Austin?"

If this boy doesn't stop staring at me, I may go a little mad. He resembles someone under a spell. And then I wonder if he's on a drug of some kind. Not weed but . . . a tranquilizer, maybe?

"Noam."

I am now so out of my depth that I feel I have no choice. "Brecht," I say, "I'm going to get Austin on the phone and can you please talk to him?"

"I won't talk to him. I will leave."

"Okay, okay. What do you want to do? Because I'm not just leaving you. And I can't stay here all night. Or even bowl. Do you bowl?"

This actually incites a smile. "Yeah. Or I used to. Like everybody in this stooge town knows how to bowl. But I'm not bowling now."

"Does Austin bowl?" I ask.

"He's pretty good."

"Oh."

"He brings out-of-town clients here. He says it's a 'novelty.' "

I reassess the place, but it looks no more appealing than it did half an hour ago. I might as well be in Paramus. There are no windows, no pictures on the walls, and the lighting is outmoded halogen, harsh and pitiless on the varnished wood lanes—and, I imagine, on my face.

"Let's get out of here. Let me walk you home," I say.

He stands so abruptly that I gasp. "Okay, let's go. I need to go somewhere else. You can go with me or not."

I knock back the rest of my drink, crunch on the ice, and grab one of the last onion rings (which are, as advertised, damn good).

"I'm with you," I say. And I have another mission, I figure. As long as I'm stuck here, why not?

Mike

He somehow thinks that I want to hear the story of how he went from poor little rich coffee heir to Harvard dropout to defender of the rain forest to nihilist bomber (though what he calls himself is a "habitat warrior"). Is he simply addicted to talking, to the sound of his own voice?

At least he does not expect dialogue. My jaw feels wired shut. I almost wish I had sent Egon with him—this man wouldn't have the nerve to kill anyone bare-handed—but Egon no longer knows where I keep the keys to the boat, and it's one he's never driven, both longer and wider than the Mako I taught him to pilot as a teenager.

It's approaching dark, and the damp chill runs bone-deep. The walk back to my apartment feels endless when all I want is to return to Margo's, where that fierce-looking woman and those two reckless boys are in charge. They are the ones I worry about. And the gun.

"We will be gone, without a trace, once we meet up with our friends," Ernesto tells me for the second time. "We will make it easy for you."

What will I do, I wonder, if we cross paths with someone I know? Will I have to stop for townsfolk pleasantries, will I have to go through pretending an introduction? Will the acquaintance be able to see that something is very wrong here—that I'm being held hostage? Ernesto has Margo's phone now, can make calls with impunity—unless I find a way to let someone know. We do pass a few people, all strangers, all attending to their damn gadgets, sparing not a glance for me and my captor. This wouldn't have been the case, I realize rather pointlessly, if Ernesto had been force-marching Deeanne through the streets of Vigil Harbor. I nearly laugh out loud at the thought. My wife would have signaled distress in some coded fashion, with hips or lashes; cop cars would have swooped in. . . . But even if a cruiser were to pass us, what could I do?

I feel more contempt than fear, as much for myself as for Ernesto, and I have the childish urge to taunt him about being an inept terrorist: not that he failed to sow terror—and really, how hard is that?—but according to the news, the intended quarry in both bombings survived, though the latest target, at Harvard, suffered superficial injuries. He was a professor of economics teaching a research seminar at the library. He was, on the side, a consultant to a large Japanese import company dealing mainly in timber.

"Here," I say. I go up the steps, Ernesto close behind me.

How different my apartment appears to me now than it did an hour ago. The overhead light illuminates a room as yet unlived in, boxes in a corner, two rolled carpets leaned upright against a wall. I try to imagine myself turning around swiftly, shoving Ernesto to the floor, knocking him unconscious, rolling him in one of those carpets and securing it with duct tape—not killing him, no, but immobilizing him.

I go to the drawer where I now keep keys: to my rarely used car, to my lab, to the storage space in Knowles I rented for the furnishings that I know my children wouldn't want me to toss—and to the boat. Another fantasy: that the keys to the boat just aren't there; that I offer the car keys by way of consolation—though there would be no escaping the town by car. I saw the news before Egon, Pearl, and I left for what we thought would be a pleasant dinner.

God, Pearl. I heard a bit of her story this morning at breakfast—was that actually this morning?—and I wonder who, out there, might be worrying about her. All I know is that she has a mother halfway around the world.

Oh, and there I was worrying for my own child's welfare in New York City. Because here, here in lofty, elitist but oh-so-liberal, end-of-the-line Vigil Harbor, up on our granite headland, we are perfectly safe! Let the seas rise over Hull and Duxbury and my poor beleaguered Essex marshes; let them reclaim Back Bay and overflow the Charles; we sit high and pretty for another two or even four generations. We could live on homegrown beans and pond algae and jellyfish pulled from the harbor when the blooms are blown this way by storms. Those Timer survivalists have nothing on us!

But I pick out the boat keys, attached to their bright, buoyant fob. Like the fake stars on Egon's bedroom ceiling, it glows in the dark.

"Excellent," says Ernesto.

He steers me toward the door but then stops. "Those phones. The ones left behind?" I know what he means, but I do not move. "I'll need to borrow them."

"Mine is the only one," I say.

He looks skeptical.

"My son left his . . . behind. He doesn't live here."

He follows me into my bedroom. The phone is on the side table. I reach for it, but Ernesto touches my arm to overrule my reach. As he conveys it toward his pocket, it glows alive for an instant, and there is the photo I like best of my children: ten and twelve, sunstruck smiles, on a beach that has since washed away. Into the pocket of Ernesto's dark jacket they go.

He makes me take him into the other bedroom, where Pearl carefully made her bed and Egon left his a vortex of blankets. He checks the surfaces, kneels nimbly, and gives a quick look under the furniture. When he stands, he glances out the window, then turns to me and nods. "Okay," he says.

Before leaving again, I stop to survey the sad living room that still feels borrowed to me.

"Not your last look, Mike," says Ernesto, fueling my rage both by saying my name and by reading my mind. Once again, I picture myself throwing him to the floor, against a wall. I must outweigh him by fifty pounds. But I have no choice here, and I lead him out to the street again, on toward the boat.

My marine research permit allows me to tie up at the harbormaster's dock. So, again, I nurture the anemic hope that authority will intervene. Barry will be there, and he will see the situation at a glance (though last I knew, Ernesto's face was not one of those being posted on every screen, searched for). Never mind; Barry is a perceptive guy. He's the best pool player at The Jetty. And wouldn't the harbormaster carry a gun? He has a flare gun, that much would be true. A strange memory intrudes, of a grisly thriller I once watched with Egon in which the climax is a cat-and-mouse chase scene on a massive cargo ship; the good guys know that one of the hundreds of containers holds a nuclear weapon. The combatants are finally winnowed down to the arch-villain and the über-hero, the former carrying some assault weapon, the latter armed with maybe a Boy Scout penknife. Suddenly they sight each other across the open deck. And there, beside the hero, is a flare gun on a rack of tools for use in an emergency. As the villain hoists his grenade launcher into place, we see a sizzling flare plunge through his chest. Agonizing death. Triumph of good over evil.

I replay this scene as we descend Wharf Street and enter the cul-de-sac that ends at Barry's dock. His office, which overlooks the dock, is dark, the slip for the harbormaster's vessel empty. My boat bobs gently at its appointed place, awaiting me like a faithful dog.

I step on board, and immediately, as I help Ernesto over the side, I can tell he has no sea legs whatsoever. But once he's in the boat, he loses no time assessing what it contains. "How many passengers can it hold?" he asks.

This seems like a stupid question to me, since clearly it comfortably holds four, with room to spare. And then I get it: of course he'll need to take his hostages along, to the transfer point. Obviously I will be at the wheel. Four captors, four hostages.

"Ten." I would lie, but passenger and weight capacity are listed on the console.

"Good."

He instructs me to open the various holds and compartments. Lines, life cushions, blankets, windbreakers, a first aid box whose contents I haven't inspected for a couple of years. A spare compass, a packet of batteries, tools, sunscreen, a thermos, several gallons of distilled water. Bungee cords with which to tie us all up before throwing us overboard.

In the small cabin, a miniature sink and countertop occupy one corner, but what little space remains is taken up mostly by racks that

I use for transporting my samples. A large toolbox—which Ernesto opens greedily—contains chemistry kits: sterile test tubes, pH strips, and various colored solutions. An old wine crate bolted in place holds half a dozen books containing charts and formulas.

"Not exactly homey," says Ernesto.

I say nothing.

"Battery?"

I tell him it's fully charged (sadly, it is) and see him deciding whether to take my word for it. I ask if he wants to attract attention by starting the engine now. He nods and laughs briefly, under the false impression that I have even a splinter of sympathy for him. To my surprise, he tells me what he has in mind: a rendezvous point behind an island off Knowles that I estimate will take us no more than forty minutes to reach. "Then you'll be free," he assures me.

I glance up and along the shoreline, toward the boatyard at the landing, the few homes perched on their granite pedestals. Lights burn in many windows, and though it's hardly a windless evening, I hear skeins of jukebox music from The Jetty. Sometimes, when I come ashore on a late afternoon, I can even smell the fries.

"Let's go then," says Ernesto. "Let's return you to your lives, shall we?"

As I step back onto the dock and give the man my hand (I could take a firm grip of his slim wrist and fling him, like a dance partner, over and off the other side of the dock), I think about that: my life. Have I been feeling sorry for myself? Whatever for?

I am going to be a grandfather. The baby's name is Eden, and I am going to meet her. I am.

Brecht

Home is where I should've gone. Seems like I have some basic knack for putting myself in the wrong place at the wrong time, because this stooge decision—to go find my old English teacher, the one person other than Mom who had solid faith in me before my life went haywire—may be the worst of my life, worse than taking Noam to see that acrobat I liked in Union Square. Whether or not she was there, the acrobat, whether or not she was blown to bits, I'll never know. For months I put dollars in her basket, but I never asked her name. She always wore this ultra-neon candy-striped skinsuit, and when she did her spins and flips, she looked like the human version of an old-fashioned pinwheel you'd pick up at a New York street festival when I was a kid.

Where I am now is not a street festival, no kind of festival at all.

Is it any consolation that these bombers aren't "my" bombers, aren't the ones who subtracted Noam from the world? There's three of them, and the two guys are basically my age. They're the Harvard students: ex–Harvard students by now. In the max-awkward moments when we meet their eyes, these two keep forgetting not to fake-smile, and then they remember and their faces clamp down. The woman is the pro, the one with the gun. Her expression's carved in ice.

We're all in Mrs. Tattersall's living room, a place I've been just once before, when she invited the Breakfast Poetry Slam to meet here one weekend. She made us waffles in her kitchen, but first she had us read our poems to one another in this room, standing in the curve of the piano like we were nightclub singers. I guess you could call it an honor, but I was queasy listening to Rosa read a poem about her nipples while she stood in front of all those photos of Mrs. T's daughters.

They have one of us tied up in thick tape, the one other guy besides me. They didn't tape his mouth, or any of our mouths, I guess because they know that we know that if we try to shout, they'll hurt us. The curtains are drawn, so you can't even tell if anybody's passing by, and probably nobody is. Once in a while the woman's phone buzzes (except that it's Petra's phone), and she'll hand the gun back to Guy One while she goes into the kitchen to deal with the call. Any talking takes place in the kitchen.

Mrs. Tattersall and Petra are in the chairs by the fireplace. You can tell that Mrs. T used to be crying; now Petra's the one, wiping her eyes on her sleeves. Me and this woman named Pearl (definitely not from here) share a tiny sofa. No way can we actually talk, but earlier, when the pro went to the kitchen, this woman whispered her name and I whispered mine. "Like the playwright?" she whispered back. When I nodded, she cocked her eyebrows and nudged me with an elbow.

The pro told us we can't hold hands, which Pearl was doing with me at first. "Just sit still," she told us. "We wait." What we're waiting for, I don't know and obviously won't be asking.

I try to remember what I was thinking, coming here. Maybe I wanted to talk about Noam. Mrs. T knew him, or she had to, at least a little. Everybody knew who he was, because he was the captain of the basketball team his last two years. In the halls, between classes, he moved in zigzags, as if he were still on the court, dodging this way, that way. He made people laugh. He seemed like a big, tame, goofy horse. Maybe he wasn't a great English student—I don't really know, because I didn't hang out with him or even really know him, not one to one, until our moms decided to send him to stay with me in New York, to think about college, since he'd spent those couple years working at one of the boatyards. (He told me he knew all about engines, that he'd always have a fallback job as a mechanic. Why fallback? I said. Sounds max secure to me. He said it was too much the same thing over and over. He wanted a job with surprises.) And then suddenly, for those two days, we were like instant friends. We stayed up the whole first night, just walking all over, down to the seawall under the bridges, over to the Battery, and up along the new El-Prom that heads north from Christopher Street. We threw pebbles in the river, Noam's flying twice as far as mine.

Back in my room, we slept some—Noam took up the whole floor between my bed and desk—and I took him to my Poetry as Politics class, which he was shocked to like so much, and then it was a Friday night, so we went out for burgers and beers, and we splurged on a little leaf (just a little), and we went to a midnight movie about samurai warrior ghosts saving Japan from a massive tsunami: they stand together and hold out their shields, and the water rises into the cosmos, smashing into the stars, totally revising the constellations. The animation felt like it was made of colors never seen before. We went out into the night and both looked up at the sky right away. Then looked at each other and lost ourselves laughing. "Yeah, right, how stooge are we?" I said. "Cities don't *get* stars." And I wondered if we were both thinking about home, about Vigil Harbor, about nights you see the stars sharp as stilettos over Harrow Point or Emmons Head.

All this I remembered no problem, all the way from that night till now. The Saturday, the next day of that time we had together, is what I had twisted up in my mind, so that we were in my room and not crossing the square, not looking for the acrobat, not spooking the pigeons just to watch them rise in clattering squalls, not zoning on those giant pretzels until everything, just like that, in an atom-splitting instant, blew up. Not that I saw it, really saw it, until after, replaying over and over on millions of screens. Not that I even remember it as something that happened to me. I remembered it as something I saw, we saw, Noam and me, from my dorm window. Except that the view printed inside my head, like a photo on a newsfeed, is from too high up to be my dorm room. But it had to be, didn't it?

And now I remember the hospital, waiting there with Austin's friend Steve (seeing the explosions on the screens even there). Except that Steve isn't fixed in my memory, either. He fades in and out. My ears are max messed up, my head like a tunnel with an endless train speeding through. I'm wearing a shirt that isn't mine, and though the pants are mine, I don't remember choosing to wear them that morning. My sneakers are their usual black, but still you can tell they have blood on them. Steve treats me like I'm a brittle old man. He keeps telling me I'll be fine when I already think I'm mostly fine, except for the train in my head. Why am I in the ER when there are people in much worse shape? Finally, a doctor looks into my ears for a long time, my nose, my eyes, my throat. I remember his Indian accent. The voices I remember better than the faces.

But Noam. I spent today sitting inside the growing structure of the boff palace just pushing at my brain, with all my mental might, to get Noam back. I felt like a snowplow grinding against a wall of ice. And then words emerged like sparks: *Horse among pigeons, laughing and stomping the asphalt, tongue salty, hair a squirrel's nest crowning into a tall tree, he tells me it's a crazy notion, but here you go: We do this together. Live like sailors on shore leave. Find ourselves a pair of selkies, keep their hides oiled and rolled tight like tapestries, window shades, magic carpets, hide them deep in a cellar. Better: Just live. You live. I live. A deal? I say, Deal.*

And I realized I've been doing it while not wanting to do it: going back to writing poems. Retrograde, but so what? So that's when I thought of my old English teacher. I knew she'd be glad to see me. Sometimes she waves from across the street if I'm in Celestino's driveway when she comes out of her house. She lives right there, across the street. So I knew she'd be glad. And then maybe we could go together over to see Connie, who by now must think I'm a loon. I'd apologize for scaring her and show the painting to Mrs. T. That's what I imagined.

Now this. I should be having some kind of PTS panic attack, I keep thinking, but I'm not. Maybe it's a comfort just to sit next to this woman Pearl, focusing on her long dark brown hand that rests deliberately against mine, between our thighs. On her long fingers she wears three thick rings with rustic stones. Viking jewels. Maybe their ancient magic will get us out of here. I'm a loon all right!

A long silence in which no one talks, that paramilitary woman and one of her student soldiers guarding us, one by each way out. The third one must be in the kitchen. I glance at Mrs. T, fishing for reassurance, but she looks beyond miserable. I conjure a chain of T words:

tempo, temporal, tempera, tempura, tempest. Torrent, torrid, tornado, torte. Tart, tight, taut.

Then here come footsteps outside the house, the kitchen door opens, and a man's voice says, "We are set. One hour. Let's eat something, shall we?" Do I know that voice? I start to stand up, I don't know why, but Pearl's jeweled hand stops me. "Hey," she breathes. I see her look sideways at the man who's tied up. They are together, whoever they are. Sometimes I see Mrs. T look at him, too, her eyes all apology and sorrow. They must be her guests, these people, and I can't stop myself from imagining a news story, the story on all the wallscreens if the bombers kill us when they leave. Just shoot us one by one. Or slit our throats because a gun's too loud.

Do not, I tell myself. No, do not think these thoughts.

And then he comes into the room, the man who was in Celestino's kitchen with all the mothers on Friday night, Celestino's old friend. He enters as if he's joining a party.

"Good news," he says, palms together like he's about to applaud us. "We leave in about fifteen minutes. Together. We will walk to the harbor."

His voice is bright and weirdly reassuring, but of course that's what he wants. He wants us to feel like children heading out on a field trip. I had a summer job one year at an art camp. Some days we'd take kids down to the harbor at low tide to collect "treasures" in small buckets, to take back to the classroom and glue onto boards in mosaics. Most of the children chose to spell out their names—in pebbles, seaglass, snail shells, old pottery chips rubbed smooth by salt. The occasional bottle cap or rusty nail or shard of Plexiglas.

Ernesto, that's his name. He holds the gun while the pro untapes the man who I know belongs with Pearl. Nobody says a word.

Now in the kitchen doorway this other man appears. He's someone I've seen around town. He looks sadder than the rest of us put together; he's maybe the oldest one here, like maybe sixty I'm thinking, your basic dad type, and I wonder if he knows something the rest of us don't. If he does, it's not good news.

The gun, which has me totally transfixed, is back with the woman. She holds it in her right hand, at her waist, its barrel resting in her left. A gun: a gun. Tautology of power. Loaded or not loaded: who takes a chance on that? If she had a suicide vest—and would we know if she did?—would one of us try to jump her?

We, the prisoners, are three guys and three women. We outnumber them—or I think we do. I don't know if there are others outside, waiting, guarding, lurking in the hydrangea bushes. If they hadn't drawn the curtains, I'd see Celestino's house across the street. And I think of that weird painting. I wish I were telepathic and could make my thoughts cross the street, just trit-trot up the front steps, like a herd of small ponies, and knock on that door. "Help!" my thoughts would shout into that warm, mussed-up, duckling-friendly house. When is the last time I asked anybody for help? That's all Mom's wanted, I think: for me to say "Help!" I want to be fitzed at her for not just telling me this thing that I am sure she knows, but can you ask somebody else to ask you if you need help? And how can you know that you need it?

Connie

Raul is upstairs, playing that damn warrior game. I try not to let it drive me crazy. I could have sworn I heard Celestino's truck in the driveway an hour ago, but it's not there. I don't like bugging him with messages or calls, and when he left, he told me he might be back late . . . but, well, enough with waiting.

I vext him that I want to know if I should just feed Raul now and set aside a plate of food. Sharing dinner with us is important to my husband. He likes the ritual of asking Raul to name the best and worst things that happened to him over the day. Then it's my turn, then Celestino's.

He answers right away, but he doesn't call. The message lights up my screen: *Don't wait. I am sorry.*

I note the formality of that last sentence. A short sentence, but one word would do. Celestino has never embraced the use of our phones as a means of filling absence with chatter. He is no more gregarious onscreen than in person. I respect it.

We'll see you later, I answer, also in full. I take out eggs, greens, apples, potatoes, cheese. My mother's kitchen-sink casserole, minus the meat. She used to grease the oven dish with bacon fat from a can beside the stove, mix in bits of leftover ham or chicken.

I am spooked by what happened to us over the weekend, not just the intrusion and the deceit, but Celestino's strange collusion with that liar. I still do not fully understand, and I confess that today, after Axel and the children left, after I settled Raul with his hour's worth of book-reading, I pulled a stool over to our closet and took down the box where Celestino keeps his scant store of papers. Letters from his mother, from years ago, dictated to one of his sisters. A few photographs of his wall work and landscaping projects, prints of the images I helped him assemble for his first website. A handful of official documents: his old green card, a transcript from the small-business course he took at a local college, his hard-won certification from the Massachusetts Arborists Association, and his letters of sponsorship. Now I understand that sponsorship in a way I never did, not fully. I lived in my Michigan cocoon when the raids took place. They happened mostly in big cities, well out of my sight.

Percy Darling, the older man with whom he shared this house before we met—who continued to rent it to Celestino after Percy died—was, I now know, far more than a sponsor. He was a man who, if only by accident, landed Celestino in trouble when he hired him to build that first tree house—along with Arturo. (I think of "Ernesto's" flattery and gushing over our own tree house and am filled with fury.)

When Celestino told me the full story of Arturo, I was angry, yet it's not as if he ever lied to me; he just left things out. He insists that he and Percy did, as he's always said, genuinely care for each other, even that his caring for this older man as he grew weaker was a private atonement for abandoning his mother, yet now it looks to me as if my husband's sense of debt was more complicated. Maybe Percy took as much from Celestino as he gave. It's not the simple white-savior story that Celestino lets others see when they ask how he's lucky enough to have stayed, even before we were married. Yes, Percy brought him here after the trouble in Matlock unleashed by Arturo's botched political protest. Yes, Percy saw to it that Celestino was able to start a business and live in this comfortable if modest house—even to stay on after he had to move in with his daughter. But in a way, he gave my fearful, reticent husband no choice. He, the older man with all the security, decided what was best. Maybe Celestino was left, because of that decision, less sure of himself. Maybe he felt less gratitude than he wanted to. Why would he tell me any of this, put it into words? And did it help that I was the one who, after selling my mother's house, bought this one from Percy's daughter?

Celestino owes me nothing for these advantages of mine, and I imagine Percy (how I wish I'd been able to meet him!) felt the same way, but the imbalance remains, and I find it unbearable to think about.

Raul stops playing his game when the timer goes off upstairs. He comes running down and asks where his father is. I tell him Dad will be late. Raul glances at the morning's collages posted on the corkboard that covers one wall of our kitchen. "I like Anya's," he says, pointing. Anya is the one the other children consider the Art Genius. She made her dream house out of paper fragments, all blue, that she tore instead of cutting. There is a feathery effect in her layering of the glossy textures, only a few identifiable as sky or water or denim. The windows in the house are eyes, actual pictures of eyes, most human, some animal, and the overall effect, if I'm honest, is creepy. Or maybe it's my mood of the moment.

"Anya has quite the imagination," I say. "So do you."

He shrugs. "Mine's okay. I don't really care."

"Why not?"

"I'm not going to be an artist," he says. "I'm going to be a tree warrior."

"Oh," I say. "That sounds adventurous."

"Yes. And dangerous. I'm just warning you."

I hesitate. So Arturo made his mark on my son in a single evening. I am tempted to say something to discredit whatever aura that man cast around himself (and for which I fell almost as surely as Raul), but I resist.

"I'm not afraid of danger if it's worthy danger," says Raul. He sits at the kitchen table, regarding me seriously. Hearing him parrot Arturo, utter the word *worthy,* with its snobbish connotations, alarms and irritates me.

"How about you grate this cheese." I hand him a board and a grater. He kneels on the chair and pushes his sleeves away from his small wrists.

"You and Dad wouldn't stop me, would you?"

"When you're old enough to make your own decisions, we won't stop telling you what we think, but the decisions will be yours."

"You always say that, Mom."

"Because it's true."

"But you can't predict how dangerous the world will be when I'm that old."

I hesitate. This isn't talk that comes from our school. When Caitlin and Trina insisted we write an actual charter, with stated philosophical ideals, one of them was *No integrity without truth. No truth without gravity. No gravity without belief in our world.*

Though I felt guilty about it afterward, I read some of the stated ideals over the phone to Harold, knowing they would inspire wicked laughter.

"No love without sex. No sex without lust. No lust—not requited, that is!—without many, many visits to the gym," he countered.

I told him how much I missed him. He told me how much my former clients missed me, how they were walking around town in shaggy overcoats of their outgrown hair and beards. "We're a city of trolls. Trolls playing on the dunes. Except that you're not allowed to play on the dunes anymore."

I hadn't been back to visit. Not since going out and packing up my apartment, after falling so outrageously in love.

"Raul," I say now, "why all this talk of danger?"

He shrugs again, a new mannerism that clearly makes him feel older. "Things are getting dangerous not just in faraway places. Like look at the bombings."

"Oh honey."

"I'm not a baby, Mom."

Of course the children know about the violence—and probably talk about it among themselves. Yet still I harbor the illusion that there's a way to shield them. I have, through great effort, kept myself away from the news for most of the day. I'm aware that all police and community sentinels in all Massachusetts towns are on high alert, that airports and train stations are at Level Red, that use of hitch cards is suspended. But we have no plans to go anywhere.

Which makes me wonder again where Celestino is.

"You know," says Raul, "planting so many trees in Canada doesn't make up for all the burned forests in other continents."

I look at him, willing onto my face a neutral expression.

"The Northern Hemisphere's trees don't do the same job as the trees in the Southern Hemisphere do. And the snow and ice in the north are what push away the sun's radiant heat."

"Is this what you're learning in science now?"

"No. But we should be learning that."

"So," I say, "let's suggest it to Caitlin."

Raul brings me the cutting board with its mound of grated cheese. "Are you making kitchen sink?" He smiles hopefully.

"Yes," I tell him, relieved that he's off the topic of danger and the disastrous state of both hemispheres.

"It's Monday," he says. "Compost night."

He's right, and I'm pleased that, for once, he's remembered one of his household chores. I hand him the small bucket of peelings, seeds, and eggshells that we keep on the countertop. "Make sure the top is tight on the pail before you put it out front," I say. "The skunks are on patrol again."

He looks at me over the bucket and says, "I do not need reminding of everything, Mom," and I relax. If he has assumed a new tone of authority, it's nothing to do with our weekend visitor and everything, I'm sure, to do with a new phase of pulling away. Not that this leaves me entirely happy.

He lets the screen door slam when he goes out the back, and I refrain from scolding him. I turn back to my chopping and slicing. I am thinking of watching my mother make variations on this dish while my father and I did our homework together at the kitchen table: me writing my papers, Dad grading his. Caleb would be out somewhere, because he liked being out for its own sake. If he could shoot hoops or skate on Little Pond in the afternoon, he would stay up far too late to finish his own schoolwork. It drove our mother nuts, but Dad went easy on him, saying that learning to manage your own time was one of the key lessons of growing up. Perhaps I and my fellow mothers regiment our children's lives too much.

But Raul is right: the world is dangerous. There are reasons to be fearful. Though hasn't this always been true? I think of Caleb when he came home after his first deployment, already looking toward the next. If you grow accustomed to living with a certain degree of fear, he said, it becomes your high-tide line, the set point at which you feel most alert. To be less than alert is to be inattentive, to live without constant motivation, to feel beached like a boat when the tide goes out.

"I do not need to live with constant motivation," I told him, though I knew it was too late to change his mind about going back—not even knowing where he'd be reassigned.

"This place," he said to me, "is all about staying. Staying in one place. Standing still. I didn't know that till now. If I were you, I'd head out, too." Then, because he died, I did. And yet, years later, I'm back. Am I standing still? Is there anything wrong with standing still if the world beyond your patch of ground feels like a quagmire waiting to pull you under?

I know, though I would never tell a soul, certainly not Celestino, that what drew me to him, urgently, was the mutation of my grief into an almost violent lust. I hurled myself into Celestino's bed, giving in to what felt like pure adolescent impulse. When we replaced that dead tree next to that absurd plaque up at the High, I understood, for the first time, that I would never get back my closest, most reliable familiar. What made more sense, at a gut level, than embracing someone as *un*familiar to me as possible? This quiet, restrained man let himself be the well into which I poured my rage at fate, my righteous sense of being wronged. The first time I woke up next to a sleeping Celestino—we didn't actually *sleep* together for a couple of weeks—I felt a wave of shame. Was I using him? But then, might he also have been using me? We didn't talk a whole lot in those first weeks, and my mother, going through her own renewal of grief (the way her medical ordeal so unfairly mirrored Dad's final months), asked no questions of me, though sometimes, over breakfast or lunch, we'd sink into a meaningful silence, during which she might shoot me a *Do I know you?* glance across the food she struggled to eat. I knew, without her saying so, that she knew what was going on at night, between my settling her as well as possible in her downstairs bed and my brewing her tea in the morning.

It was Celestino who broke the spell, who asked, "What is this, between us?" not long after we did start falling asleep together. I had slept perilously late (though I'm not sure what I thought would "happen" if my mother woke to an empty kitchen). Rushing into my clothes, I said, "I promise not to fall in love," though I didn't know yet what a lie that was. To my shock, the look on Celestino's face was one of pain. Had I offended him by implying that I was in fact using him? Or could he have jumped to the conclusion that his skin color or social status made him less significant to me? I was mortified.

"I'm sorry," I said right away, and I sat back down on the edge of his bed. "I didn't mean it like that."

"What did you mean?"

I remember sitting there, the waistband of my jeans girdling my thighs, and wondering what I did mean. "Things won't get messy," I said. "You don't need to worry about me."

"But what if I do?"

"Worry about me?" I said too loudly.

He answered solemnly, "Why do you laugh?"

I saw how insulting it was, my idiotic laughter. I had only meant to assure him that I wasn't out to complicate anyone's life (after all, he was fifteen years older than I was). But maybe I just wasn't brave enough to complicate mine.

In that moment it became clear to me that we had crossed some kind of boundary—and that he already knew we had. Or maybe we'd reached a fork in the path. I told him I had to go home, to my mother, but maybe we should meet for dinner, something we hadn't done since the night we'd first fallen into bed together.

"I will cook for you tonight," he said, "but late. I work late today."

It was at that dinner, over a rice dish bright with plantains and peppers, a dish he still makes for me and Raul, when I decided to try staying (in his bed; in this town) in a less tentative way—just try it. I would rent a room of my own, and I would try to make money of my own again: I would cut hair, or maybe I could pull strings to get a waitressing job at The Jetty or, if I could bear it, the YC. I wouldn't reclaim my roots, and I wouldn't give up my Traverse City apartment (where an intern at Harold's paper was living month to month, Harold paying the rent).

One slip of a condom and I was pregnant, six months after that dinner. I had gone on pretending that Mom was the reason I'd settled in, and the news landed on me like a felled tree. I contemplated not telling him; though it would involve a lot of red tape, I lived in a state where getting an abortion was still possible. That would have ended us, however, and much as a part of me longed for the simplicity of my former, fugitive life, I had become attached to the complexity, even the risks, of this one. I had to begin by telling him.

We were eating dinner in his kitchen, as we did often by now. He put down his fork, almost delicately, and looked at his pasta for a moment, then at me, for a longer moment. I had no idea what he was thinking. Then he said, "If I marry you, people will think I am using you. But if I marry you, I will be happy."

"Marry me?" The tears that were already in my eyes, tears of anxiety, slid down my cheeks. This I had not expected. "Honor" was hardly an issue. Religious though she was, my mother would have welcomed a grandchild even if it was fatherless.

"Yes." He looked so serious. "Marry me." He smiled.

"This isn't . . ." Isn't what? I thought. Isn't what I expected? Isn't what I want? Did I want it? He was waiting.

What the hell, I thought, and then I berated myself. Did thinking I was a dupe of fate entitle me to be a perpetual cynic?

"How would you be using me?" I said. "It's not like I'm rich."

"Connie," he said, "you are smarter than this. You are rich in how you belong here."

"Belong here?" I laughed. "Now, that is rich."

"Do not joke when I ask you to marry me. I just did that, Connie. If you say no, I won't try to persuade you." The look he gave me made me feel even younger than I was.

Awkwardly, I pushed aside our dishes so that I could take his hands. This was serious. He did mean it. I had not come to this table expecting a proposal, but here it was. "Yes," I said. "Because, look, you have to admit it's crazy—I mean, by modern standards, whatever they are—but I would never forgive myself if I said no. So yes. Yes, because it's you, Celestino. I just never thought . . . I mean, yes."

He might have beamed or gotten down on his knees, but he continued to stare at me. I could tell he was glad—maybe he'd wanted this outcome already?—but gradually his face darkened, just a little. "You need to understand something," he said. "I think I will never . . . feel at home. With you, yes. Here, no."

"What do you mean?" I made an effort not to laugh. "You're more at home in this town than I am. People depend on you."

He shook his head. "They can replace me."

"Don't be silly. You're too talented." And then I understood how naive I was being; how would I ever know what life was like inside his skin? And he'd lived inside it for close to half a century. "You'll be safe with me," I said.

He shook his head again. "*You* are safe on your own. But maybe less safe with me." I saw him reconsidering.

"Don't be silly," I said again. I put his square callused hand on my belly. "We'll be safe together. All of us. I'm going to choose to believe that, and I want you to believe me. Can you?"

He didn't answer my question, but he moved his hand in a caressing circle, stirring my desire. And in the years since, I have made myself alert to the moments when I see his fear reemerge, steering him away from it by changing the subject or turning off the news when stories about surprise deportations or "repatriations" emerge. And yet this past weekend, after seeing Celestino's reaction to Arturo, this cunning man who emerged from a far less secure time in my husband's life, I simply failed to see the fear. I willfully ignored it. I was a fool.

Thinking of fear reminds me of Brecht, his disturbing visit to me this morning. God, that strange, beautiful painting is still upstairs on my bed. I realize that though I called Miriam as soon as I knew he was gone, I never called back, to make sure he's all right. I go to the living room, where I left my phone. I tell myself that if I haven't heard from her, he must be home.

As I carry my phone into the kitchen, Raul comes in.

"Honey, please don't let that door slam," I say when he does it again.

"Sorry." He sets the small compost bucket by the sink. I remind him to rinse it.

He goes to the fridge and helps himself to a glass of water, sits at the table again. "So Dad's friend? You said he went away, but he's still here."

I turn around, setting down the phone. "Here? No, honey, he's left town."

"Nope." Raul's look is sure, even defiant. "He's in Mrs. Tattersall's house. I saw him in her kitchen. He's there with other people. Maybe she's having a party. Maybe Dad's there? Why is Dad so late?"

I don't want to argue with him. It's clearly a case of mistaken identity, though I'm beginning to wonder where the hell Celestino's gone without giving me a clear explanation. If he's meeting late with Austin, fine. Why not just let me know?

I hand my son the bowl of apples, the peeler. "Would you finish this job for me, please?"

In the living room, I turn off the lamp I left on, in order to see past the reflections in our front windows. What I see is odd, confounding. I see a group of people, maybe as many as a dozen, leaving Margo Tattersall's house and heading toward Gage Street. They move, in a close group, along the sidewalk, the streetlights not quite allowing me to recognize anyone. They all appear to be looking down, as if searching for a lost object. Their hands are in their pockets. At first I wonder if they are headed for an evening out together, but they do not seem to be chatting, let alone laughing or having a festive time. A final light inside the house switches off, and one last figure joins the group. They turn the corner, out of sight.

I go back into the kitchen.

"Did you see him?" asks Raul.

"I don't think it was him. But I think you're right. It's some kind of party." Except that I don't think so. I don't know what to think.

I pick up my phone and call Miriam. I now worry about the whereabouts of my husband as well as her son.

Margo

All my fault. All my fucking fault. And how the hell is the gun still fucking loaded? I can't even remember putting it away—Tom must have done that—after my third and final trip to the shooting range. Pia, a henchwoman straight from Central Casting, knows all about guns: opened the chamber as deftly as I might open a tube of mascara, and immediately this big fucking smile appeared on her face—the only one I've seen from that viper. Beats me how Ernesto, who looks more like a dandy than a terrorist in his stylish leather jacket and slick haircut, is apparently the boss. Back in the house, he seemed happy to let his three sidekicks pass the gun among themselves like a magic talisman, according to whoever needed a potty break, I guess, or another foray in my fridge. Cleverly, they did all the talking they needed to do outside the room where we cowardly prisoners sat like a bunch of sheep meekly waiting to be shorn. They seem to have pegged poor, dear Egon as the one potential wild card (how handsome he's grown since I last saw him, but also how thin!), the one who'd maybe martyr himself to save even a few of us, buy time for us to make a run for it. Henchwoman taped his wrists together, his legs to my piano bench—and then ripped it all off again in preparation for our leaving.

As we were herded out through the kitchen, I noticed that the makings of dinner were still on the counter untouched—the poultry, the chopped onion, the ramps wilting in a sieve—but other, more convenient foods had been pilfered from cupboards and drawers, snack bags opened and abandoned on the window seat, glasses set heedlessly here and there. And oh, look: an apple, half eaten, abandoned by the sink. Metaphors will out! I saw no alcohol; they're too smart for that.

As we leave, instructed to keep our heads down, I take a sidelong glance at Celestino's house; the lights, at least in the front, are out. Would I have dared a shout? I doubt it. I'm as acutely focused on survival as the rest of us.

The evening is cold and miserably damp, the air misted with traces of rain that just won't clear out. The moon, crisp and full, sidles in and out of the cloud cover. If the weather were different, people might be out and about, just to see that moon.

The gun goes last, right behind Egon and Brecht. Mike is at the front, next to Ernesto, and we three women are together between the men—as if for our protection. One of the two boy-fugitives has gone ahead as a scout. He precedes us by about a block; at each corner, he signals back at Ernesto.

We know the plan—or at least the alleged plan. Mike's boat will be the getaway car. If we survive, I'll make sure he never hears the end of it. That's assuming we can make a joke of it, though I figure that if we can make a joke of our spouses' running off to the woods, Armageddon's Adam and Eve (cue that half-eaten apple!), we can laugh at anything. Though at the moment I can't imagine laughing ever again.

Once we turn down the dead-end lane to the harbormaster's office and dock, any hopes I had of sudden intervention fade (though I wasn't sure what I hoped for, thanks to that infernal gun). The buildings that flank the lane are two-story wooden structures that hold a few office spaces, some empty, all dark. The light is on in Barry's office, and his official truck is in its space; his compact Whaler is tied up at the dock, but the bigger patrol boat is gone. And there is Mike's boat, with its ORCA pennant and American flag, both limp against the flagpole at the stern.

Once we are all on the dock, Ernesto faces us and says quietly, "Men first."

Women and children last! How feminist of him!

I gaze longingly up at Barry's window, wondering if an assistant might be puttering around—though from the last news I heard, right before this wrecking crew entered my house, no one in any official capacity is puttering today, not in this part of the world. I find myself wondering if maybe the bad guys have been arrested already—and then remind myself, knucklehead of the year, that no, the *persons of interest* are right fucking here, and their own persons of interest are us, six hapless individuals who came together for a convivial evening and for . . . but I have no idea why Brecht showed up, poor Brecht and that complete stranger. It's not like our captors held a circle meet-and-greet in which we each named our favorite breakfast food, our first childhood pet, or a habit we can't seem to break. Quite without ceremony, Brecht and the stranger (a tall, striking woman in a coat competing with Ernesto's for Most Modish) were ushered into my living room and shown to their seats and told (politely!) to keep their traps shut.

Mike and Egon board the boat as if stepping over a simple threshold. Seeing their ease gives me false comfort. The scout boards with them and stands between them, but before he does, I see Mike furtively touch his son's back.

My daughters. What if I never see them again? I picture Tom and that vile cunt—perhaps toting along her bow and arrow (the cuntress!)—putting on phony long faces as my daughters sob over the urn containing my ashes. Of course, that would be if anyone retrieved my corpse from the briny deep. . . .

Now I am being urged on board, Pearl and the stranger ahead of me. *Last on, first off* crosses my mind, but the last one on is the henchwoman, that gun—*my* gun—firmly at the ready. (If we're rescued, will I be in trouble for that, for owning the weapon that put us all in our yellow-bellied place? Out of some antiquated SAT drill, the word *poltroon* skims the surface of my fear.)

More instructions. Brecht and Egon, two of the gentlest, most sensitive boys I ever taught, sit on the benches to either side of the cabin. They will bear the brunt of the headwind when we launch. Egon stares straight ahead, beyond Brecht, who looks at his own shoes. Mike is at the helm, gripping the wheel. I notice only now that he dressed up for dinner at my house: a pressed blue shirt under his fleece vest; a pair of khakis in place of his oft-ridiculed cargo pants (in one of whose pockets there might have been a knife). He's bareheaded, also unlike him, and I suppose that whatever cap he was wearing, stitched with the name of some conservation group (never the YC), must have been abandoned back at my house.

Pearl and the stranger, and I, will share the bench in the stern. No one hands out cushions, of course, and our backsides are immediately soaked when we sit. And then the rain resumes—not hard, but steady. I watch Ernesto pull from his pocket a cap—and I realize that it's Mike's. *Cogswell Wind, Power from the Pacific,* it reads across the front. A hat from Mike's son-in-law. He was wearing it when I went over to keep him company . . . when? Was that last night?

Ernesto and his henchwoman both turn their heads toward me; I must have made a noise. This is how hostages get singled out, I think. I look at my lap.

"Let's go," Ernesto says to Mike.

The boat, doubtless well maintained, starts up without complaint, even quietly. Mike is looking over his shoulder, reversing slowly away from the dock, careful to keep clear of Barry's Whaler, when I see headlights looming, headed down the lane straight for the dock. The driver's door slams, engine and headlights still on, and a figure runs onto the dock. Mike, turned away, doesn't see him, but Ernesto does.

"*Alto!*" shouts the man on the dock. Celestino. He stands at the very edge of the planking, and for a moment, I think he will dive in after us.

"No," I whisper. I wave my arms frantically. "No!" I shout.

Ernesto shouts back at him, in Spanish I cannot begin to decipher. And then he turns quickly to Pia and shouts something at her, too.

By now, we are thirty feet out from the dock, and Mike has turned the bow toward the harbor, mostly an open path to the sea, few boats in the water to complicate our passage. But when he sees Celestino, he cuts the motor.

"Start it back up now," says one of the junior outlaws. But it isn't Mike I'm watching. It's Pia, who has made her way to the edge of the boat closest to land and is aiming at Celestino. Seeing the gun, he turns back toward his truck, but the shot she fires drops him to his knees.

"Oh my God, oh FUCK!" I shout, and before anyone can grab me, I am over the side, plummeting into water so stunningly cold that I feel my lungs shrink, instantly, and I feel the drag of my skirt, binding my legs together. As I shed my shoes, the instincts acquired in my long-ago lifesaving courses kick into gear. I stroke forward through the dense, dark depths, trying to stay low. If I can make it to the dock, I can pull myself up behind Barry's Whaler. If I don't go still from shock. If I don't knock myself out on a piling.

I hear a concussive noise that I know must be another shot, and I have to believe it's aimed in my direction, but all I can do is go on, forward, blind, frigid. Except for that blasted full moon, the darkness is on my side. And then my left hand, on the forward stroke, slams into something rock-hard. I come to the surface, my hand now burning with pain: it's the Whaler.

I grope along the hull with my good hand, gasping, and I pull myself up at the stern. Inside Barry's boat, I lie flat, afraid to sit up, though I can hear Ernesto still shouting, still close, as well as the hum of Mike's engine.

I am colder than I have ever been in my life, though isn't this what I trained for, those spring drills off Race Point? But I was a hardy teenager then. I know Barry will have blankets on hand, and staying as low as I can, I reach into two side compartments, groping with my right hand, until I find what I'm searching for. I am shaking uncontrollably, and my left hand, useless and throbbing, already feels swollen. Oh God, Celestino, I think. Celestino.

I peel off my cardigan and wrap myself tightly in the fleece blanket. The bad news, but also the good (I will no longer be a target of my own fucking gun), is that Mike's boat is heading out toward the mouth of the harbor. I force myself to stand and get myself onto the dock. But where is he?

I look around frantically, and then I hear him shout something incoherent. He is in the cab of his truck. When I reach him, I ask him where he was shot.

"Shoulder."

I go around to the passenger side and get in the cab beside him. He's holding a balled-up jacket or hoodie against his right shoulder. "I will drive," he says.

"No," I tell him. "I will." I realize, however, that while he's lost use of an arm, I've lost use of a hand. I start to laugh, a shivering laugh, and Celestino's eyes widen in obvious fear. I sound, to my own numbed ears, like a seagull.

"We're okay!" I insist. "I'm okay! We just, just have to—phone. Can you? For God's sake, call. Call in. Call the. Call." My voice shakes even more violently as I get out and go around the truck. I wouldn't have the strength to push Celestino away from the wheel, but he understands and does it himself.

I have to turn the truck around with my right hand alone, and I can only do it slowly. Celestino is calling, speaking to someone, his own voice broken. My skin feels as if it's buzzing, hot and cold all at once. My face is a mask of fire, my chest a block of ice.

Angling the truck forward and back in short jerks, I get us turned around and facing the other way.

"Take me home," he says.

"No. I'm taking you to the precinct. Us."

"Home," he pleads.

"Unless Connie is a nurse, and I don't think she is, no. I should take you to the ER in Knowles, but I don't know if I can get us there."

"I was there already," he gasps.

"The ER?"

"The police."

We are on Cove Road, along the seawall flanking the harbor, when I see the flare. An arc of brilliant magenta light shoots upward from somewhere beyond the mouth of the harbor, casting everything beneath it in a strangely joyous glow. I pull over briefly, to look. But I miss the moment of maximum illumination, and if Mike's boat is out there, I can't tell. Did the flare come from Mike's boat? Did it come from a Coast Guard vessel responding to the fragments of information Celestino shared? How long ago did he make that call? A minute? Ten?

I see Celestino reach for the door handle.

"No you don't," I say, and I accelerate, forcing him back against the seat. "Call Connie. Tell her to go to the precinct."

He shakes his head.

"What?" I say.

"I want her at home, with Raul. Staying there."

I barely make the sharp corner onto Beecham. I glance at my left hand, which rests in my lap. In the light from the dash, I can see that a massive bruise is already pooling like ink toward the wrist. "Fuck," I say.

Celestino glances at me. I can't afford to meet his gaze.

"Excuse the language," I say. I force a laugh. "Hey! Here we are, not dead."

"Thank you," he says quietly. Then I hear him breathing loudly, deliberately, maybe trying to keep himself from fainting. It's only five more minutes to the station, but what will I do if he passes out? That can't happen.

I hear myself say, "I used to have such a massive crush on you."

He continues to breathe audibly, but now he's staring at me, and if I wanted him to stay alert, I succeeded. He says nothing. What, even under normal circumstances, could he say?

"Oh fuck." My eloquent refrain. "I didn't mean to say that. I meant to say . . . meant to say that I can't lose you. I'm in enough trouble already."

When I glance quickly at him, he attempts a smile, but he knows it comes out as a grimace and turns away quickly, looking out into the night. We pass houses where families are dry and warm, at least for now, watching the news or willing themselves to ignore it, wondering if it's time for all of us to start locking our doors.

The more startling the news, the faster and higher into the atmosphere it travels. And when small towns make big news, for a moment everything changes.

First, the town teems with strangers. Some are detectives, some are scribes, some are artists bent on capturing a portrait of the news, the places-people-things that are *the news; some are nothing more than busybodies. In swoop drones, choppers, cars and vans with alien plates. (Who has ever seen a plate from one of the Dakotas in Vigil Harbor? What does it mean?)*

Second, town officials become far more important. Accustomed to seeing themselves on small screens but not on large, they grow alarmed at how they appear yet pleased by how much more valuable their opinions and their time have become. A few grow drunk or foolish on their ephemerally elevated power.

Barry Unwin and June Smithson have been around long enough to see this happen once before, twenty-some years ago, when a scandalously defrocked priest from a neighboring town chose Harrow Point as the place to end his life. The harbormaster brought Father Gregory's body to shore; the selectwoman spoke to the TV cameras—after they steered her toward the most scenic natural backdrop: the sunlit harbor.

But this is bigger. Homes are upended for retroactive clues, affidavits are gathered from residents as young as eight years old, and law enforcement agents from New York and Washington colonize the bar at The Jetty and take up every spare room of the Twin

Chimneys Inn the way Washington's officers might have occupied a Tory's farmhouse alongside the Delaware River.

The occupation lasts ten days, most of them gloomy and wet, after which no one is fully certain if the invaders are gone for good. The Parks and Rec commissioner waits another two days before finding the fortitude to drive up to Emmons Head and check on the rumored ruination of the old muster field. Visiting authorities and media crews used it, no permission asked, as a free-for-all parking lot. The groomed grassy commons that Fourth of July picnickers treat with such respect, year after year, looks like a cow pasture run through a massive meat grinder. He determines not to renew his appointment at the next Town Meeting; June will try to talk him out of it, but no dice.

The day is sunny and already too hot for relief. There below shines the reliable, consoling view: boats on winking blue water, masts like strokes of chalk on an old-fashioned blackboard. He pauses to watch a crane, across the harbor at the YC, as it gently lowers a wooden sailboat, scrubbed and varnished for a new season, back into its natural element. On its way down, the boat is suspended in a vast hammock, like a sleeping baby in a mother's arms as she settles it into its crib.

Things will return to normal, the commissioner tells himself. They must—and they always have, haven't they? What kind of a normal it will be, that is always the mystery, the riddle.

Miriam

My life feels as if it has come to a standstill. I am depleted. Austin has taken over cooking all our meals. Making dinner, he listens to his music through his earbuds and dances by himself, sometimes whistling or humming along. He didn't ask if I minded listening, and I wouldn't, but never mind. Last night I just sat at the dining table facing the kitchen, watching him dance and chop vegetables. He slid to and fro in his stocking feet, and I waited to find it endearing, the way I always had. Clio was watching him, too, from her bed. I hated myself for how pretentious I thought he looked, how oblivious. Had the world flipped upside down only for me?

Work at the firm paused almost completely for a week. I hear Austin taking calls, always in another room, but no one is at the office, no one—that I know of—visiting clients. We're not the only ones in limbo. When I go out, it feels as if the town is still holding its breath. I think of the pandemic lockdowns, the vacant streets and silent storefronts, though back then I lived in New York. This is different. The suspense is more focused. No one believes that the woman—Pia Suarez, we now know she's called—will return. Why would she? No, she's far, far away; of that we are assured by agencies that found evidence of her passing through Halifax. Vigil Harbor has had its waves of contagion, shared in the fatality and mourning triggered by disease as well as war, but we forgot that we are not immune to threats engendered by politics alone. If we feel righteous about a cause, an inequity, we donate rather than demonstrate. I think what frightens people the most, now that bits and pieces of the story have been stitched together, is that the threat passed right through our streets, our homes, even stayed over a few nights, while most of us carried on our comfortable lives. Any of us might have been taken hostage, might have been shot—maybe thrown overboard too far away from shore to swim back.

I asked Noam's mother to come over this morning while Austin drives around just to have a cursory look at his projects, keep an eye on them even if they are dormant. He'll end his day with a visit to Celestino.

We sit in the dining room, the stone whale breaching the surface of the table between us. Joan is telling me about her daughter, Rachel, who's getting married this summer. She's barely twenty-two, but losing her brother seems to have made her want to speed up her own life, do everything sooner.

"So I'm happy," says Joan, "and we really like him, her guy, they're lovely together, but I'm also a little sad. I mean, for her. That she has to feel even more fragile than people so young should have to feel."

You'll always be sad, I do not say. Always. It is not, I also keep to myself, like losing a husband. That's something you can get over. The slivers of grief in your flesh dissolve or work their way out. One day they're gone, even if they leave you with tiny, whisper-thin scars.

"Well, it's something they all share. They're in it together," I say.

"I know," she says. "But it's also hard because they blame us. Their parents. For having it so easy, then messing everything up."

I think, We did, didn't we? But I say, "That's the job of every next generation that comes along, don't you think?"

"I don't know." Joan's hands are flat on the table. She flexes them, and her narrow wedding band flashes briefly. "I don't remember despising my parents and their friends, as a group, the way Rachel and her friends despise us. And some generations just aren't lucky. Maybe theirs will have it harder."

"*Despise* is a very strong word." I wish Joan hadn't declined my offer of something to drink, so I'd have a mug or a glass to fidget with. She sits straight, her back against the chair.

"In any case, we'll have a nice wedding—small, because she insists on that—in our yard. We'll do it all ourselves. The food, the flowers. Rachel has musician friends."

"That sounds perfect. Too many people go overboard." I think of my wedding to Brecht's father: church, caterer, blues quartet, a rented horse and carriage. Joan just smiles, a practiced expression, looking at her hands, at the whale.

"How's Brecht?" she asks, because she knows she must. After Noam's funeral, her husband asked us if they could talk to Brecht, since he was the last person to be with their son, and I was relieved when Brecht's therapist said it wouldn't be a good idea, not yet; that maybe we could all "reassess" in a few months. When the idea of a meeting never came up again, I was once again relieved. Now I think it was a mistake, to avoid that hurdle altogether.

"He's okay," I tell her. "But there's something I thought I might tell you. I hope it's not a bad idea." Already I'm thinking that it is a bad idea. Am I telling her just because I can't stand keeping it to myself? It's too late to change my mind now.

"Brecht seemed to believe that Noam was living with him. Upstairs. He's on the third floor alone, though there's a spare room we never use, and . . . I'd sometimes hear Brecht's voice. I assumed he was talking to himself, or listening to music, and I didn't want to eavesdrop. But I understand now that he fantasized Noam as having his own life up there. In that other room." I feel as if I'm betraying my son with that word, *fantasized*. It belittles the necessity, to his sanity, of keeping Noam close, of being certain he was in fact alive. Brecht's calling off his therapy so soon was no doubt necessary to guarding that delusion.

I stop, hoping Noam's mother will say something, but she doesn't; I can't even tell if she's taking in my words. "I didn't know about any of this till last week, though I should have figured it out," I say. "Everything that happened—the boat, the police—just, kind of, shook it free."

"And you asked me over because you thought I needed to know, too?" She sounds anything but grateful.

I blurt out, "Joan, I wish . . ." I'm about to say that I wish we could be friends, but it's a lie. There is no right thing for me to say to her now. I've said all my sorrys. The upshot is this: mine is alive, hers is not. Maybe she reminds herself that mine is an "only," while she still has another child to love and worry about. Unlikely. I rush ahead with "But there's something else, something Brecht asked me to give you. You wouldn't know this, but Brecht wrote poetry, back at the High. I think afterward as well." I avoid saying *in New York*. "Maybe poetry was to him what basketball was to Noam. Not something he thought he could ever make a living from, but . . ."

"A passion." Joan nods. She is pulling herself together. She can't wait to leave, but she's going to be polite and see this through. "Well. That's wonderful. Does he still . . . write poems?"

"He didn't, for a while. But he told me he's started again. He's trying. And he wrote something for Noam before he left."

"Left?" Joan frowns.

"He's gone to New York again, for a little while at least."

"Back to college."

"No." Is she on the verge of tears? Why shouldn't she be? I say, "He's just, I guess you could say, shifting gears. Being here just isn't . . . helping. He left a few days ago." I get up from the table and bring the sheet of paper from the sideboard. I hand it to Noam's mother. I wonder if she will read it now or fold it up to read in private, later.

She reads it to herself. I know it almost by heart. *Mrs. Fletcher: This may seem weird, but it's something I wrote for Noam. It's just a draft, but I want you to have it, please,* Brecht wrote across the top. The poem is written by hand. Brecht told me that it was okay if I read it. In fact, could I tell him if it was legible? "It's corny, I'm warning you," he said. "Like, sentimental." I told him that sentimental wasn't a bad place to start. "No advice, Mom," he said, "not now." He didn't mean it unkindly. He titled the poem "Yoke."

There we were, partnered like horses:
big, rough-coated, shaggy-maned horses
pulling or dredging or hauling the hay.
Harnessed to a well-reined rhythm,
hides dusted with timothy buds,

we found a pleasure in our switchback course,
a tandem logic to the livelong day.

At the unfastening, you did a dance,
A hardy-hoofed, mane-shaking, mud-spattered dance
at the pond shaded by the tamarack tree.
Your splash was a rapture that rose in a ring
and I plunged right into your arrowing wake,
aimed for the shallows at the opposite shore.
Here was the time we'd earned to roam free.

We were yoked like horses for a livelong day,
rose-bright, sun-stoked, tail-end-of-summer long day.

I can't just sit and stare at Joan as her eyes scan the lines my son wrote for hers. I go into the kitchen, which Austin left immaculate, not a spoon in the sink. I pretend to straighten the jars of flour, sugar, and coffee, to hunt for something in a cupboard. I keep my back to the dining room, waiting for her to speak. It takes a while.

I turn around when I hear her chair scrape back. She is folding the poem, slipping it into her bag. "Tell him thank you. And tell him good luck." There's that smile, so well rehearsed.

I walk into the room, expecting to see her to the door, but then she asks me a favor. She asks if I'll show her the room where Brecht thought her son was living.

I lead her to the third floor, warning her to duck under the beam at the top. It's the first time I've been up here in a few days. Brecht stripped his bed, as he'd promised he would do, leaving the sheets clumped in the center of the mattress. His mud-streaked work boots are in their place against the wall, which feels reassuring, as if they promise his imminent return.

"In there." I point to the smaller room opposite Brecht's.

She goes in and sits on the narrow bed. It's a creaky old brass bed, one of a few furnishings left in the house when we bought it. Austin says the mattress is horsehair, that you can smell it in humid weather; we would never put a guest here.

Joan turns her head sideways to read the spines of the books stacked on the side table. She makes a noise indicating surprise or revelation.

"What is it?" I ask.

"Well"—and now she's genuinely smiling—"a history of the Celtics. The team. Celestial navigation. A history of New England cod fishing? And"—she jiggles one book free from the middle of the stack—"*Nautical Lore from a Distant Shore.*" She looks up at me. "Someone knew Noam pretty well. He was obsessed with antique accounts of mermaid and sea monster sightings. He wanted to travel to Loch Ness someday. He'd say that even with all the most advanced underwater science, people who'd been miles and miles under the ocean, even the worst skeptics had yet to disprove the existence of that creature."

She holds the book in her lap.

"Take it, please," I say.

"I don't need it." She puts the book back and straightens the stack. "I'm not even much of a reader."

She runs her hands along the bedspread before standing. Seeing the unguarded anxiety on my face, she says, "I don't believe in ghosts. Or sea monsters. But thank you for this. My boy haunted yours, in the form of a wish." She sighs. "The best kind of wish. My wish, too."

I have a folder of Brecht's poems from when he was younger. There was a haiku he wrote in seventh grade that I kept attached to the fridge door until, at the start of high school, he told me I had to take it down. "It's like max embarrassing when somebody new comes over. Not like I can foist it off on some little sister."

The haiku read, *Say the moon is milk. / Say it spills across the dawn. / How sweet the new day.* His teacher and I thought it was precocious, though maybe not. Maybe we were just enchanted that a boy had gravitated toward poetry at an age when such an affinity could brand him as a weirdo forever. At the High, he was lucky to have Margo Tattersall as his English teacher twice. Though creative writing was frowned on as distracting from more test-worthy knowledge, she would always fold it into her assignments—or add it to the same workload her peers assigned. Because they composed and delivered their work online, however, most of Brecht's poems from that class were lost to the ether at the end of the year. I heard him read a few at a class recital, but I mourned the ones I never heard or even saw. I was upset when I learned that Brecht had done nothing to save them before the teachers erased the online archive in preparation for the following year.

Margo called me the morning after what had to be the second-worst day of my life. She said she didn't have time to talk, but she was thinking of me, and of Brecht, and she would be in touch again when things calmed down a little. She was about to give testimony to some federal official assigned to the case. She apologized, and of course I told her that none of it was her fault. She laughed bitterly. "The gun?"

It wouldn't surprise me if guns lie stashed away in two-thirds of the liberal-leaning households of this town. There are a lot of closet Timers. It wouldn't even surprise me if Austin secretly keeps a gun.

It's hard to believe how much has changed in the past week, how many people's lives have shifted. Brecht insisted on going down to the precinct, to give his account, on his own. "I'm not a baby, Mom."

He was gone for five hours, and it was all I could do not to call and check on him, make sure he hadn't run off again. To distract myself, I made a complicated dinner involving numerous vegetables and herbs. When he came in the door—I knew it was him, not Austin, from the tone of Clio's barking—I made myself continue slicing an eggplant. I felt more than heard him come into the kitchen behind me. "Am I allowed to ask how it went?" I said when he did not break the silence.

"It went okay." He sounded tired. I didn't press. He'd probably used up all his language for the day answering their questions.

I turned to see him sitting on the top step to the dining room. My hands went to my chest, in shock, when I saw that he'd gotten a haircut. "What did they—"

"I stopped in at Jamie's. On the way back."

His hair was nearly buzzed to the skull. I could see the gloss of his scalp. The look was severe, but I said nothing.

"I'm going back to the city. With Egon and Pearl, when they go. They're taking Mike's car."

Don't, I warned my panicking self. This might be good news. "Where will you stay?"

"With Pearl. To start. She says there's room if I'm not picky. I'll get a job of some kind."

"Honey . . ."

"You want me independent."

"What about Celestino?"

"I'm seeing him tomorrow. I think I'm pretty replaceable."

"Oh, Brecht."

He gestured impatiently. "I don't mean it like that. Like 'Woe is me.' I mean people need jobs. He's a good teacher."

"But he's going to need you now. I don't think his arm—"

"Can we just talk in terms of me?" He sounded plaintive. "For a minute?"

He didn't bring up Noam. We'd had that talk, or really, a feverish stuttering exchange as I tried to get him dry and warm, very late on that terrible night. Austin was the one who brought him home from the town landing, from the hectic scrum of police, Coast Guard choppers, circling news drones, once the EMT had cleared him and he'd signed off with local law enforcement, promising to report for questions the following day. The FBI agent had yet to arrive.

He came in the front door shaking violently, wrapped in one of those shiny foil cover-ups you see at marathons. Even when I held him tightly, the shaking did not let up. Austin told me to get him into warm clothes and under some real blankets.

We laid a fire in the hearth, though of course they're forbidden these days except during power outages. No one in Vigil Harbor bothers to enforce the law. Smoke pours from chimneys all winter long. I helped Brecht into long underwear and sweats, coaxed him toward the living room couch, and cocooned him in the comforter pulled from my bed. I sat on the floor beside the couch and simply waited for him to speak or sleep. I convinced Austin to go upstairs.

Fifteen minutes and he had stopped shaking. Half an hour and I thought I could hear the even breathing of slumber. I reached up to turn off the one lamp I'd kept lit. But I was wide awake, unwilling to leave him. Carefully, I raised an arm and laid it along his nearest leg. I felt oddly calm—though the night was pure clamor. Helicopters over the harbor pierced the house with sudden volleys of blinding light; vehicle after vehicle passed on normally deserted streets; sometimes I heard tendrils of conversation, strangely close, unnerving at this hour in our quiet corner of the village.

At one point, Petra Coyle entered my mind, and I felt a bolt of anger. Had she been connected to the terrorists? All Austin had said to me was that he would explain. No, he didn't think she was dangerous.

Sometime before dawn, Brecht woke—or at least he spoke. He said that he was sorry. I pulled myself up from the floor to perch at the edge of the couch. In the unlit room, I couldn't really see his face. The fire had collapsed into embers. I didn't even know if he was apologizing to me or to himself or to the world in general. Then he said Noam's name.

I waited in silence.

"So if you were here," Brecht said calmly, "which you are not, the joke's max on me, like I wonder if any of this would have happened. Or, okay, so I wouldn't have been here, right? I'd've been . . . maybe in my last year? And how about you, let's see, you'd've been maybe at that boatbuilding school you mentioned. Yeah, I can totally see you there. I'd visit you there."

He sighed, long and loud, his voice catching. "But you, man, you are nowhere. So much for our bets on the big wave." I listened to him breathe for a few seconds. He said, "Hey. I get it. You *were* the big wave."

I could not resist bending close to my son's face. His eyes were closed. But somehow, I didn't think he was talking in his sleep. I waited for a long time to hear if he would say more. I realized the noise of the choppers and cruisers had ceased. When the light began to seep into the sky—the moon's milk spilling across the dawn—I went upstairs and, without removing my clothes, lifted the bedcovers and wedged myself against Austin. He woke but said nothing, just drew me close. The day to come would not be sweet.

Margo

When Prince Escalus, as one of my students so eloquently put it, rips the bourgeois families of Verona a new one, he makes of the word *punished* three ferocious syllables. *All are pu-ni-shed.* In Zeffirelli's quaintly classic version, the director made him utter it twice, first quietly, then savagely, just in case the Veronians or Veronites or Veronini, whatever they're called, didn't hear it the first time. As if their heads are so far up their velvet pantaloons that they are deaf to all reprimands.

Well, so the fuck are we, all of us, punny shed. Not that I don't deserve it. I'm sure I'm not the only one who rethinks every timid moment of our being held captive in my living room and wonders why we were such a bunch of cowards. But it was me—sorry, *it was I*—who let everybody traipse right in and join the prison party.

I can tell you this: I won't be going out on the water, not in a Sunfish, not on a tanker, any time soon. Terra firma, hold me close.

By the time I got home, even my wet underwear had dried, but I felt like a brined turkey, encased head to toe in a brittle crust of salt. And speaking of poultry, I entered my kitchen to be greeted by the stench of raw, rancifying chicken and raw onions. I went straight upstairs, however, and stripped off the clothes I'd never wear again, pushing them into the bathroom waste bin. Thwarted by my ongoing renovations, I went down the hall to my daughters' bathroom, where I decided to fill the clawfoot tub instead of taking a shower. I soaked so long, I nearly fell asleep.

And then, once in bed, despite my throbbing wrist, I did fall, swiftly and deeply. I dreamed about Mike, dreamed that he had been one of the bad guys, a member of Ernesto's posse, all along. He took the boat into open sea with all of us aboard, announced that we'd be going all the way to Guatemala. In the dream, I cried and cried and cried. He didn't care.

Having lost my phone to the eco-outlaws and then to the lawmen who caught them (or some of them), I was confused to be awakened by the sound of the landline that no one used anymore (except sometimes my daughters) but that I couldn't bear to give up. My motives are part nostalgia, part paranoia. (What if the Chinese zap all the towers?) I let it ring till it stopped—but then, a minute later, it rang again.

I sat up in bed and answered it.

I heard my name, uttered in an almost hysterical bellow.

Tom.

When I said nothing, he yelled, "Are you there? Are you there?"

"Yup." I lay back down against the pillows. My wrist was killing me, swelling around the edges of the tape the EMT had wrapped it in. That's right: I had to get an X-ray. And return to the precinct. Fun day ahead.

"Are you all right?" said Tom.

"Depends."

"Margo! You're in the goddamn news!"

Well, yes, that made sense, I realized as I brought my life into focus. I may have grunted.

"Speak to me, Margo. The girls are in a panic."

"Does the news say I'm still alive?"

"Yes! Of course! But—"

"Then tell the girls I'm fine." Something occurred to me. "So you have phones at Paleo Paradise? I thought you'd forsworn civilization and all its, what did you call them, superficial energy-hungry trappings?"

This put a plug in his absurd indignation.

"Tom, you're the last person I'm interested in hearing from. Does that surprise you? The girls can call me themselves."

I heard a television in the background.

"We changed plans," he said, perhaps sensing I was onto him. "We're figuring out where we'll be settling. Instead."

I sat up again. This was rich. "Oh? What, they don't serve Negronis or Bellinis in Arcadia B.C.E.? No room service?"

He made a noise I recognized. How well I know the face it goes with.

"Go ahead. Roll your eyes," I said. "But guess who's getting the last and very pleasurable laugh? I couldn't care less where you and Lady D decide to 'settle.' In fact, any desire to buy me out of this place? I think the thrill is gone."

"Margo, there's a lot we left unsaid. I wish—"

"I do not wish," I said. My face felt hot, and was I actually about to cry?

"Please understand. I'm not saying I want to get back together—"

Oh, the tears retreated then! "And as for me, I'm pretty much done saying anything. To you. Anything I didn't say no longer needs to be said." I hung up. I love the landline for that: the way hanging up is actually, physically *hanging up.*

That was over a week ago. I spoke with all three of my daughters at once, the evening after their father's call, their faces a triptych of high anxiety. I was at the kitchen table and felt oddly cornered by their larger-than-life gathering on my wallscreen. I felt as if I were testifying before a committee. To their admonition about my inaccessibility that day, I explained, wearily, about the testimony I had been required to give to "the authorities," the hours I had endured of their pawing through my house. I didn't tell the girls about the gun, whose case I had happily turned over, asking not to see it, or its former contents, ever again.

They told me they wanted to visit me—or Doro and Becca did.

"No," I said, a bit too strongly. "I may head out for a while. See where I might like to move."

Their expressions grew stormy again, as if I have nowhere else to go in this world, nowhere else I'm capable of making my own home. I told them I was thinking of leaving Vigil Harbor for good. If any of them had ever wanted to inherit the house, now was the time to speak up. This earned me a cacophony of protest.

I wanted to tell them that in many a divorce, sale of the marital manor is de rigueur. But this would only give credit to Tom as being somehow benevolent.

I told them I'd give them each a share of the sale price.

"But to us, it's priceless!" said Cynthia, my lawyer daughter, the one who's the most financially secure even though she's also the baby.

I told them I didn't have the energy to discuss it. I promised I wouldn't do anything rash.

Dodging calls from nosy Nellies and snooping Sams has taken up a fair amount of my energy this past week, and I so completely dread going out that I'm having flashbacks to the COVID days, except that my house is empty; no Zoom-teaching from the guest bedroom because Tom's pompous attorney voice fills the first floor to capacity; no children in all stages of antsy adolescence swearing up and down that yes there is *too* such a thing as a socially distanced sleepover!

My whole life has become a socially distanced sleepover.

I'm waiting, now, for the host of the hipster newspod *Folkflow*. It's the one interview I agreed to give, and I let her coax me into doing it here. What I wear doesn't matter—I'll be heard but not seen—yet I changed three times, settling on a blue dress that makes me feel judiciously defined, as if its well-appointed darts and lining give me the shape of integrity. My bum wrist is snug in a molded brace, which I've even fancied would make a good impromptu weapon, should I cross paths with any more scoundrels: just haul off and smack 'em across the face. It's like wearing a billy club.

Lydia Vaz, *Folkflow*'s groovy host, arrives with an audio assistant, who cases my first floor in a way that ought to give me PTS. Lydia chats me up about Vigil Harbor and all the new attention it's getting: from crime scene to bar scene. Some junior reporter, sidelined from covering the Big Story, wrote a puff piece on The Jetty and The Drome as "hidden retro gems."

Lydia is thirtyish, plump in all the right places, and wears a short sleeveless dress that shows off an archipelago of tattoos, mostly animals, and her turquoise hair is pulled into a French twist—hardly congruent with the rest of her style, but the irony works. Even Becca, my boho child, couldn't pull off this look.

The sound guy, after his pantherlike prowling is done, decides on the living room, directing us to turn the wing chairs to face each other. I was expecting some sort of wired mic attached to my person, but he laughs when I ask about it. "All remo," he says, whatever that means. "Just wanted to get the best fix on locking out street noise."

Of which there is still more than usual: drive-bys, gawkers, roving photographers. I've had to ask a dozen people to leave my backyard.

"So," says Lydia after introducing me, "we're in the place it began—your being taken captive by Arturo Cabrera, one of the chief lieutenants of Oceloti. In this cozy but elegant living room with its piano, antique furnishings, family photos. A haven of domestic privilege."

"You could say that." I wonder if my wooden smile is effectively audible.

"Books *galore,*" she adds with a nod at my library wall. "Impressive in the age of virtual everything. You're a retired English teacher. High school."

"That's right."

"I understand that, actually, two of the other hostages were once your pupils."

"Right again," I say. "And both very gifted."

I hate that word and can't believe I used it. But even *smart* and *talented* are pedagogical buzzwords these days. *Exceptional* will put you on probation.

"And the father of one of those former pupils was recently separated from a woman who's now living with your ex-husband. Quite the connection."

Her smile is predatory. I should have guessed she'd dig up and chew on this juicy morsel. Maybe her syntax is too gnarled for listeners to follow.

"Mike is the one whose boat was hijacked," I say, trying to do some hijacking of my own. "Mike was the one forced to be the pilot. And I was the one, as you know, who jumped off when we'd barely left the dock. In a way, I suffered the least of all."

"But you jumped to help save a life. Let's go right to that part of the story now, because that's when the scene first turned violent. And if you hadn't jumped, they might have escaped—the three who were captured. Who are now in custody. As of this moment, Pia Suarez is still at large." I watch her take a quick look at her gizmo, to check the current newsfeed. (Is that an anteater etched on the side of her neck?)

As I tell the part about Celestino, I'm half waiting for supersleuth Lydia to say, *So this would be the neighbor about whom you once had hot erotic dreams, when your husband had begun to seem less than appealing to you.*

Of course, I can't speak firsthand about what happened on the boat after I jumped, but Lydia says, "So I'm sure you've spoken with some of your fellow hostages in the days since the incident. I imagine you had the psychological need, as anyone would, to seek out the comfort of those who went through that harrowing experience with you, who survived."

When I merely nod, Lydia makes a talking motion with her hand.

"I have," I say, following her mimed order. "Those two young men I had as students, the three of us got together this week."

"You'll probably have each other's backs forever, though I guess that's the nature of a town like this in general, right? What was it like, seeing those guys again for the first time?"

I don't tell her how awkward it was, how we sat together in a booth at The Jetty and mostly stared into our drinks. I don't mention Pearl, though she was the one who kept up the conversation. I couldn't stop staring at her for the first half of that strange reunion. Here was a woman who'd sat across from me in my living room for a couple of hours yet hadn't said a thing to me (or to anyone), nor I to her—as if we existed that evening in different dimensions—and suddenly, there she was, her gleaming wit, her verve, her easy, droll flirtation with the two men, both of them still a bit wan with the emotional exhaustion of acute danger followed by too much close attention. I realized, looking at the two of them together, side by side in the booth, that my favorite students were almost always the introverts, the ones I drew out of their shells. It isn't true that the best actors are all outgoing, socially driven. I asked Egon about his life in New York; I heard how hard it is, but how now and then a good role comes along and he has the fever all over again. "What's hardest," he said, "is calling it quits. Which a lot of people do when they hit thirty. Break up with art." I knew he'd recently passed that mark. I told him, "So then, you're not one of the quitters. That's decided."

"It must shake you to your core," Lydia says, "to have something like this happen here, in this of all places. Some people say you had it coming."

"I did? What people said that?" I aim for cool and cynical. I miss.

"Not you personally. You as a community. Vigil Harbor is known as a place that it's hard to penetrate—almost literally. Hard to wander into by accident. Even hard to buy a house here if you're not, like, already connected."

She's partly right. It started with wanting to exclude people who turned against vaccination. But I'm certainly not going to talk about what some call "the trust," the unspoken pact between the select board and the in-town real estate brokers.

"It's easy," she continues, "in a place like this, to ignore issues of social justice. For one thing, it's a town with a jaw-droppingly white population. Wouldn't you agree that puts you kind of back in the Dark Ages? Unfortunate pun; sorry."

I don't know where she's going. Lydia's roots are working-class Portuguese, a genetic credential she flaunts in contexts involving equality or persistent classism.

"We're not apolitical," I say. "We know our good fortune, but we've made sacrifices. Just visit the war memorial, have a look at all those names. I had students who went to war voluntarily. Because they thought it was the right thing to do. It was service. Not all of them came back."

"*Service* is an interesting word," says Lydia. "I am sure Arturo Cabrera and Pia Suarez believe they are performing a great service to the world, however they must do it, whatever it takes."

"Terrorism isn't service." I sound both prissy and smug.

"Depending on the cause, it could be seen as necessary escalation, worthy sacrifice."

"No, there I disagree with you."

"But the cause of Oceloti—the urgency of putting a stop to the burning and logging of the last rain forests, even if it may be too late—you'd be on board with that, wouldn't you?"

"Of course I would."

"If saving the ecosystem permitting human survival isn't essential, what is?"

"Well, as my students used to say, there's an easy A." Hovering near the piano, Lydia's sound man holds his small black box in the air, moving it here and there, watching it closely.

Lydia is leaning closer and closer to me. "So don't you think Cabrera chose this town as his launching point to underscore his statement, that you and the others he chose—and this literally *colonial* house with its carefully curated furnishings—were meant to stand for a community that thinks it's immune to the immediate effects of global apocalypse? That gets a pass from any *true* sacrifice?"

"Oh that is not at all the—" I draw in my breath, because I remember, possibly too late, that I promised Celestino not to tell anyone what he told me about Arturo, their past connection, how Arturo had chosen him, not the town, as refuge. "Listen. If what you're trying to say is that just because we're well-off, we have no conscience or sense of responsibility, you're talking to the wrong person." To her gotcha smile, I say, "What have you read lately?"

"Read?" She stalls by laughing. "I've been reading up on the seemingly unstoppable destruction of the rain forests. Or what's left of them. I'm always reading up on my latest beat."

"Any poetry? Any fiction? There are plenty of poems and novels related to your 'beat.' "

"No breathers for that."

My turn to laugh. "Breathers. Is that what you'd call the only occasion for literature?"

"We were talking about—"

"But now we're talking about something else." I hope the sound guy's black box won't register my wonky breathing. "My students always read plenty about so-called doom and destruction. They read Dante, they read *Hiroshima,* they read plays about revolutions and poetry about hate crimes. They had an education in shadows cast across civilization far larger than those cast by any rain forest canopy.

You can grow up ignorant and selfish inside the most pious frugality. And you can grow up toward moral obligation, toward . . . humility, or how about a sense of mission? Yes, you can grow toward that light even in a place like this. See it as decadent if you wish, but it's not so simple." It's all I can do not to end with *young lady.*

"Quite the speech," Lydia says, sounding less ruffled than I can tell she is. In her lap, across the top of one fist, a yellow butterfly twitches with her pulse. "And I'll give you this much: without literature, we'd be the poorer."

Silence spreads between us like an odor: noted but unseen.

"So I have one more question for you," she says. "If you could say one thing to Arturo Cabrera and the others who held you prisoner here, in your home, what would that be?"

In the brief pause, I notice the seahorse just above her left knee, and it makes me think of Mike. "All," I say, "are pu-ni-shed."

Austin

"I did not expect to see you again," she says when she comes down to the parlor. Her tone is pointedly neutral; hearing her unembellished voice, I can't believe I was fooled by her demoiselle gushings.

"Under recent circumstances, you get a pass." I try to make it light, but she doesn't take it lightly.

"We will not talk about guilt or bad behavior. I certainly feel no guilt."

Not a productive line of discourse. At that moment, Jess, the innkeeper who's almost always on duty, comes into the room and offers to bring us a "beverage" from the small bar around the corner. We both decline. Jess doesn't try to make small talk (or, for that matter, large talk). She leaves us alone.

Petra is still standing in the center of the worn, richly patterned antique rug. It was once a fine, expensive carpet, and when I look at the garishly blossomed wallpaper somebody thought would complement the rug, my teeth hurt.

I tell her I've brought something for her, and I move the package from my lap onto the overlacquered coffee table, resting it on a stack of sun-faded books about colonial New England. "You may as well sit," I say, and she does, on an armchair that places her half in profile. She looks at the package but doesn't take it.

"This is what you've been looking for," I say. "In part. And honestly? You may not believe me, but I didn't follow your hints the other night. Over dinner. I figured it out later, but you could've just said her name."

"Would you have given me a straight answer?"

"Why not?" Though, because Miriam was there, I can well imagine why not. Miriam knows her name, but not the entire story.

When she doesn't take the package off the table, I tell her it's the one painting of Issa's I kept. "It's big," I say. "You won't be able to see the whole thing here." I'm hoping she won't open it now, because I don't want to see it.

She puts her hands on it instantly, as if she's afraid I'll change my mind. She pulls it to her lap, and she looks up at me not gratefully but with open contempt.

"Where were you keeping it?"

"Don't interrogate me. Just take it."

Miriam wrapped it in an old pillowcase, which Petra removes with some haste. I warn her that it's fragile. She carries it across the room, to a long settee against the wall, and begins to unfold it. She opens it to about a quarter of its size, draping it awkwardly against the settee. As she does this, her back is to me. I suppose she does have a right to wonder why I kept it hidden away all these years. Whether it's of any "value" isn't the point. It simply deserves to be seen—unlike the companion memories I cannot discard.

Petra stands and looks at the painting, what she can see of it, for two or three minutes. We're silent, and at one point, Jess comes to the doorway, probably wondering if we've left. She gives me a quick apologetic smile and retreats to her office. Other than Petra, there are no guests for the moment. The FBI agents who took over the rest of the rooms are gone. What they found out from snooping through the town, who knows? They must have wondered if they would unearth accomplices, moles.

Petra refolds the painting, slips it into the pillowcase, and turns back to me. She doesn't thank me, and her arms are crossed on her chest.

"You chased her away."

"I have no idea where you got that idea. She's dead. She wasn't found, but I'm sure she'd have shown up again if she were still alive."

"I don't understand what she saw in you, why she let you abuse her."

I keep my voice calm when I say, "I did not abuse her." If anything, Issa abused me—though in the end I didn't blame her. "She was ill; anyone could see that."

Petra shakes her head violently. "You just didn't believe her. Your imagination is so small." The second remark is, of course, meant to wound the artist in me.

"Sit down," I say. "Just listen, will you?"

Everyone has a mental drawer containing individual days set aside to be irrepressibly relived, retraced, perhaps regretted, in painstaking detail. My last day with Issa is one of those days. I knew at the outset that it would be the last—I knew it had to be—but I could never have known how terribly the day would end.

I knew it would be the last because of the night before. I had arrived home from work to find that she had laid out her paintings and drawings in dozens of tidy packets across every surface in the apartment, from kitchen counter to chair seats and couch. On top of each stack rested a blank sheet of paper.

She greeted me with the announcement "I've put it all together for you. All you do is write the letters!" This was a plan she'd come up with, seemingly out of the blue, a couple of weeks before. She wanted me to help her write to a long list of government agencies and corporations urging the necessary action to reverse the poisoning and pillaging of ocean life, calling on them to rise up against the vast and careless cruelties of tankers, freighters, drilling concerns, fishing fleets, cruise companies, garbage merchants, even the loopholed whaling vessels of indigenous people who lived on the dwindling ice sheets of the Arctic Circle. Stop, stop; they must all stop.

Her pictures would hold their attention, might even do the trick of convincing them! "And you have a power I don't: the power of language. And your connections—you know people the whole world over."

"Your beautiful pictures would go astray," I told her.

"Astray? Don't tell me that. Don't have so little faith. Don't you dare." I was reminded again how quickly she could move between kinetic joy and angry impatience. How easily she took on the attitude of being wronged or misunderstood.

I told her (for hardly the first time) that this wasn't the kind of work I did and she knew it. My so-called connections were useless. She had the wrong man for the job. She told me I was *her person;* others might have been chosen, but I was hers. I was the one who would make this happen, change my world and rescue hers. I would be a hero. "In my world, you already are," she told me, beaming. "Once we decided."

"Who decided? Decided what?"

She looked wounded. "Decided that you would be the one to fight for us."

"*Who* is the us?" This wasn't the first time I'd asked.

"Don't try to find words for us," she told me, her voice low but ecstatic, as if she were sharing a valuable secret.

I could no longer dodge the conclusion that she was mad. No one used that word anymore, but you could think it. What she suffered went beyond depression or delusion; the map of her madness was laid out before me, plain as day. *Look, stupid,* said the map. Was I working so hard at the firm that I couldn't see straight anywhere else in my life? It didn't matter. All that mattered was getting through the rest of that evening, somehow, getting us to the light of the following day.

Knowing it was a gamble, but seeing no other way through, I stood there, surrounded by the debris of her pathology, and suggested, in a bright voice, that perhaps she could volunteer, even find a job, with an organization that lobbied for cleaner oceans. I would help her figure it out. Nature Conservancy? Greenpeace? Trident? Save Our Seas? "So many options!" I said eagerly.

She accused me of deception and cruelty. These organizations were toothless bureaucracies! I was a coward! And then she grabbed her coat and ran out, as she had done a few times in recent weeks, whenever she worked herself into a passionate state of despair. I had reasoned before, however pathetically, that despair about the state of the world was hardly crazy. Some of us were better than others at living with big-picture denial.

Each time she'd run off, she had returned sometime in the dead of night, sliding her cool, smooth naked body against mine. I didn't ask where she went; I didn't tell her it wasn't safe to wander alone in the city at all hours. I didn't want more cause for argument. I wanted to believe that I was, in fact, "her person" and that she was mine. The alternative looked like too much pain.

But that was the pain I faced when, yet again, she ran out into the night and I was left alone with her Technicolor madness laid out before me in careful piles, each marked by a rectangle of blank white space. Each one mocked me, *What now?*

I went to bed without eating or drinking anything, and I slept well. Hadn't I tried everything? I had urged her to get some sort of counseling, which she refused, and now I had even offered to help her get a job. In exchange for which she called me cruel and deceitful!

I woke to the sounds of her returning: the apartment door closing, the bolt latching us in. I heard the rustle of her raincoat, heard her keys settle in the china bowl, up against mine. I saw her silhouette as she approached the bed, early-morning light from the living room framing her shape, a shape I had known first as something pleasing to capture in line and color on paper. But what did that shape contain?

Rising onto my elbows, I told her I had to get up, get to the office, assuming she meant to ravish me, as she could do so well, deftly obscuring whatever conflict we'd had the night before.

I dressed without taking a shower and left without drinking coffee. I told her we would talk when I came back from work. I had a client dinner, but I would be home by nine. I knew I had to end it, cut myself free—so let her sell my mother's ring; it was worth a few months' rent in Queens—and I set off for work ashamed that I worried more about the guilt I would suffer than I did about what would become of her once I told her I couldn't endure this anymore.

The day felt distant from me, like a scene in a movie I was watching. I went through meetings, phone calls, emails. I helped stage the presentation, in a darkened conference room, of a detailed budgetary breakout for a new biological sciences center at a Catholic college whose directors had, until recently, forbidden the teaching of Darwin. I confirmed the dinner reservation for the pampering of Father

Thomas, the president of the Catholic college. I noticed, looking out my boss's glass wall with its sidelong cameo view of the Hudson, that the sun was setting later and later as spring made its stealthy advance. I decided to walk the twenty blocks to the restaurant, let my boss take Father Thomas in the hired sedan.

Live in New York for more than a year or so and you will understand that it's a place where both love and sorrow are magnified by geography. The same high view that can make you feel literally on top of the world—where you imagined proposing to your girl—can make you wish you had the guts to plummet and end it all. The cobblestones preserved on certain seemingly random streets might have you telling yourself that you live in a magical place or that history is rising to swallow you whole, that you are smaller than small and doomed to fail. A favorite bar is a spiritual womb or the reminder of how, even in a place where you feel safe in your skin, you may encounter betrayal.

I concentrated on the storefronts and landmarks and awakening greenery as I made my way south, first along the cross streets of West Chelsea, flamboyant artwork splayed behind wide windows (why didn't Issa want *this*?); then across gridlocked Fourteenth Street; then angling my way to and fro along leafy streets with brick houses, hive-like bistros, and glittering perfumeries, stepping at last into the chosen restaurant, past the heavy velour drape that kept the chill at bay, fifteen minutes early.

I sat at the designated corner table with a menu and a glass of water, trying to decide what I would eat; also (as I suffered the nearby couples' enjoyment of their food and wine) trying to engrave a speech on my brain. *I owe you an apology. . . . I was selfishly impulsive. . . . I'm just not the man you . . . I will help you find a place of your own and help with the down payment. . . . Surely there's a friend or family member who could . . .*

Dinner passed in pleasantries and talk of complicated food. Semicorpulent Father Thomas told the four of us about taking a rare vacation in Thailand, splurging to attend a cooking school. He became an expert in edible flowers and varieties of fish roe; he knew how to make four kinds of noodles from scratch. I minimized my intake of liquor and was thankful when no one ordered dessert.

I returned to the apartment at nine-fifteen, taking a deep breath as I slid my key into the lock, silently reciting my speech. *I've heard there are still affordable studios in Hell's Kitchen. . . .* (Money aside, was she capable of living alone? I mustn't care.)

As I expected, I opened the door to see the living room still filled with her creations—but they were shredded, torn into a crisis of fragments, a blizzard of accusation. She sat on a chair at the dining table, in her coat, that bizarre garment she wore, rain or shine, whenever she left the apartment, and she glared at me. She did not stand.

"I already know what you want to say to me. It's written on your face. It was this morning," she said. "So all I want to say is that if you give up on me, I give up on you. And I curse you."

I thought about expressing my dismay at all the beauty she had destroyed in what was obviously a colossal tantrum. I thought of taking her in my arms and, just to calm her down, telling her that I understood her pain. I even thought of trying to get her to a hospital, convincing her to check herself in for psychiatric help.

But I said, "Issa, I'm sorry, it's over. I'll help you move out and find a place of your own."

She bolted upright, out of the chair, and threw off her coat, presenting her naked body. "Do you see what you have done to me?" She faced me, breasts forward, arms winglike. I thought of the classic statue: a marble angel guarding a grave.

What was I supposed to see? I sat on a stool at the kitchen counter, defeated. "No, Issa, I don't. I'm blind. All the things you see, for us, I can't. I'm sorry."

So quickly and violently that I thought she might attack me, she snatched up her raincoat, wrenched it back on, and said, "You will never see me again." She ran from the apartment. I walked slowly over to the door, to latch it, and saw that she had left her keys in the bowl.

It took me a long, muddled moment to become alarmed. I left the apartment and, passing our one elevator, took the stairs, hurrying. On the street, I spotted her to the west, running. There was no one else on the block, or I might have missed her. I ran, too. Never having been a runner, I felt ungainly, foolish. When I reached the avenue, the light had changed against me. I yelled her name. The next block ended at the West Side Highway, the promenade.

When I reached the highway, I might have caught her, since the traffic light did not favor the pedestrians crossing. But from half a block away, I watched her sprint through traffic, onto the promenade, and veer south. A few late dog walkers turned to stare at her, but only briefly. You could imagine them thinking, *Another crazy one. Come on now, Fido, hurry up and do your thing.*

By the time I had crossed (waiting for the light), she was far ahead of me and I had a cramp in my side. Knowing it was pointless, I yelled her name again.

I saw her turn right onto one of the recently repurposed piers. During my time in the neighborhood, I'd watched this one morph from a ruin of rotting, hazardous boards to a trim green soccer field surrounded by a walkway. The fence hemming it in was minimal, thin steel cabling, built low to preserve the river view.

I was two long blocks away when I saw her clamber onto the fence, balancing for a second on the top cable, and dive, her coat briefly extending behind her like wings. I resumed running. By the time I reached the end of the pier, the water had almost stilled. Almost—and but for that, I might have doubted I saw what I did.

I did not do the heroic thing. No, I have never claimed hero status. Nor am I an athletic swimmer. I called 911.

Petra's expression hardly changes through the course of my story. She looks like someone sitting alone in a car, waiting for the light to change. I could be an old-fashioned educational radio show, just filling the silence.

I tell her about how I found the painting, the one I just gave her, folded in the top of my closet; I'd never seen Issa working on something so large. It made her seem both more tragic and less sane.

I decide not to tell Petra about the police, taking them to the apartment, watching them survey the disaster zone it had become.

When she sees I'm waiting for her to speak, she says, "Those nights she left you? She came to me. I should have made her stay. I shouldn't have been so passive."

"Do you think you'd have somehow cured her?"

"She did not need 'curing.' She needed to be recognized."

"As what, some kind of otherworldly creature? A mermaid?"

"Well, you know what, asshole?" Petra says, and perhaps my tone deserves it. "Just maybe. Maybe a seal. Or maybe something, some spirit, about which we are clueless. There was magic in Issa. I'm not ashamed to admit I saw it. You live in a mighty small world, do you even know how small?" She extends both arms, as if to indicate that I live exclusively within the walls of this overpatterned parlor.

The door to the inn opens, interrupting us, and a young woman walks in. She stops to say hello and then, seeing our expressions, hurries past. I hear her talking with Jess in the office. I wonder if Jess has been studiously eavesdropping. I would have been.

"Well," I say, "nothing's stopping you from returning to your large world. And you are welcome to it."

Petra stares at me in a way that tells me she is deliberately withholding many, many thoughts running through her head. I have nothing to lose by saying, "What possessed you to pick up this lost bizarre relationship from way back in your life—if it was a relationship—and hunt me down as if I were some kind of escaped murderer? As if there were some kind of bounty on my head."

"All I wanted," she says, her voice unsteady, "was an answer. Some people treat past loves like garbage, to be put out on the curb, the way we used to get rid of large objects we didn't want or need anymore. Some of us keep them close, like questions we need to ask ourselves to lead a better life."

Oh God, she's crying. Why do I care? "Look," I begin.

"I *have* looked. I looked everywhere for her."

I try to soften my voice. "Yet you seem to think I knew more than you. You can't have it both ways, Petra. Either I kept her secrets or I was an ignorant cad."

She points to the encased painting beside her. "You did keep her secrets! You had this! You hoarded this!"

"Is that any kind of answer?" I say. "Does it tell you any of what you claim you wanted to 'know'?"

She will take it out again and open it fully after I leave, up in her room, I know that. And she'll see the "curse" Issa left me. I hope it gives her satisfaction that Issa ended her life seeing me as the scum of the earth. I spend a lot of energy in this town just trying to be, what . . . well regarded? *Of good repute?* as the original inhabitants of my old house might have put it?

She holds my gift to her against her body. "It's worth the shit I went through, that's all I can say." She stands up. "I have to finish packing. We won't see each other again. Or I hope we won't."

I feel like saying, *Did you get your pound of flesh?* That would only give her satisfaction. Though why shouldn't she have it? I am reminded that some broken hearts stay broken. I've been fortunate. So far.

I stand up, too, and I wish her safe travels. I don't ask where she's going. I doubt it's Texas. Or New York. Not if she's smart. And beneath all her rage and palpable sense of injustice—well, much like Issa, in fact—I have a hunch she is.

What I might have told her about, but didn't, was the visit I paid to the life-drawing class where I'd met Issa. I'd stopped going once we were entangled, but of course she continued to go, two nights a week. She'd return to the apartment, sore and stiff, to soak in my bathtub. Often I came home to find her there, up to her neck and almost dozing.

The police had turned up nothing, and I went through a scary couple of days when they turned their suspicions, if somewhat covertly, on me. They even spoke with Saul and a couple of other colleagues who'd met Issa at one of the parties I took her to. How someone could live in that big hypercivilized city without a traceable origin story defied all logic. I wonder if, in the end, the police figured I was the one who was unhinged, deluded—as Saul liked say, out where the buses don't run. Even Saul treated me differently: no more lewd remarks or offers of contacts at foreign brothels. I was relieved but also blue. I knew my days at the firm were numbered. I was once again the outlier I'd been in high school.

The police diver had found Issa's coat, which showed no evidence of foul play. I was free, but I felt no relief. Her death had rated small news items in the *Times* and the *Post;* I both hoped and dreaded that someone who'd known her in a former chapter of her life might track me down through the police.

On my way to the building where the drawing class happened, I began to dread that it wouldn't exist—that the class itself had been a dream. But people were streaming out into the night, struggling with pads and easels, just as I arrived. The same money-taker was there, divvying up the cash with a man who I presumed was the model. Once the man left, I approached the woman, who recognized me even though I hadn't come in a few months. (Probably that night I arrived with the foolish bushel of roses etched me on her memory. Maybe I was even a "story.")

"Hey," she said, without interrupting her routine. She picked up stray candy wrappers, crumpled sketches, stumps of charcoal, tossing them all in a trash bag. "What's up?"

"Issa," I said.

"Yeah." She paused in her gatherings. "What about her?"

"When did you last see her?"

"She hasn't modeled for me in over a month."

I took this in. It wasn't as if Issa ever talked about the work, or not much, but still I was puzzled.

"People liked her, too. Asked for her." She grinned at me. "You weren't the only one with extracurricular fantasies, bro."

"Do you have . . . You must have some way of getting in touch with her."

"Hoo." The money-taker's exhalation carried many meanings. One of them was, *You are not the first to ask me that, bro.* "She just showed up in the beginning. I figured she saw the notices I put up in bars. Paid her in cash. Got her yes or no for the following week. She was reliable. Never a no-show. Which I cannot say for the rest of my models."

"Did you think she'd be coming back again?"

"I go from week to week here." She told me the place was slated for demolition sometime in the next couple months. She'd be moving her operation to Long Island City. She was clearly watching my expression as she spoke, looking for another story to add to my love-lorn roses.

After an awkward pause, she said, "Can I make an unsolicited comment?"

"Shoot," I said.

"I wouldn't pursue a girl the police are looking for, too. You know? Because in case you didn't know it, I got a visit from a cop. I mean, I'm not the IRS here."

Of course the police had beaten me there. I knew this, but I'd forgotten.

"Good advice," I told her, and back I went into the sharp spring night.

It's the same kind of spring night I pass through on the short walk home from Twin Chimneys.

To my surprise, Miriam is making dinner for the first time in over a week. Maybe she's snapped out of her trancelike anxiety, ever since Brecht left with Iliescu's son. It stunned me, too, his sudden move, but something had to give. I told him to come back, no questions asked, if what he has in mind (what does he have in mind?) doesn't work for him.

The kitchen smells like mushrooms. Miriam is wearing a red apron and chopping parsley. The wallscreen is dark, and no music plays. Clio clamors for my attention, and I give her the minimum it takes to send her back to her bed.

"You were gone awhile." Miriam glances at me over her shoulder but continues her task. She knows where I was.

"Sorry," I say, realizing how worn out I am from talking.

"When is she leaving?"

"Tomorrow."

"Good."

I know the frost in her voice is meant for both of us, me as well as Petra.

"Can I just say one more thing about this whole weird business?"

"Who said you couldn't say whatever you like about anything?"

I watch Miriam scrape the parsley from the board into a bowl. When she starts in on an onion, I can smell it the minute she cuts it loudly in half.

"I told her the story she wanted to hear. Or needed to. But it reminded me what a spell that woman, I mean Issa, could exert on people."

"On you, you mean."

"Not just me."

She chops quickly, efficiently, upends the onion into the bowl. From behind, I see her wipe her eyes with the apron. The onion is pungent; my eyes sting, too, though I'm sitting across the room.

"I still don't really get why you told me almost nothing about that intense time in your life. About her."

"Obviously, I was embarrassed by it, that I was with her for months. That I asked her to marry me." But also, and I don't say this, for the longest time after, I pined for her. I'd come home from the office half hoping to find her in my tub. After I found the red painting, sometimes I would take it out and unfold it on the floor of my living room. I'd sit in a chair, with a drink, and simply stare. What I didn't tell Petra is that I, too, began to wonder if Issa was still alive somewhere. I looked for her—not actively, the way Petra did, but among the faces all around me everywhere: not just in New York but in Dubai, Cleveland, Fresno, Miami Beach, whatever random places my work took me. And the uncontrollable searching frayed my nerves. It may have contributed, I now realize, to my longing for a kind of burrow, for settling and working in one place, a place where I would come to know all the faces around me.

Miriam fusses in a drawer, clattering skillets. Did she hear me, or is she ignoring me?

"Before I forget," she says, "Tyrone wants a meeting."

She wouldn't forget such a thing. I know our conversation about Issa is over, but only for now.

She sets the pot she was seeking on a burner, turns around. "You're not going to talk him out of a bunker, not now. He went to check on the site yesterday, and he says you can tell someone's been camping out there."

"Camping out?"

"Nothing damaged. But he found some wrapping. Food wrapping. A piece of clothing. He doesn't care what it costs."

Bunkers, shelters from catastrophe: if I build one, I'll end up building more. I want to believe that we can all go on living with our faces to the light, no matter what comes our way.

"I said you'd meet with him tomorrow. I made an appointment."

Clio, who sometimes seems to know everything, comes over to me, presses herself against my legs. I scratch her throat.

"Okay?" Miriam says.

"Of course I'll meet with him. Obviously."

"Good." She turns on the screen. Pia Suarez is still on the run. I imagine she's on a trawler, crossing the equator by now. One side of the screen shows us her square, obstinate face, as if we haven't memorized it, and the other shows us an aerial view of burning trees.

Outside, it's dark, but the sky is refreshingly clear. The waning moon broadcasts its light across the sliver of harbor we can see past our neighbor's house.

Miriam says dinner will take no more than twenty minutes to cook. Before then, she'd like to see if she can speak with Brecht. She unties her apron, hangs it up, and walks past me without touching me. I hear her footsteps on the stairs. Clio looks up at me with what I could swear is not just love but pity.

Connie

Raul is impatient for school to start again. "Why don't we just do it at Jordie's house? Jordie's house is bigger than ours." And then "Are we not meeting here because of the agents?"

Nearly all the other children's houses are bigger than ours, but I would never point that out. And the FBI agents have finished their work here. They even combed through Raul's room and took away all our electronic gadgets for a few days. I found it a relief to have nothing but my own phone with which to connect to the outer world. I did not allow myself to turn on the wallscreen. And if Arturo had planted any kind of bug or virus in our lives, I wanted it ripped out from the roots. If they found any evidence of meddling, the agents kept it to themselves. They asked a thousand questions but gave us very few answers. They were civil, however, and their presence became a bizarre consolation.

I tell Raul that we're taking a pause, a pre-summer vacation. We'll start again on Monday, adding a week in June to square with the school days the state board requires. The town's public schools are back in session—they took off only two days—but the other parents agreed that we would let Celestino come home first, have a few days of quiet.

His arm is in a sling, and he is taking painkillers. Shattered bone, torn muscle, extensive neural damage. Since the surgery, pain from the regenerating nerves keeps him up at night. And bad dreams, from which, when he does sleep, he wakes awash in the kind of sweat that smells like undistilled fear, not at all the kind of sweat that drenches his clothes after a long day of outdoor work in July. I will get up and help him sponge off his body in the bathroom. It helps tether him back in reality, too. "Everything," I keep saying to him, "will return to normal. It will. You just have to heal." Sometimes I rest a cheek against his damp back, careful not to jostle his aching arm. We'll stay like that, silent together, for a few minutes before I lead him back to bed.

For a few days, while he was still in the hospital, he suffered spells of panic in which he was certain that Arturo, from whatever place of detention he'd been taken to, no matter how distant, would find a way to ruin our lives.

I told him it seemed pretty clear to me that Arturo had used him (and deceived me) but held no hidden grudges and had no desire to ruin our lives. "I think he liked Raul," I said. "And me," I added, foolishly affecting a tone of flirtation.

"What are you talking about?" Celestino seethed through the torpor of pain muddled with drugs. "The man is a killer."

He was right, but still I want to believe we are out of danger. The way I see Arturo, his flaw is fanaticism, not malice. The world is full of fanatics now, a dime a dozen, and many of them are justified in their drive to destroy the destroyers. They become killers despite themselves. Or is a killer merciless and malignant by nature? "Bring on the bombs and the bombardiers!" Harold used to say in response to headlines about conservative Supreme Court decisions, elections won by bigots, hideous housing developments that sprouted from rolling pastureland. Some people told him it wasn't funny in an age of proliferating violence, much of it wrought by actual bombs. Bombs are no joking matter, they'd say. Never.

For most of that sodden Monday, Celestino went AWOL from work. He told Brecht to take the day off, and he drove obsessively around the town, searching for Arturo. He had an uncanny feeling that, just as the younger man had done back in Matlock, he was lying low somewhere. (If only he'd looked just across the street!) Late in the day, he gave up and came home, but while he sat in the driveway, grimly transfixed by the local news, he heard the latest statement released by Oceloti, their obstinate claim to the rightness of the bombings. The language, its haughty cadence, echoed similar statements made by the student group whose foolish acts led to the burning of that old house in Matlock. (It was easy to agree with Arturo's contempt for institutions like Harvard, yet I had to wonder if his time there had also given him access to people with the means to back his kind of mayhem.)

The statement included the dictate to *denounce our greedy society.* Celestino told me that those words struck him so hard that had he been out on the road, he'd have had to pull over from shock—because those very words had formed the name of that defunct student group, its silly acronym: the DOGS. *We will unleash the DOGS!* its childish leaders had declared as they deployed one destructive prank after another.

Almost without thinking, Celestino went straight to the Vigil Harbor precinct, his instinctive fear of uniformed authority eclipsed by the realization that we had been harboring a murderer. He told me he was willing to be arrested, locked up, sent away; he was done forever with Arturo Cabrera and wanted the world to be done with him, too.

Only after Raul and I had eaten dinner did I check my phone and find his message: *Lock all the doors and do not answer.*

The police spoke with him, and they believed him, and then, too busy with the urgency of acting on what they had learned, let him go. Told him to go home, lock the doors, and wait for their call. But on his way back to us, he passed the town dock and saw something that struck him as wrong: a crowded boat at the dock. Opening his window, he heard Arturo's voice.

One of the reasons so much of this town closed up for the next few days is that an antiterrorism brigade, trucks carrying men and women in hazmat suits and dogs with keen noses and drones armed with sensors, arrived to sweep through all public buildings, the parks and shoreline, and even our neighborhood—especially our house and Margo Tattersall's. Our appliances were dismantled, our attic and cellar cleared of cobwebs, our carpets overturned. The strangest sight, something I almost wish I'd photographed, was the tree house being searched by two women in puffy white suits. High up, inside the tree's blooming canopy, they deployed a tiny drone that buzzed about like a monster mosquito. Raul wanted to watch from the porch, but we were asked to stay deeper inside the house. They were looking for explosives, of course.

The only thing they found, on the uppermost platform, slung from a slender branch, was a pair of high-powered binoculars that did not belong to us.

That day, I was glad Celestino was in the hospital. The sight of those women up in our tree, which I did not describe to him, would have added to his nightmares. Or he'd have insisted on coming home too early.

Now his living nightmare is how to go on working. The surgeon forbids him from overworking the arm for at least a month—light work only, no lifting. Brecht has left (for which Celestino doesn't blame him), and Finn is someone Celestino has kept on only because he hasn't had the heart to fire him. Austin claims that he can put most landscaping on hold for a month. Most. Some jobs Celestino will lose.

I'm spending my evenings taking a fast-track certification webinar. According to Margo Tattersall, there will be an opening at the High later this year for a part-time art teacher (the only art teacher). I've told Celestino I plan to apply—Margo, who still inspires awe up there, will recommend me—and if I get it, Raul will go to what he and his friends scornfully call "regular" school. Of course it's the fault of their parents, including me, that they have this disdainful attitude toward the way most of their peers will travel toward the shoals of becoming a grown-up. This past week, watching the "regular" world intrude—its outlaws and then its enforcers—and doing so mostly on my own (Raul over at Axel's house, with Jordie, so that I could go back and forth to the hospital), I've wondered what it is that makes me feel as if we and our child are exempt from the norms. At the end of the day on which Margo told me about the job, I was on my way back from the hospital, in the truck, when I decided, on impulse, to turn right off the main route into town and drive around the loop in front of the High. I know that Celestino makes this small detour now and then, just to check on Caleb's tree, but I hadn't driven up there myself in a couple of years.

It was dark when I made the detour, but even before my headlights reached that far, I could see the riotous blossoms. It's dogwood season, and I'm fully aware of that from driving around town, where even last week's persistent rains did little to dislodge those sturdy flowers, yet still I was stunned at the sight.

I hadn't intended to stop—I was overdue to pick up Raul and get him to bed—but I pulled around to the school entrance and shut off the engine. I got out and crossed to the island with the tree and the plaque. I laid both hands on my brother's name and spread my fingers, to cover as much of it as I could. I pressed hard, to warm the chilly bronze.

The tree has grown so tall that I can nearly stand upright beneath its lowest boughs. In the motion-sensor lights of the high school, activated by my presence, the lacework of white flowers above me took on a greenish hue. Some had fallen to the grass, like stars spun free from the sky.

I was dry-eyed, and that surprised me. Maybe I'd used up all available emotion just getting through the drama of recent days. Or had I, like the crown of the tree, grown far enough from the root of my loss that I could see well beyond it? I looked at the face of the High, a place and a community I had blamed for driving Caleb to choose the path he had, the path on which he got himself killed. I'd gone to no reunions, lost touch with the few classmates who might have turned into lifelong friends.

Yet here I was: living right here, even raising a child in this town I continued to resent in a suspiciously adolescent way. If Raul had followed the usual routine of school in Vigil Harbor, he'd be starting fourth grade next fall, heading to the High five years later. Was my decision not to have him follow in my footsteps there just an overprotective attempt to make sure he didn't follow in Caleb's? Well, that was magical thinking.

I wondered what it would be like to pass this tree, maybe a dozen times a week, countless times a year, going in and out of that too-familiar door (though now it led to a bulletproof vestibule before opening to the school offices, the yawning hallways beyond). Would I, after a few weeks, give not even a glance to the tree and to the tiny place it marked, honoring the uncle my son would never know? And would that be any worse than avoiding the place altogether, as I did now?

I walked back across the drive to the front of the school. I put my face up to the window, hands cupping my cheeks, in an attempt to see past the vestibule. I could just make out the reflective curve of the long glass display case still lining the lobby. The case had been used, back in my time, to display students' artwork. Over my four years, I'd had numerous sketches, photographs, block prints, even a clumsy but piercing self-portrait pinned up there. If things hadn't changed, and if I applied for that job and got it, would I be displaying the art of my students here, not on the corkboard in my kitchen-turned-classroom?

Brecht came by to see me the next morning. I was about to leave for the hospital again; Raul was taking a long time to pull his things together so I could send him for another day at Jordie's. Brecht had sent me a message that he wanted to retrieve the painting he'd left behind, but I had forgotten and was, for a moment, both surprised and worried to see him on my doorstep.

"Hey, how is he?" he said before I could even invite him in.

"He's getting through it," I said. "The surgery took longer than they thought it would, and they want to make sure there's no infection before he comes home."

Raul came galloping down the stairs at the sound of Brecht's voice. He asked if Brecht was taking him for the day. "No," I said. "He just has to pick something up. And then we have to go."

Raul stood still for a moment, and Brecht smiled at him in a way that slowed me down. Maybe I didn't need to rush.

"Can I show him something on my game, upstairs?" asked Raul.

"For a quick minute," I said, and let them go up together. I sat down at the kitchen table and stared out at the yard, the tree, the row of vacant birdhouses standing at the back.

Until a week ago, we had, I only now realize, a very insular circle of friends and acquaintances. Unlike Austin Kepner, Celestino does not socialize with the people he works for. They may stop him in a store or on the street, to say how pleased they are with such and such a planting or walkway—and how is he doing, and where's he working now, and how is his family? And they go on their way, and that's fine by him. It's not even something he'd comment on; I'm the one who takes that in when we're out and about together, and if it doesn't bother him, it shouldn't bother me. But it's me who can't help feeling conscious that I'm married to one of the dwindling number of "working-class" men who live in this town.

Once, I asked him if he was conscious of this—I struggled for a word—distance? Difference? At first, I thought he wouldn't answer me, and I told him, "Never mind." But then he did answer. He told me that he'd spent his whole adult life inside a zone occupied by no one else. The odd stroke of fortune that lifted him out of his village and brought him to this country—and he would always see it as *good* fortune, despite what he'd lost because of it—meant that he would always be isolated. I must have looked sad, or even offended, because he left the room and returned with one of his much-used, well-soiled binders. He opened it to a highly detailed map of micro–growing zones in Massachusetts. The map resembled a colorful jigsaw puzzle.

Celestino said, "Here," and pointed to a tiny sliver of purple north of Vigil Harbor, on the part of our coast where the last of the state's salt marshes continue to shrivel, a rare liminal zone. "That is me," he said, and he said it cheerfully, then moved his hand from the map to my shoulder. "You are with me there," he said. "Raul will be more in the world." He swept his hand westward on the map, to broader swatches of color where temperatures are, at least for now, a bit more reliable.

If we have friends, they are the fellow parents to whom we open our house on most days of the week—all of us sharing and trusting one another with our children. That is a high degree of trust, and perhaps it amounts to friendship, but if so, it's a conditional friendship. This past week has shown me its limits, or maybe just its specialized nature, ever since that handful of other mothers realized they'd spent a couple of hours in my kitchen being so deceptively charmed ("bamboozled" was how Caitlin put it) by a terrorist. "Is there such a thing as a gentleman terrorist?" said Trina when she called me, though instantly she apologized for making light of it.

The morning after Celestino's surgery, three of them dropped by with food, and after I assured them that he would be fine, though the recovery wouldn't be easy, they wanted to revel in the collective sensation of having had such a close brush with death and mayhem. How lucky I was not to have been one of the hostages! They wanted to know the *true* story of the past this man shared with my husband. After all, Celestino hadn't raised an alarm, hadn't seen through the ruse, and shouldn't he have? Shouldn't the false name have alarmed him, alerted him to some kind of danger to them all? I couldn't—or didn't want to—tell them about the dangers that Celestino feared more, that had made him so passive. I felt caught between loyalty and shame.

All I told them was that people change radically—become radicalized, as we all know—so that the man Celestino had known decades ago wasn't the man who had ordered the making and setting of bombs. (Because now we knew, as everyone following the news knew, that Arturo was what our children might call a "mastermind." Like any corporate executive, he was more of a manager than a doer. Who knew if he could even have fired that gun?)

What disturbed me most that morning—other than the delay in getting myself to the hospital—was that I found myself more the object of intense curiosity than of love and concern. Is this why I withheld so much from my friends? For the first time, I wondered if my alliance with these women would last beyond our children's going out into the world (something I couldn't, at that moment, imagine surviving).

Alongside the subtle shift in my sense of where I stood among these women, there was the shock of a new and sudden closeness both to Brecht, whose unraveling I had witnessed up close, and to Margo, who had swum—actually jumped into cold, night-black water—to my husband's rescue. She insists, and technically she's probably right, that she didn't "save his life," but I told her we'd never know that. And to her also insisting that it was her fault the gun had been fired, because it was her fault there'd even been a gun, I said that desperate people will find ways to get what they want. I assured her that if I'd been one of the hostages, I'd have been just as meek. I'd have told myself it was for Raul, that if I behaved rashly or bravely, he might lose his mother. "But you," I said, "you *jumped*."

I am not saying that Margo Tattersall and I will become best friends, crisscrossing our street for companionship, consolation, and neighborhood gossip, but I see her now in three dimensions, as far more than the archetypal middle-aged fading blonde, the onetime champion sailor, the strict teacher I managed to dodge (though Caleb didn't); mother of three attractive girls now flown, ex-wife of a man who pontificates and poses, whose loud voice on summer nights often forced me to close my front windows. She is funny, smart, and fearless about sharing her opinions—one of which is that in creating this idyllic school of ours, we mothers should be careful what we wish for. "Like it or not, the world has its own ideas for what your children ought to be learning, and the world is not a generous place," she said to me last night when I asked her to come by and talk to me about the high school.

I sat quietly for a moment, in my small safe living room, and thought about what she was saying. No one, of course, needs to tell me about the world's lack of generosity. "You know," I said, "I keep thinking about the glib and flattering things Arturo said to me the day he showed up, when he was holding court in my kitchen with the children and their mothers. After I showed him the children working, writing in their journals, he said something like, 'How proud you must be, to put this together and make it work!' And I said something probably self-deprecating, I'm not sure what, but then he said, 'You have all these choices. Most people don't. Be careful not to take your choices for granted. Too many choices mean that many more chances to choose wrong. More chances for regret.' "

I had been thinking about the warning in that remark, though he'd said it lightly, and I hoped Margo might comment on it, but she said, almost cutting me off, "That fucker—sorry, but he is, a fucker I mean—may he rot in the country's most illicit dungeon. May he enjoy philosophizing to large, hungry rats."

"But the thing is, he wasn't out to deal in human slavery or extortion or torture."

Margo shook her head vehemently. "Murder is murder. Even murder by proxy. And he meant to kill. He meant to blow shit up. He almost blew us up. Not that we don't deserve it, but leave us to dig our own graves, buster."

I watch the boys—though of course Brecht isn't really a "boy"—come downstairs, moving quickly, laughing. Raul swings himself down, three steps at a time, by hoisting himself on the twin handrails that flank the staircase—a vestige of the time when Celestino lived here as caretaker to an older man. I enjoy the way they travel through space, so heedless of physical mishap, of tripping or falling.

I think of something I heard Trina telling the students when she was teaching them dance out on the lawn last fall. She was talking about proprioception, explaining why some people just seem to move more instinctively than others or catch on to sports with minimal practice. "You might call it our sixth sense," she said. "We're all wired to have an awareness of where our body—our limbs, every part of us—is located in the space around us. It's how we balance on a bike or skip rope. We couldn't get anywhere without it! And you can work on it, and that's what we do through yoga and dance, but it's also true that some people are just born more proprioceptive than others. That expression 'natural athletes'? Those folks exactly."

I wouldn't count myself among such people; no sport ever came naturally to me, and one thing I loved about the end of school was the end of so-called physical education. But maybe I've felt that I am emotionally proprioceptive, that I know my spiritual place among others—and suddenly, all at once, I think I've been a fool to believe that. Suddenly my orientation to the space around me isn't what I thought it was. My emotional balance is shot.

"Brecht," I say, "you went to the high school."

"Yeah," he says.

I ask him if he liked it—I mean, granting that high school isn't much of anybody's notion of paradise—and he shrugs. "If you'd asked me while I was there, I'd've said the place was a jail. That's what I would have said. We all said it. But that wouldn't have been the whole basic truth. Am I like nostalgic about it? No. Do I like running into people I knew there? Hardly ever. But then there were teachers who I guess kept me sane, pointed me in certain directions. Mrs. Tattersall's one."

Raul is watching him and listening. He knows how Mrs. Tattersall rescued his father. "But I'm not going there, to the high school." This he addresses to me.

"I was just curious," I say.

"Curious," says Brecht, "is maybe what the best teachers make you. Or they make you stay that way. They don't"—I see him mentally reword what he's saying for Raul—"mess up your head too much. Not *too* much." He lays a palm on Raul's head and musses up his hair.

Mike

I'm going to be having these dreams for a long time, I'm sure. Maybe I'll get to the point where at least, inside the dream, I'll know it's a dream. If I hadn't felt the need to leave so quickly, maybe I'd have bushwhacked through and beyond the dreams, but from this house on a wooded California hillside, surrounded by greenery, not ocean, Vigil Harbor itself might be a dream.

In last night's version, the boat is, as usual, speeding out to open sea, but this time Pia Suarez is in control, holding the gun to my head, pressing me back against the railing at the bow, while Arturo pushes the throttle full out. The Coast Guard is in pursuit but cannot catch us, and tied up in the stern is Marinda, my pregnant daughter. There is no way I can go to her without being shot, and if I go overboard, she will be defenseless, in the hands of these maniacs to do with as they please. As we leave the harbor, I look to the yacht club, high on its granite pedestal. A party is in full, buoyant swing, revelers dancing on the wide porch, and I yell in their direction, desperately hoping that someone will hear me, but the musicians—somehow a full symphony orchestra's playing up there—drown out my voice.

I would like to say that what I remember of that night, of what actually happened, is a blur, but quite the opposite is true. I recall every moment, as if in some three-sixty full-focus panorama, like the virtual tour I sampled of the house I put on the market a month ago now. (Despite Broker Babs's expert staging, it has yet to sell.) If Barry hadn't been in the vicinity, if the Coast Guard hadn't arrived so swiftly, if we hadn't been so close to Ruby Rock, and if the water temperature hadn't been at another all-time high for April—if any or even all of these things had not been in our favor, I am pretty sure some of us would be dead. And then there was the foolish risk I took, not because I'm so "brave" but because I could no longer control my rage.

Halfway out of the harbor, making my way between the few boats moored at random stretches, going as fast as I could not just in obedience to our captor but in the feeble hopes that we'd be stopped for speeding, and wondering if my heart might explode from beating so fast, I realized that the woman holding the gun was focusing more on the path before us than on her hostages. No doubt she presumed that Arturo and the gullible young men they'd roped into their miscreant scheme would be intimidation enough to keep us in our places. I knew, because I'd overheard the two novices discussing it in English, that we were headed to meet the trawler that would take the four of them north. My hunch was that if our fate were left to the three men, they'd let us return to shore on our own, but watching the woman shoot someone on the dock made me doubt she'd let us off so easy. She'd just as soon throw us to the jellyfish and scuttle my boat.

But what enraged me was my fear that her second shot had struck Margo—after that crazy valiant dive—and my shame in not finding a way to short-circuit the engine, stranding us. Back when we relied on fuel, not electricity, it would have been easy to flood the engine, but would I have done so? How, in the first place, had these outlaws chosen Margo to leverage their freedom? Or had I been the one in their sights all along? What did any of that matter now? Why the hell was my mind, as tediously as ever, treating the situation as a puzzle in logic, not a call to action?

We were abreast of Ruby Rock when I did three things simultaneously: I shouted, "Egon, the flare!"; I released the wheel; and I lunged at the woman from behind. Her strength and reflexes stunned me; I was the one thrown off balance by the sudden pitch of the boat as it veered toward the island. Arturo grabbed the wheel and corrected our course, but just then the harbormaster's boat came toward us, on the port side, from around the back of Harrow Point. I was trying desperately to use my weight to pin Suarez to the deck when I heard Barry's voice over his PA ordering us to power down and halt—an order Arturo had no intention of obeying. A powerboat is easy enough to steer, and he cut the wheel hard to starboard. Pia Suarez and I, wrestling against the port-side bow, pinwheeled into the water. The momentum hurled us in separate directions.

When I came to the surface, I saw my boat streaking out past Barry's larger but less agile vessel, and I heard a flare gun discharge, casting the scene in a wide, sudden nimbus of red. Under the candle-glow of the flare—was it mine? Had Egon heard me?—I could make out the island, a few hundred feet away, and I swam toward it for my life. I pulled myself up on a slice of shingle—a place I dimly recalled as a wider beach from my children's few summers at the camp that used to occupy the island. Once I got to my feet and climbed toward the summit, where the flattened remains of the camp buildings slumped in an overgrown field, I found myself surrounded by gatherings of seals, the island's current occupants. Until the commotion, they had probably been fast asleep. From my vantage point, I saw a Coast Guard security boat come into view, making a wide swing from the south to cut off Arturo's outbound trajectory. I know those boats, and they are well armed.

Don't shoot! I wanted to bellow across the water.

All I thought of then was Egon. I knew that by removing that evil woman from the boat, I'd also removed the gun, or so I hoped, but desperation is a weapon in itself. The three outlaws still on board might try anything, drawing fire from the agents bent on their capture. I reminded myself that Egon's friend Pearl was also still aboard, along with the two remaining hostages—that young man who worked for the tree guy and the woman he'd shown up with, someone I'd never laid eyes on—but all I cared about was my son's survival. Wasn't that exactly what I'd been thinking a few short days before, when I longed for him to return from New York to the "safety" of Vigil Harbor?

Standing among the throngs of seals, I watched Barry and the security boat maneuver to either side of my smaller vessel, and I heard the loud hiss of the Guard boat firing a grapple hook to bring my boat to a halt. Around me, the seals began to murmur, garble, and bark softly, probably more alarmed by my agitated presence than the human drama unfolding in the water. "Shhh, go back to sleep," I told them, as a parent might tell a child spooked in the middle of the night. I knew I would have to wait to call attention to myself. I also knew someone would have already called in a search for me, as well as for (perhaps especially for) Pia Suarez. Cold as I was, I knew I wouldn't freeze. The rain had stopped, and a dry breeze blew in from the south, uncloaking the moon and stars.

The moon was breathtaking, a platinum disc as bright as a shield, as lucid as a wide, watchful eye. I stared at its timeless marbled surface and willed it to calm my pounding heart. I had nothing to do but hope and wait. My rage was spent.

I took a seat on a low, crumbling cement barrier, part of the foundation to what had been the counselors' cabin, their sole refuge from the constant assault of heat-intoxicated six-year-olds. Inside the remains of the building huddled a dozen gray seals, and as I looked down at them, I noticed that one stood out for its pale hide; not the mottled dove-gray of a young seal but a luminous silvered white—the color of the moon. She—somehow I felt certain the seal was a she—appeared daintier than her companions, and her pelt seemed to glow. Maybe it was, in fact, a trick of the moonlight. She looked up at me with the round imploring eyes of a seal you'd see on an old-fashioned wall calendar, one of those glossy giveaways that conservation groups used to send as a plea for money to help save another doomed species. Her whiskers and doglike nose glistened in the sparring search beams cast out by half a dozen boats, all converging on the scene of the arrest. How easy it was to look into her dark eyes and project human questions onto her expression. I held her gaze for several moments before her larger bunkmates nudged her into shrugging free of the crush, propelling herself away from me, toward an opening farther off in the scrum.

I might have waited half an hour; time hardly mattered. Even as choppers began to pulse overhead, the seals settled themselves. I watched the Coast Guard security boat peel off toward Boston, a patrol cruiser aim itself to the north, and a few local boats, including the harbormaster's, pass by en route to the town landing. After I stood and waved my arms, I heard Barry's voice, over the PA system, tell me he'd return to pick me up.

Ten minutes later, as he helped me aboard and handed me an old military-issue blanket, he told me that no one had been injured in the arrest, but they hadn't found Suarez.

We both knew that if she was a decent swimmer, it was plausible she'd made it to the mainland. She'd never make it past the roadblocks, but our town border was hardly impenetrable. She could sneak out through a chain of suburban lawns or the patch of scrubby swamp that tumbles across the border we share with Knowles. I told Barry I needed to find my son, and then we docked at the landing. Seeing the chaotic crush of emergency vehicles, variously uniformed officials, hearing the media drones buzzing overhead, I realized that no one, or none of us who'd been on that boat, would be going home any time soon.

Before we disembarked, Barry told me that my boat had been impounded by the Guard. He was apologetic, but I was relieved. They could keep it for weeks, as far as I was concerned. I asked him if any of my fellow hostages had been harmed before the arrest. I was thinking of Margo; I couldn't bear asking about her directly, because I was so dismayed at how I'd failed to protect her. But Barry said, "Mrs. T's already down at the precinct. T as in T. rex, we used to say. More like T as in titanium. Sheesh."

For the first time in hours, I smiled. Barry had almost ten years on Egon, but I suppose he'd endured those poetry recitals along with everyone else.

Two hours later, Egon and Pearl and I returned to my apartment. Egon and I made Pearl go straight to the shower, and we put a frozen pizza in the oven. The EMTs had given us weak, tepid coffee, of which we'd drunk too much, and stale protein bars. My mouth tasted like old nuts.

The three of us made only practical conversation (*Plates up there. Drink water. You warm enough?*) as we opened beers and collapsed on couch and chairs. When we finished the pizza, we went to our beds. We took the tranquilizer tabs the EMTs had doled out and lay down to sleep off our shock.

I was the first one up in the morning. I was making coffee when I heard a muffled buzzing: my work phone, which mostly lives in my boat pack. Opening the closet door, I could see the thing glowing with urgent self-importance right through the nylon skin of the pack. I nearly closed the door and let it ring out, certain I'd be disregarding nothing more than invasions by reporters and calls of concern from associates I barely knew, but fortunately, I pulled it out to look at the number; I answered instantly.

"Dad, I'm sorry to call you at work, but I thought you promised to stop ignoring your phone," said Marinda. Only then did I remember that the police had my phone, which they'd confiscated from Cabrera. "The first thing I want to say is I'm okay, everything's going to be okay, but I'm having some . . . issues. The baby's fine, she's a good weight, and they've given me some hormones, but I'm going to be in bed for a couple of months."

I didn't know what to say, because to speak would be to cry. Her mother's two pregnancies had been textbook normal, hardly any side effects, my children arriving as punctually and free of fuss as well-mannered dinner guests.

"Really, I'm going to be fine, I trust my midwife totally, but I wanted to let you know. They can induce me early, she said . . . but until then, until I'm farther along, I'm going to have to learn to love the life horizontal."

"I'm coming out," I blurted into the phone.

"Oh Dad, I didn't mean—"

"Let me tie up some frayed ends, give me a day or two, and then I am there." But my heart slumped. "Unless you want your mother."

Marinda laughed. "Mom? Are you kidding? Do you know where they are, Mom and that . . ." She sighed. "They're at some club on Lake Michigan that has reciprocal privileges with the yacht club. Like they . . . No. Mom's not the company I'm looking for."

She insisted that she didn't need me. They were already looking into hiring someone to help out when Harkney had to make offshore inspections. The company would be sinking a new field of turbines in waters west of Crescent City.

"Let me," I said. "Please?" Was I begging for an excuse to put my life, like my excess belongings, in storage?

In the background, Harkney was offering an opinion I couldn't hear.

"If you want to come out," she said at last, "we'd like that. But you don't have to stick around."

But stick around is what I've been glad to do. The house is one of those glass boxes inside which one never feels entirely private, even with the hemp blinds drawn. The views are mesmerizing—subtropical woodland tucked snug in a fertile canyon, interrupted by only a few other distant dwellings—especially from the main bedroom, where my daughter reclines all day in a king-size bed, a bunker of pillows that faces not a screen (as so many beds do nowadays) but a great window broadcasting the cinematic joy of all that verdant biomass. Most mornings, after I've brought her a tray of eggs and fruit and a bright red herbal tea, we sit side by side and stare out, looking for the elusive birds or watching the clouds revise themselves endlessly; drifting, shifting, dispersing, making way for those in pursuit. Perhaps because our only way of staying in touch these past few years has been through exchanging words long-distance, it surprises me to find that this grown-up daughter, like me, knows how to coast along stretches of silence. Now and then, she will reach over, take my nearest hand, and place it on her belly to feel her baby's body in motion, shifting as inexplicably as those clouds. We may not say much of anything for an hour or more.

It felt a bit embarrassing, the first few days, to sit on Marinda's bed with her, but that's how she likes it, even if we're engaged in separate pastimes. She wears what she calls her yogajamas, I wear my daily jeans and buttoned shirt. Though she might have figured out how to do it with her torso pitched back at a forty-five-degree angle, she's quit her graphic design job and jokes that it's "lockdown all over again"! A dozen years ago, she was in middle school and Egon a freshman at the High when we endured that first year of house arrest. When the schools sent students home, poor Egon had just emerged from the worst of the nerve pain following the terrible burn of the summer before, and he had hoped to find a new sport he could embrace, something to replace his gymnastics. At least my work, in the so-called great outdoors, allowed me to get away from the house once spring arrived. Back then, I ran a ditch remediation project, an attempt to forestall the surrender of the marshes in Ipswich and Essex to encroaching salination. I gave fundraising talks on Zoom, speaking in lofty terms of "vulnerability assessments" and "coastal buyback," describing the plight of our "living shoreline" and how our hidden dependence on the ocean commits us all to a "blue economy." But suddenly, and for quite a while, all the science news coverage converged on the epidemiologists. Ecologists, oceanographers, conservationists . . . who were we? The economy was blue all right, but water had nothing to do with it.

At night, after unshackling our children from their screens—the zone that had become the classroom, office, marketplace, and watercooler of all our lives—Dee and I would focus on the grim news together, over a bottle of wine, keeping the volume low. As if our teenagers weren't dipping into the apocalyptic bulletins all on their own.

If homework was finished, we'd pull out the games of their childhood: cribbage, Bananagrams, Risk, and two outliers called Tantrix and Rummikub. We toyed competitively with geometry, geography, words, and numbers. We kept a diary of scores. I remember wishing we were one of those musical families like the von Trapps or the Marsalises, that we might have entertained one another as families in previous centuries had done, no sitcoms or social media or online shopping to fill the hours of indoor confinement. But we did have those games, and on some mornings, after taking my coffee to the kitchen table, I'd sit on a chair and feel something small and hard beneath my bottom. I would stand to find a plastic tile showing me a 3 or a Q or a cryptic web of colored lines. I would return the tile to the pouch or box where it belonged and feel grateful, for a moment, that we had the luxury of games.

Eventually, we returned to the world and resumed most if not all of our old habits, the bad with the good. There were periodic retreats, but we soldiered on. Now we searched the news for emerging new diseases, mutations of those we already knew, and we gained a greater, darker respect for the lethal mosquito. All too soon, those who swore they'd never be comfortable at another YC dinner or dance shed their fear of carousing. I returned to the lab as well as the marshes. I remember how badly my skin was burned that first summer; I'd leave the house with my masks and my gloves and my sanitizing potions, too often forgetting my sunscreen.

Those years were part of the collective memories Marinda and I shared and compared in the first days of our intimate two-hander lockdown. In the beginning, we brought up only the best of those memories—as if her mother hadn't cast a shadow over all of them by blowing up our marriage. (I don't tell Marinda that maybe I hadn't been all that happy, either. It would bring her no comfort.) But now, a few weeks into our arrangement, we sometimes fill our time by listening to a book Marinda's chosen, some modern novel that would never have caught my interest before but in which, perhaps, families not unlike our own live out their dramas, work out or bury their heartaches and grudges and scandals and joys. I begin to understand that storybooks are never outgrown. I offer to read the books to Marinda myself. She's touched but turns me down. "Dad, no offense, but Egon's acting genes didn't come from you."

The house is almost vertiginously vertical, its glossy butter-colored bamboo stairs connecting five narrow floors, descending from my compact guest room and deck at the top to Harkney's office at the very bottom. Harkney is a businessman, but his business keeps company with science and we are both nerds. The day after I arrived, he gave me a tour of the house's various carbon-sparing features, each of which he'd researched and installed himself over two years. I listen to him with genuine interest, an interest that I realize grows from and also deepens my fondness for a son-in-law with whom I'd barely exchanged more than this or that holiday pleasantry. If Marinda overhears our geeky banter, she'll laugh and tell Harkney to watch out or I'll make him disassemble and reassemble an outboard motor. Except that, thank God, there are no outboard motors in sight. There is no ocean in sight—though I know the Pacific is less than an hour's drive away. After picking me up at the airport, Harkney took the "scenic" route, following the coast before turning sharply inland, pointing out a distant scattering of his company's leviathan turbines. Not my ocean, not my problems, I thought with relief. And then I had a strange thought: What if my ocean had become, to me, like a wife? What if the problem I had with my work was that I expected to yield from it comfort, loyalty, a warm body to greet me each day with reliable affection? How silly and grandiose was that?

I grow accustomed to running a laundry machine that appears to use about a thimbleful of water, to thermostatic microzones that awaken in response to my proximity, lights that rise and fall at my gestured commands, window shades that bow down, all on their own, to the intensity of heat from the sun.

How fortunate I am to be able to flee my ordinary life for months on end, even put my job on hold. Without saying so, I let my coworkers believe that my self-appointed furlough was triggered as much by the trauma of being taken hostage as it was by a family emergency. I suppose my recurrent dreams hold a different opinion, but I feel like I'm over and done with the events of that ghastly night, done with telling the tale to yet another friend or stranger, done with whatever "emotional process" was somehow expected of me. Deeanne vexted me three times over the following week, and I finally wrote her a short message saying I was fine. I didn't say I hoped she was, too, because I actually hoped she wasn't. Marinda speaks to her once every week or so, and Dee knows I'm here, so perhaps she represses details of her life with Commodore Giraffe. Turns out they've wound up in Boston, deciding that what they'd wanted all along was a modern city life. *Vive la différence,* and good luck to them when Boston's underwater, which, despite billions of dollars spent on holding back the harbor, could well happen in their lifetime.

In other urban tales, Egon is back in New York, apparently undaunted. Why do I worry less, especially now that he's so inaccessibly far away? Marinda says it's because we went through something dangerous together and survived. From our cushioned command post, she talks to him every few days, which gives me the assurance of his continued survival without having to stalk his voicemail. And if I'm sitting beside her, maybe attempting to read some dry, data-driven article, she'll sometimes conclude her conversation with "I love you, here's Dad," and hand the phone to me.

When I ask him about Pearl, he tells me she's getting ready to leave the country. She's joined the Restitution Corps. It's a little like the army: you don't know where they'll send you, though she has asked to go anywhere in Africa and will, with her history, probably get her wish. Along with the hard work of helping people simply survive, she wants to bring theater to children who've never known such a thing.

"Oh you young idealists," I say.

This doesn't amuse Egon. "Do we have much of a choice? Unless you count slitting our throats. Extreme times call for extreme beliefs."

I think, Aren't all times extreme to those living through them? I ask him, "Are you really still happy there?"

"Happy? I hear what you're thinking, you know. *Why doesn't he quit with this dream and figure out a real life?* But have I asked you or Mom for any money in the last ten years?"

"I'm sorry," I say. "What I don't mean to do is insult you."

His voice softens. "I know that." He pauses. "Dad, if I remember correctly, you used to tell Mare and me that sometimes you have to keep on doing what you care about even when it seems like a lost cause. And not to insult you, either, because I think you're one of the good guys, but doesn't that describe your work these days?"

Next to me, I sense that Marinda can tell the conversation is tense. She looks at me with concern. I smile at her and say to Egon, "At times it does."

Both of us are quiet for a moment, resting from the work of what I hope is growing closer, though maybe I'm fooled. We tell each other to take care, be well, and stay in touch.

I know better than to ask if he has any acting work. He'll tell me (or his sister) if he does. When Marinda reports that it sounds like he's "met someone," I say, "Don't tell me anything yet. What children don't realize is that such news comes with a very long kite tail of multicolored hopes for the parents."

"Dad, I think you're becoming poetic."

"That's what happens when you take me away from my lab bench and my centrifuge."

One morning she asks, "Aren't you lonely here? I feel selfish holding you captive. You know, *I* won't be lonely if you go." She lays a hand on her globe of a belly. "I have built-in company."

"Sweetheart, this is the cure for my loneliness. This is the opposite of loneliness." But when I see her expression, I say, "Don't worry, I'm not moving in. I'm passing through. When I'm no longer needed, I'll strap on my tanks and face the music." This is an expression the divers use at the lab when they don't like the results we're getting, and it brings a smile of relief to Marinda's sun-starved face.

Harkney joins us for most dinners, even sometimes for lunch. I moved a small drop-leaf table and a couple of folding chairs into a corner of the bedroom; each evening, once I arrange the table, Marinda pulls herself to the edge of the bed. One thing I realize as the three of us sit and chat together is that my daughter married an optimist—and, as far as I can see, a man without a temper. This makes me happier than anything has in a very long time.

After dinner, I always leave Marinda and Harkney alone. I ascend to my guest room at the top of the house. It opens onto a small deck that gives me a bird's-eye view of the canyon. Seen from aloft, our surroundings are a paradise, but when I venture down and out and along the trails that roam among the trees, I notice the dearth of birdsong, never see a snake or lizard flash by underfoot. There are plenty of insects, of course; there will always be insects.

On my overlook, I stand above the world—it reminds me of the time I visited a fire-spotting tower in the White Mountains, back in my grad school days—and I wish I could feel as high above the pull of my suspended life, because this retreat won't last forever. Little Eden will be induced in a month or so, and while Harkney says I'm welcome to stay on, I know they've hired a doula, and tall as this house may be, it's not large. Four, plus the demanding little newcomer, would indeed be a crowd.

Other than Egon and a couple of my colleagues, the one person I speak with fairly often is Margo. She's usually the one to call, though if she misses me and leaves a message, I will always call her back. She does make me laugh.

She keeps up with the news (the charges against Arturo and those two misguided students whose lives are ruined, the attempts to extradite Suarez from Venezuela, and of course the diminishing buzz around town), and I let her vent about it, but I don't follow any of it directly.

"Tyrone's Taj Mahal is going great guns, now that the monsoon season appears to have passed. He's put a big fence around the site so nobody can watch it go up," she tells me. "Unfortunately, it doesn't block the noise of the heavy machinery blasting the rock. Like, didn't they do that already? But now, get this: a fucking underground bunker. Here in Trusty Town, U.S.A."

"I'd say the bloom is off our rose."

"Well, we can no longer pride ourselves on obscurity. I'm thinking maybe it's overrated."

"Obscurity?"

"Off-the-mappishness."

"I'm learning a lot about being off the map. Off mine, that much for sure." I'm standing on the deck, in the dark, watching lights wink on in homes across the valley that normally hide behind the trees. By day, I can see only two. In the dark, lights betray the covert location of five more. Once in a while, tendrils of music make their way this far. Not classical or jazz or the kind of music on which my taste fossilized decades ago; the music is decidedly young, much of it discordant and mournful, the singers' voices plaintive or harsh. The inhabitants of these tucked-away homes are members of the generation on whom it has fallen to save the rest of us or go down fiddling in the flames.

"When are you coming back?" Margo asks.

"The baby gets her marching orders by mid-July. I should clear out a week or so after that." What I don't tell her is that I may stay on the West Coast a bit longer, visit two marine biologists I've collaborated with long-distance, one in Seattle, one in Vancouver.

"But how can you miss the Fourth on steroids?"

"I hadn't thought of that. My God, what a relief."

"Yeah," she says. "Maybe I don't actually love watching the fireworks crammed together with dozens of people who greet me with phony cheer while thinking of the C-minus they got on that paper about *Beloved* or *Winesburg, Ohio.* I didn't do grade inflation. I still don't. In my opinion, most of the world gets a solid D these days."

"Pass/fail for me," I tell her. "Please."

"Actually"—she sighs loudly—"the reason I hoped you'd be getting back sooner is to rescue me from my bossy daughters. I can't get rid of them. One goes, another shows up. Gaslighting by tag team. They're determined to get me into counseling through some local 'victim services' bureau. They also tell me I drink too much, that I am unaware of all the 'stressors' in my life. Excuse me, but *they* are the ones unaware of all those fucking stressors, and they should thank me for keeping them in the dark."

"Margo, all our children think we drink too much. We do. The thing is, most of them don't drink enough."

My turn to make Margo laugh.

"In other news," she says, "I finally sold the damn boat. To someone in Maine, so I'll never have to lay eyes on her again. And resigned from the club. Which should reduce my bar tab if not my drinking. Wait. Mike? Do I hear a piano on your end? A real live piano?"

And yes, from downstairs, the scales have begun, the plucked notes rising readily up the uncarpeted stairs. "My son-in-law, at age thirty-four, is taking up an instrument."

She laughs again. "Now, that takes guts."

"I'd say having a baby takes more."

Margo sighs. "All I can say is, you beat me to grandparenthood."

"Not yet." But I think of the baby inside my daughter—my daughter's daughter, a concept that stuns me all over again—rolling against the curve of my palm. She is so very close to the world, and sometimes I wonder if I can bear the extra weight of her arrival, the weight of that love.

"Soon enough, my friend," says Margo. "Soon enough. And there'd better be pictures within twenty-four hours of the birth."

"I live in fear of the consequences."

After a pause, she tells me that she likes her new bathroom so much, she's thinking of letting Kepner's juniors attack her kitchen—especially since mine is on hold. She got a good price for the boat.

"I guess that means you've decided to stay."

"Or it means I want to sell. Could go either way, couldn't it? The Drome is still for sale, Mike. We could join forces and turn it into a strip club. Strippers of all genders. They'd dress as famous historical figures and disrobe from there. I think I've struck gold. Who'd you pay more to take it all off, Thomas Jefferson or Sappho? Mahatma Gandhi or Sojourner Truth? We would leave no cultural icon clothed. Gandhi was scantily clad to begin with, so never mind him. What about . . . oh, Supreme Court justices. Popes. So many layers to fling off! A field day."

It's not the first conversation I've had with Margo, lying on this chaise on this deck, in which I've realized that we go on talking beyond having anything of consequence to say. It's like we're treading water in a warm lake, no waves, no wind; maybe, if this were ten years ago, bats conducting their business right over our heads.

But we do say goodbye, and I lie still for a while, eyes closed, listening to Harkney labor earnestly at producing a tune chosen for a six-year-old to learn. It ought to fray my nerves, but it doesn't. Is it a measure of hope that even if bats are nearly extinct, people keep on learning the piano? Harkney wants to be able to play lullabies for his baby daughter. (I asked him why not the guitar. He told me he'd inherited the piano and couldn't bear to let it go. Sometimes, he said, the instrument chooses you.)

When Harkney stops playing, I go inside, to my diminutive yet perfectly proportioned, energy-efficient yet gracious bedroom. Many nights here, after I turn out the light, I find myself picturing that odd little silver-skinned seal, the one who kept me company while I waited for someone to take me off that island. It's easy to see why people, especially lonesome sailors and fishermen away too often from home, believe in selkies. Her gaze was so girlish.

I think of small Marinda, who loved it when she could go out on the Mako just with me, no mother or brother, just us. I taught her to fish. We'd take our catch home for her mother to clean and cook. It was on these occasional outings when she would turn her eyes to me, as we waited for a pull on our lines, and ask me sudden, important questions: Why is it okay to eat fish? Why can't we see to the bottom of the ocean? How can that giant metal ship out there float? Why can you sometimes see the moon—but not always—in the middle of a sunny day?

"What would you do if I died?"

She was seven when she asked me that one. "And don't say," she said, "that it won't happen for a really, really long time. That's the dumb answer."

Never had I felt so alone as a parent. The answer on my tongue (however unlikely in truth) was that if she were to die, I would die, too. But I told her that her spirit would be inside mine, alive with me, always, like a favorite treasure you like to carry everywhere in your pocket. "Not inside Mom's?" she wondered, frowning. Yes, I told her, inside Mom's—and her brother's, too. (No surprise that it was Egon who'd told her about death in the first place, big brothers the reliable source of life's worst and most sensational news.)

"And what if we all went extinct?" she said. "Where would our spirits go then? Everyone's spirits?"

I didn't know that she knew about extinction—but then of course, she'd studied whales in first grade, gone into Boston to see the IMAX movie at the aquarium.

"Maybe into the ocean," I said. "The ocean is forever."

"Maybe Mom and I will be mermaids, and you and Egon will be mermen."

"Maybe so," I said. "Not a bad life."

"Oh Dad, that's just crazy." She sounded exactly like her mother for a moment, startling me. "Dad, I was joking."

Brecht

My job works me to the core, uses every joint and every little hinge on my spine, and then my commute to Jersey eats up a stooge amount of time, especially when the river gets a tide surge and the ferries have a hard time docking. But some days on my way home, and some weekends, if it's nice enough to sit outside, I go to the place where we lived in the Village when I was a kid, and I sit across the street and just look at the building. It's your basic five-story brickpile: tenement style, Mom calls it, and it looks pretty much exactly the way I remember it, though it's been spiffed up at the margins—bricks scoured and repointed, windows washed, the cast-iron fencing limousine black, not a lick of rust. "You can be sure only rich people—well, relatively rich people—live there now," said Mom when I told her I'd walked past it. "No more rent control, I bet. We could never have lived there now."

The weird thing to contemplate, kind of a thought pretzel, is this: my father's last home was my first. I'm twisting it into a poem, that pretzel.

I watch the people going in and out, maybe for as much as two hours if nobody kicks me off the stairs where I like to sit. I totally get all these city suspicions. How could you not respect them? Me in particular: how could I not?

Through a connection of Austin's, I landed work on a city construction crew. We're rebuilding a section of the East River walls, so to get there from Jersey, I have to cross the Hudson and then cross the whole island, too, but it's a union job, and I'm saving up to find my own place, even if it has to be farther away from the city. The boss is nice enough (he told me he had to take a social justice course to get his promotion, so I guess you could even call him "just"), but he's not the kind of boss to teach you much of anything beyond the skills of building this reinforced flexcrete structure to hold back the river when it rises or gets unruly. He's no Celestino.

The worksite is a scorcher—all tarmac and cobble, no shade, and now the August sun—but we get some river breezes and there's an epic view of the bridges to the north and south. I'm writing about them, too. I remember when Mrs. T gave a talk one time about looking at poems as bridges: making connections, carrying you over, snubbing the gravity of prose. What makes them so strong is rarely clear to the naked eye. With prose, she said, you hunker down; with poetry you rise and soar. Not that they can't take you down to subterranean places. She made a slide show of different bridges, from an ordinary trestle structure, all bolts and corrosion and graffiti, to some delicate birdlike suspension bridge in China that looked like it was made of translucent fishing line, and she put up a poem next to each bridge, and we took turns reading them out loud. She paired the Zakim in Boston (lit up at night, a leviathan rib cage) with a modern love sonnet, the Brooklyn Bridge with a Beat poem, that trestle bridge with something by Jericho Brown. So now I think about these bridges, wonder if I could make a poem to pair with each one. Maybe I'll surprise Mrs. T with a postcard, just to tell her.

A month ago, when I talked to Celestino, he told me her house is for sale. Where is she going? I asked him. I was surprised to feel worried that she might go somewhere else, somewhere unreachable. After all, here I am somewhere else.

She told Celestino she's "testing the market." Or maybe, he thinks, she's trying to bluff one of her daughters into taking it off her hands.

He called out of the blue to ask me a favor, teased me that I owed it to him because of deserting him. Not that I feel guilty, especially now that he says business is back to normal. His shoulder aches, but it's getting stronger, and for now, he's hired kids through the summer listings at the High. Connie's going to teach there starting in January, he said, and that news gave me a jolt. I thought that little school of human ducklings was a kind of micro-utopia.

The favor (and really, it's Connie's idea) is that I be an old-fashioned pen pal to Raul, write him actual cards and letters. Weird, but I get it. What I usually do is send him a poem, with a note at the bottom. I asked him to send me poems, too, but that part hasn't worked so far. He wrote me back, *I'm not a poem guy but don't tell Mom.* Instead, he responds to my poems. He's my critic-by-mail.

The only problem with the favor is that where I live has no services. It's Pearl's place, where people live on the sly; off the grid, my mother would say. So Raul mails his cards and notes to me at Egon's address, and I don't mind the excuse to see Egon. We share a pizza if he's free. Or I stop by the theater where he builds sets. For now, we're both in the business of building. He's also an understudy to the lead in a big-deal play about a future nuclear holocaust. When he offered me a ticket, I asked for a rain check. "Bombs aren't really my thing," I said. I laughed, so he wouldn't kill himself apologizing.

I snuck in an hour at my watch post on those stairs this morning. Not all that logical, since I have to end up for dinner back in the city, and I'm not going to spend the whole day wandering around. The thing is, I don't mind doing the ferry turnaround twice. Unless it's stormy, the ferry is a good place to write. Today is fair, one of those Saturdays you wish you'd embarked on a few hours earlier, just to make it last forever, and on my way back, I ride outside in the stern, where I find a sleeve of shade from the midday sun. I have a look at a draft of my gestating poem.

West to east, like a river of chrome,
Traffic flashes past my post.
My father's last home, the building I spy on,
was also, before that, my first.
I turned eight the month he died.

Awning to awning, a boy
who must be the age I was then

sprints to stay ahead of his mother.
"Wait!" she yells, but she's laughing.
He lets her almost catch up, then bolts.

Story on story, brick and cornice, stairway and sill,
the long block is an unbroken chasm of shade.
Small trees, like prisoners,
survive each day on the briefest libation of sun.
Noon pours down like joy, the cocktail hour.

Cellar to rooftop, our old building
is a city by itself, a stack of spooling lives.
They come and go, in-a-big-rush or pausing-to-chat,
all strangers to me now.
No telling who took our place when we left.

Birth to death, the hospital down at the corner
is busy; that's where the boy stops, surrenders the chase.
From there, my mother bundled her baby home on foot,
but Dad caught a ride the short distance back.
The ambulance, glittering, hastened there in silence.

I have to pretend that the hospital's still there, at the end of the block. It's not, and that was a shock, the first time I made my pilgrimage. It's totally gone, replaced by a sleek glass cube of apartments.

Stepping from ferry to shore, I think about titles. The title to a poem is its threshold, Mrs. T once said. How you enter a room is always important. Will you slink? Will you dance? Maybe you pause in the doorway until you have everyone's attention.

I think about "Revenant." Too snooty. "Voyeur." Too pervy. Or maybe just "Saint Joseph's on Twelfth Street."

"Twelfth Street."

This pinball thinking keeps me occupied on the bus to Pearl's. She left a month ago, but I still think of it as "Pearl's place." That strikes me as a title, too. I could write about the things she left behind: futon, table, two chairs, dishes, a fan that turns into a heater, a colorful shaggy rug and a big floozy of a plant she found on the street. Pearl said she regards it like a good mutt; she doesn't worry what it "is." But I was curious and shot a pic to Celestino. It's an aspidistra, he says, a houseplant that grows just about anywhere for anyone. I decided the plant deserved a name: I decided on Celia.

I'm not as hardy as Pearl, I guess, or even as Celia, because I can't imagine toughing it out here through the winter. I want to find my own place by then. I still have a few months. I asked Pearl if she needed me to be her basic placeholder till she gets back, because if you vacate one of these spaces, in a blink someone else will claim it. She said she'll be gone a few years if the Corps works out the way she hopes. She'll know by fall. If she makes it till then without getting kicked out, she says, she'll be fine and I'm free to go my own way.

We overlapped here for a few days so that Pearl could show me the quirks and unwritten rules of this place, make sure I knew what I was in for. "Look at it one way," she says, "it's a crime story waiting for a plot. Another way, you are a prince in a palace."

So my new home is this plain old industrial building on a block that sits so low, it's in the flood zone, making it basically worthless. For now, nobody wants to touch it for renovation or demolition. The ground floor is empty, because a week or two of rain and you could be sloshing in ankle-deep water. But Pearl's on the fourth floor, where she has one of three big open spaces. The other squatters up here are two single guys. I'm friendly with the one who's a painter (also the one who feeds the all-important cat); the other is elusive, and Pearl says just to ignore him. I think of him as The Enigma. He keeps weird hours and, if I pass him in the hall, doesn't speak. Which is fine, since it means no questions—and nobody said this was a social club. I do my own thing. We share an old restroom, and one floor down, there's a charging station, installed by Sergei, the guy who knows how to pirate the power.

We're at the end of an alley, which means there's no breeze. August is max brutal, especially with nothing but the rigged-up shower we share in the space behind the building, a cement canal we call the moat. Water pools there if we get smacked by one of those Hand of God cloudsplitters. Which means more mosquitoes. I'm thankful Pearl put in good screens.

Mom worries it's dangerous here or that there will be some kind of an eviction raid and people will get hurt. I could have lied and told her I had a "real" apartment, but then she'd want to visit, and there would be no stopping her. She seems filled with some new resolve now that she's not working at the firm anymore. She told me she's thinking of moving out of the house to "take a break and figure out what's next."

"Next?" I felt my nerves spur my heart. "After what, Mom?"

"Everything," she said, as if this were obvious to anyone.

"But you and Austin . . ." I realized how worried I was—for me as much as for my mother.

"Oh, Austin and I are probably fine." From her tone, the opposite was true.

"But like—move out? You're moving out?"

"Honey, it's more about this place than about Austin."

Should I just believe her? "So, okay, you're leaving Vigil Harbor?"

She told me that she is plant-sitting for someone up in Gloucester for a month, a friend of Filene's. "A change of scenery is what I need. And, Brecht, if anyone can understand that right now, you would, wouldn't you?"

Her tone, even if it's impatient and a little wounding, implies that maybe she thinks of me as an adult, not the kid who had to be coddled through a crisis. She tells me that she misses me, and when can I come up? (Not "come home.")

I haven't been back to Vigil Harbor since leaving in April, but I remind her that I promised to return for Thanksgiving. She reminds *me* that's three whole months away. Egon said he'd show me how to get a hitch card, though I've heard rumors the program might be suspended.

There's been no more mayhem here, at least not the terrorist kind, but still there were crackdowns and pop-up checkpoints after what they now call the Boat Basin Bombing. I get randomly asked for my license on the ferry; once in a while the official doing the random checks will notice the town I'm from and ask if I was there when they caught the Oceloti bombers. I say something vague.

Even if I'm not living there, I've been wandering around the city a lot. After being under my own personal rock for so long, I suddenly itch to explore as much as I can. Not travel, just walk everywhere and observe. High summer is a good time to spend weekends in botanical gardens and parks. Like Wave Hill, in the Bronx, where Celestino got his start as a tree guy. I sent him some pix, but he didn't answer. I asked later if he got them and he messaged me that he did; he'd been too busy to reply. I tell him busy is good. He tells me yes, and that I should never take busy for granted.

There is one place I haven't been to, have totally and deliberately avoided. It's Union Square (like you couldn't have guessed). I go under it by subway, and sometimes I have to change trains there. But aboveground: no.

This is kind of a challenge today, because I agreed to have dinner with Austin's friend Steve, who lives just a couple blocks from there. Steve is the guy who took care of me on the day from which my memory saved only a few paltry scraps. I feel grateful, of course I do, but it's in this abstract way, and even if he gets it, that I was max traumatized, what does he think we can talk about unless we at least begin with that day? But Austin would be hurt if I didn't go, and it would be rude.

I spend the afternoon on the futon, writing. The problem with my poems, I realize, is that I'm trying too hard to tell stories. Which might mean I should just surrender to prose. But that's the thing: it would feel like surrender. So I think about trying to use poems as portraits. I want to write about the borrowed objects around me, Pearl's things, not as a collection but one by one; to each a poem. The plant is a good place to start, because it's the one that feels most emphatically mine. Wherever I go next, that's the one thing I'll definitely take along.

Some days Celia droops
Until someone swoops in
To tend her thirst and trim her skirts.

Then she vaunts her fronds
Like wands flinging spells
Through the ceiling at the sun.
She flirts with any light that comes her way,
Delights in her undeserved fortune:
Found, rescued, the bride lifted
Up the stairs and through a door.
Pride of place, scent of soil,
Watered to a fever gleam.

Sometimes writing makes me drowsy, so I let myself sink into the rare luxury of a nap. I key a quick message to Mom (*all fine, dinner in the city*) and set my phone to take its own nap. When I wake, I go down the hall and sponge off the sleep-sweat at one of the sinks, put on a clean T-shirt. Then I am off again: walk, bus, ferry, walk. The air is cooling in the slow approach of evening, and the surface of the river is smooth as a rink. I face west and watch the wake of the ferry. That word, *wake:* how can it mean so many things, not just this band of roiling water but to rise into consciousness and then, how illogically weird, the ritual of keeping vigil over a corpse? If truth is stranger than fiction, words are stranger than truth.

This morning I thought about *sentence:* a coherent chain of words—or, no, a prison term. Crazy, right?

To get to Steve's, I walk a few blocks north of the ferry slip, then straight east all the way to Third, then up the few blocks to his address. I focus on my feet as I walk those northbound blocks, not wanting to catch a glimpse of the place I don't go. It looms just a short ways uptown.

Steve's building is tall and plain, an undistinguished tower with a cramped foyer and one elevator. I contemplate the stairs, but he's on the top floor. Not a penthouse, though I'm guessing it'll be nice, and it is.

When he opens the door, he looks the kind of familiar that people do on the street when you know you know them from *somewhere,* but out of context you're out of luck. He's this superfit-looking white guy, handsome like a polished stone. His pants match his pure white hair, and he's wearing a sleek shirt the innocent green of honeydew melon, its buttons like road-flattened pearls.

He hugs me, which is a shock, and he tells me how glad he is I've come. I feel the slippery cocooning of air-conditioned air as I hand him the wine I bought, and at the same time I smell a collision of spices, a meal that might be Moroccan or Greek or Israeli, and I'm happy to have worked up an appetite on my walk. Quiet solo flute by way of music. I get this irrational hit of panic that maybe he thinks this is a date. But that is stooge. He's just a really nice guy, and he knows me in a way I do not know him and wouldn't want to. Relax, I scold myself.

"You might not even remember me," he says.

"Well, yeah, that's sort of the case," I say. "Sorry."

"Don't be sorry! That's ridiculous. I also realize it might not be easy to see me, but I wanted to welcome you here. I wanted to offer you whatever help I can. I'd have had you over before now, but I was on a project in Toronto. It's definitely the new New York."

"Like they say." Nerves make my voice sound parched.

He urges me into the living room, a gathering of soft white places to sit. While he gets me a glass of water from the kitchen, I have a look around. Unlike the sofa and chairs, everything else—the rug, the museumy objects in the shelves, and the pictures on the wall—is crazy with color. Though it works. Out the window, I see the sun sinking toward the collage of rooftops across the avenue. On the glass table before me sits a black plate holding seed-speckled crackers, olives, and tiny tomatoes that must have cost a fortune. A stack of folk-embroidered napkins. Everything in the room seems to have come from a different country: napkins Mexico, vase Denmark, mosaic Tunisia or Greece. The star of the show is an oil painting of a snow-covered mountain against the drapery of northern lights, a landscape of sharp icy edges.

When Steve returns, he sits across from me and asks about Austin. I know he wants to hear about the work, so I tell him about the boff palace and some of the other projects I know about. When he asks about Mom, I don't mention that she seems to be taking a break from the marriage.

"Austin was smart to go his own way," says Steve. "Not sure how many more years of this ping-ponging all around the globe I have in me. It gets harder and harder, not just because of my age. We say yes to a project in Johannesburg or Saigon and then have to cross our fingers the borders won't close."

Before I can respond, maybe ask him about his favorite places, he does the good-host thing and focuses on me. How am I spending my days? Where exactly am I living? Is it true I'm writing poetry? (At least he doesn't tell me how brave I am. When did *brave* become a synonym for *stooge?*)

I'm not sure why, but I tell him everything straight, not with the omissions I apply when talking to Mom and Austin. So of course he doesn't like the sound of where I'm living. "I know how hard it is to find anything remotely affordable here in the city," he says. "I do pretty well, but could I afford this place if I hadn't found it decades ago? Doubtful!"

I admire how he can gesture with his glass of red wine yet never spill a drop on his impeccably perfect pants.

I tell him I'll have to find something else in a few months, and he tells me he has an old boyfriend who runs an artists' residential co-op out on Staten Island. There's a wait list, but if I apply now, and if the boyfriend handles my application . . .

"It's not like I'm published," I say. "I don't exactly have creds. Like, I'm basically a practice poet."

"They look at the work," he says. "Don't undersell yourself! They have spots for people just getting into the swing of their art. And you'll meet people there. It's very collegial. People share kitchens and meeting rooms, but you have your own space."

Look at the work. That phrase blows around in my head for a few seconds like a large colorful leaf. I think of looking at a wall I've helped build, a tree I planted, a hedge I pruned. I think of standing back to look at any work I've done, whether it's made of words or stones, letting in a sense of completion. I feel a splinter of sorrow, remembering what it was like to ride along in Celestino's truck, just a passenger, waiting to arrive at the next place, do the next work that needed doing. Plant. Fertilize. Mulch. Water. Executing other people's wishes can be a comfort. As long as they're decent wishes.

Dinner is just about ready, Steve tells me, and why don't we move to the kitchen? I pick up my water glass and follow him through a narrow arch into a room that you can tell is flooded with light even before you enter. It's larger than a lot of city kitchens, and he's explaining to me that it's the one big thing he changed about the apartment when he got it—knocked out the second, smaller bedroom he didn't really need—because he loves to cook and entertain. We're having a vegetable ragout that is *heaven* at this time of year because the ingredients are at their freshest, especially if you buy them at the open market the same day, knowing they were harvested possibly even *this very morning*. . . .

Which is what he's saying when I see the source of the late light cascading onto the table set with linens from France or Spain or maybe Sweden . . .

The one large window, next to the table, opens mostly to sky, because this building is one of the tallest around, but it also looks directly north, and center stage is a view of Union Square, a view in which the divide is clear between the surviving old dowager trees along the east side of the park and, to the west, the brand-new junior trees that must have been planted to replace those that died from the blast.

Steve is slow to pick up on my fixed attention to the view, and I no longer hear what he's telling me about the meal or the apartment. Then, abruptly, he shuts up and comes to stand beside me at the window.

"I'm an idiot," he says. "I'm sorry."

"Was I here that day?" I ask him. "I mean, in this apartment?" I can feel him wanting to put a hand on my shoulder, but perhaps he noticed my shock when he hugged me at the door.

"You don't remember being here."

"I think I stood right here and saw the smoke."

"You did. Which was stupid of me. To let you see it. Idiot again."

"It's okay," I say. "I actually had this memory, like carried it around with me, of standing at a window seeing the smoke. I didn't know where the window was. I told myself it was my dorm, though that didn't make sense. It was like a piece that lost its puzzle." I look down at the table, the basket of bread. "I'm hungry, and it smells really good in here."

Once we're sitting, the fear fades from Steve's expression, and he starts to talk about the wine we'll be having with his ragout. It's certainly not the cheap stuff I brought along, but it's not like I'm ashamed. I know that when I leave, he'll want to send me with the leftovers, and I won't tell him that I don't have a refrigerator, that they'll probably spoil. Steve's wine touches my tongue like some supreme elixir, and I let myself glance at the view now and then. The light changes quickly at this hour, the hydrangea blush of the sky snuffed out, like it is every day, by the brassy sparkle of city lights, the firefly trails of bikes and cars moving in every direction.

I ask Steve about Toronto. I ask him about the colorful possessions in his living room. I ask him about how he decided on being an architect. I listen to all his answers, and either he forgets to ask more about me, or maybe he's worried that it will take us where we shouldn't go. He most certainly does not ask about what happened in the spring. Which I appreciate yet also, not very logically, resent.

I'm a place where lightning struck twice. And I came out alive. (Well, second time around, everybody came out alive. Even the villainous Pia Suarez, who's thumbing her nose at the government goons who are trying but failing to get her shipped to this country like some coveted back-ordered doodad from one of those cheap-ass Singaporean websites.) But the lightning's still in me, buzzing through my veins, shaking my brain cells. Maybe it's calming down a little.

At first when I returned to the city, sometimes I still found myself talking to Noam. It's weird how I knew him only a couple of days, but we were max simpatico. We had the High in common, sure, but we got way beyond that subject. He had micro-obsessions that mirrored mine: me the inconsistencies of language, Noam the mystery of why cars and buses are shaped the way they are. Me: our passive acceptance of meanings assigned to colors. (Why shouldn't red, the color of blood, be what we wear to funerals? Envy, if anything, is black.) Him: the very real possibility of mythical creatures that aren't in fact *mythical.*

That morning we joked about how, no matter what he did or where he ended up, we should plan a summer road trip. With a theme, I said. Coastal ghost towns, he said. Too many mosquitoes, I said. Museums on ships, I said. Now that's not a bad idea, said Noam. And let's include a submarine.

He said he'd never been on a submarine. I said, Who has?

It's easy to like someone based on a couple of days, I know that. Even to fall a little in love, though I'm not gay. But if that person vanishes, especially from right beside you, you will be haunted. You will. Especially because no one understands what you lost. You didn't really know the guy, right? Who are you to *miss* the guy?

After we finish dinner, Steve won't let me help clear the table. He does that, and while he does, I stare out the window. In Union Square, streetlamps illuminate the young trees from above, the older trees from below. The edges of the greenery are crisp, like they'd look if you were a raptor scanning those trees for your supper. The whole picture reminds me of a before-and-after diorama or a simulation Austin might show a client in the Vroom, a mimicry of how your new place will look one year in, then twenty years out.

We say goodbye awkwardly, me and Steve, though he doesn't try to hug me this time. He lets me refuse the leftovers—I just go ahead and tell him I don't have a fridge—and he reminds me about his friend on Staten Island. I promise to be in touch with him about that, and I decide that I will.

On the street, I think for a minute that maybe I'll just make a right and walk through Union Square. No, I decide, not yet. The ferry won't be running at this hour—I'll have to take the PATH—but it's the perfect kind of summer night that used to be an ordinary thing. Your body moves through the air the way your head rests on your favorite pillow. You happily walk on and on.

I head south and west, aiming for a detour through Washington Square. This is the place that holds the best memories of my dad, because there's the playground he took me to, and there's where we walked with Mom on summer weekends, where I ate lemon ice cream and watched the dogs in the dog run and the old guys playing chess and the skateboarders flashing by like they rode on invisible wires. Their speed looked like pure joy to me.

It's crowded, people craving this rare gift of a night that feels so kind. The community patrol is out in force, except that whatever authority they're meant to project is basically canceled by how happy they look to be here. Three or four groups of musicians are playing near the basin of the old fountain. Couples crowd the benches. Dogs lie on the paving stones, panting, waiting for their owners to call it a day. (Those stones have yet to cool.) I cut through at a diagonal, listening to guitars and drums, even a violin, but also to the shushing leaves. I slow my stride from brisk to browsing.

The violinist, a woman with short hair dyed like a rainbow, has the most impressive audience, maybe thirty people. As I pass behind her, I take in the arc of appreciative faces. And for an instant, my attention snags on a tall woman in a sleeveless moth-colored dress.

I stop, and if she weren't transfixed by the violinist, she'd probably see me—but then I realize, no, it's not her. The shifting shadows from lamplight carousing with leaves confuse everything.

The day after I got home and slept off the ordeal of that boat ride, the rescue, the police, my mother told me the story about why that woman was stalking Austin. It creeped Mom out, that's no surprise, but I was puzzled by how upset she seemed at not having known the whole story of Austin's sad, mixed-up girlfriend, the one who thought she was a mermaid or selkie or some kind of underwater creature here to save the ocean.

And Mom says Petra believed her. "So," I said, "wouldn't you say crazy cancels out crazy?"

Mom asked me what I meant by that.

"Well," I said, "so here's this line, running through time from that other woman to this one, connecting Austin's old life with what he thought was a completely separate new one—like life is a cake and you can cut it into pieces. But no. So he has to wrestle with that. He has to explain it to you. He never thought he'd have to do that, and I sort of feel sorry for him, because really, why would he? So what I mean is that without this crazy woman, the one who showed up, you wouldn't know about that one. If you can put this one, Petra, out of your mind—and she's gone, so you should—then can't you just let the other one go?"

Mom just looked at me for a minute (maybe I wasn't making sense), and then she said, "But she's the one who took you to Margo's, who put you in danger—"

"No," I said. "I'm the one who took her there."

"But why? Didn't you know I was looking everywhere for you?"

"I didn't know that," I said. "All I knew is that something was breaking up inside me. I was trying to run away from myself. Here—this house—was a place I couldn't be."

I think my mother still resents that I didn't go to her right away. I told her I was sorry, that all I could really think about was me. And I really wasn't up for the two of us having to acknowledge another anniversary of my father's death.

If I were to decide to return to Vigil Harbor—say a year from now, if I'm tired of the city or if something violent happens again to scare me away—one thing I know is that I wouldn't be able to retreat to an attic. I know too many people now, and too many people know me. Or think they do. Or simply know who I am—can point to me on the street and say my name. I guess it's what you call notoriety. Which I don't relish. And though I know I could always work for Celestino, would that be a good idea? That chapter in my life is over, the stanza complete.

In that house, and then in that boat, I was scared. We all were. But there was a kind of weird exhilaration when Mike was driving us straight out to sea, like an arrow pointed at a far continent—at Spain—and I thought about the tsunami Noam and I talked about when we were together the day before he died. We were eating those puffy street pretzels with spicy mustard, and for some reason we were obsessing on tragedies wrought by nature: hurricanes, tornadoes, mudslides, wildfires. We remembered where we were during Cunégonde; how we first heard about the Seattle quake. Noam, zoning on the ocean, had a thing about tidal waves.

So there I was, a hostage on a speeding boat, thinking about deadly waves and my dead brand-new friend, never mind wondering if I might die on the same date my father had died. And then we saw another boat speeding our way, and then two, and we had no idea if they were the bad guys or the good guys, if we were toast or about to be saved. And then there were megaphoned voices, and all of a sudden Mike and that woman are going overboard, so fast there's no time to absorb it as true. Snap, they're gone. And the liar from Celestino's kitchen is grabbing the wheel, and Egon is holding what looks like another gun and, thump, the sky is on fire.

Under that cherry-colored glow, a Coast Guard officer leaped from his boat to ours, and though we knew it was about to be over, that's when I was the most frightened I could ever remember being in my life. *Remember* being. The shouting and struggling, the flash of weapons, the sulfuric smell of the flare. Sensory overload. It cracked open a lode of fear I had obviously forgotten, though only later, in the middle of the night, did I feel the actual sensation: like a floor collapsing under my feet.

That's where I am in the rehashing of it all when, just as I am about to leave the park, head east toward Sixth Avenue, I see her: the acrobat in the striped bodysuit, running in place on a large red rubber ball. Here she is, alive as can be, and at the thought of it, I laugh out loud. Was she in Union Square that day, and she escaped—or had she taken the day off? Does she avoid that park now, the way I've been doing? People are clapping as she jumps off the ball and, at the same moment she lands on the pavement, lifts the ball straight up into the air with her left sneaker and catches it on top of her head. She spins like a top now on one toe and bounces the ball high off her head, ten times in a row.

"You've got to see this trickster woman," I told Noam that morning. "She's always in the same place, and she's amazing."

"I'm not into clowns or magicians," he said.

"No, no, she's someone who just makes her body do fantastic things."

"An acrobat."

"Yeah, but no trapeze or rings."

"You're the tour guide, man," said Noam. "Tour guide away."

Which is why we went where we did when we did.

The bench facing her act is full or I would sit. I watch for five minutes or so, see her flip and dance and shimmy and stretch her limbs out with the grace of a ballerina. I have a silly, wicked thought. Suppose I could distract her enough to steal her brilliantly striped acrylic hide? Would she be mine? I laugh out loud again, and a few people stare at me, wondering if I'm tame crazy or dangerous crazy. I release them from the worry by going on my way, leaving the park.

When I reach Greenwich Street, the river reveals itself a few blocks away, a vertical sliver of reflective gleam framed between two high-rise apartment buildings. When I cross the highway, I can hear the water wash against the pilings. A few late-night runners crisscross the view. Here there are no performers and the benches are empty. I find one of my own on a patch of browned grass.

I pull out my pocket notebook and flip to a blank page. I write, *what we wagered on a wave.* I write, *tsunami betting pool.* I write, *the day you disappeared.* And *the day you went under.* Also, out of left field, *our selkie's bright pelt in a flat-file drawer.*

My phone vibrates. "I can't sleep, and I miss you," says Mom. "And I knew you'd still be awake."

"I'm here," I say.

"Home?"

"No. Sitting by the river. With plenty of people around." Mom is a believer that there's safety in numbers, so I try to humor her.

"How was dinner?"

"It was good," I say. "He's a pretty amazing cook, so the meal was skilling."

"I'm always glad to hear you're being well fed."

"Why can't you sleep?" I ask.

She hesitates. "I suppose I'm beginning to miss Austin."

"Well, sure." A surge of hope.

"I'm still mad at him."

"Well, also sure."

"But it gets old."

"You're not asking me for advice, are you, Mom? How weird would that be."

"No, Brecht." She sighs.

"And you're not asking me to come home."

"No, sweetie. No. You're doing all right there. You are, aren't you?"

I tell her it's true, and I leave it at that. If I spelled it out, I'd say this: I'm on an island whose shoreline is threatened, there are guards and cops and rangers and all kinds of uniformed people keeping an eye out for trouble, there are flood basins where there used to be basketball courts, there are stretches of summer when the temperature hits one hundred degrees five days in a row, and there may loom storms, bombs, contagions, pandemics, and pandemonium, but I'm doing all right. I'm working my mind, working my body. I'm eating—sometimes very well.

"Can I ask you something?" I say.

"Of course!" she exclaims, glad to prolong our conversation.

"I don't remember coming home after. From the city."

She's thinking. "After Union Square," she says carefully.

"Yeah."

I can almost hear her anxiety, that she might say the wrong thing.

"Are you asking me to remember it for you?" she asks.

"Well, okay. I guess so." I laugh, to reassure her.

"We picked you up. Austin borrowed a bigger car, for your stuff. You were quiet the whole way. We listened to music."

"Austin's music," I say. I picture him dancing, from the waist up, while driving the four or five hours from the city to Vigil Harbor.

"Do you remember arriving at our house?"

"No. But maybe I remember unpacking."

"Okay," she says. Meaning *Good.*

"So I didn't tell you stuff then, stuff that, like, I don't remember now? About that day."

"No, honey."

"If I did tell you stuff, you'd tell me—now, at least. Right?"

"Sweetie," she says, "of course we would."

"Thanks," I say.

After a silence I don't choose to fill, she says, "Can I ask you something?"

"Hey, I owe you one."

"Will you send me a poem for the fridge?"

This surprises me so much, my laughter turns the head of a passing runner. "Mom, I will write a poem *to* the fridge. Ode to the fabulous fridge, by me, Brecht, amateur poet and professional builder of walls."

She tells me that's perfect, and away we go to our separate though always connected lives. I picture the fridge, the kitchen—except now I remember that wherever she is tonight, it's not in the house containing our kitchen, Austin's kitchen. But I can make bets, with myself, about whether she'll go back. I'm going to bet that she will.

It's time for me to make my trek, catch the train and ride under the river, back to Pearl's; to the palace where I am the prince. Check on Celia. Jot a card to Raul, tuck in a poem. Think about my long Sunday to come and how I might fill it. Write about smoke; about boat wakes, funeral wakes, waking from a dream; about the perfect meal. Write about the acrobat: celebrate that she's alive.

A boy stands inside the crown of the tallest tree for miles around. Once more it's withstood the assault of a storm. (Who could count how many times the tree has prevailed? Someday, like all living things, it will not.) The boy's view, through thinned but still shimmering leaves, includes the stark pathway that last week's high winds carved straight across the headland, marked by trees felled or fractured. Men and women are busy cutting up timber and hauling it away in trucks; technology hasn't done much to ease the backbreaking labor of remedy after violent weather.

No one was killed, or even injured badly, but roofs buckled, windows shattered, fences were crushed. Last night the boy heard his parents say that some people are petitioning for the oldest and tallest trees in town to be felled out of caution. They can't make us, *thinks the boy, and for now he's right. As June Smithson said at the emergency Town Meeting, "Our ancient trees are to be treasured, like our ancient houses." But June is well past the customary age of retirement; many residents think the same of her opinions.*

He has always been proud that his father built this tree house, and he remembers when, two years ago, he was finally allowed to climb to this platform, the one at the top. He was also reminded (as if he'd forget!) that he and his friends are forbidden to carve initials or words of any kind into the bark. When he heard about the binoculars left up here by the terrorist—or, he prefers to think, the tree warrior—he wondered if maybe the man had also carved his initials or a secret message up here. No, he did not—and somehow that is a disappointment. Maybe the boy hoped for a personal sign from that man. So much of what he said seemed sensible and right, but no way would Raul say that to his parents.

He still does not understand completely how his father was shot with a gun or who did it. But it wasn't the man; he knows that much. Yet now the man is in prison—well, yes, for setting the bombs or directing others to do it. Even though there will be a trial, Raul's parents tell him, the man is sure to be in prison for a very long time. They seem to think this is reassuring.

Yesterday he went for a tour of the school where he'll be starting next week. He went with his mother and Mrs. Tattersall. His mother kept saying things like Oh my God I remember this room! and They still have the vegetable garden and the orchard! She was the one acting like the kid, like she'd be the one going there every day. She talked much more than she usually did, and the teacher who gave them the tour said he had such fond memories of Raul's grandmother and her work in the church. Raul did like the gym. Brecht would call it skilling.

He has to answer Brecht's new poem. It's about the color of smoke. Weird, but Raul loves the weirdness of Brecht. He misses having that weirdness right here in person. He has to settle for it on paper. He wishes he could visit Brecht in New York. (Not a chance of that, and he knows it.)

His mother promises that he can still spend time with his friends from their home school—which is moving to Jordie's house. Why Raul is moving to the bigger school, he doesn't understand any more than he understands why his father was shot, but he's old enough to know that sooner or later changes will happen. Some are sudden: just look at how the storm took down that avenue of trees, all in a minute or two; they heard it when it happened, and it sounded like a train passing through—or a fierce wild creature from a myth. Others are gradual, like getting taller, whether you're a kid or a tomato plant or a house being built—a house going up, as his father will say. Going up; growing up. He'll suggest that rhyme to Brecht; in his opinion, Brecht's poems could use more rhymes.

You have to pay attention to the things you love, and you have *to fight for the ones that matter most: that's what the tree warrior said to the mothers that night in the kitchen. He was talking about their school, wasn't he?*

Raul's mother is calling him down. The two of them are meeting Jordie and his mother at The Drome for lunch and the last afternoon of bowling. The Drome is closing. Another sudden change for which he sees no logical explanation.

What happened was this: an inspection of the bowling alley structure by a potential buyer revealed that it falls within the recently updated floodplain. It will be torn down, and, at least for the time being, the adjacent boatyard will lease the land for expansion. Boats of all kinds have grown in popularity.

Raul turns toward the top of the ladder but hears a boat horn go off, then another and another. He returns for a moment to the rail. A very large old ship is passing the mouth of the harbor, slowly, sails swollen by a breeze. The noise of the horns comes from a group of smaller boats saluting the ship. Boat horns can be warnings, but they can also be applause, like after the fireworks show every Fourth of July. Raul watches the grand ship glide along until his mother calls him down a second time.

On the ship, passengers stand on deck enjoying their opposing view: the passing coastline. They are a select two dozen who, while paying a minor ransom for the cruise from New York to Newfoundland, will assist in the simpler chores associated with a marine mammal census being conducted by a team of scientists who hail from Woods Hole, Cape May, Halifax, and St. John's. The cruise will carry the passengers only one way, after which they must find their own transportation back to wherever they came from—or wherever they want to go next.

One woman on board recognizes this stretch of Massachusetts coast and, as she does, feels a crosscurrent of rough emotions. She expected this, yet still she feels powerless in the undertow. All passengers must carry binoculars with them at all times, to help in the search, and now she lifts them to her eyes, partly to hide those emotions but also to see what she can see as the ship draws abreast of the harbor.